You Get
What
You Pay
For

Also by Larry Beinhart

NO ONE RIDES FOR FREE

YOU GET WHAT YOU PAY FOR

Larry Beinhart

William Morrow and Company, Inc. • New York

Library of Congress Cataloging-in-Publication Data

Beinhart, Larry.
    You get what you pay for / Larry Beinhart.
        p.   cm.
    ISBN 0-688-06613-5
    I.   Title.
PS3552.E425Y6 1988
    813'.54—dc19   88-7295
                                                      CIP

Printed in the United States of America

2 3 4 5 6 7 8 9 10

BOOK DESIGN BY LINEY LI

FOR ANNE BEINHART
she of great love and little faith

AND IRVING BEINHART
a very clear vision, but different

JEZEBEL, "Nashville" Katz, 1983
by permission of Memphiz Muzic, Inc., 400 W. 45 St., N.Y., N.Y. 10036
U.S.A. ALL THE WAY, The White Rapper/H. Stucker, 1982
by permission of Honky Tunes, Ltd., 111 Lexington Ave., N.Y., N.Y. 10016
WHITE BOY DO IT 2, The White Rapper/H. Stucker, 1984
by permission of Honky Tunes, Ltd., 111 Lexington Ave., N.Y., N.Y. 10016
CRACK-CRACK, The White Rapper/H. Stucker, 1983
by permission of Honky Tunes, Ltd., 111 Lexington Ave., N.Y., N.Y. 10016
SAY NO, NO, NO, Mary Jo Parker, 1983
by permission of Gospel Faith Music Publishing, Inc., Faith, N.C.
OLYMPIC FEVER, The White Rapper/H. Stucker, 1984
by permission of Honky Tunes, Ltd., 111 Lexington Ave., N.Y., N.Y. 10016
DECADES A GO GO, "Nashville" Katz, 1983
by permission of Pussykatz Muzic, 400 W. 45 St., N.Y., N.Y. 10036
CYRANO DE BERGERAC, Edmond Rostand, trans. Jean-Lauren du Chien, 1988
by permission of William Morrow & Company, Inc.

CONTENTS

Contents

PROLOGUE · JANUARY 1984
There Goes the Neighborhood

Bronx Park is just south of Woodlawn Cemetery. It contains the New York Botanical Gardens and the famous Bronx Zoo, where the tigers sometimes eat a keeper.

One way to get there is the Seventh Avenue/Broadway line. It runs underground in Manhattan, over the streets in the Bronx, and it's called the El. It rattles along on seventy-year-old iron curves. Gutted buildings gape windowless at the passengers. Where kids once came running home to eat Momma's liver and onions, four solid walls around them, there are rubbled lots.

That's old news. The mayor has been on TV to tell us that the Bronx is coming back. Now or sooner or sometime. But come the ass end of January, you could empty the projects, apartment flats, tenements, brownstones, by offering a free ticket to anyplace warm. Nicaragua. Beirut.

Even Arthur Scorcese, rolling warm and easy through the ruins in his two-door white long-hood Lincoln Continental—knowing more often than not which buildings had been torched by the landlord and which by the tenants—might have gone for it. Though where Arthur wanted to go, and had been trying to go for three years, was Arizona. The Sunbelt. Warm, clean, and still reasonably well segregated.

The day had started with great expectations and positive ones. Arthur's father, Santino "The Wrecker" Scorcese, was in Manhattan, a

9

mere twenty-minute drive from Arthur's Long Beach, Long Island, home. How the Feds loved to call Santino "The Wrecker," they never missed a chance, they had the moniker right off the wiretaps, and never once did they point out, or did you see in the *Daily News,* that it was real literal, as Santino had a big finger in the tow-truck business and a couple of junkyards.

That was a real treat in that for the last three years, Santino's residence had been the State Penitentiary in Dannemora, in the frozen wastes somewhere between nowhere, nowhere, and Canada. A sixteen-hour drive on the New York State Thruway, with rest stops where the coffee tasted like Styrofoam and they had discovered a method to make even the pepper you put on the cardboard-flavored food taste like cardboard: probably a refinement of the same process that decaffeinates. Or, almost as bad, all the way through the city, out the other side to People Express in Newark, to Burlington, Vermont, to Avis, then cross-country on two-laners skinned with ice and sprinkled with 35-mph logging trucks.

Santino was scheduled to stay there two more years. He'd been busted on a federal rap, but there was also a parole violation, which meant he had to do some state time. When he got out of Dannemora, he'd move to a federal pen, Danbury probably, for another five years of federal time.

Arthur himself was clean. Not like rice is white or the pope is holy, but clean as could reasonably be expected of someone in the construction business in the greater metropolitan area. Most of his business was in Nassau County, so he was a Republican besides.

Naturally, he had built the day around the visit to his dad, which was scheduled for nine in the morning. Then he was going up to the Bronx to meet a couple of guys who'd told him it was important to have a meet. That was good scheduling too. From there he would go check on some renovations he was doing, in case the mayor was right and the place had made a comeback while he wasn't looking. He didn't think so, since he had been there yesterday, and the Bronx was looking as bad as the Bronx can look, which is like shit.

From there, at least, he could head home over the Throgs Neck Bridge —pleasantly pondering what a throg could be—beat the traffic, and avoid the Long Island Expressway, a seventy-mile six-lane parking lot.

Naturally, the Feds had screwed everything up. They were petty and vindictive people. They rescheduled Santino and made the father-son meeting for the afternoon. Which Arthur had to discover for himself when he arrived at the federal courthouse on Foley Square. After he had already paid to put the Lincoln in a lot. The Feds claimed they had tried to call him.

Arthur knew that that was a crock, because he had a brand-new pager. It was a Christmas present from his family—Angelina, his wife; Santino II, his five-year-old son; and Krystal, the two-year-old he doted on, never mind the dumb name Angelina had insisted on, from *Dallas* or *Dynasty* or maybe one of those daytime things she watched—he could never remember which. It was not your old-fashioned beeper. It was a miracle of modern microchippery. It had a digital readout across the top, in red, that told him the number from which the incoming call was being made, provided the dialer punched the right code. It required a little cooperation was all, and he had taken great pains to give the Feds their own code, at least for this little time that Santino was in town, because he knew they would pull this crap on him. Now everything was reversed, and he was going to end up on the LIE right at rush hour. They were petty and vindictive people.

There was a cheaper model, where the readout was green, but Angelina had gone for the best.

He took it off his belt to admire it. Also to see if it had gone off and he had missed the beep and there was a number printed out for him to call. There wasn't. Sitting as he was, deep in the big, soft Continental seat, it was awkward to put the thing back on his belt beneath the fold of his thickening belly, so he clipped it to the inside pocket of his jacket.

The closer he got to the park, the higher the quality of the habitations. On the last block before parkside, the change was so clear and linear it could have been lifted off a graph. Not that the top end was Fifth Avenue alongside Central Park, but it did reach a level where a self-respecting person would live, the supers mopped the halls, and the tenants didn't remove the plumbing for resale.

Arthur turned and drove along the park until he found a space across from the 2400 block, Park East, between Waring and Mace.

He was early. He turned off the engine and put on the radio. An oldies station came up. Mick Jagger sang something about shelter just a shot away, while Arthur opened the *Daily News* from the back, the sports section. He was disgusted with the Knicks, who hadn't even had the sense to get Mullin, who was going to be the next Larry Bird, out of St. John's.

Ten minutes later, a slow-cruising Buick pulled up alongside and a little behind him. Little Louie Mangiafrino was driving. Frank Felacco, who Arthur knew as a sometime associate of his father, sat in the shotgun seat. Fat Freddy Ventana rode in back.

Arthur pushed the button that electronically popped the door locks. Fat Freddy got out of the Buick, then Felacco.

Fat Freddy was not of those invert names where some gorilla is named Tiny. Fat was fat, and it was with great effort that he bent, finally almost squatting on his haunches, to find the little lever that let the front seat flop forward. He wasn't any more graceful with the contortions required to maneuver through the low trapezium of seat back, slanting roof, and doorframe, into the backseat. There was butter on his tie.

Frank, impatient and shivering in his cashmere overcoat, was a normal-shaped person, even on the lean side. He had to watch his diet because he was diabetic. At sixty-two, ten years older than Freddy, thirty more than Arthur, he moved slow but dignified.

Bob Dylan whined about other people getting kicks for you and chrome horses. Arthur shut the radio off. Freddy fell back with a grunt. Frank pushed the seat back to upright with an annoyed gesture, got in quickly, and closed the door behind him.

"Long time," Frank said. "How you been?"

"OK. Yourself?"

"I take my shots, watch the sugar. You know. I'm alive. . . . Nice car, right, Freddy?"

"Yeah, nice car," Freddy said.

"Thanks," Arthur said.

"How's Santino?"

"He's all right. You know."

"That's a rough thing," Frank said. "Ten years for using an interstate telephone for a felonious conspiracy."

"Yeah," Arthur said, "but they had—what?—eighteen felony counts. I guess that was the one that sounded the least bad. You know how Momma is about the neighbors, so if he was gonna plead, you know. . . ."

"It was a good idea, though," Frank said. "Synthetic cocaine. Fuck the fucking spics right where they live. Santino told me the Nazis, they invented it. You know, during World War Two."

"But it was all over the papers anyway," Arthur said. "Hundred million dollars. What a crock! You ever see a hundred million dollars' worth of anything?"

"Nah," Frank said. "Did you ever, Freddy?"

"Nah, I never," Freddy said.

"The Feds," Frank said. "The Feds are like that. You know, they figure how it might be after it, you know, gets cut and cut and cut all the way to the bottom, like when it's dimes in tinfoil down Avenue D or something. That's how they make up those numbers; make 'em feel like heroes."

"Every which way they can, they fuck me around," Arthur said.

"Anyways," Frank said, "it was a good idea. I had some money in it."

"You did?"

"Yeah. A lot of us did. How 'bout you, Artie?"

"Ahh, you know I don' get involved like that—you know that, Frank."

"Well, that's good, I guess. Anyway, it wasn't just me, you understand, a lot of us had money with your father. Different things."

"I don't know much about his . . . financial arrangements."

"No?" Frank said, indicating neither belief nor disbelief.

"All I know," Arthur said, "is that everything is fucking tied up in this forfeiture-of-assets thing."

"Is that right?" Frankie said.

"Yeah. Yeah. RICO and Continuing Criminal Enterprise crap. You want to hear something. Listen to this. See, I got fucked by it too. They got nothing on me, 'cause there is nothing to get, and they still got every nickel I got tied up."

"Howzat? You so clean?"

"When I started my thing, my construction thing," Arthur said, "Santino, he loans me ten, you know, to get things off of the ground. Well, the Feds claim that that money, it comes from 'racketeering' and a 'continuing criminal enterprise,' which means, according to them, that what I make by busting my ass is part of his thing. You ever hear shit like that? My house—I'm working my tail off paying the fucking mortgage. The Feds, they got a first lien on it."

13

"That's rough," Frank said. "Isn't that rough, Freddy?"

"Yeah, that's rough."

"I heard even worse," Frank said. "Some Colombian spic, down in Lauderdale, I think it was, he bought a raffle ticket. Two-dollar ticket, like at the church or something. And he wins this Cadillac. I don' know, coulda been a Seville, coulda been a Coupe de Ville. Well, you know these spics—first thing they do, they always buy some foreign car, so probably he already has himself a Mercedes and a Porsche, so he don't need the Caddie. So he gives it to his father. Which, I personally think, is a nice gesture, what with how kids are today.

"So they come at this kid with the RICO thing, like with you, and they claim that this two dollars he put on the raffle, it was money from peddling nose candy—like he couldn'ta picked up two bucks in the street, even—and they take his father's Cadillac away. Do you believe that?"

"Yeah, I believe that," Arthur said ardently. "With me they didn't even prove anything. With me they know they can't prove anything. But until I can prove they can't prove anything, which I have been trying to do going on like two years now, everything I got, it is either escrowed or liened. If there are pay toilets, I got to ask the judge for permission to use a dime."

"You got any idea," Frank said, "what kind of bread your father, he owes us?"

"I told you—"

"Counting all the various things he was into."

"—his business was his, not mine."

"Two of the very large," Frank said. "You know, six zeros. Give or take a couple of hundred thousand."

"That's a lot of money," Arthur said, impressed and intimidated.

"Yeah, it is. Isn't that a lot of money, Freddy?"

"A lot of money," Freddy said. "It is."

"See that—Freddy thinks it's a lot of money," Frank said.

The redundancy hung there for several otherwise silent moments. "Are you," Arthur finally said, "asking me to do something about it?"

"Nah," Frank said, shaking his head. "We know you don't have that kinda numbers."

"And like I said—"

"Like you said," Frank said, looking straight ahead. "Though the Feds, they think different. You told me yourself, he laid ten on you for starters. I think that sounds modest, you know, for a man of your father's standing. And generosity. I know if I had a kid, and I had your father's business connections . . . But you say it, I believe it."

"What are you saying? You want ten grand from me?"

"Nah, nah—" Frank began.

"Hey, that's all right," Arthur said, "You go down Foley Square, you get the Feds to cut my money loose, you can have it. I think it's a little fucked, but you want it . . ."

"Slow down, kid. I'm talking here about two million. You think I wanna drive around the fucking Bronx in January for shit like ten thousand? Hey! . . . What you think, Freddy?"

"The fucking Bronx in January," Freddy said.

Across the street, Carlos Ortiz, *el super,* came out to chip the ice from the sidewalk. He noticed the two cars because the Lincoln was parked behind his Honda Civic, his first brand-new car ever, only four years, six months left to pay.

"They got your father down for this grand jury, special prosecutor— what's his name? Jew lawyer . . . Freddy?"

"I don' know," Freddy said. "Jew lawyer."

"Fenderman. Stanley Fenderman," Frank said. "Right?"

"Yeah," Arthur said.

"Why is that?"

"I don't know. Why is that?" Arthur said.

"Well," Frank said, "do you think he's maybe tired, living up there, up Dannemora, practically fucking Canada. You think that's it?"

"What kind of crap is this, Frank? I mean it, what kind of crap is this? You asking me if my father is gonna sing to the grand fucking jury?"

"I'm asking you 'bout your father's health. His, you know, morale, state of mind. A man, he done three, looking at seven more . . . his perspective, it can change."

"I don't know; I never been in the joint. You have." Arthur said. "What do you think? Freddy, he's been in the joint. What does Fat Freddy think?"

"Freddy," Frank said, "tell the man what you think."

"I don't know, Frank; I never done more'n eighteen months."

"So tell me, Artie," Frank said. "Santino, you think he's looking for early release?"

"I respect you, Frank, I do," Arthur said, "but fuck this shit. My father, he coulda taken the witness program and never done a day. You know that. I don't have to tell you that. Also, who are you to be asking me about Santino? I tell you what—you got some reason, something between you and him, you're entitled to ask this shit, you ask him yourself."

"Hey." Frank held his palm up and spoke softly. "We got nothing to fight about. I got nothing but respect for your father. I figure Santino, he's a stand-up guy. I came to do you and him a favor."

"A favor?"

"When your father, when he's done his time, I bet he would like to come out, find the slate clean. Not owing nobody nothing . . . Don't you think he would like that?"

"Yeah," Arthur grunted, wondering what quid would pro for quo.

"And we are not asking," Frank said, "anything your father would not do anyway, you understand?"

"Of course, sure, whatever you say, Frank."

"It would be a good thing your father, he don't say nothing to this special Jew prosecutor, 'specially about Gunderson."

"About Randolph Gunderson?" Which was who the grand jury was investigating. It was at his own request. To silence the "scurrilous and unfounded rumors" that his business dealings, before he entered government, had been less than immaculately conceived.

"How many Gundersons you got in your social circle, Artie?"

"What you want, you want that my father doesn't say anything about the attorney general of the United States." The rumors had started almost immediately after Gunderson had been confirmed by the Senate.

"Yeah, yeah, the Head Fed," Frank said.

"What could Santino say about Gunderson?"

"Your father never mentioned his name?"

"He mentioned his name, you know, sometimes. But you know how he is. If he went to Atlantic City on a high-roller junket, and they brought Sinatra around, like they do, to make you feel big after you drop a hundred grand, he would come home talking 'Me and Frank this' and 'Me and Frank that.' One time they had Diana Ross sing a couple of tunes for just about fifteen of them, and everybody got introduced, personally. You woulda thought my old man done a number with Diana, which I don't figure she would've gone for it. Also you ever hear him talk about him and the mayor? How they're like this? Well, I know fucking well him and His Honor ain't. So he mentioned Gunderson's name, so what?"

"Hey, if that's all there is, then it's painless. Right, Artie?"

"Whatever you want, Frank," Arthur said flatly.

"You telling me you don't know anything about your father and R.G.?"

"I got my own problems," Arthur said. "How deep into things is he?"

"Ask your father," Frank said.

"My father tells me what he feels like telling me. What's the big deal with Gunderson?" Arthur said, and wondered if there was leverage there somewhere, a little something to get the heavy federal foot off his hard-earned, and entirely legit, money. And let him move to Arizona.

"Artie, Artie," Frank said, in that tone that means: We are wise guys; we are supposed to understand these things. "What business is Gunderson in? Where did he raise all that money, for the President's campaign fund?"

"Are we talking something specific here?" Arthur asked.

"Maybe we're not talking at all," Frank said sharply. "Except about who owes who how much."

Mrs. Estelle Kalmanowitz came out of the apartment building across the street, leaning on her cane, on her way to White Plains Road to buy a chicken. She nodded, somewhat grudgingly, to Ortiz, who gave her an unreserved *"Buenos días"* in return.

From the park side and down the block, Mrs. Inez Rodriguez approached. Padded and downed against the cold, she was a magenta-and-gold snow woman. She was dragging her four-year-old, Paco, to all appearances a teddy bear in a puffy maroon swaddle. Paco was dragging his sled.

"You want to tell my father," Arthur said, "that you cancel the two mil if he doesn't talk about Gunderson."

"Yeah," Frank said. "It's getting cold in this fucking heap. Whyn't you turn the heat on?"

"Sure," Arthur said. He bent forward to turn on the ignition.

As the engine caught, the new pager, gift of Angelina, Santino II, and

Krystal, came tumbling down from his jacket pocket. Frank's eyes were caught by the falling object. Arthur reflexively reached to snatch his toy before it hit the floor. It looked like something he wanted to hide.

"The fuck is wired," Frank yelled. "Hit 'em, Freddy."

That was one thing the fat man could still do quickly and smoothly. The .38 came out from his shoulder holster. As Arthur straightened, maybe about to say something, Freddy fired. The bullet entered the back of Arthur's skull, nicely centered. It came out the front and took most of his forehead with it.

Arthur's body folded forward. His arm hit the gearshift and pushed the automatic from Park to Drive. The big Continental shot ahead into the car of Carlos Ortiz. Even though Carlos had taken care to put on the parking brake and leave the car in gear, the disparity in weight was so great that the Lincoln shoved the Honda into the car in front of it, fenders crumpling and lights crackling at both ends.

Frank bent to the floor. He snatched the beeper from under Arthur's feet, then he flung open the door and jumped out. Little Louie, who was experienced in these things, had his motor running. He opened the back door of the Buick so Frank could slip in.

Fat Freddy, however, was having a problem. Getting out was even more difficult then getting in. To begin with, he couldn't get out of the driver's side, what with the dead weight of Arthur Scorcese blocking the way. He had to hump his way, heave and grunt, to the passenger side. Then he had to bend, from a seated position, for the latch to release the front seat back.

As soon as Frank settled in, Louie started the Buick. All of Freddy, except his head, was still in the Lincoln. "Hey, Frankie," he yelled, the way Andy Devine used to do when Wild Bill went galloping off. "Wait for me!"

Louie realized that he had, indeed, left one of the living behind. He began to back up.

Carlos had ignored the shot. But at the sound of taillights cracking, his ears stood up. He always reacted to the sound of a fender crumpling, knowing in his fatalistic Latin soul that someday the crumple would be for him. As, this time, it was.

"Come back here," he screamed as he saw the hurters of his beloved Honda making their escape.

"Hurry up, you fat slob," Frank snarled.

Freddy squeezed out through the door in a sort of half twist, then stumbled. Carlos grabbed his ice chopper, a wooden broomstick with an eight-inch-wide metal wedge at the end, and began racing across the street. Inez Rodriguez carefully looked both ways. Since there were no vehicles in motion, she began to cross the street, dragging Paco behind her. Paco dragged his sled.

"Move, you stupid fuck," Frank yelled at Freddy.

"I'm tryin'," Freddy said, one foot in the Lincoln, one hand on the icy street. He scrambled and stumbled half upright and made a rhino charge, crouched and headfirst, into the Buick. As soon as the bulk of his body was in, only his feet still out, toes pointed at the ground, the Buick started moving.

Carlos arrived, slipping and sliding, as Louie hit the gas. Screaming "Motherfucker car fuckers," Carlos busted their taillight with a savage slash of the ice chopper. As they escaped, he raised it, a spearman as fierce as any Aztec ancestor, and flung it javelin style. His aim was good. It hit the rear window. But it bounced off as harmlessly as an Indian spear against the Castilian steel of conquistador armor.

Inez Rodriguez looked up as Carlos yelled. She saw the Buick leap from a standing start, skid, and roar directly at her. She froze as the metal monster came down upon her. And her child. She snatched at Paco, throwing him out of harm's way before she moved herself. Paco snatched at his sled. He missed.

Louie swerved as Inez finally started to move. Inez was hit only by the breeze. The sled was less fortunate. Paco wailed as it turned to splinters. "Motherfucking *maricones*," Inez screeched.

"Oy, the neighborhood," Mrs. Estelle Kalmanowitz sighed to her cane.

Part I

FEBRUARY
•1984•

1.

Have You Seen a Bergman?

Ninety Percent of the Universe Is Missing
New York Times, *science section*

Luis, the super, had left a note under the door asking me to call our landlord, Jerry Wirtman. Glenda, the woman I live with, was irritated. She thought the note should have been addressed to her. Quite right; the lease was in her name. It was, she said, a sign of disrespect to her as a woman.

Wayne was oblivious. He was reading the science section of the *New York Times*. The science section is published every Tuesday so that the *Times* has advertising space to sell to companies that sell computers. Whenever a particularly good deal appears, Wayne shares that information with us. We are aware that we, as a family, can enter the computer age for under two thousand dollars. Wayne is ten.

It was a comfortable time. Without anger, without fear.

We had, by New York standards, space. Two bedrooms on the upper West Side. Prewar construction, before the builders had figured out how to maximize profits by lowering the ceilings, shrinking the rooms, thinning the walls, and eliminating closets. We even had a real kitchen. Time and rent stablization had turned it into a good deal. A very good deal. By New York standards.

My income still came in fits and starts. But the fits had been frequent enough to allow the illusion of fiscal stability. My partner and I had even taken to banking our fees and then paying ourselves weekly. Just like real people with real salaries.

23

So there was a home. And a relationship. Seven years old. No deliriums of love, no demons of lust. But enough sex for health, enough affection for stability, enough closet space that we didn't have to keep the baggage of the past and fears of the future on top of the TV set.

Jerry Wirtman's note, it turned out, had nothing to do with the landlord-tenant relationship. He had heard from Luis, the super, that I was a detective. Luis has always been very impressed by my profession. Like Wayne, he has some very childish and romantic ideas. Wirtman was interested, perhaps, possibly, maybe, after we discussed the matter, in utilizing my services.

I told him there was no fee for a first consult. When I got there he asked if I had any problem working for a landlord, against a tenant.

The detective agency D'Angelo Cassella gets a variety of jobs, but we maintain our hard-won illusion of stability because of four clients—two divorce lawyers, one general-business law firm, and one of the last remaining bail bondsmen in Brooklyn, Alan Bazzini. But Bazzini was talking about retiring. To Sanibel, in Florida. Or Tucson, Arizona. Without Bazzini we'd be dining at a three-legged table.

So I lied. I said it didn't bother me at all.

"Landlords have a bad press," he said. There was a softness about him, pudgy rather than fat, not nervous but eternally defensive. "We really do. If people don't want landlords, let 'em move to the suburbs or go co-op. Does any other business get treated this way? Do they?"

"Never thought about it," I said neutrally.

"You live in one of my buildings. Do I gouge you?" Wirtman asked. "No," Wirtman answered. "Do you freeze in the winter? No. I give plenty of heat. Plumbing's good. Elevators work. Security is good. The halls are kept decent. Somebody complains, we take care of the problem. That, despite rent stabilization, rent control, union janitors, union doormen, inspectors with their hands out, garbage men with their hands out. You try to find a super who isn't an alcoholic, a junkie, a thief, and can speak English. You try it."

"I see what you mean," I said.

"I get carried away sometimes," Wirtman said, and gave me a silly little smile. It was a nice smile.

"Rent control," he said, titling the next subject. "You understand rent control? Rent stabilization?"

Everybody in New York does. It's a fact of life more significant than the failure rate of condoms. Rent control was established after WW II. It was fine when an inflation rate of 4 percent seemed high. Then the dollar started acting like a peso and rents lagged so far behind rising costs that the landlords were able to make a decent case for its repeal. Anytime a controlled apartment was vacated, it entered the free market. Once. Then it came under a new system called stabilization, which permits regular raises at each lease renewal at a percentage determined by the Rent Stabilization Board. That number, arrived at after much screaming by landlord and tenant groups, is supposed to allow landlords a fair profit, but no more. When a stabilized apartment is vacated the jump is larger, but still limited. Rent is therefore determined by how long the apartment has been stabilized and how often it has turned over.

Some rent-controlled apartments still exist. The tenants pay amounts keyed to the days when the subway was a nickel and thirty-five dollars bought an ounce of gold.

"There are people who abuse the system," he said. "Twelve C."

"Twelve C?"

"The Bergmans," he said.

"Bergmans?"

"Have you ever seen a Bergman?"

"Have I ever seen a Bergman?"

"Have you ever seen," he said, very pointedly, "a Bergman in Twelve C?"

"I'm sorry," I said. "I don't think I'm following this."

"Of course you haven't seen a Bergman. Nobody has seen a Bergman in fifteen years. But the name on the lease on Twelve C is . . . Bergman. For twenty years it's been Bergman." He wasn't smiling anymore. He looked sad. "Since rent control," he sighed.

"What you're saying is that the Bergmans still have the lease, but they don't live there."

"Look at this, look at this. . . ."

```
                                                              205
        Samuel & Ethel Bergman
        754 WEST END AVENUE, APT. 12C
           NEW YORK, N.Y. 10025            _____19_____

    PAY TO THE
    ORDER OF_____| $ _____

    _____DOLLARS

    NEW YORK FEDERAL

    MEMO_____        _____
    ⑆021000089⑆ ⑈04 ⑈66525218⑈ 0232
```

"For two bedrooms. High floor. In a good building. A clean building. A safe building. With elevators, yet. Abuse. This is abuse. By subterfuge. Abuse by subterfuge."

If the Bergmans were subletting, they were making a profit of at least a grand a month. If Wirtman could regain control of the apartment and put it on the market, he could raise the rent between 800 percent and 1,000 percent.

"Could you prove for me," he said, "that these Bergmans live elsewhere?"

"If they do, I probably can. Do you have any more information about them?"

"Yeah. They came with the building."

"Did they fill out an application, ever?"

"It's ancient," he said. But he took it out of the file.

APARTMENT APPLICATION

3/12/56 DATE

NAME: *Samuel N. Bergman*
EMPLOYER: *Sultan Sports Wear*
276 7th Avenue
POSITION: *Vice-President*
INCOME: *$12,500*
AGE: *42*
OTHER TENANTS: *Ethel Bergman.* **RELATIONSHIP:** *Wife*

26

BANK ACCOUNTS:

Checking—*N.Y. Federal*

Savings—*Dime Savings Bank of Brooklyn*

"Am I being an exploiter? A leech? A Dracula landlord?"

"I don't think so," I said.

"They," he said, "these Bergmans, they are stealing from me, they are the gonifs. I am entitled to have real tenants. So how much?"

My rule of thumb is $250 a day. I've gone lower, but I prefer to go higher. I said $350 a day, fifteen a week, and warned him that expenses might be the big number. It was worth better than $20,000 a year to him, but he still wanted to haggle.

"Mr. Wirtman, you seem like a nice man," I said. "And your cause is just. That's important to me. But the thing is, there's a union. . . ."

"A detectives' union?"

"Well, it's called a guild, but it's the same thing. I violate the minimums and I can get in a lot of trouble."

"A union. Who would've thought . . ."

"Hey, they're everywhere. The doctors got the AMA. Luis, the super, he's got a union."

"Don't I know it."

"My hands are tied," I said.

"Unions. That's why everybody's driving Japanese cars. What they've done for this country. Thank God we finally have a President who stands up to them."

"Oh, yeah," I said.

"OK. You better go ahead with it. But watch the expenses."

"Of course," I said. Thank God for the Private Investigators Guild. Someday we really should organize one.

It was a fairly simple case. The first step was a credit check.

There are several multimillion-dollar corporations that keep track of us and sell the information for a profit. That data is confidential, not to be released without our permission. Something we give, for example, every time we fill out a credit application.

I use *TRS* Inc., because their computer is the easiest for Thayer

Sturdivon, hacker, to enter. I had to wait until 3 P.M. Thayer doesn't get out of school until then. He's in the eleventh grade.

In the movies, people who are very smart wear glasses over odd-shaped noses and baggy clothes from Sears over skinny bodies. Thayer has lots of biceps and pecs, which he shows off with muscle shirts and designer slacks; his hair is stylishly short.

There was no Samuel N. Bergman at 754 West End Avenue. At least not one who had ever had a credit card, car loan, mortgage, or judgment against him. Nor was there a Samuel N. Bergman with Citibank checking account number 16652521. I had no other number to cross-reference. All we could do was pull every Samuel N. Bergman in the United States.

Thayer charges me one hundred dollars for the first name and fifty for every other name. Which, depending on how many Samuel N. Bergmans there were, could get excessive. We settled on a five-hundred-dollar cap. Which was fortunate. There are thirty-two Samuel N. Bergmans in the United States. Probably more if we counted those who never applied for credit. But we don't.

None of them lived in Manhattan. The closest one was in Piscataway, New Jersey. But he was born in 1952. My Samuel N.'s DOB was 1914. That gave me a cross-reference and cut the list down to one. In Tucson, Arizona. That particular Bergman listed his main source of income as a teacher's pension from Atlanta. Which did not sound like my Bergman.

I asked Thayer if we could run it the other way. Through the bank account number. That pleased him. "Citibank." He smiled. "I love fucking with Citibank. I'll only charge you fifty for it."

Account number 16652521 turned out to be a business account. It belonged to P.O.B. Services. Their address was a post office box, No. 23784, at Peck Slip Station, New York, N.Y. P.O.B. Services was not listed in the New York phone book. Another dead end.

Mr. Bergman was turning out to be a serious pain in the ass.

Desmond Kennel called shortly after I got back to the office. I hadn't heard from Des in ten years. When last seen, Des had been a semiradical, somewhat investigative reporter for the *Village Voice,* the establishment paper of the counterculture. Des had been very hip in those days: Italian slacks, leather jacket, and Tony Lamas.

He wanted to meet me. And he didn't want to tell me why until he saw me.

I asked when. He suggested we meet for drinks, around eight. I had a six o'clock squash game. What with a shower and all, there was no point in going home in between.

"That's all right," I said.

He named the newest, trendiest spot on the West Side.

2.

Frankly Ferns

Frankly Ferns specializes in vintage California wines with French château prices. They have an all-video room. At Frankly Ferns, real men eat quiche.

I was early. They didn't seem interested in letting me in. I told them Desmond Kennel had probably made a reservation. They admitted he had. I would be permitted to wait at the bar. I asked the bartender for water.

"Apollinaris? Saratoga? GustaAvis?" the young man behind the bar asked. He spoke with verve. He was an actor. I might be a producer. There are no real bartenders anymore. Or waiters. There are only underemployed other things. Coloratura sopranos, prima ballerinas, video artistes, mosaicists, nouveau choreographers, auteurs de cinéma. "I recommend the GustaAvis. It's new. It's Swedish. Glacial."

"Tap?" I said.

"I don't tap," he said. Very apologetic. "I just do jazz and a little classical. But I'm a quick learner."

"Tap water," I said. He looked at me, wondering how I'd gotten past the bouncer. "And a beer," I said.

"Amstel? Beck's? Heineken? Guinness? Molson Golden? LA? Grolsch? Dos Equis? Dortmunder? Pschorr Kulmbacher? St. Pauli Girl? Mitsubishi? Kirin? Coors? Grizzly? Nordik Wölf?"

"Schlitz," I said.

Once it had made Milwaukee famous. He hadn't heard of it. I settled for Mitsubishi. I thought it might taste like a car.

Des was late. He bustled in. Reporter on the make, still. There was a girl on his arm. The leather jacket had become a leather coat, he wore a suit underneath, and he had shoes on his feet. His hair was a little thinner and the mustache was gone. Des was pushing forty, the girl was pushing Bloomingdale's. I understood why Des had picked Frankly Ferns. She was a Farrah Fawcett–cut border-states blonde with that natural look, all hypoallergenic. The tint in her contacts made blue eyes bluer, her lipstick was oral-sex coral, her designer breasts were in off-white cotton with dimple-pink trim.

"Sorry I'm late. Really am. Late breaker," he said, hitting his attaché case. "This is Kimberly, this is Tony; Tony, Kimberly. They have my table ready for us."

We slithered between tightly packed tables. Credit cards glittered.

"You still with the *Voice?*" I asked Des.

He looked at me in shock. "You don't know?"

"I guess not," I said.

"Action News. I'm Action News!"

"Action News?" I asked.

"Come on," Des said. "WFUX Eight, New York's leading independent. 'The Hot One.' "

"Hey, hey," I said. I had never actually watched it, but I had seen their posters in the subway. *"Action News. 'The Hot One.' Great going, Des. It's a long way from the *Voice.*"

The waiter arrived. Kimberly stared at him. He asked what we would like. She said, "Don't I know you?"

"Two Chivas," Des said. "What about you, Tony?"

"Some food," I said.

"The Dark Before the Dawn," the waiter said.

"Greg Diamond," Kimberly cried. "You're supposed to be dead!"

"Yeah," the waiter sighed.

"You went over a cliff in that terrible crash. After you seduced Jessica, and her mother, and stole the secret formula for Dr. Horton's immune vaccine."

"It was my agent's fault. I was up for renewal. There was no stopping my charming villainy. So my agent asks for double. There I am, a week later, over a cliff. The stupid bitch. I got rid of him."

"You poor man," she said.

"I have a new agent. There's a good chance for resurrection."

"Two Chivas," Des repeated.

"Now, now, Des," Kimberly said. "Perrier with a twist."

"Come on, have a real drink," Des said.

"My new agent is also the agent for one of the head writers," the waiter said. "There are all sorts of possibilities. Maybe I wasn't really in the car. Maybe I was, but I survived. Or I might come back as my brother, seeking revenge, of course. Death is no obstacle."

"Two Chivas," Des said.

"Des-s-s," she said. A whole history of skirmishes in her tone. "It's a work night."

"We don't have Perrier," the recently deceased Greg Diamond said, "but we do have a fine selection of mineral waters, imported and domestic."

"I recommend the GustaAvis," I said. "It's new. It's Swedish. Glacial."

"Exactly," the waiter said. Impressed.

Des sighed.

"And a menu," I said.

"It's been a long time," Des said to me.

"Yeah."

"I never told you about Tony Cassella," he said to Kimberly. "You're looking at an authentic American hero."

"Oh," she said.

"You remember the Knapp Commission?" he asked her as if she would. Which was foolish. She wouldn't know the Brooklyn Dodgers, Walt Frazier, sex without the pill, illegal abortions, Khe Sanh, Yippies, or any other ancient histories.

She nodded tentatively. But she had the same expression on her face that Luis has when I'm speaking English too fast and he's embarrassed to admit he doesn't understand.

"Frank Serpico?" he asked. "Serpico was made into a movie, with Al Pacino."

"I like Al Pacino," she said. "That's an Italian name, isn't it?"

"In those days, Tony was a prison guard—" Des said.

"Corrections officer," I said. Auto reflex. Black men to boy, sanitation workers to garbage man, and liberal politicians to liberal.

"Back then," he said, "corruption was pretty institutionalized."

"Still is," I said.

"And here is this young, idealistic guy—"

"Come on," I said. "What did you want to see me about?"

Des ignored my question and went on making a major drama out of a relatively simple investigation. Corruption is easy to find once you're on the inside. The waiter brought the drinks. Des's media style was meant to be flattering to me or exciting to her. I didn't care to hear it.

"Come on," I said. "So how did you end up with 'The Hot One,' the *Action News?*"

"I went into crime. I realized crime is where it's at," Des said. "You got to target your market." Des swallowed some Chivas. "Print is dead. The future is electronic, and the future is now."

"So you moved to TV. Terrific. What you wanna see me about?"

"Things are popping. I'm talking cable. I'm talking satellite superstation. I'm talking news."

"Des is tuned to the pulse of things. It's important to be tuned to the pulse of things. Planning does not mean rigidity," Kimberly said. Unless she said, "Planning does not mean frigidity."

"I have a plan," Des said.

"It's important to have a Life Plan," Kimberly said. "Do you have a Life Plan?"

"No," I admitted.

"I have a Life Plan," she said. "First, school. I'm done with that. Then Career Start. That's where I am now. Then Career Firmly Established. When I reach that strata, that's when I'll get married."

"I see," I said. "When's that?"

"When I'm twenty-four."

"Hard news is one thing," Des said. "Just the facts and nothing but the facts. Wham, bam, thank you, Ma'am. But there is another dimension. It's called life. Real life. You can't deliver real life in twenty-two-second clips. Make the viewer feel. Make 'em laugh, fear, cry, yearn. Do you understand what I'm talking about?"

"Oh, yes," Kimberly said, concentrating.

"I'm talking magazine format. Video column," Des said. "My own show."

"Oh. When?"

"Right now," Des said. "I'm in development with the pilot. The city. That special energy. That nitty-gritty. Downtown, uptown. The Urban Experience. A show with heart and guts. And cheap to produce."

"Heavy," I said.

"Very," Kimberly said.

"Exactly," Des said. "It's not just the opportunity to do a different kind of journalism, which is my first priority. It's name recognition. A whole new level."

"It's a Life Plan," Kimberly said. "Des has a Life Plan now. He's in the process of formalizing it. Once it's Formalized, you move on to Full Realization."

"A Formalized Life Plan and Full Realization. I'm happy for you, Des," I said.

"LPW makes a lot of sense, Tony," he said a little defensively. His eyes went to her off-white pink-trim breasts.

"LPW?"

"The Life Plan Way," Kimberly said. "Des was an Instinctive when we met. He was pushing very hard to become Master of His Environment, but he just didn't know how. Now, with his Full Life Plan being Formalized, I'm certain he will achieve his each and every goal. Including wealth and happiness."

Des gulped down the rest of his first glass of Scotch. He waved for the waiter.

"So what can I do for you, Des?"

The recently deceased Greg Diamond returned. I asked for the smoked-mozzarella-and-tomato platter and another beer.

"Two Chivas," Des said.

Kimberly, who had finished her first Scotch, said "Des-s-s, I'm drinking water."

"I want you to visualize this," Des said to me. "From the towers of power to the back alleys. Des ·Kennel and the Insiders. I have some very heavy people lined up. So heavy that some of them, *you will never see their faces.* A Wall Street heavy. This is the eighties. Money is sexy.

A City Hall power broker. Power is sexy. I have a madam. Sex is sexy. It still is. Really.

"The Insiders," he said. "I want you to be one of them."

"It's great, Des," I said. "But what do you want?"

"Can you dig it?" He punched me on the arm. "Do you love it?"

"Well, Des . . ."

"Tony . . . it's going to do you a lot of good."

"You know your business better than I do," I said. "So if you say I'm right for this, maybe you're right. But I have to warn you, my business is divorces, employee theft, in-law embezzlement. Like that."

"Right. You got it," the waiter said—my food, a beer, two Scotches, and one water.

"All right," Des said, "let's put some cards on the table. It's no secret"—he put a forefinger to the tip of his nose and pushed it sideways—"you're connected."

"Gimme a break, Des," I sighed.

"Vincent Cassella," he announced. My uncle.

"So?"

He looked at me, significantly.

"I'm not even going to bother to discuss it," I told him. I don't, in fact, know the man very well. I don't know his business at all. Our lives haven't crossed since I was ten. Well, hardly ever.

"Sure," he said. Letting me know that he knew a lot more than he was supposed to know about me being connected, though he most certainly did not know what there was to know, and what he thought he knew was not there to be known.

Then he made another nasal gesture. He raised his pinkie to one nostril, like it had one long scoop-shaped nail.

"Yeah," I admitted. "Once upon a time. Who gives a fuck?"

"My only point is that you've been there. Been to the bottom. And clawed your way back up."

"Hey, Des. By now, half the world's been around that block."

"It's chic! It's hip! It's the eighties!" he said. "This is the age of the Betty Ford clinic. Get straight and you get on the cover of *People*. Donohue'll bring you in to talk to the housewives."

"Would you excuse me a minute?" Kimberly said. We watched her walking away. She was good at it.

"She's a great kid," Des said, "and I have a lot of feeling for her. She's very, very cerebral."

"Cerebral?"

"Yeah. Analytical. Analyzes everything; very sharp."

"I can see that," I said.

"But underneath that serious exterior . . ." he said. "Once she gets a little drunk, she's hot. She thinks sex is dirty. So when she does get to it . . . it's hot. Sex as sin. It makes me feel like a teenager. A teenager stud. You know what I mean?"

"Is she Catholic?" I said.

"It's really hot," he said. "Things go in cycles. I think sin is going to make a comeback. And big tits."

"They both have a lot of potential, Des."

"What I'm offering you," he said, "a press agent couldn't get you. You could pay him fifty, sixty grand a year and he couldn't deliver what I can deliver. Media power. I can make you a star. . . . Are you on board?"

"I'm giving it serious consideration," I said. And I was. It was time for some kind of move. Even if we got a client to replace Bazzini, we were just treading water. And the water was rising. Our insurance had doubled in two years. Our office lease was coming up. Commercial rents are not controlled or stabilized. It was going to go up 400 or 500 percent.

Kimberly came back while Des was saying, "Tony, let me say this, and I won't say any more. You've always made other things more important than money. I respect that—"

"Anyone who leaves money out of their Life Plan," Kimberly quoted, piously, "is unrealistic, or a fool." She returned to her drink. She was the only person I'd ever seen drink Scotch through a straw.

". . . But you're shortchanging yourself," Des said. "Until you've had it, you don't realize what money can buy. Not just materially, but in self-respect, in the respect granted you by others, even in social and romantic relationships." His words ricocheted around the table, a silent clicking slide show of what we were, relations that were, that had been, that could be and couldn't. "The higher you go, the better it gets. Believe it."

"OK, I believe it," I said.

"Are you on board? Can I count on you?"

Television has made successes out of people who are far bigger assholes than I am. "I can see the potential of the idea," I said. The last time I'd been in the spotlight, it had torn me up. But that was about real things. That was about accusing my brother correction officers of corruption, and convicting them. Destroying them. Des's "concept" sounded a lot more soft-core, an *Entertainment Tonight* of crime. Pleasant, profitable, and bullshit. "Yeah, I could get on board."

"I'll drink to that," Des said.

We all touched glasses and had a swallow. Des finished his.

"Hey, can you help me with something?" Des said, offhand, waving for the waiter.

"What?"

"Did you catch the *Six O'Clock Report?*"

"Mostly I read the papers," I said.

"You been following this special prosecutor thing with Randolph Gunderson?"

"The attorney general?"

"That's the one," he said. "The grand jury came to a decision today."

"Wasn't one of the witnesses killed?" I said. I'd read about the Scorcese murder. And the papers had tied the murder of Arthur Scorcese directly to an attempt to silence his father, Santino Scorcese.

"Two," he said. "Two 'mob-style hits.' Like we like to say."

"Did the grand jury indict?"

"Background," Des said. "You have to dig the background. That's what makes it tasty. It starts out standard: President nominates, the Senate holds hearings. The guy's not much of a lawyer; he's more a big-time real estate dealer. But who cares. There's an FBI check on the guy. They do that on everybody. The FBI says he's clean. The Senate approves the appointment.

"Two weeks later, the rumors start to fly. The Senate reopens the hearings. It turns out the FBI knew of some kind of links, through wiretaps, between Gunderson and organized crime. And they lied about it. It looks even worse because the agent who lied got promoted practically the next day." Des opened his briefcase and pulled out a clipping from the *Times.*

You Get What You Pay For

New York Times

WASHINGTON TALK   *(September 22, 1983)*

Briefing

Promotion Deferred at DEA

Ex-FBI Special Agent Vernon W. Muggles, who had been promoted to Deputy Director of the Drug Enforcement Administration, is now temporarily Ex-Deputy Director and a Special Agent again.

Mr. Muggles was the agent in charge of the background investigation of Attorney General Randolph Gunderson. His promotion, a jump of three steps in GSA grade, came only one week after he testified before the Senate Justice Committee about that investigation. When those hearings were reopened, it appeared that the FBI had information that Mr. Muggles admitted had been "overlooked."

The Committee's senior minority member, Senator Orin Steele, said, "Overlooked, my petunia. The man is an old-fashioned country liar."

A Justice Department spokesman said that Mr. Muggles' promotion "has not been withdrawn, it has only been suspended, pending."

"Anyway," Des went on, "the allegations started piling up. Gunderson got up and said he wanted it settled once and for all. Innocent or guilty. His day in court. He called for a special prosecutor in the Leon Jaworski mode. You remember Jaworski," he said to Kimberly.

She looked a little blank. Very cerebral, but light in history.

"The special prosecutor that was appointed to investigate Watergate, Richard Nixon, and all that," Des explained. She nodded with more positive understanding than I think she actually felt. "That was a tragedy," Des said, talking about Gunderson again, "for us newsies. Senate hearings are wide open. What the hell—they're not fact finders, they're publicity forums. But you move the thing into a grand jury room and everything is secret. So there's no news, and if you're Gunderson, no news is good news."

"But with two witnesses getting rubbed out . . ."

"You really didn't catch my story on the *Six O'Clock Report?*" he said, as if it actually surprised him. He looked at his watch. "They have TVs in the back. We're going to watch 'The Hot One, on 8 at 10.' "

Four giant screens graced the walls of the video room. Three of them were tuned to MTV, which was broadcasting the new White Rapper video, *Talk Show Hostess*. He had a John Travolta face and a Rodney Dangerfield body. Women with long legs and smiles tossed batons around red and white satin crotches. *I Love Lucy* silently filled the fourth screen. There were individual TV sets at various tables. It was a place for people who don't want to sit home and watch TV.

Des found an unoccupied table and switched the TV to Channel 8.

Action News, with the Action News Team, had, like most TV news shows, developed to a point beyond parody. They spent more time telling us what they were going to tell us than they spent telling it to us. And when at last the story came, it was less than what they'd promoted it as. For example, they promised "Action Tape" of the President's bowels.

The Gunderson story was promoted four times. "Coming up," the anchorette said breathlessly, "Desmond Kennel with Action Tape. Surprise finale," she said four times, "in the Gunderson trial." Although it was not a trial.

When at last the tape came, it displayed Randolph Gunderson standing on the steps of the federal courthouse, raising his fingers in a "V" sign. Just like Winston Churchill. Or Richard Nixon. "The court has ruled. I am Innocent. This is Vindication." Reporters tried to ask questions. "I have been the victim of politically motivated innuendo and a campaign of smears. The court has seen justice done. Let the scandalmongering stop. I'm going back to Washington to do the job the President asked me to do."

Then they switched to Stanley Fenderman, special prosecutor. "The court does not rule that someone is innocent," Fenderman said, rather limply. "That is not legal phraseology."

"How would you describe the court's decision?" Des asked him on camera.

"The court did not make a decision," Fenderman said. "The grand jury made a finding."

"Which is that you found Gunderson innocent?"

"I would say—which is what our report says—that there is insufficient corroborated evidence to indict."

" 'Insufficient corroborated evidence to indict,' " Des said. The live Des, not the previously recorded Des. "What the hell kind of unstatement statement is that? I'll tell you what it's not. It's not good copy. What does it mean?"

"Why don't you wait for the report to come out?" I asked him.

"Ah hah," he cried. He flung open his briefcase. "Take a look," he said, waving a printed report as thick as a book. He dropped it on the table and it landed with a thunk I could hear even over the White Rapper.

4/5/83

**Report of the Special Prosecutor and the
Findings of the Grand Jury**

UNITED STATES OF AMERICA vs RANDOLPH L. GUNDERSON

HON. DUDLEY R. DAMSKY

DISTRICT COURT

SDNY

U.S. COURT HOUSE

SPECIAL PROSECUTOR STANLEY FENDERMAN
Appointed under 1978 Ethics in Government Act
SANFORD L. TOMPKINS III
STEPHEN EKISIAN
ALICIA BRONSTEIN
WILLIAM F. CROOKE
NATHANIEL SIMONOV
PETER DIMMER-LODES
SYDNEY COBERLAND

The Special Prosecutor was appointed on October 5, 1982, by a Federal Appeals Court Panel under the procedures established by the 1978 Ethics in Government Act to conduct a Grand Jury probe of possible violations of federal law by Randolph L. Gunderson.

This investigation was intended to examine the specific allegations arising from or included in the testimonies of ██████████████████ ██████████████████████████ Gerald Maldonado, Peter Ciccolini, ██████████████████████████████████████ ████████████ ; transcripts of authorized federal wiretaps of ██████ ████████████████████████████████ pursuant to the investigation of the ████████████ Crime Group, of ████████

40

██████████████████ , ██████████████████
████████████████████ pursuant to investigations labeled FBI Case
#2397-78; but not limited thereto and inclusive of any such other infor-
mation and matters that the Special Prosecutor and the Grand Jury might
deem relevant under the charter of this investigation. . . .

"One hundred and thirty-six pages, and eighty-four pages are deleted!" Des said. "Protecting protected witnesses and ongoing FBI
investigations. Now what kind of report is that—eighty-four pages of
investigations and the kind of witnesses that have to be kept secret, and
the guy is proclaimed innocent."

"You read it?"

"Just flipped through in the cab, picking up Kimberly, and then on the
way here. It's not good copy. That"—his finger jabbed at a black
block—"under there, that's the good copy."

The recently deceased Greg Diamond had found us, bringing another
round of drinks with him.

"You should be able to get a copy of the original," I said.

"You think so?" he said. Excited.

"Yeah," I said. "Piece of cake."

"Fabulous," he said. "Absolutely fabulous. I knew I came to the right
man. How would you do it?" he asked.

And I figured that he had come to the point. At last. "Well," I said,
"the first thing I would do is find a client to pay me to do it."

"Could you get it?" he asked.

"Yeah," I said, sipping at my beer, feeling fuzzy but certain.

"OK then," he said. "That's it. That's the key. We're looking at
opportunity here, you and I. We need something, something big, something hot, to kick my show open. To get these syndication guys to wake
up and realize Des Kennel is the man to back. . . . *This is it!*"

"I'd love to help you, what with you buying all these drinks . . ." And
by then we were on the third round. Or the fourth.

"I thought we were in this together. I thought you were on board,"
Des said. "The Insiders. That's *us.*"

"Des, you know my rate."

"What the fuck," Des said, and added, "Pardon my French," for
Kimberly.

"Don't worry about me," she said. "I've heard the *f* word before. And cock. And cunt. And all of them. You boys just go on and have your conversation." People have different ways of showing their inebriation.

"I don't work," I told him, "on the come."

"And that word too," Kimberly said. She was reaching under the table, groping for Des.

"I can't pay you," he said. "You know that. Even if I wanted to. Journalistic ethics."

"Des is very ethical," Kimberly said.

"You know what I think," Des said. "I think you just realized that you were shooting your mouth off. That you'd be in over your head. I'd lay money you couldn't get it."

It was a very juvenile ploy. "How much?" I said.

"Fifty bucks," he said. I shook my head. He offered a hundred.

"Look," I said, thinking very rationally, "I gotta figure it would take me, I don' know, two, three weeks, maybe, to nail it. So what we're talking about, we're talking about three, four grand to make it worth my while. So if you want to bet four grand that I can't get it, then we're talking."

"My four grand against your four grand. Can you afford it?"

A sober, cold sober, thought cut through the fuzz. The thought was: No. But I was very clever. Very clever indeed. "Your money against my time," I said. "All I got to sell is my time and my smarts. If I go looking for all this deleted stuff and I don't find it, then I'm already out four grand. Plus it costs me a grand in expenses."

"That's a crummy bet," he said. "If you lose, I don't win anything."

"Yeah, but if I lose, I lose," I said. "And if I win, you win too."

"Life is tough, then there's a commercial break," Kimberly said.

"The two of you," I asked her, "how long have you been together?"

"A week," she said. "Well, we haven't been together for all week. We met a week ago."

"It's gotta be two weeks," Des said. "News gets old real quick. You'd have to do it in two weeks."

"You got a bet," I said.

42

3.

A Polish Hypothesis

In the morning I regretted the bet. That's what people get high for. To do things they'll regret in the morning. But a bet's a bet.

The report was full of government secrets. As with most government secrets, a lot of people knew them. Eight attorneys. Their support staff—secretaries, stenos, typists, researchers, paralegals, proofreaders. The FBI had to read it to censor it, and the director of the FBI reports directly to the attorney general, who was Randolph Gunderson.

As did a judge, his clerk, a bailiff, a court reporter, and sixteen grand jurors.

With that many people, there was no question that someone could be gotten to.

> When the group reaches the size of five, a traitor is a
> statistical inevitability. Jesus was lucky that he only
> had one out of twelve. As a son of God, he knew the
> odds, and that is why he was so phlegmatic about the
> event.
> STANISLAW ULBRECHT, *Centripetal Forces in
> Group Dynamics* (University of Grenoble Press,
> 1961)

I had studied with Ulbrecht for one undergraduate semester. According to his thesis, the forces of cohesion can be quantified, and the forces of dissolution are open to statistical analysis. Which sounds like babbling academia. But it's just different language for the way cops and prosecutors operate, which is more like: "If there's two scumbags on a job, one'll rat out the other to save his own ass. If some junkie whore doesn't rat him out first for a nickel bag."

Ulbrecht's ideas were fascinating. And disturbing. It was hard to tell which side of fascism he was talking from. But his statistical methods were flawless. Which he pointed out. The undergrads naturally nick-named him "Flawless Slawless." I would have taken more courses with him, but when Stony Brook was shut down by the students in '69 one of the issues was the discovery that the CIA was paying all or part of Ulbrecht's salary and he resigned.

It was not a question of if someone would spill, but how to target my limited resources in a limited amount of time. The best bets, simply because I had their names and because they were the most likely to have the actual physical document, were Fenderman and his seven associates.

The morning paper had a profile of Fenderman as a sidebar to the Gunderson story. Colby College. University of Chicago Law School. Federal Appeals Court clerkship. Senior partner with Wharton, Scully, Fundament & Elhaus. His clients all had initials: IBM, LTV, T&A, GTE, ITT, RVS, B&D. His assignment as special prosecutor had been temporary. A citizen soldier serving his country in her hour of need. In fact, he had donated his billable hours, $200,000, bringing the cost of the investigation down to only $1,200,000. His staff was, likewise, a temporary posse, enlisted for the duration of the pursuit. Personally selected. Four of them, Tompkins III, Crooke, Simonov, and Dimmer-Lodes, came from Fenderman's firm. Ekisian and Coberland had been borrowed from another Manhattan firm, Wilfree, Madison, Madison, Montague & Reach. Ms. Bronstein had been on loan from the Brooklyn district attorney's office.

Once again, I had to wait until after three, when Thayer got out of school, to run a credit check.

Remarkable things, credit reports. The staccato abbreviations and coded designations are dot matrix abstracts of character and life-style. They catch the truly significant points in the human lifelines. Not birthdays or anniversaries, but the points where income soars or floors, where spending is under control or running like blood from an open vein.

All of them had Visa/Mastercard/Amex Gold/Diners Club/Brooks Brothers/Bloomingdale's/Exxon/Sears cards, margin accounts, mortgages, Keoghs and/or IRAs. They were lawyers.

When Ulbrecht developed his theories, he was a prisoner in a concentration camp. In fact, he wrote the first draft of his first book there, a way of taking the foulest and most dehumanizing experiences and, by dealing with them on the plane of the intellect, transforming them into an affirmation of human capacity. His later studies, and those of the academics who followed up on his theories, were conducted in police states or in police situations, where force in varying degrees could be employed. I didn't have the power of the state behind me. But the theory remained the same. Find the soft points and then apply leverage.

Of the seven, three seemed to have potential.

COBERLAND, SYDNEY: 121 E. 74 St. NYC // Emp. Wilfree, Madison, Madison, Montague & Reach // salary $98K // outside income $42K // Mortgages, Old Westbury and New Hampshire // Auto, leased, Mercedes // C/S (child support) $54K // A (alimony) $30K // SLC (auto loan, co-maker) $10K and $7K. // 4 Judg Vacat // Suit Dismd // 2 Suits // Age: 48

Four judgments vacated, one suit dismissed, and two suits in court. Syd was a very litigious guy. A fighter. Yet after the alimony, child support, and mortgages on two homes he didn't seem to live in, his $140,000 was down to thirty or forty thousand a year. Before taxes.

No question, his wife had something on him.

DIMMER-LODES, PETER: 234 Third Ave. NYC // Emp. Wharton, Scully, Fundament & Elhaus // salary $58K // outside income $60K ('83) // outside income $12K ('82) // Mortgage, 234 Third Ave. // Auto, leased, Saab. // Age: 28

In 1983, Peter's outside income had jumped $48,000. Maybe he'd gone long in yen. Maybe his rich spinster aunt had died. Or maybe it was something interesting.

45

BRONSTEIN, ALICIA W.: 182 Hicks St. Brooklyn, N.Y. // Emp. District Attorney, Kings Co. // salary $28.7K // outside income $0 // Auto loan $3.6K, Mitsubishi. Age: 30

Alicia stood out because she made less than half what anyone else made, because she was a law enforcement professional, and because she was a woman. I like women.

I went after her first.

The old-time machine is dead in Manhattan. Now Manhattan belongs, quite nakedly, to the real estate interests.

But it's different in the boroughs. In Brooklyn, Queens, the Bronx, the machine lives. With patronage, no-show jobs, the rake-offs, kickbacks, schemes, scams, and a boss. Andrew Skelly in the Bronx. Gerry Gutman in Queens. Alfonse Alioto in Brooklyn.

Beneath the bosses, there are district leaders. That is an elective office. Obscure, unsalaried, with few defined duties, they are the *capos,* the cardinals, of urban politics. Gene Petrucchio has been one, in that part of Brooklyn called Sunset Park, for twenty-five years or more. His financial condition is probably "substantial," and substantially unknown. He lives in a modest one-family house on a residential street, surrounded by other neat one-family houses. It is remarkable only in that the entire block is very clean, with sidewalks in good repair, and there is not a single pothole in the street.

We met at Dom & Angie's Luncheonette on Prospect Avenue. It was three in the afternoon. Two men were at the counter; Gene was alone at a table in back.

Gene knows people. It's his profession. He knows my partner, from when Joey was a cop. And he knew my father. All of which made me a paisan. Someone who could be spoken with. Casually, off the record, up to the point of indictability.

"You're looking more and more like your father every day," Gene said.

"You're looking good, Gene. You're gonna run Brooklyn forever."

"Hey, Tony, I don't run no Brooklyn."

"Just your part of it."

"I wish it were like that. I wish it were like that. I work real hard. You gotta stay on top of things."

"I know that, Gene. You do. You work real hard."

"You want some coffee? Sandwich or something? They got a meat loaf special today. Side a spaghetti. Dom makes it, so it's pretty good. So long as Angie don't make it, it's pretty good."

"Just some coffee."

"Nothing else? A danish? A roll?"

"Just the coffee."

"Hey, Angie," he called out. "Coupla coffees."

"How's Donna?"

"The wife's real good. Had a little trouble with her back, you know. Regular doctor couldn't seem to do nothing. Had her in a corset. Ever seen one of them things—a medical corset, I mean? Like something outa the Middle Ages for torturing. Maybe something the priests put you in, you didn't say enough Hail Marys, did too many venereal sins. So we tried a chiropractor. The health insurance covers that now, and I think he fixed her."

"And the kids?"

He sighed. "Anita, she's getting a divorce. I don't know, we brought her up right. Two kids and she's getting a divorce. I tried to talk to her. The wife tried to talk to her. Talkin' to your own children, sometimes that's the toughest thing in the world. Sonny, he's up at RPI. Doing real good. Gonna be an engineer. Which leaves me batting .500, I guess. Which isn't bad in life."

"Not bad at all."

"What's with the Bronstein?" he asked.

"I just want to know about her."

"Yeah? You got a client got a case coming up against her?"

"Nothing like that."

"Oh," he said. "You telling me this is something you don't want to tell me about? Or you telling me this is something I don't want to know?"

"If you want me to tell you, I'll tell you. I'm in your ballpark, Gene, we play home-team rules."

"All I would wanna know is, is this something that could hurt us some way 'other?"

"No way I can see."

"The thing is—"

"If I thought it was something could hurt you, I wouldn't come to you

47

with it, you know what I mean. If it was something that I had to do and it was gonna hurt you, I would go somewhere else. Not to friends."

". . . The thing is, if we got a problem, I don' wanna be the last to know it."

"If it's gonna be a problem, Gene, I'll let you know."

"Yeah, well, I checked her out for you, plus I know her a little."

Angie brought two cups and the pot. Some women have cleavage and it's a pleasure to see. Then there are some who have it and you wish they'd kept it a secret. The coffee was in those heavy old luncheonette cups, at least a finger thick around the rim. Only one was chipped. The coffee was fresh and strong. I added cream. Gene added cream and sugar, two spoons. He blew on it and took a thoughtful sip.

"Whatever happened to a woman's place is in the home?" he said.

"I don't know, Gene."

"I mean, I understand the argument they got, mentally. But don't family mean nothing no more? My mother, she's got Alzheimer's, senile. Whyn't we say senile? She lives with us, 'cause that's the way it's supposed to be. What're we supposed to do, put her in a home or someplace? What kinda thing is that to do? If Donna goes out with a job, how we gonna look after the old lady? You see what I'm saying? So women got a right to work, I understand that, but maybe it's not right that they work, you understand what I mean?"

"Yeah, but times are changing."

"Yeah, times are changing. Anyway, I'm saying all that to say that maybe where female D.A.s is concerned, I'm maybe not exactly un-prejudiced. I think she's a cunt."

"Oh."

"You know, you're in politics, you learn you gotta got along with all kinds. You don't like niggers, you don't like niggers, but you got to recognize that they're here, that they're people and they're gonna do what they have to do like we all do. So you get along. I get along. With the Jews, with the P.R.s, with the blacks. With guys you know the score. With women you don't."

"You don't like her?"

"Well, you know, she gets herself hired with affirmative action. There wasn't a whole lot of women lawyers in the D.A.'s office. So she gets out of law school and applies. She comes in for an interview, makes all the right noises. She's supposed to understand that you don't become a star overnight. Even with lawyers, there got to be infantry. But from the day she got hired, she's complaining. She's better than the work she got. And talks like she could run the whole office better."

"She smart? Or dumb?"

"Book smart. Reality dumb. You know what the D.A.'s office is. Hell, they like winners. We like them to like winners. Come campaign season, D.A. he wants to say his office it got like a ninety-two-percent conviction rate. You know, I know, that just means they didn't take anything to court unless it was a lock.

"The D.A.'s office, it's not like sanitation, or the DMV, or parks, nobody knows you're working or not. A prosecutor, they can keep score. D.A. got someone can get the job done, he moves him, her, up fast 'nough. This she don' understand. She doesn't wanna wait for Reuben to move her up. She wants homicides. She wants O.C. She wants this and that. That's why she got sent over, work on that Gunderson thing with a special prosecutor, something."

"Not because she was good?"

"She's good, you think Reuben's gonna let her take a leave of absence?"

"So she's not good?"

"Fair's fair." He shrugged. "It's not so much that she's bad but that she's a pain in the ass. . . . Other thing is, Reuben, he's gonna pack his bags next year or in four, but mos' likely next. Now things being how things is, that's no big deal. We got Landsman—"

"Landsman?" I said. "You got to be kidding."

"The man has paid his dues. Loyalty, you got to remember loyalty. . . ."

"I once saw Landsman in the john," I said, "down the courthouse. He looks at the stalls, he looks at the door, he looks back again, finally he has to ask directions which way is out."

". . . He's been Reuben's assistant twelve years. Knows the office. And he ain't got no enemies," Gene said. "Thing is, there's a couple different people making noises at making a run for Brooklyn D.A. There's Bill Vassey and Edith Bloom."

"For D.A.?" I asked. Vassey was a civil rights type, black, usually found attacking the police or being attacked by the police in the course of being civilly disobedient. Bloom had been a liberal congressperson from Manhattan, a one-term media phenom. Then she lost her seat to redistricting.

"If they both make a run"—he smiled—"they split the reformers, Bloom gets the divorced women, the faggots, Vassey gets some of the colored votes, we keep the party faithful, the married women, all the Catholics including the P.R.s. Bloom against Landsman, one on one, we got trouble. . . . So. You want an introduction to Alicia Bronstein."

"Yes," I said.

"I'm not the best person to do that. She thinks you come from me or from Al . . . So what I got to do is think of a back way."

"Thanks, Gene."

"You know, Ant'ny, it's funny, I miss seeing your father around. He was . . . you know what he was like."

"He's a long time gone," I said.

"We didn't agree 'bout everything. . . . You live by what he taught you, you'll be all right."

"Yeah, Gene. I'll be in touch about Bronstein."

"Call me day after tomorrow, something. Hey . . . and it might be a good thing, you get close to her. You might get a sense that she's doing some business with Bloom, even Vassey maybe, but I think Bloom. If you do, you lemme know."

4.

Bergmanesque

In the meantime, I did what I should've been doing, the job I was being paid for, searching for Bergman. I went down to the county clerk's office, looking for P.O.B. Services. It was listed. Thank God. It was a simple DBA—doing business as—of Finkelstein-Magliocci, Inc. P.O.B. was described as a personal financial management company.

Finkelstein-Magliocci, without the "Inc.," was listed in the phone book. Dominic Magliocci and Morton Finkelstein, attorneys, had individual listings with the same phone number and address. I gave them a call. I told the receptionist that a friend of a friend, at a party, had recommended Dom as someone to handle my money. She put Mr. Magliocci on the phone.

"Look, Mr. Magliocci," I said. "I'm a free-lance person. A photographer. I do a lot of traveling. I get my money in lump sums. And I am not what you call a natural-born checkbook balancer. So what I'm looking for—and this friend of my friend Johnny, who I met at a party, said you would be good for it—is someone who can collect my checks when they come in, make sure they get in the bank. I want you to handle my bills too. You know, make sure the rent gets paid, even when I'm out of town, and Con Ed and the phone company. And take care of keeping a reserve for income tax. You know, all of that."

"Yes. Mr. . . . uh?"

"Crispy, Tony Crispy," I said. It sounded like a good name for a photographer who couldn't keep track of his bills and all of that.

"Mr. Crispy, we do exactly that sort of thing. Our fees are in the neighborhood of three percent. . . ."

"That sounds real reasonable."

"Would you like to make an appointment?"

"Sure. Yeah. Today? Tomorrow?"

"Well, I don't think I can fit you in until next week. . . ."

"Mr. Magliocci, it would be great if you could squeeze me in. Either this evening or tomorrow." I didn't want this thing to linger on and on. "I have an assignment tomorrow. So maybe it's a half day and I can squeeze some time. Day after that I'm off to Bhopal? Aplab? Someplace like that. In India. Photograph a chemical plant. Big place. Lots of pipes. So I'd like to get with this. Discuss it. Then, you know, when I get back, I can set it up right away. So I don't get caught like this again. Frankly, I'm going to spend most of tomorrow night prepaying bills and catching up on old bills, and I don't have the time—"

"Why don't you," he said, "come by around six tonight?"

Dom Magliocci had a standard gray two-piece suit. He was five feet seven, about 175 pounds, his hair was still dark but thinning. He impressed me as a straightforward small-time attorney offering a straightforward service. He did exactly the sort of thing I would have wanted him to do if I were that world-traveling photographer Tony Crispy. Or if I were Samuel Bergman, retired somewhere sunny and warm, wanting someone to collect the rent from my sublet, sending me my profit and the landlord his rent-controlled cut.

Insofar as it was a scam, I didn't know if there was anything actually illegal about Dom Magliocci's carrying out his client's instructions. And unless I wanted to black-bag the place, it was a dead end. It could be done. Security in the building was a sign-in sheet requiring neither ID nor legibility. The guard was severely astigmatic. Office security wasn't any better. A simple Yale lock. No alarm system was visible. The files in standard file cabinets. But I wasn't going to do that. I wasn't some crazed FBI agent.

APARTMENT APPLICATION

3/12/56   DATE

NAME: *Samuel N. Bergman*

EMPLOYER: *Sultan Sports Wear*
276 7th Avenue

POSITION: *Vice-President . . .*

Finding Sultan Sports Wear should have been simple. It should have been in the phone book. It wasn't.

I went back down to Centre Street. Back to the County Clerk's Office.

It had existed. It had even been a New York State corporation. Bergman's title, VP, had been faintly misleading. In actuality he had been a founder and one of two major shareholders. The other was a Moses Fishbein. They sold out to LMC (Leading Man's Clothes) Ltd. in 1976. LMC Ltd. was not on record at the county clerk's office. That meant nothing in particular. They could have been a Delaware corporation or registered in New Jersey or even in England, what with their Ltd.

The Manhattan directory had three Marks but no Moses Fishbein. I struck out with the Brooklyn, Bronx, and Queens books. East to Long Island. There were two M's in Great Neck. The first turned out to be Minerva. An old woman answered the second number. She turned out to be the widow Fishbein.

"I don't know where Mr. Bergman is," she told me. "I haven't seen or heard of Bergman since 1977, when he set off on his around-the-world cruise. One postcard we got. One. Hong Kong. To my husband, God rest his soul. 'Moses,' it said, 'wish you were here. These people don't have unions.' That, from a partner of twenty years. I bet he doesn't write to his mother, either."

I figured that people who had taken over Bergman's company would have had to maintain contact with him, at least for a while. Although LMC Ltd. wasn't on record at the county clerk's office, it was easy enough to find. It was listed in the Manhattan phone book and in the red-book index of advertisers as well.

LMC Ltd.
(212) 247 2598
863 Madison Ave.
NY. NY. 10022

Approx. Sales: $25,200,000

Leading Man's Clothing
　(Mfg. HK)
　Ex.Rep:
Scandinavian Ski Wear
Lilith of France
Burma Road Cotton
Marie Christine—Costume
　du Soleil

Chm: Harvey Ginsberg
Pres: Sheldon Ginsberg
Sec. Treas: Adela Ginsberg

Rather than approach the Ginsbergs directly, I decided to reach them through a mutual acquaintance. The organization that touches everyone in the garment industry is the union, the ILGWU. I dropped in at their headquarters to see Ralph DeLillio.

Before he said hello, he asked, "What the fuck are we supposed to have a government for? To protect us? Or to destroy us?" He lit a cigarette before he answered his question. "They're cutting our hearts out."

I said, "Hello," then asked him if he knew the Ginsbergs at LMC Ltd.

"Yeah. Real schnorrers. They had two factories. In the Jersey place they had union workers. Then they had a sweatshop out in Queens. Like something out of 1911. No ventilation. No fire exits. No overtime. No workers who speak English, or even green cards, probably. And they're slapping union labels on garments from both places."

"So you figure they'll be difficult to deal with?" I said.

"I got 'em on safeties," Ralph said. "One spark, you got dead Dominicans and Taiwanese all over a four-story factory. So I go to OSHA. Violations up the wazoo. You know what OSHA tells me? They're not doing field inspections in the Northeast. 'Are you outa your fucking minds?' I ask them. They mumble budget cuts and duplication of state services. I push up to the district supervisor, because this is a load of shit. What does this sonuvabitch tell me? Huh? This sonuvabitch, he tells me that 'it's time to get government off the back of the people! Free America from overregulation!' "

"That bad?" I said, making agreeable noises.

He sighed. "It's worse, Tony, worse." He stubbed out his cigarette. "Does anybody believe in unions anymore?"

"I don't know," I said. "So I guess you couldn't talk to the Ginsbergs about Bergman?"

He lit another cigarette. "I took those bastards up on charges," he said. "Litigation, you know what litigation is? Something that Jews invented to let us Guineas get old watching. A year passed, we're making motions, they're making nonunion garments, slapping union labels in them. But what they're really doing is stalling. So they can move the whole thing to HK. Which they did."

"I'm just trying to find this guy. Bergman. Used to own Sultan Sports Wear. Sold out to Ginsberg, eight, ten years ago. I'm just trying to find a way for Ginsberg to talk to me. But I guess you're not on real good terms with them."

"Those motherfuckers?" he snarled. "Sure I'm on OK terms with them." He shrugged. "It's nothing personal."

"Thanks, Ralph. I owe you one."

"How you doing?" he asked.

"I'm doing OK," I said.

"What's that mean? OK? That mean you're gettin' rich and famous, or that mean you getting by?"

"It means OK."

"How would you like a job?"

"I already have a job."

"I could use you," he said.

"Free-Lance, I'm always available."

"We gotta work staff. What kind of stuff you do? Divorces?"

"Some," I admitted.

"Insurance fraud, employee theft, all that stuff?"

"Yeah," I said.

"Tell you what, Tony, money ain't what it's all about. I look in the mirror and I see this ugly mug and I know I'm beating my head against the wall. But I look in the mirror and I see a guy who's trying to do something for people. Something useful . . . How about it? Working for the union."

"I'll think about it," I said. Not meaning it. But maybe I should've said yes. Then I could've been a happy guy. Like Ralph DeLillio.

5.

A Fate Worse Than Death

COBERLAND, SYDNEY: 121 E. 74 St. NYC // Emp. Wilfree, Madison, Madison, Montague & Reach // salary $98K // outside income $42K // Mortgages, Old Westbury and New Hampshire // Auto, leased, Mercedes // C/S $54K // A $30K // SLC $10 K and $7K. // 4 Judg Vacat // Suit Dismd // 2 Suits // Age: 48

I got his face from WFUX footage of a Stanley Fenderman press conference. I followed him as he left his office. He took the subway. Went to the supermarket. Then home, East Seventy-fourth Street between Lexington and Third. Posh but not overwhelming.

He came down in forty-five minutes. His Adidas tops and bottoms matched, blue with a silver stripe. Running shoes with a logo on the sides. Runners are a pain in the ass to tail, for obvious reasons. But ninety-nine out of one hundred times, all they do is run in a circle and end up where they came from. So they can take a shower.

I figured him for twenty minutes. I went out for pizza.

I was wrong by eight minutes. I watched from the corner as he went upstairs. His apartment faced the front, and I saw his lights go on. I waited. I gave him an hour, getting on to 10 P.M. then let it go. Which is a lot of what my job, maybe a lot of jobs, is all about—a lot of nothing. Joey does crossword puzzles. That's better than thinking.

57

The next night promised to be more of the same. He left the office a little later. Subway home. Drugstore this time. Quick stop at the liquor store. One bottle of wine. A man of moderation. He went up. I waited. The air was thick. Edging toward rain. Getting right to the edge of precipitation. But something—wind, a distracting shove from the cold front, a downdraft—kept keeping it back. Like the sky was just another woman who couldn't quite come.

A half hour later, Syd came down. He had a gym bag. He went to the New York Health and Racquet Club on York Avenue. I waited out front. He came out, fresh and blown dry, in forty-five minutes.

He went west to First Avenue, then south. I ambled along behind. Down along First, he glanced, as he went, into various restaurants and bars. He looked at his watch. Considered. He decided he had time for a beer. He turned to face the bar beside him. Looked at the door, looked at the name. Hesitated, shuffling his feet. Then he turned and walked on.

I gave the place a look as I went by. It was called Hunks. All the customers were male, and the windows had black leather drapes.

Instead he went into McDimples, your normal semi-neighborhood, semi-singles, standard East Side bar. So did I. They served their beer in mugs. Syd had one. There were two empty stools beside him. I sat at the further one. I ordered a beer. While I waited for it, I turned and surveyed the room. When the beer came, I raised my glass to the bartender, then to Syd, being as they were the people closest to me. "Cheers," I said. The bartender said the same. Syd nodded. Neutral.

I looked down at his gym bag.

"Been working out?"

"Yes," he said. Neutral. Careful in New York. Someone talks to you, they want something.

"The machines, I bet. Nautilus. I can never get myself to do that. I'm a squash player," I said. A genteel credential. Few out-and-out ruffians in the sport. Far from its roots in debtors' prison. "You ever play?"

"No," he said.

"Try it. It's a good game."

"Several of my colleagues play. But I play tennis, and they say it ruins your game to play both."

"Could be," I said. "I bet you are . . . an attorney."

"What are you?" Syd asked. "A detective?"

"No." I smiled. "An accountant."

He smiled. I held out my hand. We shook as I gave him my name and he gave me his. We chatted. Syd was a careful man. He revealed little, and I could feel his calculator pawing me. To what end, besides native caution, I didn't know. I asked him what kind of law he dealt with. He was a litigator. Corporate things. Lately his firm was moving into labor law. What with business getting tougher with unions, regulations changing, and the regulatory bodies changing even more. He meant union busting, but he didn't say that.

His favorite sport was skiing. He had been lucky enough to have a Christmas holiday with his kids, without the ex, out in Colorado. It was beautiful. And their condo was in the same complex as Jerry Ford's.

"You're lucky, having kids today, if they're not in trouble. Dropping out, doing dope, falling in with cults and stuff. It's scary," I said.

"We've had a couple of close calls. But they seem to be doing all right," he said, knocking his knuckles on the wood-top bar. Then he looked at his watch.

"Early day tomorrow," he said.

"Yeah," I sighed. "Me too."

He threw a bill on the bar. I did too. He got up to go.

Out in the street, he looked at his watch again. I looked at him.

"I think I'll have one more beer," he said. "I have some Heineken's in the refrigerator. Care to join me?"

"Yeah," I said. "A beer sounds good."

The first execution for "sodomitical" activity [in America, took place in Plymouth Colony in 1642]. . . . William Hackett, an eighteen year old servant, was observed on a Sunday copulating with a cow. Hackett confessed his crime and the cow was burned before his eyes after which he himself was hanged.

VERN L. BULLOUGH, *Homosexuality: A History*
(New American Library, 1979)

"Sit down," he said, and went into the kitchen to get the beer. He had gestured at the couch. But I wasn't ready to sit there, where he could sit beside me. I chose the chair. When he came back with the beer, I wasn't quite in reach from anywhere. He couldn't quite decide where to position himself. So he stood over me, cool but anxious, obsequious yet macho.

"Pretty good," I said about the beer.

"Yes. I find that it's an excellent beer." God, he didn't want to talk about beer. And he was bulging all over his groin. Just for me. I could read his fantasy in his eyes. What he really wanted to do was pull down his zipper and pop it out in my face. "You look like you have a pretty good body," he said. His basic mask—self-contained maturity and the dignity of corporate law—was melting across his features. The son of a bitch was leering at me like a teenager. "Squash must keep you in shape." And as with a teenager, there was a nervous anxiety that he might handle it wrong and get put down for getting his cock up.

It was a hiccup away from grotesque. It must've been what I look like when I have lust in my pocket and a woman in the corner. God save us from mirrors.

"I like to get to know people. Find out what makes them tick," I said. That's what the girls say when they mean: I want to talk first; what sort of slut do you think I am?

"Yes," he said, trying to calmly put his mask back. "I have the same inclinations." He decided he was going to have to sit down after all and looked around for the best spot, tactically speaking.

We made chitchat. His work. My work. Very dull. We sipped our beers.

"How about another beer?" he said.

"Sure," I said.

I spotted photos on the wall. His kids. I got up to look at them. When he returned, he found me there and came up close. Close enough so that his body brushed mine when he handed me the beer.

"Your kids?"

"Yes," he said, putting his hand on my shoulder. I could feel his warm breath against my neck. It made my hair stand and my stomach churn. I tried not to let that show.

"Do they know?"

His mouth tightened. "We've never really discussed it," he said shortly. His hand moved across my back.

I slid away from his hand, turning to face him. I looked him squarely and sympathetically in the eye. "It must be especially tough. Someone of your generation, and situation, coming out. Your ex knows, doesn't she?"

"Yes," he said shortly.

"I bet that was nasty. Vicious divorce, I bet."

"No, actually," he said, "it was quite civilized."

"This is a nice apartment," I said, "but not for the kind of money you're making. She got the house, right?"

He nodded.

"Hefty child support," I said, looking at the portraits, "and some heavy alimony. Right?"

"I don't see that that is any of your business."

"Just making conversation. You know . . . hey, things are tough. I'm sympathetic."

"Sure," he said, willing to ignore the trespass. If he could just get into my pants.

"She used it against you, didn't she?" I said. "They're such bitches."

"If it makes any difference, she knew. I knew that she knew. We didn't make an issue of the matter. Yes, there was a very generous settlement, but that is because I felt generous. I am happy to provide a good home for my children. Whatever their needs might be, whatever that may cost, I am fortunate enough to have the means to provide. Having the means, I am happy to do so."

"Sounds reasonable," I said. So many things that aren't true sound reasonable.

Our little chess match in sexo-space went on. I sat on the couch. He followed me eagerly, certain my queen was exposed.

"And the job—they know on the job?" I asked casually.

"It's one of those things," he said, man of the world, "that's understood, where necessary, and properly unspoken." He put his hand on my knee.

One cool sliver of brain acknowledged irrationality. With my eyes closed, we could put orifices and appendages together in ways that were virtually indistinguishable from places where I had been before with great pleasure. But what has sense got to do with it? I felt his touch like a disease.

I took his hand. Lifted it off my knee and held it from the back.

"Your clients," I said. "Do they know you like to fuck men?"

He yanked his hand away. "I keep my private life private."

"Tell me, Syd," I said, "are you into 'safe sex'?"

"What kind of game is this?" he said warily. "I'm not into games. I am a very straight person."

"What a bitch it must be, Syd." I was going to shake him up. "All those years in the closet. Closing your eyes and pretending that the wife underneath is a guy. And the sneaking around. Sucking anonymous cocks in men's rooms. Going down to Forty-Second Street and paying little hustlers to suck yours. Is that what it was like—"

"I think you'd better go now," he said, standing up, the bulge in his crotch deflated.

". . . And then you finally come on out. Only to find the plague waiting for you," I said lazily, putting my feet up on the coffee table. "Jesus, you got handed a tough one."

"I think you'd better go now," he said.

"Sit down, Syd. I want to talk to you."

"Perhaps you think I'm not capable of throwing you out," he said.

"Oh, man," I sighed, "it doesn't matter. That's not what it's about."

"Out. Now. Before I call the police."

"Five years, Syd," I said. "You got five years, from the last time you fucked a guy, of fear. Wondering if you got It."

He crossed the room and picked up the phone from the end table. I was right behind him. As he picked up the receiver, I reached for the clip connection in back and pulled it out. Enraged, he swung.

I thrust my shoulder up to protect my head, instinctively.

But he was better than I thought he was. He was balanced, and that swing was just a feint. The real blow came from his right hand. A karate-trained thrust, with a twisting fist at my solar plexus. I never saw it coming. It's what you get from underestimating people. Just because they're old and take it up the ass from time to time doesn't mean they can't hit.

I went down, with the wind half knocked out of me.

Gasping, sitting on the floor, I looked up at him, in his spread-foot karate pose. "You're over . . . reacting," I said.

"Out," he said.

"We have some things to talk over, Syd," I said, letting my breath come back.

"No we don't," he told me, reasserting his karate pose.

"Oh, man," I said, "don't make this difficult."

"On your feet, and out! Now!"

"Slow down, Syd."

"Out. And you can tell that bitch, not another nickel. Nobody's gonna bleed me."

"I'm not—"

"Out! Out!" he screamed.

Moving slow, calm, getting to my feet, I said, "Take it slow. Take it easy."

"Out. I want you out."

"Why don't you hit me again, motherfucker," I snapped. "Come on, faggot."

I faked with my right. He yelled, "Hai!" Blocked with his left. Stepped in and hit with his right. Which is what I was waiting for. I snatched his forearm and, holding it, turned hard. I had the weight and, in spite of his Nautilus machines, the strength. It spun him off his feet, and he went stumbling past me. I slammed him hard, with my forearm, across the spine. He lost it and went face down on his rug.

I came down on top of him, my knee in the small of his back. I snatched his wrist and bent his arm up.

"Syd, Syd, why you wanna do it the hard way?"

"Get out of my house. I'll call the police. Don't think I won't."

"Fuck it, Syd." I jammed his arm up, hard. "Stop and listen. I don't want to hurt you. I don't want your money. I don't work for that bitch. . . . Now you gonna listen to me?"

"Let me up," he asked.

"No more fuss?"

"What do you want?"

"I just want you to listen. Then I'll go."

"OK."

"No more fuss?"

"No. OK," he said.

I released his arm and moved off him. I stepped back far enough to watch him get up. "You all right?" I asked him.

"Just a little . . . stressed, in the shoulder," he said.

"Sorry. I'd massage it for you, but you'd get the wrong idea."

"I already had the wrong idea, didn't I," he snapped.

"It's the Gunderson thing," I said. "I saw the report of the special prosecutor." I was thrusting my finger at his face. "A farce. A cover-up. I want that report. The whole thing. Without the blackouts."

He shook his head no.

"Yes," I said. "That's the only way for the rest of the world to find out the truth."

"That would be a breach of ethics," he said stubbornly, wrapping his face in his mask as well as he could.

"Tell me something, Syd," I said, suddenly soft, reasonable. "What did you think of Gunderson? You think this is an honest kind of guy? Who should be the highest legal officer in the land?"

"That is not for me to judge. That was not our mandate." He had found his balance again. His role.

"Man, it's such a goddamn shame," I said like I meant it, and I probably did. "After a couple of hundred years of hiding, it's finally OK to be a homosexual . . . and bam! They're slamming the closet doors again. They're coming back after you guys. They're gonna use AIDS, family values, anything they can. It's pariah time again. You got to protect yourself. Not Gunderson. He's not worth protecting."

"I have ethic—"

"I'm talking ethics," I rode over him. "Real ethics. You know what I want this report for? Just to show it to the public. Just so the world knows the truth. Let the people judge."

"I cannot—"

"You stupid shit," I snapped, switching back to bad guy. "I don't know if you're bullshitting me or you're crapping on yourself. I want that report. Complete."

"I don't have it," he said weakly, down to his second line of defense.

"You can get it. Do it because it's the right thing to do. Or because if you don't do it, you're gonna be destroyed. Not by me: I'm the nice guy. They'll drag you out of the closet with a dress on. Pictures, tapes.

Rumors of AIDS. And your clients, they're gonna know. All those Fortune 500 fuckers, they won't eat lunch with you. They won't go in a conference room with you. They won't shake your goddamn hand. Because you're a plague carrier! You understand? All that money, it's gonna disappear. Your kids, they're gonna hear—"

"You bastard. You bastard. How dare you—"

"Syd, Syd," I said, soft and reasonable again. "Not me. I wouldn't do that. I can't fuck a guy over just because he likes to put his dick in the wrong place. I'm the one that's trying to help you. I don't want that to happen to you."

"I don't feel well," he said, swallowing, sweating. "I have to get my pills."

"Sure, go ahead."

He walked toward the bedroom. Hit 'em high, hit 'em low, keep 'em off balance, let 'em know they're beat, then tell them they can trust you, and only you. I had him.

The gun he held in his hand when he came out of the bedroom was a large-bore automatic. It looked like a Luger, authentic WW II Wehrmacht vintage. And ever so macho.

"Oh, shit," I said.

"I'm gonna kill you," he said, his voice tight and near to hysterical. That wasn't good.

"You don't want to do that," I said. "That would really ruin your career."

"Not killing an intruder in my own home," he said. The same tension-filled notes were in his voice. He even sounded as if he believed himself.

"Well," I said, "maybe if I were black and had a rap sheet, you know, you might get away with it."

"You bastard, you motherfucking bastard," he said, something close to tears in his eyes, his hands tight, too tight, on the gun. "You come up here, pretending . . . pretending . . ."

"No. You asked me up for a beer. And to chat."

"I ought to make you . . ." he said, coming toward me, holding the gun in front of him. "Get on your knees, you bastard."

"Let's not let this get out of hand," I said. Smiling.

"Oh, it's gonna get out of hand. I may shoot you yet," he said, not smiling at all.

6.

Foreplay

We were over and under them days,
then tomorrow changed,
and even the body betrays.

"Nashville" Katz, "Jezebel"
(© Memphiz Muzic, Inc., 1983)

"I was lucky to escape with my life," I said to Glenda.

"Every time you come home late"—the clock over the bed said, with that excess of precision typical of digital devices, 11:56 P.M.—"you tell the most marvelous stories. And you expect me to believe them." Though this time she did.

"Come on. I almost lost my virginity."

"Oh, horrors," she mocked. "A fate worse than death."

"You're goddamn right," I said.

"It might serve you right," she said, smiling. "Turnabout is fair play, hoist by your own petard, or something like that." She snuggled against me as I lifted the covers and slid into bed. She reached for my petard. I put my arms around her. She was wearing a nightdress, a thin, soft flannel. It felt good to the touch, soft, feminine, sexy in a ladylike fashion. And I loved the way it bunched up around her waist when I raised it.

"It's been too long," she said, spreading her legs as my fingers opened her lips, seeking moisture.

She was right. It had. I wished she hadn't mentioned it. I like my lust unalloyed. Instead of losing myself, disappearing, one layer of brain circuitry was trying to nail down the why. Another, who's to bless and who's to blame? Another going through back files, tangent tracking, comparing past and present, this woman and others. Another, wonder-

66

ing if the whole thing was a condition, which is a thing that is, or a problem, which is a thing with a solution.

I didn't disappear at all.

NEW TV SEASON: SEX IS OUT, OLD VALUES IN.

U.S. News & World Report

"How did you get away?" she asked me at breakfast.

"Get away from what?" Wayne asked.

"There's this attorney," I said. "He has some papers I want. . . ."

"What papers?" Wayne asked, giving up both his cereal and his *New York Times.*

"Transcript of a government report on Randolph Gunderson, the attorney general. I went over to chat with him. I ended up in his apartment, and when he found out what I wanted, he pulled a gun on me. And said he wanted to kill me, or worse."

"Or worse? What's worse?"

"Uh . . ." I said. Though I believe in frankness, truth, honesty, openness, with the young, I didn't feel like presiding over a sex-education class at breakfast. "Well, you know, it was actually not the toughest corner I've ever been in," I said. "The toughest corner was when I went out to the Rocky Mountains."

"When was that?"

"I never told you about that?"

"No!" he declared.

"There was a bail skip, a bank robber, who went out to Wyoming to hide out. I didn't know the territory too well, so I hired a local guide. Where I heard the suspect was, was in a cabin hidden way up in the mountains. Well, we traveled two days by jeep. Then the jeep couldn't go any more. So we hired a couple of mules. Mules are real unpleasant."

Wayne was totally fascinated.

"It was spring, early spring, and the snows were melting. The rivers and creeks were high. The water was really rushing, pounding down through these rocky riverbeds.

"Suddenly, while we're crossing this river—well, either a small river or a big stream, somewhere in there—suddenly there's a wave of water. What can happen, sometimes, is that snow is melting up on the mountain but there's another section below, in the shade, say, that isn't melting. That forms a natural, but temporary, sort of dam. Sometimes it lets go all at once. The water breaks through and comes crashing down through the creekbeds.

"That's what happened. Rick, my guide, was in the creek when it hit. It swept his mule out from under him. Then it swept him along. I went racing along the bank, trying to keep up.

"Finally there came a point where the water slowed, and I jumped in and grabbed him. He was hurt medium bad. Concussion, severe bruises. Contusions. I set up camp for him, we talked about it, then I went on, on my own.

"The last thing he said to me was 'Watch out for grizzlies.'

"I should have listened. But I'm a city kid, and what do I know? The next morning, I'm waking up, and I hear a noise. I look and there is a mostly large bear. Actually, he's bigger than that. There's big, then there's big, then there's bigger? Well, one size larger.

"Mr. Grizzly is in the act of stealing my food. The idea of being in the mountains of Wyoming, alone, three, four days from my jeep, with no food, does not appeal to me. So I decide to shoo this large and ugly creature away.

"I jump up. 'Shoo, shoo!' I said, except that I used stronger language. The bear mostly ignores me. So I pick up a stone in one hand and my rifle in the other. I don't want to shoot him, not right away, because that's against the law, a one-year prison term or a ten-thousand-dollar fine, whichever comes first. I threw the rock. I thought it might get his attention, chase him away. After all, you can chase a shark away by punching him in the nose—"

"Is that true?" Wayne asked.

"Tony," Glenda said, thinking about her son trying to punch sharks in the nose, then dying of a wrong supposition, "is that true?"

"Oh, yeah, it's true. Anyway, that's where I hit the grizz, in the schnozzola. It did get his attention. He roared. He stood up straight. As big as I thought he was before, I now find out he is even bigger.

"I'm scared. The hell with the ten-thousand-dollar fine. I want to live.

I raise the rifle. But apparently this bear has seen rifles. Or been warned about them on forest ranger posters. He doesn't like rifles, and he is very fast. Before I know it, his giant paw swipes out and knocks the rifle out of my hands.

"I started to run. I'm going as fast as I can, this old bear coming after me. Then suddenly I'm at a rock wall. Sheer face of a cliff. There's no climbing it. I turn. I face the bear. The cliff behind me. The bear in front. I'm unarmed. He's enraged. He wants to kill."

"What did you do? What did you do?" Wayne cried.

"Nothing I could do," I said sadly. "That bear done killed me."

"Oh, boo," Wayne said.

"Oh, hiss," Glenda said.

Wayne picked up his things and headed off to school. "Oh, booo," he yelled again on his way out.

"You didn't tell me about this case," Glenda said, walking away.

"No," I said, looking at her ass, just concentrating on it. Trying to ease on down below the surface tension of householding, down to where the passions flow, muddy waters. "No, I didn't," I mumbled, following her bottom into the bedroom.

She went into the closet to get her coat.

"Who's it for?" she asked as I came up behind her.

My hands began fondling the roundness wrapped in her business skirt.

"Cute," she said, apparently unenthusiastic about the paw on her ass. "Involving yourself with Randolph Gunderson could be serious," she went on.

"It's not actually a job," I told her, my hands sliding around to feel the slight rise of her mound in front, the half swelling in my pants pressing against her back. Please let us find it. She must want to find it too. She's said so. "Not actually a job. A bet."

"What?" she said, turning around, breaking loose.

"A bet. Let's fuck."

"You're out getting yourself . . . almost killed, on a bet?"

"It's a big bet." I wanted to want her enough to grab her, toss her on the bed, skirt up, panties down, and play rape. But I couldn't find the urgency all by myself. The sea that carries free-floating lust was dry.

"When are you going to grow up?" she said.

"Grow up? When am I gonna be young again," I grumbled, "fight grizzlies, take you to orgies, get stoned."

"Our financial situation—"

". . . is OK. More or less."

"OK. But not what you could go out and gamble. How much is this bet?"

"Four grand," I said casually.

"What? What are you dreaming ab—"

"Cut it, will you? It's four thousand, to me, when I win. Not if I win. 'Cause I'm gonna win."

"You are sure of yourself. Why are you only happy if you're walking on the edge of a cliff? You can't possibly afford, we can't possibly afford, for you to lose four thousand dollars."

"In the first place, I am not happy only if I'm walking on the edge of a cliff," I said. I liked that description of myself, very macho romantic. But it's not true. "It's not true. I've worked goddamn hard to even our income out, keep it steady. And believe me, I like it that way and want to keep it that way. In the second place, if I lose, it doesn't cost me four thousand dollars. It doesn't cost me any money at all. So I know what I'm doing. So cut the crap."

"What do you lose? What did you bet against four thousand dollars?"

"Wayne," I said, straight-face.

It almost caught her. But with a little effort, she managed to retain her indignation. "Very funny. What did you bet against four thousand dollars?"

"Your fucking sense of humor. See, so if I lose, I don't lose anything."

"I have a sense of humor. But not about things that aren't funny."

"Fuck off, Glenda. . . . I'll see you later," I said, grabbing my jacket and my keys.

She moved around in front of me, blocking my way. In all fairness, she's a better man than I am when it comes to fighting. I like to storm out. She likes to finalize, get to it, get through it.

"No you won't. You tell me what's going on."

"I don't have to tell you shit. I'm tired of you being on my case. I'm tired of you watching me all the time. I'm not Wayne. I don't have to answer to you."

"You don't tell me about this bet. I never know what you're involved in. I still don't know how you got away."

"What difference does it make?" I said.

"Oh, forgive me. I'm not entitled to care if you live or die."

"I fell down on my knees," I told her. "I told him I liked the idea. He didn't believe me. I told him that I had always had secret homosexual feelings and was ashamed of them. But if I was forced, I might like it. I fluttered my lashes a little, looked fetching. The tension was going out of his trigger finger. It's funny—you get to a state of mind where you can see things like that, I don't know how.

"Then I took him," I said, gesturing with my words. It still felt ugly. "Knocked his arm aside, came up hard, hit him between the legs. Then I picked up the gun from the floor where he dropped it. He told me he was going to make me pay. He told me he was going to get me. I politely gave him my card and told him to call as soon as he got the report. I gave him a week.

"There, satisfied? . . . If I recite my day in the detail you seem to need," I said, "I would need forty-eight-hour days, 'cause I would have to get through it twice."

"Communicate. Why can't you communicate?"

I started shoving her out of the way.

"Don't you dare push me," she cried, trembling. "Don't you ever hit me. If you hit me, we are really through."

"Hit you?" I snarled. "What kind of crap is that? Standard woman weakness crap. I've never hit you. And I never will, so don't fucking worry about it."

"You've raised your hand to me," she declared. As proof of something.

"Raising my hand and hitting are two different things. You idiot."

"You're the idiot. You're an emotional idiot. You don't share anything. I don't know what you're doing. You don't tell me anything. Except to scare me, like that story you told me last night."

"Scare you? I told you that story because it's funny. It's funny; don't you understand that? Me as the reluctant virgin—I thought you would find it funny."

"Oh, don't worry," she snapped. "I know how much of a virgin you're not. I know all about your conquests. Oh, tell me again about all your other women."

"I didn't say anything about other women. You're a nightmare. You're a goddamn nightmare. With your goddamn jealousy. You're jealous of the past. You're jealous of . . . of I don't know what. Now let me outa here. And maybe I'll think about coming back."

"No. No." She started to cry.

"Not that; not the tears," I said, even as I knew I was climbing down off my anger to be sorry, maybe even guilty, that I had hurt her. I reached out for her. She pulled away. I reached again, trying to hug her. She moved back again. Me forward. Her back. Until she was against the wall. Then I got her. I shoved my hands around her back, between her and the wall. She was trapped. She made herself small, tight, inward.

"I didn't mean to hurt you," I said.

She sniffled. I tried to raise her head. She fought that.

"Oh, come on, Glenda," I said.

"Let me go," she said.

I grabbed her chin in my hand and forced her face up. She struggled.

"Please, baby," I said.

"Let me go," she said.

So I bent my face to hers and put my mouth on hers. She kept her lips tight and cold. I softened mine. She went limp. The I-won't-respond-you-are-kissing-a-dead-fish defense. My tongue forced its way between her lips, then pressed against her teeth. They pried open. The whole length of my body pressed against her slenderness.

Then she was sucking on my tongue, her hips moving. That thing I was looking for was finally in the goddamn room. I hauled us both to the bed. Her skirt hiked up to her thighs and rode up to her waist as she spread. I was thick inside my pants and pressed into her center.

She had on panty hose, the unfortunate successor to the horror of girdles. There's only one way through. I grabbed the fabric in my fingers.

"Don't. They're seven dollars," she said.

"Yeah," I said, tearing them.

"Oh, good," she said.

I unzipped. I pushed her panties to the side. She was wet and I was in, pressed tight and furious. Our mouths came together hard, and her fingers dug at my buttocks.

"Fuck me," she said.

"Fuck me," I said.

"Oh, love me, love me, Tony," she said.

It was good for me. It was good for her. So good she even made it without the vibrator. But if our only successful form of foreplay was a fight plus tears, it was going to get real enervating.

7.

Rubbers

DIMMER-LODES, PETER: 234 Third Ave. NYC // Emp. Wharton, Scully, Fundament & Elhaus // salary $58K // outside income $60K ('83) // outside income $12K ('82) // Mortgage, 234 Third Ave. // Auto, leased, Saab. // Age: 28

Mohammed Salim, headhunter by profession, specializing in the financial fields, blew me off the squash court. He does that a lot. He's Pakistani, like the Khan family. A Khan has been number one in the world for three generations. It's a genetic thing, or a cultural thing, or a biochemical thing, like Jewish lawyers, Black basketball players, Irish cops, Italian designers, and French women.

Afterward I asked him if I could have several of his business cards. I told him that I knew a couple of people looking for jobs. Mo works on commission. He was happy to give me as many as I wanted.

Then I called Peter Dimmer-Lodes. I told him that we, at the firm of Search Inc., had heard very good things about him and might have a position for which he would be suitable, at a considerable raise in salary. To let him know that we were serious in our search, I invited him for lunch at Smith & Wollensky, an old-timey steak house on Third Avenue.

I arrived first, and the maître d' showed him to my table. Peter was

74

a big guy. I imagined that he wrestled in high school, then switched to beer in college. He had a power wardrobe.

"You're Mohammed Salim?" he said.

"You bet," I said, and handed him Mo's card with a flourish.

"That's an Arab kind of name," he said.

"It is indeed," I said, as if I wasn't insulted. "My father was from Pakistan. A ranked squash player. But he moved to America and married an American woman. I was raised here."

He peered at me. "I can see it now," he said. "When I heard your name I was expecting an Arab. But I can see where you look Pakistani."

We ordered steak and brew. Then we talked about Peter's favorite things—Peter, money, mergers, and acquisitions. He was eager to tell me the part he had played in B&D's merger with Watkins Steel, Pontraine Chemical's takeover of California Micro, T&A's divestiture of Carolina and its acquisition by People's Products. The partners, as always, had taken all the credit, while Peter did all the work. Peter said.

I made dutiful notes. I asked if he'd worked in any other areas. He had. It had taken him a couple of years to maneuver himself into mergers and acquisitions. His arrival there marked the time when his outside income made its phenomenal jump.

Although I hadn't said a word about insider trading, he volunteered definitive reassurances. "If you run the game films of any of those deals," he said, "you won't see any significant market action until the principals went public. No insider trading on our club."

"Of course not," I said, wishing that I were with the SEC. I would have subpoenaed his broker's records in a minute. If the trades didn't show up there—if he was half smart enough to have had his father or brother or best friend or girlfriend make the trades—it would still show up in his bank records. Then let him explain the extra money under oath.

"The reason I'm willing to talk is that considering the order of magnitude of the deals that I'm putting together, I am actually undercompensated."

"Absolutely," I said. "You belong in six figures." Which he was, counting his side action. I was wondering why he was considering giving it up.

"But just salary is not where it's at. A guy gets traded from the Raiders to Tampa, he's not going to be happy about it, even if they raise his salary. You want to be on a team that's got a shot at the Super Bowl. I want to be with a championship team. I like the big deals."

"What I can tell you is that it's a major financial . . . umm . . . group. Very major," I said. He frowned. "Until recently they have been rather passive investors. T-bills. Gold. More a matter of protecting their earnings then maximizing their leverage. Now, with the price of oil down . . ."

"Ah hah," he said, feeling terribly shrewd. "It is the Arabs."

"I didn't say that," I said, "although I did mention oil. In any case, there is a great deal of money that is looking for action. Real action."

"That's what's important to me," he said, outwardly under control, neither drooling on his tie nor barking. "More important than the money. Being where the action is."

I was certain. If I had subpoena power I could've opened him up on the spot. I didn't have it. I had to figure out something to bluff him with. And I couldn't yet.

BRONSTEIN, ALICIA W.: 182 Hicks St. Brooklyn, N.Y. // Emp. District Attorney, Kings Co. // salary $28.7K // outside income $0 // Auto loan $3.6K, Mitsubishi. Age: 30

"Welcome to Brooklyn," Alicia Bronstein said. She was full in the hips and thighs. She wore a full skirt and a jacket that hung over the skirt.

I was at a fund-raiser for Fernando Santana, a reform candidate running for City Council. It was classic New York insurgent politics. Independent versus The Machine. Housing versus Real Estate Interests. Civil/women's/gay/minority rights versus everything else.

Gene Petrucchio had done well, arranging for Fernando himself to make the introductions. There was something odd about it, since Gene was most definitely part of The Machine. Brooklyn politics has a Byzantine aspect. Fernando had laid it on thick with Alicia. The correction officer thing again. How I'd gone undercover, then testified and put some people away. Usually it's a story that works against me. This was one of the times it worked for me. Mostly I think of it as a previous life, like the one in which I did drugs, and wish that other people saw it that way as well.

I gave Alicia one of my sweeter, laid-back smiles, and looked at her like my interest might be erotic. I wanted me and Alicia to get along real good. "Are you involved with Fernando's campaign?" I asked.

"You bet," she said. "It is about time the old order passed on." She had a glass in her hand. Not her first. She raised it. "To the old order. May its passing be swift, but painful."

"You take this personally."

"You bet," she said. "Read my lips."

"Bitter, aren't we?"

"Aren't *we*," she said. "How did they treat you? When you stood up for what was right, and did your job, did they back you up? Give you subsequent promotion and reward? Elevate your status? Either your own people or the D.A.?"

"Yeah," I said. "They fucked me over."

"Right," she said. "Bastards."

"They are not the best of people," I said. An alliance forming. You and me against the world, baby.

She put her hand on my arm, speaking confidentially, warm blears of wine breath coming with her words. "Very petty people."

"That's exactly the word. Petty."

Alicia and I left together.

From a distance, and even more with darkness, Manhattan is a movie set. So, too, the river. Get close and you see the oily scum. Look over the edge. Garbage is collected in the shore's nooks and crannies the way butter, Thomas' boasts, fills their English muffins.

The River Café sits below the Brooklyn Bridge. Mostly it sells the view. Alicia was into the gin and tonics.

She lived a few blocks away, in the Heights, in a studio, which was overpriced, pricey as Manhattan, but walking distance to the court-house and the office. Where they hated her and denied her her proper rungs on the ladder, she told me, again, because she was a woman.

"But Fernando told me you were put out on loan to Stanley Fender-man for the special prosecutor's staff. . . . I mean, that puts you in the public eye, you the only one selected—"

"Is that how Fernando made it sound?"

"Yes," I said. Her glass was empty. I waved for the bartender and pointed at her glass. What the hell. I ordered one for me as well.

"Fenderman went to the Manhattan D.A. first," she said. Bitter about it. "The Manhattan D.A. wouldn't give him anyone. You know why? Caseload. Everyone has a caseload would kill a normal person. Same over here. We have as much crime as Manhattan, you betcha. You think that was an honor? A special commendation? . . . Read my lips. N. O. It was a way to get rid of me."

"We gotta do something about that," I said.

"We sure do, and we will," she said. She leaned forward and told me, as Gene Petrucchio had, that the current D.A., Reuben, was on his way out.

"Ahh," I said. "So things are gonna change?"

"Not if *they* have *their* way. But yes if I have my way."

"What's your way?"

She nodded significantly.

"Ahh," I said.

"Their way, they got Landsman." She put her hand on my arm and wet her lips. "Landsman's been Reuben's assistant forever. Waiting his turn. He sits there in his office, waiting, sort of like a cross between a basset hound and a vulture. If I were married, I wouldn't let Landsman handle my no-fault divorce. He's a disgrace to the reputation of the Jew lawyer. If Landsman is in, I stay one of the outs. You know what they got me on? They got me on DWI. Why am I doing drunk drivers?"

"It's a shame," I said, "that you didn't nail Gunderson. . . ."

She scowled.

". . . If you had nailed Gunderson," I said, "it would have given you a rep. Like the man who shot Liberty Valance. . . . I'm trying to figure out some way you can deal with the assholes. . . . How come Gunderson got off the hook?"

"Fenderman," she said with a sneer.

"He was in Gunderson's pocket?"

"No," she said, with contempt. "Mr. Fenderman is a corporate attorney, which means—read my lips—a jerk. An emasculated, no-ball masturbator . . . Oh, I'm certain he's as tough as polished steel, hard as a marble bathroom stall, when he's negotiating bond declivities or whatever they do over there. . . ." She pointed, and yes, we could see it. "Wall Street."

"What do you mean?"

"Tony, read my lips: Fenderman is not a prosecutor. He takes testimony like he's taking depositions from corporate vice-presidents. The kind of people, they take an oath and someone tells them the penalty for perjury, they actually think they have to tell the truth. Not just Fenderman; all the Park Avenue clones he recruited. A witness says something, some guinea wise-guy punk tells Fenderman, 'I don't know nothing,' Fenderman believes him. Fenderman even believes Vincent Calabrese. He believes Vinnie the Hook. Who came to us as a perjurer."

New York Times

Witness Fails Polygraph

WASHINGTON Dec. 5 (UPI)—

. . . An alleged organized figure, Mr. Calabrese had testified that he "did not know this Gunderson," had "never met this Gunderson," and that "I ain't got no knowledge of no one else's knowing Gunderson, or having dealings with him, especially not 'Tony Provolone' not having dealings with him or knowing him." "Tony Provolone" is the street name for Raymond Anthony Prozzini, ex-president of New Jersey Teamsters Local #331, alleged underboss of the Gonzoni family, currently under indictment for murder, extortion, and loan sharking.

"And if you don't believe me," Mr. Calabrese said, "I'll take a lie detector test to prove it."

According to FBI sources, Mr. Calabrese failed the polygraph. At the subject's request, the tests were repeated six times, with the same results.

"Did Calabrese finally testify about Gunderson?" I asked her.

"This is typical Fenderman. What he should have done is a couple of days of depositions from Calabrese. Comprehensive but not tough, you know. Taking him over territory you know about, stuff you can prove. Because you know Vinnie; he's gonna lie. Then, when you got him on perjury, cold, nailed, then you cut a deal.

"But no, not Fenderman. Fenderman takes him before the grand jury. Starts to ask him about Gunderson and Tony Provolone. This is about three in the afternoon. On Friday. At four we recess. Fenderman is certain that Calabrese is gonna sing, something, I don't know what, so he subpoenas him back for next week and sends a subpoena to Provolone."

NEW YORK POST, JANUARY 14, 1984

SLAUGHTER ON 10TH AVENUE

Mob Rubout on the West Side.

Vinnie "The Hook" Calabrese, missing mob witness, found in the trunk of his own Coupe de Ville, 10th Ave./45th St.

"The way you nail someone like Gunderson, you get someone else cold. Someone in fear of his asshole, so he doesn't want to do hard time. Then you turn them. Then you turn the next person up the line," she said. "But you can't just call in everybody who volunteers, listen to them ramble, and then check your Crim Law 101, federal statutes, to see if something will fall out of the sky. You have to work at it."

"Was that all it was?" I asked. "He didn't work at it?"

"He didn't know how," Alicia said. "And when I told him, told him how, he got just as insulted as any other male chauvinist pig does when you tell them anything more complicated than 'you're so big, you're so big.' "

I walked her home. The branches of Brooklyn trees threw lacy shadows on deeper shadows. Windows were traced with frost. Streetlamps had a hazy glow and yellow warmth. Well-kept brownstones and a kind of quiet felt like the preserve of either an earlier time, a good old day, or a future time, when we'll all be gentrified out of our minds, kept clean and sweet by the landmarks commission.

She took my arm. Her hip bumped my thigh. "Come on in," she said. "One for the road."

Up the steps to the first-floor apartment. High windows, high ceilings in the front room. High windows, high ceilings, and a big, big bed in the back. It was warm inside. I opened my jacket, she stripped out of hers. She brought me a bottle of beer from the kitchen. Déjà vu. Sydney, read my lips. We sat on the edge of the bed. In the light of the day she

80

might have been barely the safe side of ugly. What matter? What matters is the moment.

"What do you want from me?" she said.

"What do you think I want?" I said coyly. There's something about fucking that's something like love, which is something like trust and sharing. And I wanted her trust and sharing. Maybe I was wanting Alicia. Just because she was female. A different female, and there'd been a long stretch of fidelity. I understood that cheating could get complicated, very complicated.

"I don't know, but you won't get it from fucking me," she said.

"Oh," I said.

"One thing about being a lady lawyer, it's easy to get laid. The guys in the office, they wanna fuck me because I'm there. The cops, they wanna fuck me 'cause they're the horniest sonofabitches in creation and they wanna brag about something. The defense attorneys wanna fuck me because I'm the only woman around. The perps think if they could only fuck the D.A., she would be so overwhelmed she would cut them loose. Join them in a life of crime. Men," she announced, "are so impressed by their cocks."

"And you're not?" I said.

"Now you figure I'm a dyke, right?"

No. That's not what I figured. I figured it was the defense of a woman who knows that men only leave with her at closing time.

"Uh huh. You're a good-looking guy. You wanna do it, I could do it with you. But I warn you right now," she said, "I don't fuck around with fucking around. You do me, you wear a rubber."

"Oh," I said. She made it so unromantic.

"So what do you want? Come on, Tony, I know when someone wants something. Just 'cause I'm ugly doesn't mean I'm dumb."

"You're not ugly," I said with male-o-mat sincerity.

"It's something to do with Gunderson, maybe," she said.

"Yeah," I said, "yeah. Since you ask. I would not mind at all getting hold of the special prosecutor's report. Without deletions."

"Why? Who for?" Her face changed, and it was more than a switch from boozy to business. I was going to have to ease her back to that good-time mood by tantalizing her with a different kind of yearning.

"WFUX. 'The Hot One,' " I said, since truth sometimes works.

"They want to know. Inquiring minds want to know. But the thing is, then I'm in a position to do you a lot of favors. See, I don't know what you plan to do about Landsman, or what anyone plans to do about Landsman, but right now he's got a lock. The party regulars they get line A in the primaries, and unless people got a real good reason out here in Brooklyn, when they walk into the booth they pull the lever on line A, just like they've been doing all their lives, all their parents' lives.

"I don't know if anyone is gonna make a run at Brooklyn D.A., like Fernando is making a run at the City Council, but unless they get lots of noise, nobody is even gonna pay attention."

"If—if—someone is making a run," she said, wanting it but afraid of it, "and they're better, really better, than Landsman, better for Brooklyn, and better for me, then you might have a deal. I'll give it some thought."

"Don't wait too long. Do it while what you got is still worth something," I said.

"I will definitely consider it," she said, sounding so close to yes.

"See, it costs you nothing. And gets you a lot."

"I want to sleep on it," she said.

"OK," I said as we moved to the door, just praying she would slip off the hook. "Let me know tomorrow."

"A good, hard sleep," she said. "I'll let you know end of the week, beginning of next week."

"It's not like you're doing something wrong. You're doing something right," I told her.

"I had you figured," she said, holding the door open for me, "for the kind of guy who wouldn't wanna do it with a rubber."

8.

Scrupulous

It has been common practice that a person arrested for a crime has to post a bond or await trial in jail. That makes the bail bondsman a significant feature of the criminal justice system. The bondsman has very peculiar and unique powers. If people for whom the bondsman has posted bond fail to appear, the bondsman or his designee can go after them, exactly as if he had police powers. Chasing bail skips has been, traditionally, a lucrative source of income for private investigators. Some bondsmen pay a percentage of the bond recovered when the skip is returned to the court's jurisdiction; others pay a fee. It's a lot like bounty hunting.

The bail bond business is not what it once was.

Because the prisons are overcrowded with people awaiting trial, because it is a fact that those who await their trial in jail are almost always convicted, while those who await trial in freedom frequently get off, and because bail has a very limited effect on whether the accused turns up for trial, bail is no longer standard procedure in New York.

Only three bondsmen are left in Manhattan. In Brooklyn there were five, including Alan Bazzini. Now there's four.

My partner announced that Bazzini was definitely retiring. He had found a buyer for his business. One of his competitors, Bernard "Snake" Silverman.

I'm in a business that helps people. Should a person
languish in incarceration vile merely because he does
not have the means? No. That is not right and that is
why I am here. Always thank God for the Magner
Carter, which has put such persons as myself here.
Yet here is a person who has abused my trust. What
am I to do? What am I to do? . . . Bring me his
head. Dead or alive.

> BERNARD "SNAKE" SILVERMAN,
> Brooklyn bail bondsman

"I went over and spoke to Snake," Joey D' said, "and Bazzini, he
called him for us. We're going to get a piece of his business."

"Do we want it?" I said. "Is that the kind of business we need or
want? Where you don't know if you're gonna get paid, though you do
know that if you don't get the guy you won't get paid."

"How much *we* out," Joey D' said, "on your bet with Des Kennel?"

"There's a difference," I said, "between one isolated stupidity and
making a policy of it."

"Hunting bail skips is not like going to the track," my partner said.
"It's good business. So you miss a few; the ones you score, they more
than make up for it."

"Yeah, right, like roulette," I said. "The city, if it didn't pay cops
unless they got the perps, you know how much the city would save.
The cops are too smart to let the city do that. Now what are you going
to say, that we are dumber than cops? What we have to do is get to be
more like a business. This is supposed to be a business, but it's two
guys, renting out their bodies."

"We're doing OK," Joey said. "Making more than we were a couple
years ago. And," he added "*you* are doing a whole lot better than you
were a couple years ago," which was a personal remark.

"Fuck you. My progress as a human being is not the point. Things
. . . cost of things is going up faster than our income. Case in point." I
held up the letter from the health insurance company. "Premiums up
twenty-eight percent over last year. And the deductibles have doubled.
We're not going up no twenty-eight percent a year. What the hell are
we gonna do when the lease comes up?"

The phone rang. "Have you found my Bergmans yet?" Jerry Wirtman said.

"You know, for what should be a real simple job," I said, "Bergman is remarkably elusive."

"So how much is this costing?"

"He isn't in the metropolitan area. That I've established. His bank account is a blind. Those checks, with his name on it, that's an account that's owned by a law firm. His ex-partner's widow hasn't heard from him in fifteen years or something like that. The ILGWU, they don't know where he is, but they're looking for him too. For me. Which means for you. It's not like nothing's happening."

"So how much is this costing?"

"I'd have to sit down and add that up. I don't have a figure off the top of my head."

"Is that a stupid question for me to ask? Is it rude? Am I being pushy? I have something being done. I would like to know: How much is this costing?"

"Hang on a minute," I said. I covered the phone. I took a deep breath. I'd put in maybe three days, with at least one more to go. Expenses, seven hundred, maybe. "It's around two. So far."

"Around two? Around two what? Two hundred? Two thousand? Two dollars?"

"Around two thousand dollars," I said.

"How much around?"

"Without pulling the paperwork, which I can do if you wanna give me a couple of minutes, I'd say around twenty-one, twenty-two."

"And for this I have what?"

"Nothing yet. Which I'm sure you understand. With a job like this, you have pretty much all or nothing."

"So. So. How much longer? How much more money?"

"Mr. Wirtman, I have no way of knowing. I doubt it will be much more."

"I am not happy."

"That's understandable—"

"You're right, it's understandable."

"Look, Mr. Wirtman," I said, getting irritated. "You own a car?"

"Yes. I own a car. An Oldsmobile."

"Fine. Well, sometimes you take it in to get repaired and you figure it's something simple. A tune-up, new spark plugs. But then it turns out you need gaskets, and when they take it apart to put the gaskets in, they discover you need your heads reground. So you get pissed at the mechanic. Fine. So do I. So you go somewhere else. You still have to get gaskets and the heads reground. And it costs about a hundred times more than you were expecting when you drove in. But that's what's wrong, and that's what it costs to fix. You can pay it, or you can junk an eighteen-thousand-dollar car. That's the situation. You got a problem. I tried to fix it quick and simple first. It doesn't happen to be a quick and simple."

"Well done," Joey mouthed, nodding approval and miming applause. I bowed to him.

"You understand what I'm saying, Mr. Wirtman," I said into the phone.

"Yes, I do," he said.

"Good."

"I should get a written estimate!"

"I'll do what I can," I sighed.

I did feel I'd been neglecting him. I called Ralph DeLillio, over at the ILGWU.

"I been meaning to call you," he said.

"Yeah. You get in contact with the people over at LMC, the Ginsbergs?"

"Hey, I did what I could. Talked to them myself. They haven't heard a word from Bergman in years. Last they heard from Bergman was back around '77, '78. He was on an around-the-world cruise. They got a postcard from him. From Hong Kong. It said 'Wish you were here. These people ain't never heard the word union!' . . . 'Hah hah,' I said. Ginsberg swore that's what the postcard said. . . ."

"It did," I told him. "That's what it said."

"Yeah, well, that's what started Ginsberg thinking, according to Ginsberg. That's why LMC pulled outa New York, wenta HK. You find this Bergman, do me a favor: Kick him in the balls; make sure you got a union label in your shoe when you do."

"Will do," I said.

"Hey, sorry I couldn't do more," he said.

"It's OK, Ralph. You did what you could. I owe you one."

"Come to work for me. Put on the tattered plume, join the good guys."

"I'll think about it," I said.

"Nah, you won't," he said, and hung up, as he does, without saying good-bye.

"Well," Joey said, "there ain't much else doing, except for your bet, so I took one a his bail skips. Snake's. I figure I'm more likely to find my guy than you are to win your bet."

When I got home, Glenda said she'd spoken to Philip, her ex-husband, Wayne's biological father. "Wayne's tuition is up," she told me. "Philip doesn't want to pay the increase."

"I didn't know the tuition went up," I said.

"There's no reason you should," she said. There wasn't. Philip's supposed to pay it. That and a medical policy is the extent of his child support. Less than she could have gotten. If she had had a tougher lawyer. If she had been a meaner bitch. "But he doesn't want to pay the extra."

"Take him to court."

"Because of you," she said. "He says that his lawyer says that we are a common-law marriage. Living together. This long."

"Bullshit," I said, speaking to the issue. "New York doesn't recognize common-law marriage. What the hell's wrong with him, not wanting to take care of his kid, not that he sees him that much."

"No. He doesn't."

"With as much money as he makes, he can well, well afford it."

"He just bought a new house. And Buffy is pregnant. Again."

"Oh, are you your husband's attorney now?" I heard undertones in everything she said. Was she telling me that as long as we were *like* married maybe we should *be* married.

"I'm not defending him. I'm just explaining."

"Just tell me what you want to do. You want me to pay the difference? You want me to find a lawyer who'll make sure Philip sticks to his agreement? Or do you want to send Wayne to public school?"

"I'm not sure. That's why I am attempting to discuss this with you."

"All right," I said. "I'll call Palmeri, the world's nastiest divorce attorney."

"Then we have to pay attorney's fees."

" 'Palmeri guarantees,' " I quoted, " 'the husband pays the attorney's fees.' "

"That's not what I want," she said.

"What do you want?"

"We didn't fight about things like that, even while we were getting divorced. We made our agreement, between us. Then we even used the same attorney."

"I know. You're a good woman. You are. A decent person. That's nice. It's terrific. And mostly I don't get into what goes down between you and Philip, but you're talking to me about it, and Wayne's school is something he can and should pay for. The man can afford it. You don't want to tell him that, I'll call and tell him that."

"Usually I don't realize I'm dependent on him," she said.

The other woman in my life, Alicia Bronstein, did not return my calls.

Sydney Coberland was out. I asked his secretary when he would be in. His secretary said she didn't know; he was out sick.

I called a contact at the SEC. I asked him if he would help me do a number on Peter Dimmer-Lodes. I suggested that he might want to prosecute Peter after I was done. My contact wasn't interested. I decided to follow Peter and see what happened.

He left work at seven. He was in a hurry. He got in a cab. I followed. He went home. I waited. He came out in thirty minutes. Blown dry, Pirelli peg pants, Bally shoes. He took another cab, they went about seven blocks. He picked up a girl. She had lots of salon-perm curls; she'd put a touch of blush in the center of her breastbone to make the deeply cut neckline look like cleavage; I guess you could say she was that *Cosmopolitan* girl. They got in another cab. I followed them to Border Town Rose, where everything was grilled on real mesquite and served with arugula.

I waited outside until they were seated. Then I went in and sat at the bar.

Peter had ordered the laaarrge—that's the way it was on the menu—margarita. With two straws. For him and her.

The bartender was an actor; he seemed heterosexual. I ordered a beer.

Another couple entered and joined Peter and the *Cosmo* girl. Peter and the new guy were clearly dear friends. Slug on the back, let's get really polluted, we're fine fellows, friends. The two women were strangers. They looked at each other competitively. The new arrival was plainer of face, built more for comfort and less for speed. Women know superior packaging when they see it. They know it when they are it. *Cosmo* girl won.

Peter's friends thought a two-straw laaarrge margarita was cute. They got one as well. Peter and *Cosmo* girl ordered a second.

I made myself friendly with the bartender. I talked to him about acting and art and mourned the death of the New York stage.

Across the room, the Dimmer-Lodes foursome were very merry. The important dynamic was between the two guys. When two people have a special relationship, it shows. A quicker, almost coded communication, a way of looking at each other, of touching. Not that I thought that Peter and his buddy were lovers. More likely, almost certainly, unindicted coconspirators. Partners in crime. Secret fiscal buccaneers. Pleased with themselves, like two sixties college boys dealing ounces of Panama Red in the girls' dorm.

I could smell it. If Peter Dimmer-Lodes had a partner to do the actual buying and selling based on the insider knowledge he obtained at his law firm—and he certainly would, that being the half-smart kind of thing that white-collar criminals think will make them undetectable—this was the guy.

"See that table over there?" I said to the bartender, gesturing toward Peter. "Foursome. One medium-size guy, one big guy . . ."

"You mean 'ain't no margarita too laaarrge for me'?"

"That what you call him?"

"Ah—" He stopped in midsyllable. "That guy a friend of yours?"

"No. I know him slightly," I said.

"Asshole says, 'Ain't no margarita too laaarrge for me,' every single time he orders one. He thinks it's funny. Every time."

"What I want to know is about the other guy." I put a twenty on the bar. "What's his name? Where's he work, if you know."

"Be right back," he said.

He moved to the end of the bar and talked to one of the waiters. The waiter went off. A few minutes later, he came back and spoke to the bartender, who came back to me.

"Arthur Collinson," he said. "Young stockbroker. We think Shearson Lehman—They Breed Apart, or have Minds Over Money, I forget which."

"Great buddies, those two," I said.

"Yeah. High school sweethearts, or something."

"You think they're like that?"

"No, I didn't mean that," the bartender said. "I can tell. Even the ones deep in the closet. I'm a judge of character."

"I can see that," I said. "But they got something going. . . . If it's not sex, it's money, I would guess."

"It could be," he said. "They hang out a lot together. And they tell the waitress they do big deals. Especially the big one. He's going to own Wall Street someday, is what he said, when it was closing time and he was trying to get Paula"—he pointed out one of the waitresses—"to go home with him."

Two drinks later, Peter's bladder suggested that he rise. He swaggered through the restaurant, head full of tequila and pocket full of credit cards.

I was certain that Collinson was Dimmer-Lodes's partner in crime. And I figured that if I moved fast enough and hard enough, I'd get Peter just enough off balance to open him up. I followed him. The men's room door was marked by a silhouette of a vaquero, to remind people that it was macho to piss standing up. I paused, to make sure that when I got inside, Peter would be in that psychologically defenseless position of having his zipper down and his pecker in his hand.

I locked the door behind me and said, "Hello, Peter."

He kept his body facing the urinal, but his head swiveled around to see me. When he recognized me, he gave me his good-buddy grin. He thought he was pleased to see me. He thought I was someone who was going to do good things for him.

"Mohammed, buddy," he said. "How they hangin'?"

"Peter," I said pleasantly, "you're an asshole."

His face went through a series of changes. He'd had a lot to drink, and it took time to get to "Duh?" and from there to "Who you talking to?"

Cops come on hard. There's a reason for it. They don't want the suspect to get his balance, to realize he should keep his mouth shut until his lawyer gets there. Or, in Peter's case, before he remembered he was a lawyer. I put the flat of my hand against the back of his head and shoved his face into the wall. He tried to shut off his bladder and put his penis away. He flailed at me with his other hand. It was a gift. I took it and put it up between his shoulder blades.

"Don't even think of moving," I said. "I want to take you down."

He was a big guy. He was tough. He wasn't going to take that. He tried to move. I lifted his arm till he thought it would crack. Then I slapped the back of his head with my free hand. The punk was guilty, and I didn't want him to slip away with lawyer's tricks.

"It hurts," he said. "You're hurting me. What's the matter with you? You some kinda crazy?"

"Peter, you're so fucking stupid. That's what this is all about. You and how stupid you've been."

"What do you want?"

"You're gonna take a fall."

"What are you talking about?"

"Insider trading."

"I didn't—"

"Don't bother with denials. Don't fuck around. Mergers and acquisitions. You have the information. Your buddy Artie, out there, he's got the setup. Couple of phony trading accounts. Two punks think they're half smart. You think the accounts can't be found. You think you left no traces. God, you're not even half smart."

"I don't know what you're talking a—"

"Asshole," I snapped, putting pressure on the arm again. "You take a fall, you know what happens to you? Disbarred, just for starts. No more BMWs, no more credit cards, no more *Cosmo* girls. The SEC, they're thinking that maybe it's time they really set a serious example. And you're just the kind of small-time punk they would choose to get serious on—"

"I didn't do—"

"Maybe you get to do time. You think you're tough. You got any idea what a punk you are and what they'll do to you in the joint?" I shoved my knee into his ass. "You get out, you're gonna be stretched so wide, you can take a taxi up your asshole."

"What do you want from me?"

"That's better," I said.

"Look, what you're saying, I never—"

"Come on," I snarled, pushing up the arm again. "You think once they start running Artie's accounts through the computer they won't turn it all up? How stupid do you think they are?"

"If . . . if Artie . . . Artie wouldn't."

"You think your buddy's a stand-up guy. Asshole. There ain't no stand-up guys no more. Even the Mafia, they don't have stand-up guys. Once the SEC gets started, federal prosecutors, your buddy Artie, he's gonna sell your ass so fast you won't even see it happen. This is 1984, the year of every man for himself."

"If Artie. . . . if I let something slip and he did something on his own . . ."

"You think they'll buy that?" I slapped the back of his head again.

"Stop it, stop it. Who are you?"

"I'm your worst nightmare come true."

"All right, all right. You want me to say something, do something—what is it?"

"OK. You and your buddy been making a small fortune. You're up for it if it comes out. But I can show you a way out."

"If you say so, but it's not so."

"Asshole," I said, "I'm trying to help you, and you're still playing games."

"I've been scrupulous," he said.

Scrupulous. From a guy with his face to the toilet wall. He was doing a lot better than I thought he would.

"Right. Integrity personified. With an extra sixty grand a year in outside income. As soon as you move into mergers and acquisitions. Sure. You're a good little yuppie. Ain't no dirt on you. How you gonna account for that?"

"That . . . that's my trust fund," he said.

"Oh, of course it is."

"Really. I . . . I came into it last year. That's the way my grandfather set it up. I don't know why. But you can check it. You can check it."

I believed him. It made the whole thing terribly embarrassing.

9.

Muggles

Alicia Bronstein was in conference, at lunch, in court, then gone for the day.

Sydney Coberland was still out sick.

I warned Mohammed Salim that someone named Peter Dimmer-Lodes might make some sort of fuss. The best thing he could do, I suggested, was act as if he'd never heard of Peter, never seen him, and never spoken to him. Mohammed was irritated with me.

I was going to lose that four grand. Plus my time. Plus seven hundred dollars cash out of pocket. It was because I'd been too sure of myself. And, at the same time, afraid to commit myself fully, hesitant to spend too much money or too much time on a job that didn't guarantee a payback. There was more that I could have done. I could have gone after the other four attorneys. I could also have looked for a resentful secretary or a proofreader with a need for cash.

There was no time left for any of that.

At five-thirty, I put on a suit of blend-in gray and an unmemorable tie. I took the subway downtown. At least I was going to close out the Wirtman job. I called Dom Magliocci. There was no answer. That was good. I only wanted to go see him if he wasn't there.

I carried a standard brown leatherish attaché case. It contained what are legally classified as burglar's tools.

There was a moderate flow of people leaving, not many coming in. I rode the elevator up alone. The office of Finkelstein-Magliocci was down the hall to the left and around the corner.

The older and saner I get, the more doing something stupid upsets me. Had I looked for an alarm system? Yes. Had I missed the alarm system? Probably not. Sonic sensors, had I thought about sonic sensors? Was Dom out for a meeting and on his way back to the office? Was the lock on the door as simple as I remembered and would my fingers retain their skill? Why was I doing it? Because the answer was inside that office, and I knew it.

When I turned left at the end of the corridor, the office door just ahead of me swung open. I started, like a fool, and jumped back. Looking ridiculously furtive, I peeked around the corner.

It was one of the cleaners, an old woman shaped like a loaf of Wonder bread, walking away from me. She was hauling a cart with a trash bin and a broom.

She opened the door of Finkelstein-Magliocci. When she entered, she left it ajar. The hall door opened on the reception area. Each attorney had his own office through a connecting door, one to the left, the other to the right. I moved up. I could hear the cleaning woman. She grunted when she bent for a trash basket, then grunted again when she bent to put it down. After she did the center room, she turned right to do Finkelstein's office. I heard the twin grunts. She closed the intraoffice door, then trundled across to Magliocci's office. As soon as she did, I dashed into the reception area. All I had to do was step into Finkelstein's office, which she had finished. I knew how long I had to do it. Two grunts. One grunt and I was in. Two grunts, my hand was on Finkelstein's door.

It was locked. I was standing there, with nowhere to go, and I heard the wheels of her trash cart squeaking toward me.

I dived behind the secretary's desk. As I went down, I could see her coming out. So I was certain she'd seen me.

She trundled out, dragging her wheeled wastebin behind her. Without a backward glance.

It was that simple.

The file cabinet was a piece of cake. And Bergman was filed under "B," right after "A" and in front of "C." I pulled it out. There was another Bergman file behind it. I pulled that. And another. All in all, there were sixteen Samuel N. Bergman files.

On Eighty-eighth Street, between Park and Madison, Bergman was paying the landlord $286.78 and charging his subtenant $2,100. On West End Avenue he was getting $1,100 a month for a one-bedroom and paying out $187.52. On West Fourth Street he was netting about $1,000. Each file was a different apartment. Except the sixteenth. That was the dead file. Seven apartments on which Samuel had lost the lease for one reason or another.

The Bergmans were having a very satisfactory retirement. Averaging over a thousand a month on each, better than $180,000 a year.

I looked at my watch. I stopped and listened. There were no noises in the corridor. I gave myself ten minutes. It was worth the extra time to give the rest of the files a quick once-over and see if Mr. Magliocci, Esq., was handling the same type of scam for anyone else. To my deep disappointment, Bergman was the only one.

Still, I had stumbled on my own little bonanza. Each and every apartment had a landlord. Each and every landlord would be willing to pay something, anything from one thousand to ten thousand, for the proof that would allow him to evict a rent-controlled tenant who didn't really live there. Win or lose on my bet, the short-term problems of D'Angelo Cassella were solved.

I turned on the copy machine and started duplicating the files.

It jammed. I started to sweat. That's the sort of thing that takes the extra five minutes that make the difference between success and incarceration.

I opened the copier up and read the instructions printed on the inside of the casing. They had been translated from the Japanese by a Korean and were applicable to either building a microchip or running a fruit stand. No matter; I could see the sheet of paper that had twisted itself between two rollers and a gearshift. We wrestled, the machine and I, and in time, and in bits and pieces, it gave forth the errant sheet.

Copying recommenced.

I read as I fed. There was one thing missing from all the files. Bergman's actual address. That was the crucial bit. With it I could make the same case fifteen separate times. I could not say that the man had fifteen apartments, because someone would want to know how I got that information.

Many police officers, all TV producers, Attorney General Gunderson, and President Reagan take the position that a criminal act against a bad guy is justifiable, pardonable, and even laudatory. But those people are not to be trusted. Just because Reagan pardoned and praised FBI agents who were convicted of break-ins of leftist and antiwar groups doesn't mean he's going to stand up and be counted on my behalf. Even if my break-in was absolutely essential to solve the heinous case of the Bergman apartment-hoarding ring.

I went back to the file cabinet. There was nothing else about Bergman there. Then I found it. Exactly where it should have been. On the Rolodex. Samuel N. Bergman, 42 Avenue Jean Moulin, 75014, Paris, France. Oh-la-la. How *très bien. Que merveilleux. C'est si bon.* I have gone many places in my detective work: Erie, Pennsylvania; Camden, New Jersey; Gary, Indiana; Birmingham, Alabama; the Bronx and Brooklyn and Secaucus. *Mais jamais Paris.* My feet felt like Gene Kelly's, my ears heard Gershwin.

I waved to the security guard as I left; he nodded politely. He could tell I belonged. I walked up to the corner, turned left, heading for Church Street. It was a fine evening, still light in a gentle way. The air was soft and warm. A car, driving the wrong way along the one-way street, pulled up on the curb in front of me. The door swung open. The man who got out was large. About six feet three, 240 pounds, wrapped tight in a light-brown suit made of 100 percent virgin acrylic. He was looking at me. Like a cop.

I looked over my shoulder.

I saw what I expected to see. His partner. He was smaller. He had his hand at his waist, pushing his jacket back. Presumably, his gun was there. They must've been sitting out front, waiting for me. Now they were going to pick me up. No muss, no fuss. With my attaché case to testify against me. Full of burglary tools. And the papers in my pocket to prove I'd made use of them. Nowhere to run. Nowhere to hide.

"Hello there, Anthony," the driver said when I got close to him.

"I don't believe we've met," I said politely.

"Well, now we have," he said, in that slobbering, I'm-in-control manner that cops learn from watching too much television.

"We would like a few words with you," the one in back said. His diction was too good for the NYPD. And his accent hadn't come from one of the five boroughs.

"Sure, why not," I said. "There's a pretty good coffee shop back on Broadway. Elaine's. She once sang the national anthem at Yankee Stadium."

"Why don't we go for a ride," the man in front said, opening the back door of the car.

"Sure," I said. "But I would sort of like to know who you are."

A hand came down on my shoulder from behind. Big deal. "Get in," the guy behind me said.

"Hey, hey, slow down. No need to get physical. I just would like to know who I'm dealing with."

The man in front of me pulled out a wallet and flipped it open. "Ferguson, FBI," he said. He was impressed.

I didn't know what the hell they could want from me. Unless they were already on to Finkelstein-Magliocci for something. Maybe I had stumbled into a federal investigation. When the Feds go in, they wire everything. Sound and picture. I could see it already. A video of me diving behind the secretary's desk. Opening the file cabinet. Making copies. When I got to the federal penitentiary, I could get a job in the library, fixing the copy machine.

"Let's," I said, "go for a ride."

It was a short ride. Federal Plaza was only four blocks away.

Upstairs, they sat me down in an interrogation room and left me alone. I waited for half an hour. To meditate on my sins, no doubt.

The door banged open. A different guy stood in the doorway. He looked at me coldly. His suit had pinstripes. It was a poly-wool blend; he was obviously a very senior agent. Ferguson and his partner were behind him. They came in and surrounded me.

"This Cassella?" the new one asked.

Ferguson said, "Yes."

"What kind of wise guy are you?" the supervising agent said.

I shrugged.

He opened a file on the table. The FBI has a lot of files. They like them. "Private detective . . . God," he muttered, "what jerks. . . . But you have a very impressive background. A year at Yale Law School. Did they teach you anything up there, wise guy?"

I looked at him.

"Well, did they? Do you know anything about the law?"

Of course I did. I knew I had the right to remain silent. I knew that I had the right to an attorney. More than that, I knew that shutting up and having an attorney does not make the police think you have something to hide. It does not make them certain that you are guilty. It makes them respect you, as someone with some self-control, not easily manipulated, who can cope with the system. As someone it would be more difficult to convict. Randolph Gunderson, John Mitchell, Richard Nixon, would never talk to the cops without an attorney.

"Do you understand that it is a felony to reveal the secret proceedings of a grand jury?"

I looked at him questioningly.

"We decided to be nice; that's why you're here, Cassella. A polite warning. Stay away from the Gunderson thing."

"The Gunderson thing?" I asked.

"You've been looking for the special prosecutor's report on Randolph Gunderson."

Oh, that. That was what they'd picked me up for. Nothing to do with Magliocci, Bergman, the burglary. That was good. I was relieved.

"Let me explain a couple of things. The information that was deleted from that report was deleted for excellent reasons. To protect ongoing FBI investigations. To protect witnesses. Some of them in the Federal Witness Protection Program. To save their lives. To save the lives of their wives and children. . . ."

It has been my experience as a law enforcement professional that those are not the things that bureaucrats care about. They care about protecting themselves first and protecting the department second first.

SENATE JUDICIARY COMMITTEE
Hearing 2/12/82

SEN. ORIN STEELE: You were the agent in charge of the background investigation of Randolph Gunderson?

DEPUTY DIRECTOR DEA VERNON MUGGLES: Yes, sir.

SEN. STEELE: At that time you testified that there was nothing in the background of Randolph Gunderson that would render him unfit to serve as attorney general. Is that correct?

DD MUGGLES: Yes, sir.

SEN. STEELE: Would you like to change your testimony at this time?

DD MUGGLES: No, sir.

SEN. STEELE: At that time you were a supervising agent in the Federal Bureau of Investigation. Subsequent to your testimony, two weeks subsequent, you received a promotion to Deputy Director, Drug Enforcement Authority.

DD MUGGLES: Administration.

SEN. STEELE: What?

DD MUGGLES: Drug Enforcement Administration. You said "Authority."

SEN. STEELE: Thank you for the correction. It has come to our attention that Randolph Gunderson's name appears in conversations of organized-crime figures, on tape recordings, that the FBI made in New Jersey.

DD MUGGLES: That is not correct. . . .

Hearing 2/14/82

SEN. ORIN STEELE: Mr. Giuliani, you were the field agent in charge of the investigation of Randolph Gunderson.

AGENT GIULIANI: I was one of several agents involved. I was the supervising agent in the Northeast.

SEN. STEELE: Did you ever happen to come across organized-crime figures dicussing their involvement with Mr. Gunderson, or one of his companies, or in any way implying a relationship?

AGENT GIULIANI: Yes, sir.

SEN. STEELE: Did you report this information to your superiors?

AGENT GIULIANI: Yes, sir. . . .

Hearing 2/15/82

SEN. ORIN STEELE: Three days ago you denied that there were wiretaps of organized-crime figures in which Mr. Gunderson's name was mentioned. You lied, under oath, to this committee.

DD DEA Vernon Muggles: No, sir. I didn't lie, sir.

Sen. Steele: We have testimony—

DD Muggles: If I may, Senator. I have a transcript of the hearing. . . .
You specifically asked me about organized-crime wiretaps in New Jersey.
Mr. Gunderson's name does not appear in any FBI wiretap in New Jersey.

Sen. Steele: We have testimony that his name was mentioned. That you
were informed of this. A long time ago. The first time you testified to this
committee. Do you deny that?

DD Muggles: No, sir.

Sen. Steele: Then you did lie to this committee.

DD Muggles: No, Senator. The wiretaps in which Mr. Gunderson's name
was mentioned were not recorded in New Jersey. They were recorded in
New York.

Sen. Steele: A whole river away.

DD Muggles: Yes, sir.

Congressional Record

". . . Am I getting through to you, Mr. Cassella?"

"Answer the man," Ferguson said from behind me.

I could see how it would be very important to the Feds for the
Gunderson affair to die away and be forgotten. I nodded yes.

"Very good, Mr. Cassella. Now, to the point. Revealing that information, or attempting to reveal that information, is obstruction of justice. If you obtain it, it is probable that you used bribery or extortion or
stole it. We will go to great, great lengths to determine which. Then we
will prosecute. Another felony. Or two or three.

"I will personally—and I am speaking on behalf of the Director—see
to it that, when convicted, you will serve your time in the most unpleasant of federal penitentiaries.

"In addition, while we are proceeding, we will make every effort to
make your life hell. We will investigate you from birth to the present.
We will investigate your finances. We will ask the IRS to assist us. We
will request that your license be suspended, preferably forever, but at
least until there is a finding.

"And if we can't get you for obstruction of justice, we will find something. We will find something."

He stood up and marched out.

Then Ferguson's partner marched out. Finally Ferguson marched out. I was alone. It was over. I picked up my attaché case with the burglary tools, which they had been kind enough not to open, and I, too, walked out. Just followed the exit signs.

10.

Par-lay Anglais?

The marvelous thing about Paris was that it was just like Paris.

Chic, sharp, meticulously intense about all and every object, particularly if it was edible. Gray stone, gray mist, gray river. But a different gray than New York or misery. A historic gray, designed in the sixteenth century, conscious of its own longevity and significance. The inhabitants lived up to their billing: bourgeois, rude, and rich in attitude.

Wirtman had insisted on a written estimate. His concept of expenses was not four-star, but my travel agent was delighted that I was going somewhere I couldn't get to by Greyhound. And the dollar was strong against the franc. I was supposed to get the job done in two days. Anything more would require written authorization or be at my own expense. Mr. Wirtman was not "financing vacations disguised as business. You are not, after all, a doctor."

About an hour before I was supposed to leave for the airport, twenty-four hours, give or take, before the time limit on the bet I was losing, a messenger, wearing cycling tights, soft helmet, and Campagnolo shirt, arrived. The nature of New York traffic and the get-it-here-yesterday New York attitude have called forth an urban pony express, the bicycle messenger. Paid a percentage of what they deliver, they ride at remarkable, even reckless speeds, when it's freezing, when it's steaming, when it's raining.

He gave me a large envelope. Clearly, by weight and shape, it was some sort of document. The return address was only the name of the messenger service, City-Speed. I tore it open.

The cover page said: "REPORT OF THE SPECIAL PROSECUTOR. UNITED STATES OF AMERICA VS. RANDOLPH GUNDERSON." There were no deletions. No WW II V-mail black ink. None. It was complete. It was the unexpurgated original. It was four thousand dollars.

The messenger asked if he could use the phone. They do that to confirm delivery and be assigned their next mission. I asked him his name. It was Speedo.

"Where'd you get this, Speedo?"

"From the office, dude."

"Where'd they get it?"

"Yo, dude, how am I gonna know?"

"You want to ask them at the office?"

"Sure, I do that for you. But time is money, dude, and time is all I got."

"Don't worry about it," I said, but he was already dialing anyway.

"This is Speedo, got a customer inquest. Gimme Dispatch One. . . . Hey, dudess, I'm here at"—he looked at his book—"D'Angelo Cassella. Got a package and we is the address returnee. Dude wanna know where we got it. . . . OK. What you say. . . . You got anything for me? . . . Yo. Good. Got it." He hung up. "Dudess gonna check it out, then she give you a shout. She got your number."

"Thank you, Speedo," I said, and I gave him a twenty. Tony C, last of the big-time spenders. I surprised myself.

He snapped it, he looked at it, pocketed it, and peered at the package.

"What?" I asked him.

"Look like paper, don't look like blow. But what do I know?"

"Yeah, it's paper," I said. "Why'd you say that?"

"When the green get long, someone doing wrong."

"You ever tempted to reach in?"

"Hey, what you take me for, dude? I got my thing. I'm good at my thing. Maybe one of the best. Dig this, dude: I once done a thousand-dollar week. I got pride."

"Sorry, dude," I said. "Dispatch One, she's gonna call me?"

"Yo, the dudess," he said, heading out the door.

I looked at the clock. There wasn't much time. I called WFUX and asked for Des. He wasn't in. I asked where he was. They offered to take a message and have him call me back. I said I had to reach him immediately. They weren't eager to help. I pushed it until they said he was on a beeper and they would beep him. "Tell him it's urgent. I have to speak to him in the next ten minutes, then I'm leaving the country."

He called five minutes later.

"Where are you?" I said.

"What's up?" Des asked.

"Where are you?"

"Why? What's happening?"

"I gotta see you right away. You'll see."

"I'm at a fire. Eighth Avenue and Forty-fifth."

"Stay there," I said, and hung up.

The dudess had still not called. I dialed City-Speed and asked for Dispatch One. The dudess said she hadn't had a chance to track it yet and would get back to me. When? Soon. Thanks. I was out the door.

I jumped into a cab. We stopped and went, stopped and went, the traffic clogging from Thirty-seventh to Forty-second in front of the Port Authority bus terminal. It opened up for a block, then tangled itself again around the fire at Forty-fifth Street. At Forty-fourth, I tore a twenty in half—a paranoid gesture on behalf of the luggage I was leaving in the backseat—and told the driver to wait.

The fire was mostly out, but the trucks were still there and the air had a sodden smudge. Forty-fifth was closed to traffic, but bike messengers cut around the barriers and wheeled up on the sidewalk, pedestrians hopped over hoses and slid between the men in boots and thick black slickers.

Des was easy enough to find. He was one of four camera crews competing to talk to the only available victim, a lightly scorched wino. I grabbed him.

"Hey, I'm on camera," he said.

"You think you could gimme a quarter, just a quarter?" the wino said to the man shoving a camera in his face.

"I gotta talk to you. Now."

"What about?" he asked.

"For a cup a coffee," the wino said as the paramedics lifted him away.

"Des, I don't have a lot of time here."

"OK. . . . Stop tape, Bobby. Shut it down a minute. . . . What's the big deal?"

"Here you go, Des," I said, handing him the report in a new envelope. "Take a look, dude."

"All right," he said, mumbling. "What's the big deal?" Then he saw it. He did the same thing I'd done, looked for the blackouts that weren't there. "Son of a bitch. You did it. Jesus, I forgot all about it."

"You owe me. Four grand."

"Wait a minute," he said.

"Don't fuck around about it," I said. "We had a bet."

"Tony . . ."

"I gotta catch a plane. I'll be back in a couple o' three days. See you then. Cash, check, or money order."

"I can't give you that much . . ." he started to say, but then he saw the look on my face. "All in one chunk, I mean. I mean, first I gotta check this out. . . ."

"Go ahead."

"Then you gotta, I mean, give me some time on it."

"No sweat." I grinned and dashed back for my cab.

The flight was full, the seats were narrow. I fell asleep breathing the breath of the bodies on either side of me, dreaming dreams of clients who would fly me on the Concorde. I woke up to a seat belt announcement and turbulence forty-five minutes out of Charles de Gaulle. Sunlight was coming through the windows.

Then we were on the ground. The signs for the bus that went to the train to Paris said "Le Train." I could follow that. In the station there was a combined train and metro map, just like the subway maps at home. Unfortunately, as with the subway map, without a knowledge of the city to mentally transpose over it, it was nothing but a random assemblage of unpronounceable names.

The seating was two across, facing each other, with lots of standing room. The middle-aged couple across from me were chattering away in Parisian, but I asked them anyway if they spoke English.

"*Mais non,*" the man said. Contempt twitched his mustache.

I asked the people back to back with me.

"Sprechen Sie deutsch?" they replied.

"English?" I said to the people across the aisle. *"Parlez anglais?"* They shrugged and looked so blank that I figured I didn't even say that right. A woman, a girl, standing beside her suitcase, looked down at me. She wore an oversize sweater, blue and yellow, a belt at the waist giving it some shape, patched blue jeans, bright green sneakers. She was built for comfort, and looked like she'd look as right with the morning as cream does with coffee. Her black hair was in an uncombed tangle, chic au natural, tied with a scarf folded into a band. Her eyes were dark, eyebrows thick; her nose was strong, her generous lips were a breath away from laughing. A Gallic face, a Mediterranean face. I could see the human animal living in her eyes. She was welcome to laugh at me.

"You speak English," I said. She had to.

"A little bit," she said.

"It had to be that way," I said.

"What?"

"I said," I said very slowly, "that I am very glad that you do."

"OK." What a lovely accent.

I asked how I should get to my hotel. She didn't understand the name of the street as pronounced by Cassella, so I showed it to her and she repronounced it, correctly.

"How do I get there?"

"Do you have a map? Of Paris? Of the metro?" she asked.

I shook my head. She sighed with exasperation and smiled at the same time. (Translation from the French: *You are a foolish boy, but what can one expect from a boy. Even so, I still like boys.* Who teaches them to talk like that?)

"You are American? English?" she asked.

"I'm from New York," I said.

"Oh, la la. You are American."

"No. New York is not America. My name is Tony."

"Is short for Antony? Yes?"

"Yes."

"I want to go to New York. You think I will like?"

"Hey, you'll love New York. When are you coming?"

"En été. End of the summer. Uh . . . Au-gust, yes?"

"Yes. August. When you get there, you call me, I'll show you around. It can be difficult for a stranger."

She suddenly looked very shy. A good girl would not do that.

"Here," I said. I reached into my wallet and gave her my card. "You call me when you are coming."

"Maybe," she said, sounding very much like maybe, and took the card. "I will show you where to go. To get to your hotel. It is in the arrondissement twelve. You know arrondissement? It means district, yes? An area."

"OK. Thank you. Thank you. What's your name?"

"It is Marie-Laure."

I caught the Marie, but the second part was a sound that can't be formed with a New York tongue.

The train slid into Paris, and at the Gare du Nord we got off and changed to the metro, buying small yellow cardboard tickets with a magnetic stripe down the back. These went into the turnstile and came back out. "You must keep this," Marie said, "to do the exit."

"Right. To do the exit."

"If I do not say it right, it is better if you correct my English."

"OK. 'To get out.' "

When we got out of the metro, she took me to a magazine shop and picked out *Les Rues de Paris* for me, an encyclopedic directory, maps in the book, plus two foldout maps, one for the rues, one for the metro, cross-referenced to each other and to the book.

"Now we go this way," she said.

I offered her my arm. She didn't take it. "Thank you for this," I said. "I would like to take you to lunch."

"It is nothing; it's OK."

"Yeah. What about lunch?"

Again she looked shy, but a look so full of flirtatious charm . . . (I'd seen that look before. Nineteen forty-four. Dropped behind enemy lines. The countryside. Moonlight. Wounded. The SS on my trail. A farm. A barn. A place to hide. Troops outside. Someone entering the barn. . . . It is her. The farmer's daughter. I know at a glance she will save me. And oh, la la.) I asked if she would join me for dinner.

"Maybe in New York," she said. "The hotel is on the street. There."

"A coffee. Let me buy you a cup of coffee."

"Thank you," she said, smiling, a dance around her eyes. She looked at her watch. "But it is the hour that I must go."

"I'm sorry."

"Me too." She made it sound like she meant it. Every woman who turns me down should do it with a French accent. "Ciao."

"I'll see you in New York," I said.

She spoke to me with her eyes. I understood every word she didn't say. Then she was walking away. In a few steps, she disappeared into the purposeful bustle of the Parisian street.

After I checked in and showered, I found Avenue Jean Moulin on the map. It was to the south, only a few blocks long, coming out of Avenue du Général Leclerc. With or without the map, I wasn't up to finding it on my own. I hailed a cab and told the driver the address. He said what I understood to be "Huh?" I repeated it. He said, "Huh?" I wrote it down. "Ah, oui!" and we took off with enthusiasm. It was an interesting drive, and I saw many things. New York cab drivers are equally courteous to foreign visitors, always picking the most scenic routes.

When we arrived, the meter showed forty francs. But there were additional charges. Because it was a Tuesday. Because it was *l'heure de déjeuner.* Because we had to cross the Seine. Seine-crossing alone is an extra twenty francs. Ah, Paris, city of lights, you are what I had always dreamed you would be.

No. 42 was, like the buildings around it, a six-story apartment building. I rang the bell beside the door. The lock released. I pushed my way into the foyer. There was a double door in front of me, a smaller door and a directory to my left. While I was reading the directory, the concierge appeared from the small door. She was exactly as she should have been, gray-haired but vigorous, short, stout, with the territorial instincts of a terrier, guardian of her domain. Entry to America is controlled by the immigration department. Residence in Paris is dictated by a casting director. She spoke to me in French.

"Mr. Bergman," I said. "Oo ay Mr. Bergman. Samuel Bergman."

"*Que?*"

"Par-lay English?" I asked.

"*Non,*" she said, and then something else, which contained a lot of syllables attached rapidly to each other.

I wrote down the name and showed it to her. She was even more emphatic. *"Pas ici, pas ici,"* ushering me toward the door as if she had a broom and I were litter in her lobby.

What do you do in Paris when what you're there for isn't there *et vous ne parlez pas français* and you can't figure out what to do next? I decided to see the Eiffel Tower. I had my *Les Rues de Paris* in my pocket and I thought I could walk across the city. To anyone raised with the utter simplicity of Manhattan's grid street plan, Paris is a nightmare. No street is complete, no street is through, no angle is right. Soon I was in a *cimetière*. The *du Sud,* if it matters. Which meant I was going in the right direction. For the tower, not for a Bergman. A zig, a zag, I left the dead, and I was on Boulevard Raspail. Which went to Boulevard Montparnasse, a name I had heard somewhere, probably in a movie. But I was turned around and found myself at an intersection of a whole lot of streets. About six of them. All with different names.

There was a café. *Est bien.* Seats outside, umbrellas over the tables, a waiter in a soiled white jacket and a mouth that made moues. I ordered a croissant and *un café con leche.* Service was leisurely. Except for presentation of the bill. That was instantaneous. Written with an insouciant flair and placed before me: 8.4 francs. I handed him a fifty.

"Vous n'avez pas dix francs?" he said. I think.

"What?" I said.

"Dix, dix francs," he said, holding up ten fingers. *"Vous avex dix francs?"*

"No. Sorry," I said.

He took the fifty with great weariness. Or perhaps, since he was Parisian, it was ennui.

Once again the open door had led to nothing. I had the feeling that if I failed, Wirtman was the kind of guy I would have to sue to get my money, a landlord.

The waiter placed my change before me. I looked up, said thank you, then looked out at the street. There she was. My pretty woman. Roy Orbison burst into song in my head.

"Marie," I yelled.

Fourteen out of twenty women, and two men, turned around when I called. Half the population of France is named Marie-*quelque chose;* the rest are named Jean-Paul, Jean-Claude, and Jean-Louis. My Marie smiled when I jumped up from my seat. She laughed when I hopped over the railing that surrounded the café.

"I need your help," I told her.

"Oh, yes?"

"Yes. Definitely. Come. I will buy you *un café* and I will explain," I said, taking her arm and turning back to the café. The sonofabitch moue-mouth waiter was not only collecting my unfinished coffee and my half-eaten croissant; he was gathering forty-plus francs as a tip. "Hey, leave that," I yelled.

The waiter calmly dropped the forty francs in his pocket. Probably slightly deaf in his left ear. I dragged Marie after me into the café. The waiter was hiding behind the bar.

"Give me my money back. And where's my coffee and croissant?"

"*Pardon?*" he said, a double moue on each vowel.

"Come on, Jacques. Gimme," I said, with my hand out.

The waiter turned to the bartender, and in rapid French, they discussed their incomprehension of what I'd said. I explained to Marie what was going on. Marie put on a new face and voice, inherited from *Maman,* a devastating set of expressions handed down through generation upon generation of the housewives of France to deal with thumb-on-the-scale, sou-stealing shopkeepers.

It brought my waiter up short, like a French poodle caught on a choke collar. "*Pardon, pardon. Excusez-moi,*" he mouthed, handing back my forty-one francs. Marie watched the money, then turned those eyes upon him. He coughed up an additional six centimes.

Only then did she look back at me. *Maman* had disappeared. The shy girl with flirtatious eyes was back. I was the man and in charge. It was up to me to show her to the table. Which I did.

"Tell me something, Marie: You got a housing shortage in Paris?"

She said, "What?" and I repeated it slowly and carefully.

"Oh, yes. It is very difficult to find the apartment. Very, very expensive." Her franglais description of the problem was interrupted by the arrival of the waiter. I ordered two *café con leches* and two croissants. Marie was kind enough to wait until the waiter left to let me know that it was *café au lait.*

"The reason I'm here," I said to Marie, "is to find this guy named

Samuel Bergman, who's wanted for multiple rent-control fraud back in the States."

Rarely have I seen someone look blank so attractively. Intelligently. Bergman's crimes and the labyrinth of real estate regulations from which they arose were not really worth explaining. So I told her, simply, that I had an address for a man. When I went to the address, the concierge had shooed me away.

The waiter returned with our order and *l'addition.* I reached to pay the 16.8 francs. Marie took the money from my palm, extracted a ten-franc piece, gave that to the waiter and the rest back to me. He moued. She looked at him. His eyes drooped. The world was a very sad and unfair place.

"Will you help me talk to the woman?"

"I think so, yes."

"Thank you. Listen. I . . . do not want to be rude."

"Rude?"

"Not polite."

"Yes, I understand. You do not want to be not polite."

"Right. But I can pay you for your help."

"No," she said.

I accepted that. She dipped her croissant in the coffee the way Americans dunk doughnuts. Oh, the thrill of seeing another culture.

This time we went directly to the concierge. Marie told her that I had come from America in search of Samuel N. Bergman. That I was certain that Mr. Bergman lived or had lived . . .

This time the greeting was completely different. *"Bien,"* the concierge said, and something else, which I think was: "I am pleased you have returned." She held her door open and ushered us into her apartment.

It was a room filled with overstuffed furniture, paintings on the wall, mementos and do-funnies on every available horizontal surface, doilies on the arms of every chair and on top of the huge old console TV. A man in a blue suit and pale blue tie sat facing us.

The concierge slammed the door shut, blocked it with her body, and cried with malignant triumph, *"Il est ici!"*

He was a cop. I surrendered my passport. Marie showed her identification. The cop spoke rapidly. Marie translated haltingly. I spoke slowly. The concierge watched us all balefully.

Gradually, sense and order came to the conversation. After I left, Madame DeFarge, the concierge, had called the police. The police now wanted to know who I was and why I was looking for Mr. Bergman. At the name Bergman, Madame DeFarge once again broke into a tirade, a cascade of syllables, a torrent of agitation. Marie scaled that down to a few phrases. "She is upset"—I could see that—"that such a thing has never happened before . . . or since. This is a good habitation . . . apartment building."

"What thing has never happened?" I asked her.

She shrugged, her face neutral but her eyes laughing.

The cop finally barked loudly enough to stop Madame DeFarge. Silenced, she wrapped herself in a cloak of righteousness and sat. She picked up her knitting, jabbing left, left, right, as she listened. Again the cop turned to me. I explained slowly and as simply as I could, Marie translating, why I was looking for Mr. Bergman. I finally had the sense to show him my investigator's license. He looked at it, raised his eyebrows, and put it in his pocket.

When I finished my story, he sat and looked at me. Finally he spoke. "You have to go to the police station with him," Marie told me.

"What's going on?" I said.

Marie asked. He repeated that I was to go with him.

"Am I under arrest, or something?"

He repeated the same phrase. With less patience. In France they do not say, "You have the right to remain silent . . . anything you say can and may be used against you . . . you have the right to an attorney . . . if you can't afford an attorney the court will provide you with one." This omission was not due to his inability to speak English. It is because those rights don't exist in France. The anarchy it would engender is unthinkable.

The three of us exited under the glare of Madame DeFarge. An unmarked Citroën was parked out front. He opened the back door and gestured for me to get in. I held it open for Marie.

"Non. Vous," the cop barked.

I got in. He slammed it shut. It did not open from the inside. He got in front, then gestured at Marie to go. Rarely have I felt so bereft. She stood looking at me.

"Come to New York," I called through the window. "Call me."

The engine started, and we left her behind.

Police stations are more or less universal. So are cops. He sat me down in a dank corner office—a table, a chair, a small, high window—and went away. Five minutes later, the door opened. I was led to a much grander office. Now we were four.

I was introduced to Capitaine Renaud, Officer Zucchero, a translator, and Détective Jean-Claude Solaise, who had brought me in. Jean-Claude took out his notebook and recited a précis of his initial interrogation. Capitaine Renaud took out a Gitane. Officer Zucchero lit it for him.

When Jean-Claude was finished, *le capitaine* asked Zucchero to ask me how I had obtained that address for Bergman.

"Can I have a lawyer?" I asked.

Zucchero laughed, but he translated. *Le capitaine* said, "No."

"Can I call my embassy?"

Zucchero laughed, but he translated. *Le capitaine* said, "No."

"Mr. Bergman is supposed to live in an apartment in New York," I said. "Each month he sends a check with his name on it to the landlord. But the account from which the check is drawn does not belong to him. It belongs to a lawyer, in New York. I went to the office of this lawyer. I looked in his Rolodex. I found the address on Avenue Jean Moulin."

Le capitaine said something.

"What?" I asked Zucchero.

"He said it is a barbarity the way you said Jean Moulin."

"Yeah, well, is mispronunciation a punishable offense over here?"

"Yes, *monsieur*, it is," Zucchero said.

Le capitaine began to question me, through the translator, about Bergman's apartment scheme. They sounded very skeptical. We went through it three times.

"*Vous êtes Italien?*" Renaud asked, looking at my passport.

"American."

Zucchero translated his reply as "The captain says your name is Italian."

"I am American," I repeated. "My father came from Sicily."

I picked out the word "Mafia" from what Renaud said next. "Tell your captain," I told Zucchero before he had a chance to translate, "that he's seen too many movies."

They asked me about the dates rent control had changed to stabilization. I didn't know. They had me spell Magliocci, asked for his address, and wanted to know if he was Italian. Again they said "Mafia."

I told the captain again that he saw too many movies.

"Oh?" Zucchero translated. "America is not run by the Mafia? Are we in France misinformed? We hear that they reach into the highest in the government."

"Some things are very exaggerated." I sighed. "Yes, they exist. No, they don't run America. They are a dying breed. Almost history."

Renaud snorted. "We know better," was the translation. "Did the Mafia not assassinate witnesses against your attorney general?"

Odd that they had noticed. Nobody in America seemed to have. There was nothing I could say. I shrugged. Gallically. They looked at me.

They asked what I had done before I was a private detective. I told them. They wanted to know why I was dismissed. I explained that I had resigned, and had to explain why. Back to Bergman. They all talked among themselves. I knew their decision was favorable when Renaud shrugged and said, "America."

"*Café?*" Renaud said to me pleasantly.

"Do you want some coffee?" Zucchero translated.

"Yes, thank you."

"*Oui, merci,*" Zucchero translated. Renaud and I both looked at him. Jean-Claude went out for it.

"*Monsieur Bergman est mort. Elle été assassiné.*" That made the whole thing comprehensible. "It appears," he went on, through the translator, "that Attorney Magliocci has maintained Mr. Bergman's dishonesties. . . . It is an unsovled murder. Paris is not New York. We are not accustomed to police inadequacy. Is it true that police in New York only solve one third of their murders?"

"They solve more than that," I said. "Maybe two thirds."

"What about Miami?"

"I don't know."

"I would like to visit New York," *le capitaine* said, "but I would not like to live there. Do people really eat at McDonald's every day?"

"Would it be possible for me to get a copy of the death certificate?" I asked.

There was some discussion between Zucchero and Capitaine Renaud. Jean-Claude returned with the coffee. It was in real cups, proving that French civilization is superior. Officer Zucchero brought me a cup and took the opportunity to say, by way of apology, "My family, they are also Italian. Zucchero."

Renaud spoke again. Jean-Claude looked very interested in the question. Zucchero said, "The program *Magnum, P.I.,* do you think it is realistic?"

"No," I said. They all looked very relieved. "Do you think I could get a death certificate?"

Then Jean-Claude spoke. "It was a particularly brutal crime. . . ." He paused for the translation. "Mr. Bergman was an old man. . . . He was hit, several times, with perhaps a club? perhaps a pipe. . . . Then the body was thrown out the window . . . from the *étage* four, the fourth level . . . to disguise the assassination as self—as suicide."

"What about his wife?" I asked.

Jean-Claude looked at his file. "He is, in our files, a widower. He was. His death occurred in September of . . . 1979." He spoke to Capitaine Renaud. Zucchero didn't translate. Then back to me, with translation. This was why I hate foreign films: I always wonder what the subtitles leave out. "We will give you the papers you require. We would like to ask a favor of you. In return. Would you send us photographs of Dominic Magliocci . . . also of his partner, Mr. Finkelstein."

"Yeah, sure," I said.

Jean-Claude gave me copies of the death certificate and of the police report. I asked him if he knew Marie's last name or remembered her address. I had watched him copy it from her ID. He claimed that he didn't know.

My one night in Paris. I decided to go out on the town and learn if Marie's charms were part of the national character or uniquely her own. I went back to the hotel and fell asleep across the bed, fully dressed. In the morning, with the help of the hotel's concierge, I changed my booking for an early flight. I bought the *International Herald Tribune*—a joint publication of the *New York Times* and the *Washington Post,* printed simultaneously in Paris, London, Rome, Zurich, Hong Kong, Singapore, The Hague, Marseilles, Tokyo, and Miami—because it has U.S. sports and *Doonesbury.* I saw why Capitaine Renaud had gone on about Randolph Gunderson and the Mafia. The *Trib* had picked up on an exclusive, giving credit where credit was almost due, to Desmond Kennel, WFUX, New York. Des had revealed some of the allegations that had not been sufficiently corroborated to indict. An ex–loan shark and bagman now in the Federal Witness Protection Program, Sal Minelli, said that he had received money "in the tuna bag," a brown paper sandwich bag, from Randolph Gunderson, for Tony Provolone. Benito "Little Benny" Caputo had alleged that he had seen Gunderson with Santino "The Wrecker" Scorcese and several other O.C. figures and some "very tasty bimbos" in a private box at the 1976 World Series. Scorcese himself had said—on the telephone, as recorded by the FBI—that "R.G. and me, 's all right," and also that "hey, Empire, I'm in with all the top people, like this, [at] the Empire." A large number of Mr. Gunderson's businesses and real estate investments, the paper explained, were organized under a holding company named Empire Properties, Inc. The attorney general had replied that this was "scurrilous rumor mongering, . . . the most irresponsible sort of journalism." Sanford Beagle, the President's press secretary, commented that "the courts have done their work, we intend to abide by their decision. This is a government of laws."

11.

Rock 'n' Roll

I'm a rock 'n' roller
don't want no Ayatollah
that mean old U.S.S.R.
they can't beat God and a rhythm guitar

U.S.A. all the way
home of rock 'n' ro'
we got Ronnie
we got Rambo
sea to shining sea
from Maine to Miami
it's the land of the free
'cause we got MTV

The White Rapper (H. Stucker),
"U.S.A. All the Way"
(© Honkey Tunes, Inc., 1982)

When I returned to the United States, I got a finger up my ass.

12.

I Confess

*The Justice Department is not a domestic agency.
It is the internal arm of the nation's defense.*

Randolph Gunderson

WFUX was not a twenty-four-hour station. So the FBI did not arrive until the morning after Des Kennel's broadcast. They had arrest warrants, search warrants, and several injunctions. They picked up Des at home. He was charged with theft of government property, violating the secrecy of the grand jury process, obstruction of justice (thirty-four counts), conspiracy to do all of the above, and probably some other things too.

Desmond Kennel was not a stand-up guy. He was not the kind of reporter who would go to jail to protect his sources and the First Amendment to the Constitution of the United States. He looked the Feds square in the eye and said: "Cassella."

A bored-looking black woman took my passport and punched my name into the computer. Something came up beside it. She pushed a button under her table and two other agents appeared.

I said, "I'd like an explanation." They each took one arm. They marched me into a small room. I said, "I'd like to call my lawyer." They took my bag and left. I tried the door. It was locked. I waited. Then waited some more.

An hour later, the door opened. A new agent appeared. He had my bag. Still open after their inspection. My best pair of underwear was hanging out. "Is this your luggage?" he said.

118

"I want to call my lawyer," I said.

"Is this all your baggage?" he asked.

"I want to call my lawyer," I said.

"Would you remove your garments, please," he said.

They have the right, I understand, to do this. I stripped. I didn't like it. He fondled my clothing, he felt the inside of my sneakers. He asked me to bend over and spread my cheeks. He put on a rubber glove, greased it, and stuck a finger up my ass. They have the right, I understand, to do this.

"Thank you," he said when he withdrew.

He stripped off the glove, tossed it in the wastebasket, then left. I got dressed. And I waited. The greasy feeling of the petroleum jelly lingered. It was another hour before the door opened again. This time it was the FBI. They handcuffed my hands behind my back. One of them mentioned that I was under arrest.

"I want to call my lawyer," I said.

"Downtown," Agent One said. Agent Two nodded.

Agent One held the door. Agent Two shoved me out.

"How about my bag?" I said. Agent Two shoved me along. "It might be evidence," I said.

Agent One thought about that. He nodded grimly to Agent Two. Agent Two retrieved it without bothering to close it. They marched me out through the terminal. My best underwear, a lovely hue of blue, 100 percent cotton, made in France, slid inch by inch out of the bag, to be left behind on the floor of JFK.

They hustled me into the backseat of their car.

Agent One had just moved to Tenafly. His daughter was a pep squad reject. That had broken her heart. She had been a Chattanooga Cougarette. And let's face it, Tennessee girls are a lot prettier than Jersey girls, and his daughter was one truly pretty, real classic, blond, blue-eyed American Beauty Rose. Something was clearly not ko-shure.

Agent Two had read an article in *Reader's Digest*, "Are Americans Eating Too Much Meat?" He was wondering if he was eating too much meat. He had a lot of gas.

I made some mention of a phone call, to a lawyer.

Lot of minority types, Agent One said. Blacks, Italians, Jews, Latins, all kinds of stuff, out in Tenafly, which he had thought was a good community. He suspected a little affirmative action going around, which to his way of thinking was all wrong when it started causing pain to the most innocent, loveliest, never-hurt-a-soul-in-her-life, teenage American girl that you ever did see.

"And you got her in school with guineas," I said, admonishingly. "Italians, man, they get around that blond, blue-eyed pussy, they are outa control. And blacks, that's even worse. They got those big, big things. Once your daughter tries that, she'll be ruined for life. Send her back to Tennessee. Quick."

They didn't even look at me. I gave up.

We ended up in Federal Plaza. They had even saved me the very same room in which I'd had my last federal interview.

Before they left, Agent One put his face up close to mine. "Where you're going," he said, "you are not going to see any sort of pussy whatsoever, let along young, blond, blue-eyed. And you're the one who's going to have to worry about nigger dick. Have fun, asshole." He'd had tuna for lunch.

They left me there with the cuffs on.

When the door finally opened, I saw two familiar faces: Ferguson and the supervisor he had brought me to the first time.

"Can I call my lawyer?" I said.

"Of course you can," the supervisor said. "Absolutely. You may have to wait a bit; we got a problem with the phones."

"How about a pay phone?"

"With the regular phones out, there's a line, about a mile long. It might be a half hour, an hour even, until it's free."

"I'll wait," I said.

"Do you mind if we talk a bit while you're waiting?"

I shrugged. He had his Cassella file, legal pad, tape recorder. He turned the machine on and uncapped his Bic. "My name is Special Agent Vernon Muggles," he announced to both myself and the machine. By then I knew who Muggles was. The man who'd covered up for Gunderson. And he would never get his promotion back as long as the affair was in the public eye. I was in trouble. A lot of trouble. He added the date and my name as "the suspect, who has of his own free will agreed to a discussion."

"The suspect," I said, "asked to speak to his attorney, but was told there was a problem with the phones. We want to get everything recorded, right?"

"Sure."

Ferguson leaned closer to me, speaking too softly for the machine. "Me you already know, don't you, punk."

"Why'd you do it, Tony? We warned you," Muggles said. "We know it was you. Kennel told us. Your prints, they're on the report, on the envelope you delivered it in. I want you to understand, we have you on ice."

"You think we could take the cuffs off?"

"Nah, but we could make 'em tighter," Ferguson said.

"Take 'em off. We don't need them," Muggles said.

"Chief . . ."

"Ferguson," Muggles said.

"Go ahead, Fergie, be a sweetie—take 'em off."

Ferguson moved around behind me. He lifted my arms enough to hurt while he was getting to the cuffs. I grunted. He squeezed the cuffs down hard before he released them.

"That hurts, and you know it, Fergie. . . . Damn it."

"Uh, sorry," he said, making it clear that he wasn't.

"What am I charged with?"

"Theft of government property. Violating the secrecy of the grand jury process. Obstruction of justice, thirty-four counts. Conspiracy to do all of the above." He held up a warrant, but he didn't show it to me. "I told you, we think of this as pretty serious stuff. I mean, maybe you think it's just a piece of paper. But what you've done is you've endangered lives. You've contributed to the slander of a very, very prominent man. Who has already been through a very, very trying ordeal and been cleared by the courts. And you've jeopardized some very important investigations."

"You guys really screwed this one up, didn't you?" I said.

"You're in serious trouble here, Tony. I wouldn't worry about anything but myself if I were you."

"Don't bother with him," Ferguson said to Muggles, for my benefit. "We got him cold. Let's not waste our time. Hey, punk"—he smiled at me—"I'm gonna see to it you do your time in Atlanta. That way, you won't keep coming back."

"We are a nation at war," Muggles announced, working himself into

121

a fine lather. "A war between Society and the Criminal. What you have done . . . as far as I'm concerned, that makes you a traitor. As much a traitor as a guy who sells atom secrets to the commies." He took a deep, deep breath, bringing himself under control. "In my heart, in my guts, in my soul, there's nothing I want more than to put you away. Put you in a cage where one of the other animals will take care of you for us. But they tell me . . . they tell me I have a job to do. My job is to get information. Now. If you help us open up the rest of this conspiracy, then . . . then you might get lucky."

"Lucky? How lucky?"

"God, you don't deserve it. But if you come clean, no more than a year."

"Forget it." I couldn't afford to take any kind of bust at all. Bye-bye license. I'd be washing dishes for a living. Or have to go back to law school.

"If you tell us everything, without reservation—now, right now—when we're done, we'll go for a dismissal. If we get everyone else involved."

"Even that," I said, my eyes cast down, "might . . . it might be dangerous."

"We can protect you," he said, eyes bright, eager now.

"No. Forget it. I won't. I can't," I said.

"All right, punk, it's the slam for you," Muggles said.

"Hey, Vernon—you don't mind I call you Vern, do you, Vern?"

"It's Special Agent Muggles," he snapped.

"Yeah, Muggs. You know, you're doing this all wrong. You're supposed to have a good guy and a bad buy. But you got yourself playing both parts. Whatsamatter, you don't trust Fergie the Gorilla to use his mouth for anything but sucking?"

Fergie got angry. He stood up from his chair and loomed himself over me. "You show some fucking respect, punk," he growled.

"Ouuu, did I hurt your li'l feelings?" I mocked him.

"Just shut your mouth, punk."

"You know what I think?" I said in a teasing voice. "I think you're a little strange." I reached out and patted him, lightly, tenderly even, on his cock.

Fergie lost his cool. He telegraphed the big roundhouse right that came at me. I got my hand up enough to protect my face, but the force of the blow knocked me off the chair and onto the floor.

"Get away from him, Ferguson," Muggles yelled, but not soon enough to keep Fergie from kicking me.

"You didn't see what he did," Ferguson said defensively.

"It doesn't matter."

"He . . ." Ferguson started to say, then he blushed and shut up. I watched from the floor while he backed away from me. When he was out of striking distance, I picked myself up.

"I'm sorry about that," Muggles said through tight lips.

I wasn't. I glanced over at the tape recorder. Muggles hadn't turned it off. "What . . . what do you want to know? I'll tell you," I said, weakly.

"Let's take it from the top," he said. He got his pen poised over his pad. "Who first approached you?"

"To get the special prosecutor's report?"

"Yes."

"Nobody actually approached me. It just sort of happened."

"Look, this is up to you, Cassella. You help us, you help yourself. You want to screw around, you hurt yourself. Am I clear?"

"*Claro,*" I said. "You asked the wrong question."

He frowned. "Who paid you?"

"Des Kennel," I said.

"Oh, come on. We have his testimony. You came up to him. Out of the blue. You said"—he looked at his file—"and I quote, 'I got the goods. You gotta get it on the air. The people who gave me this, they'll do good things for you if it gets on the air. Listen,' you told him, quote, 'I got to run. I'm leaving the country. I'll be back when it's over.' "

I shrugged.

"Let the record show," he said to the machine, "that Mr. Cassella shrugged."

"I thought it was a Gallic shrug. Didn't you get that feeling? A tray fran-say type of gesture?"

"Do you deny the statement?"

"That I shrugged?"

"Don't play wise-ass with me," Muggles said.

"What Kennel said I said? . . . Not true."

"Who paid you?"

"Des. Or he will. He hasn't paid yet."

"You went and stole a top-secret document without payment. I find that difficult to believe. It couldn't be idealism. I don't care how perverse you are; there is no way that anyone could conceive of what you've done as being anything but detrimental to the good of society."

"Muggs, I gotta deny all of that."

"You deny that?"

"Yup," I said.

"You deny you stole the special prosecutor's report?"

"Yup. I also deny that it was top secret. And I deny that there could not be any idealistic reason to publish it."

"What are you? Some sort of radical?"

"He's a pinko fag," Fergie said. "He's a pansy."

"Muggles," I said, "you say you want to talk, then you insult me. You don't listen to what I'm telling you, you have me cuffed—"

"You're not cuffed now."

"I was. When you knew you didn't need it. You brought in the gorilla, you let him hit me, kick me. You threatened my life—"

"I didn't threaten your life," he said.

"The gorilla said you were going to send me to a prison where I would be set up to be hit. You made the same suggestion. I take that as a threat on my life. Now you're scrambling my brain. You got me where I can't think," I whined, "let alone talk. So if you want something from me, why don't you back off and . . . and talk to me like a person."

"All right. Let's slow down. Would you like a glass of water?"

"Yes, please," I said.

He gestured to Fergie to get me some water. Fergie lumbered out reluctantly.

"What was it you were trying to say?" Muggles said with forced politeness.

"I'll tell you how it was. Me and Des, we were having a drink. We got drunk. The night the report was issued. He had an expurgated copy. His girlfriend, great boobs, was talking about LPW, the Life Plan Way. I don't know how we got to it, but we ended up making a bet. That I could get the original. In two weeks or less."

Fergie returned with my refreshment.

"I don't believe you," Muggles said.

"That's how it went down. I don't know, maybe you can talk to the girl."

"We'll get back to that," he said. "Tell me how you got it?"

"This," I said, "you're really not going to believe. . . ." The truth was a true mind fuck for Muggles. I didn't tell him about Alicia Bronstein, but then, I didn't really know that she had sent me the papers. I did tell him about City-Speed, Speedo, and The Dudess. It brought Muggles pain. He had Fergie take my water away.

Muggles dispatched Fergie to find Speedo. I wish I'd been there to see it. The skinny kid on his Atala with all-Campagnolo parts, slicing between cabs and trucks, with Fergie stuck behind, his government-issue Ford overheating in midtown traffic.

"Enough," I told Muggles. "No more until I see my lawyer."

"Yeah, Cassella," he said. "Talk to your lawyer." He smiled and left, carrying my taped confession with him.

13.

Miranda

"You did what?" Gerald Yaskowitz, attorney for the defendant, said, belly and jowls quivering. "You did what?"

"I confessed."

"You? Without your attorney? You spoke. Without an attorney. I am at a loss. You—"

"Gerry . . ."

"A confession. Who would believe? Without his attorney—"

"Gerry . . ."

"It's a death wish," he said to himself. He looked up and addressed the ceiling. "Lord, why? Why such clients as this? Am I a bad man? Do I fail in my duties?"

"Gerry . . ."

"What?"

"They didn't read me my rights."

"They didn't read you your rights? What do you mean, they didn't read you your rights?"

"You know those little cards they carry. That they read from. 'You have the right to remain silent' and all that."

"What am I? An idiot? Of course I know."

"They didn't read it."

"Really?" he said, his eyes lighting up. "The FBI?"

"Right. Immigration didn't, either. Or customs."

"That's wonderful, wonderful news. You know what? That's wonderful news. Maybe—maybe—I can save you after all. Oh, oh"—he chuckled—"the FBI didn't read him his rights."

"They refused to let me call my lawyer. And I asked. Several times."

"That's good, that's good," he said.

"They stuck a finger up my ass. Then they hit me."

"At the same time?" he said, genuinely shocked.

"Separately," I said.

"Heaven. Perfect," he cried. He looked up. He apologized to the ceiling. "Lord, I doubted. I'm sorry. You did good on this one. They hit him! Don't worry, I can take it from here."

"I really thought they had me. When I delivered the special prosecutor's report, there wasn't just Des, who couldn't wait to give me up, there were cops, firemen, and four other news crews."

"Confession," he sang.

> The worst sort of people use this incomprehensible
> legal loophole to subvert the law. Crimes of which
> the police have proof positive go unpunished. Over-
> turning Miranda will be among the most important
> achievements of this administration. A giant step in
> restoring the power of self-government to the people
> of the United States in the suppression of crime.
>
> RANDOLPH GUNDERSON,
> attorney general of the United States

> The attorney general is right. If it weren't for techni-
> calities and police incompetence, we'd all be in the
> slammer. Including him and me.
>
> ANTHONY CASSELLA,
> Suspect

Gerry demanded, and got, immediate duplication of my taped confession. He wanted it before Muggles woke up and realized his triumph would leave him sucking lemons in Saskatoon. Of course they could have prosecuted. Their failure to Mirandize me, the elements of coercion and physical abuse, did not disqualify their other evidence. But the

point of the exercise had been to minimize embarrassment, not protect
the integrity of the judicial system. That aim was best served by
dropping the matter.

My arrest was briefly noted in the press. When charges were
dropped, it was not, to the best of my knowledge, reported anywhere.
Including WFUX.

Randolph Gunderson continued as attorney general. No more tar-
nished by the new revelations than by the old.

Des tried to welsh on the bet.

My partner, Joey, has a long, long-standing relationship with his
bookie, Angie "The Cat" Canterello. Angie, me, and two of Angie's
larger goons visited Des at home. I told Des that I had sold my action
to "The Cat." Who explained, in turn, that the vig was only 10 percent
a week. Actually pretty reasonable by Canterello standards, what with
bank interest on personal loans up to 22 percent.

I told Des I was sorry. Then I left.

I waited out front. The Canterello group joined me in less than ten
minutes. Angie had requested that Des make out his check directly to
me. "If there's a problem, like it's a bum check, you call me, you hear,
kid?"

"What do I owe you?" I asked.

"Joey and me, we go back practically forever—'s on the house. Four
bills'll cover it." Angie was one of nature's gentlemen.

I gave him cash. The check cleared.

Capitaine Renaud, upon further consideration, contacted the New
York City police. They contacted me. I gave them a lightly censored
version of the story, claiming that I had merely sneaked a peak at the
Rolodex while I was at Finkelstein-Magliocci in my Tony Crispy, ace
photographer, disguise. There was clear and compelling evidence of
fraud, based on Bergman's death. They went after Dominic and Morty
with warrants and all that official stuff. They found what I had found—
the other fourteen apartments—which killed the side action that was
going to make me rich.

Jerry Wirtman was ecstatic. Death was such unequivocal proof of
nonresidence. He paid quickly and cheerfully, even apologizing for
doubting me. He evicted the illegal subtenants in a record thirty days.
He offered me more tenant cases. I was not delighted. But I took it.

The big news in my partner's life was that he finally found someone to keep him company. A dog. He had also, while I was in Paris, found Snake Silverman's bail skip, a certain James Monroe "Rusthead" Robinson, armed robber and manslaughterist. Snake Silverman gave his standard speech about the "Magner Carter," reached into his desk drawer, took a stack of hundred-dollar bills out from under the sawed-off pump-action Remington shotgun, and paid Joey 10 percent of the $100,000 bail. In cash.

Part Two

SPRING – SUMMER •1984•

14.

Red Herring

I was sitting in my office, reading a threatening letter.

It was convoluted, opaque, and had been addressed to Glenda. It came from Jerry Wirtman. It was called a red herring, the first open move in the desperate game called Conversion, in which rental apartments become co-ops and condos.

Not that I wasn't forewarned.

It crept up Columbus Avenue from the Seventies. A few years ago, people were afraid to walk there after dark. Now the evening streets are impassable, clogged with pedestrians wearing New Jersey license plates, wandering from bar to bar, boutique to café to bootery, hoping sophistication will strike.

I knew they were getting close when the apparently nameless Cubano-Chinese joint down the block closed and reopened as a Mexican restaurant named Jalapeño Baby. *Comidas China* sounds baroque, but in the ethno-food code of New York it is bargain chow, found only in neighborhoods where people still earn money the old-fashioned way— physical labor, welfare, and a soupçon of street crime. For reasons unknown, the cuisine created by desperate poverty in rural Mexico— rice with yesterday's beans refried and served on unleavened corn muffins—fetches Amex Gold Card prices in Manhattan. Margaritas come in three sizes, all described with synonyms of "large," each with a brief paragraph outlining the florid machismo of those brokerage trainees who dare to drink them. The price of the least large is at least $5.95. Only people who accrue capital by donning ties, fast-tracking, networking, and managing each other's mutual funds spend that way on a drink that is 95 percent recycled water.

Those same people go into heat over the concept of property. Owning cues their estrogen cycles.

There had been more specific signals.

Wirtman made no effort to replace the tenants in 12C. It wasn't the only apartment in the building left empty. He was warehousing.

Conversion requires 15 percent of the tenants to agree to a non-eviction plan and 5 percent or more to an eviction plan. The tenants have an automatic first option on their own apartments. To get that vote of approval, the landlord offers an "insider" price, usually 50 percent to 75 percent of the market value. The tenants, should they sell immediately after they buy, participate in the windfall. The average price of a Manhattan condo is $100,000 per room. The landlord, therefore, makes an extra profit of $25,000 to $50,000 per room on the apartments he has warehoused.

I was not looking forward to tenant meetings, dealing with real estate lawyers, or filing applications with bankers. And just the idea of a mortgage made my feet feel like they were set in concrete.

When the phone rang, I was delighted to toss the red herring into the bottom drawer, face down.

It was my congressman, John Straightman, calling. I wondered what wild, wonderful, wacky new form of trouble he had gotten himself into. I should have expected the call. It had been at least a year since he had been caught with a no-no up his nose or his penis up a no-no.

His penthouse windows, high and wide, faced east, Con Ed smokestacks straight ahead, bridges to the left, bridges to the right, the oily gray river beneath. The interior was Art Deco, soft gray over all, highlights in back-beat pink and tropic-vice blue.

He offered a drink. I turned it down.

"And none of that other stuff," he said with a wink. "We're all clean these days." He made us cappuccino from his brand-new cappuccino machine. He'd bought it for a mere million lire while he'd been in Italy on a NATO junket. Then he asked me what I thought of him.

The first time I'd worked for John Straightman was when a coke dealer who supplied John offered to give Straightman to the D.A. as part of a plea bargain. I got the congressman out of that completely clean. The second time, he had been caught with two thirteen-year-old girls sucking his lolly. I was able to establish that both teenyboppers' moms had been peddling their kiddies for over two years. That took the sting out of things. The D.A. then accepted a plea bargain from five felony counts down to one class A mis. And when John-boy said to the judge, "I'm sick, I'm sick; remand me to a shrink," the judge agreed.

I said, "Ahh," lifted my coffee to my face as a stall, burned my tongue, coughed, and got steamed milk up my nose.

"You know more about the worst of me than anyone else," he announced, answering the question himself. Which was much better manners. "You know my dark side. It is problematic. Excessive. Self-indulgent. You know that. And I admit it; I do. I admit it. That, by the way, is the first and, my doctor says, the most important step in my therapy."

It sounded like one of Wayne's jokes. How many psychiatrists does it take to change a light bulb? Only one. But the bulb has to want to change. I said, "That's good, John."

"I draw a clear and distinct line between my private life and my public life. You can say what you damn well please about my private life, but when it comes to my public duty, my record is impeccable. I am a representative of the people. What I do in Congress, I do for them. . . ." He gestured vaguely out the window, to the little people so far below, somewhere out there in the boroughs where such live. "The world recognizes the difference. Look at JFK and Bobby. Look to old Ben Franklin, Tony. Just look to Ben Franklin."

My congressman crossed the room to an Art Deco desk. It unfolded like a magician's trick to become a bar, complete with sterling gewgaws—stirrers, shakers, whatnots—and a rich selection of beverages. It was a genuine Prohibition piece, from the good old days when hypocrisy was stylish and handcrafted.

"Drink?" he asked again.

"No, thanks," I said.

"Are you political?" he asked.

"Not especially," I said.

"Let me tell you a story. I'm on the Labor Committee. Back in 1969, we passed the Federal Coal Mine Health and Safety Act. It worked. Every year since '69, the number of deaths in the mines has gone down. Right up through 1980. Then Reagan came in. He appointed administrators whose purpose was to get government off the backs of business. They couldn't change the law, so they decided just to enforce it less. For the first time in eleven years, more men died in the mines than the year before. It went up from 133 to 153.

"That's twenty men. Good men, bad men, who knows, but twenty more were dead. For no other reason than they went to work in the morning to pay the rent and put dinner on the table.

"For some people, the politics of 1984 are life and death. Life and death.

"The Reagan administration wants to go backwards. That's no secret. That's what he promised in his campaign. But what does that mean? Does it mean a white picket fence and an apple tree in every yard? Back to a Jimmy Stewart movie? Or to some darker past? Say, back to when we really had rich and poor. When women knew their place. And so did the darkies.

"Not a joke. Every Justice Department since Ike has gone to court to help end the division of this country into two races. Not these guys. This Justice Department has appeared in court only to oppose integration."

"Slow down, John," I said. "I don't even vote in your district."

"Patience, Tony, patience. You have to see this in context. You have to get the big picture. . . . You been paying your taxes?"

"As little as possible," I said.

"You rich?" A rhetorical question. "Too bad. If you were rich, the '82 tax cuts would have been real nice. I'm talking about the $100,000 range. They saved $3,300. But somebody on payroll, making ten grand, all they saved was $52.

"We're talking about government by the rich, for the rich, and screw the working stiff. The strange part is, the working stiffs love him for it."

"Stop," I said. "Tell me, John, what you want from me."

He went back to the bar. "Here is the problem. We, the Democrats, liberals, whatever, we've been knocked on our ass. It's not issues and it's not rational. He hurts people, they get up and say, 'Thank you.' The bankruptcy rate has tripled under Reagan. That's mostly small businesses. Result? According to our polls, the small businessman gives Reagan an approval rating around sixty-eight percent, plus or minus two points. Out in the Midwest we have high, chronic unemployment. Courtesy of Reaganomics. Then he cuts back on unemployment benefits. Result? Unemployed white males, *union members,* give Reagan a fifty-four percent approval rating.

"Somehow, in a way we can't yet get hold of, Ronald Reagan has captured the high ground. Of image. Of the media. He's even stolen Roosevelt and Kennedy, *our* heroes. Plus they have a lot more money than we do. So how do we stop him?

"The Teflon President. Well, I want to scratch the Teflon," he said. "If we can find the right thing to hook the media's attention. Just that one thing, that when the hook is in, set, it doesn't go away. With Nixon it was Watergate. With Ford it was his pardon of Nixon. With Carter it was the hostages in Iran. I'm looking for something that will stick to this administration and refuse to go away."

"What were you thinking of? Specifically?" I asked.

"Randolph Gunderson," he said.

"Oh, no," I said.

"Oh, yes," John said. "He could be the weak link. If he's indicted. Not this secret grand jury crap. A criminal trial, right out in public. Every day new witnesses. New testimony. New denials. Every day a new story. To remind America that the FBI covered up, that Reagan knew about the allegations but still stood by Gunderson. It's got to cling to the President. It's got to say something about his judgment. Once they start to question one item, they question the rest."

Maybe it was worth considering. It might be fun to try to bring down a President. And it was certain to be a long assignment, steady money. On the other hand, Vernon Muggles would be delighted to have a second chance to read me my rights. The days when prisons provided such amenities as squash courts are long gone. Then there's prison food. And prison sex. I said, "Forget it."

"Why not?"

I wanted to decline gracefully. Straightman had been a client before and could well be again. So I pointed out that the special prosecutor had already failed with a million bucks to spend, and the FBI, and a team of attorneys, and subpoena power.

"You underrate yourself," Straightman said. "You really do. There were a lot of people looking for the complete version of the special prosecutor's report. CBS, NBC, the Gambino family. You're the one who found it."

"John, do you realize how much money this'll cost? For something that might not work."

"You should think about that. That you underrate yourself," he said. "The reason I called you is that I think you're the best. But look at yourself. Working low rent on low-rent cases. Living low rent. All it takes in this world is that one big score. You win the big one, it all changes. You're Joe Namath, Reggie Jackson. You're Woodward and Bernstein. Just that one big win and you become a winner. Forever."

A great rush filled me. It was eager and cool all at once, and I had the sensation of seeing many things simultaneously. On the one hand, Gunderson had all the weight of the federal government behind him— FBI, IRS, DEA, Justice, Treasury, even the President. On the other hand, he had at least one of the five families willing to kill to protect him. I had seen the light. It was the light of sanity.

Quickly, while I was still in that peaceful golden glow, I said, "No."

15.

The Other Mario Cuomo

Q: Why do Italian dogs have flat noses?
A: From chasing parked cars.

A joke (Courtesy of the Wayne Collection)

The first thing Glenda said to me when I got home was, "Did you read the red herring?"

"Not yet," I said.

"Hey-y-y, Tony-y-y," Wayne said from in front of the TV set. "You wanna come watch this with me?"

"Want to," Glenda corrected reflexively, not for Wayne, who couldn't hear her anyway, but for herself, so that she wouldn't end up speaking like a ten-year-old, and for me, so that I might, someday, come around to setting a better example.

"It's *Rocky,* the big fight scene! Pow! Pow! Uh! Uh! . . . Bam!"

"We can't afford to ignore it. It would be financially irresponsible to ignore the issue," Glenda said, meaning the actual money matters, not the issue.

"We don't want to be financially irresponsible," I said, mimicking just enough to be irritating. I felt that what she said was a barb, pricking at my earning powers. A neat little nip in my macho. But it probably wasn't. Or it was, but not intentionally.

"There's a tenants' meeting next Tuesday. And you probably should go," she said. "For once."

"I'll do my best," I lied outright. "If it's possible."

"This should really be *our* decision. It concerns both of us." Which was getting close to the real issue, the issuance of binding fiscal ties, the

139

creation of a relationship of property. Still not marriage but close enough to the heart of marriage that it would alter the pronouns of separation from "thee" and "me" to the possessive forms, as in have "your" attorney call "my" attorney.

"If I can't make the meeting," I said, "—and I really will try—if I can't and you can, you really can just tell me what happened. Really."

"I don't think that's fair. Or responsible."

"Look," I said, "I have a light day tomorrow. I'll read it tomorrow."

"Why not tonight?"

"Gimme a break."

"Will you really read it tomorrow?"

"Yeah," I said.

When it came time to turn the lights out, we found separate rooms in the double bed.

The next day was, in fact, an easy day. Organizing another report to evict another illegal tenant for Jerry Wirtman. If my father happened to stick his head out of the grave and snatched a look at whose side I was on, he would have grabbed a shovel and dug himself back in. I itemized the bill.

My partner was out in Brooklyn. Criminals continued to betray Snake Silverman's trust. It wasn't cause for alarm when Joey didn't call in or return to the office, but he'd been a little erratic lately. Feeling poorly. He didn't answer his phone, so I decided to drop by his apartment on my way home.

He lives on Forty-fifth, between Ninth and Tenth avenues, a neighborhood that vacillates between calling itself Hell's Kitchen and Clinton. It no longer deserves the melodrama of the former—a *nom de guerre* that dates back to the Civil War—but neither is it entitled to the posh sound of the latter. Yet. But the deals have been cut for a super cleanup. The players are in position. The moment the thirty-eight lawsuits opposing the Forty-second Street depopulation-reconstruction project are settled, the economic energy will sweep west and wide, fast as fire, through Hell's Kitchen, making it Clinton at last.

When he got the apartment, New York had rent control, Brooklyn had the Dodgers, and Joey had a wife and two kids. His wife and kids went to Florida in '59, the Dodgers had gone to Los Angeles in 1957, and

Joey hasn't gone to a ball game since. The apartment is very empty, but still rent controlled.

From Times Square I walked west across Forty-second Street, the block with the highest arrest rate in the city and thirteen movie theaters. A cheery glow announced triple-action sex action—*Sleazy Rider, Nympho Sizzle!* and *Bodacious Ta-Tas*—flanked by a double Rambo on one side and triple-action action on the other: *Fists of Fury, Fists of Fire,* and *Sister Fist and the Seven Shaolin Monks.* The Superfly Boutique offered suits at drastic reductions. Sneakers were on special. Porn was specially discounted. There was the special glass flicker of base pipes in the windows of narrow-slot head shops. After all these years, my eyes still see, and my neurons remember. Drop in a rock, hit it with the bright blue flame, watch your brain go up like neon gas in high-volt rain. Preachers with porto-mikes ranted at each end, bookending the glandular street with Jesus.

All will vanish, we have been promised. And vanish with it will be all tieless dark-skinned persons, especially those who make eye contact that is not contact as they mutter with still-lipped ventriloquism, "cheba, crack, blow."

All will be replaced by high-rising monuments of corporate rectitude, stolid, solemn Philip Johnson shapes. More monochrome, better-mannered, they will bring Midtown West a better breed of people, those who breed apart and keep their minds over money.

I let myself in the front door, walked up to Joey's top-floor apartment, and knocked. There was a shuffling sound. I knocked again.

"Come on in," he called. "I'm too tired to move."

He had fallen asleep with a bottle of beer in his hand, two empties on the table beside the gun, and he looked tired. The phone was disconnected. Mario, lying on the floor beside him, just looked lazy and maybe a little stoned.

"The Snake has called upon us, once again, to defend the Magner Carter and the Seventh Amendment."

"That's good. Who this time?"

He pointed at the file on the floor. Elijah Sampson, eight post-juvenile arrests, including murder, three convictions, not including murder, and still entitled to the presumption of innocence. Like Randolph Gunderson. There was an address.

"The address is no good," Joey said.

"You look like hell," I told him.

"He's got a girlfriend," he said. When fugitives flee, they head for the familiar. "Look at his rap sheet, victim on the second assault charge. Angela Moreno."

I looked. "He cut her?"

"Cut each other. It's a sure sign of an enduring relationship."

"You been out there?" I asked.

"Yeah," he said. "He's been around."

"Living in?"

"Nah. And he's not the only one she sees. Goddamn six-floor walk-up, and she's on top." He sighed. "But I miked the place, so's I can sit in the basement and just listen for him."

"When you going back?"

"I don't know; maybe tomorrow. . . . Jesus, I'm tired. Will you get me a beer?"

Beer is one of several words Mario knows. His tail thumped against the floor. Literate doggie. I got two beers from the '53 Frigidaire. I poured a couple of drops in Mario's bowl. It's easy to get the wrong idea about Mario, but he's only a social drinker, not an alcoholic. I rubbed the loose flesh beneath his chin. "You're a smart guy, aren't you, Mario, even if you are a police academy dropout." Which is something we say to be polite. The truth of the matter is that he was expelled, unable to control himself around bitches.

"Time is money," I said.

"Well, I ain't moving."

"He's gonna turn up there at night, you know that," I said.

"Am I outa beer?"

"I'll go out there," I said. I hadn't read the red herring, and if I went home, all I'd find was an argument.

"Whatsmatta? You don't wanna go home?"

"You know what I did yesterday, Joseph? I turned down a job. From Straightman. He wants us to go after Randolph Gunderson."

"You turned it down?" Joey said.

"Yeah."

"Good boy. Showing some sense for a change."

I went down to the bodega and bought him another six-pack. When I

142

got back, he was asleep, pale and snoring, in his chair. I put the beer in the refrigerator and took Mario Cuomo out to Brooklyn to keep me company.

Angela Moreno, Elijah's dear one, lived on Halsey near Atlantic Avenue. Parking was not a problem, since the radio is already gone and the hood is secured with a lock and chain so no one can steal the battery. I took the last remaining hubcap with me to serve as a water bowl.

The basement—storage, boiler room, and what had once been a laundry room—was supposed to be locked. I found it open. I let Mario go first. It was deserted, no one blowing crack, turning tricks, or stealing the plumbing. I bolted the steel door from the inside, put water in the hubcap from a still functioning sink, and set up the receiver.

Angela Moreno's life came in loud and clear. It consisted mostly of rap music. I put my ears on autofilter.

Around 2 A.M. she turned on the TV. Without turning off the radio. Run-D.M.C. meets *Gilligan's Island.* There were also toilet flushes, a baby crying, and something boiled over on the stove. Crazy Eddie announced that his prices were insane, and I thought I heard a knocking.

"Hello, baby. Lemme unlock the locks," Angela said. I waited for her to call baby by name.

"I miss your sugar lips, sweet thing," a male voice said. The music was up as loud as ever, and I was straining to hear. Mario started to growl, which made it more difficult.

"Shut up," I told him.

He didn't. He barked. I put my hands over the earphones to block him out.

"Wha'd you bring me? Wha'd you bring me?" she said.

"I got something else for you, even better," he said.

"Come on, call him by name," I said.

"Arf! Arrrf!" Mario barked.

"I'm a straight white dude," the radio announced. The White Rapper with his all-time classic, "White Boy Do It 2." " '. . . *come from Minnesota/I wear Bass Weejuns/I'm a Republican voter/I ain't lyin', I ain't struttin'/I'm selling futures at E. F. Hutton . . .'* "

"You rushin' me," she sighed, not complainin'.

"I needs what I need," he said. "I ain't waitin'."

"You so big," she said, and "You so strong."

"Baby, I got to put it where it belong. You know what I can do, it's my claim to fame."

"That's what they all say," I said. "But what's your name?"

Then Mario barked. He ran to the door. He put his paws on it, then howled some more. Upstairs they were panting, he was ready to score.

" 'Lemme do it once, lemme do it twice,' " the White Rapper requested, " 'one for nasty, one for nice/I learned to do it watching Miami Vice/sugar, sugar babe, lemme do it to you/white boys, white boys do it two.' "

"Don't fuss with my clothes, you tearin' my dress. Lemme slip it off, before you make a mess."

"Let me see yo legs, let me see that bottom," he said. "Uh, yeah," then, "Yes, yes, yes."

There were *Ooo*s and *Ahh*s in my earphones. Mario had a problem, and was starting to moan.

"Baby, ohh baby," he said, "spread 'em wider."

She said, "Tha's wide's they go. Come on, Elijah."

With great relief, I tore off the headset. He was here. I had him. All I had to do was climb six flights and pick him up.

Mario grabbed my pants near the ankle. He was tugging at them. It wasn't time for play. Then I saw what was making him excited. Smoke coming in, under the door. I could smell the fire. I could even feel the heat, beating its way in from the hall, through the steel door.

I told Mario to shut up. I told myself to stay calm.

I went over to the door, and it got hotter as I got closer. I didn't really want to know what was on the other side. As I reached for the knob, I could feel the heat beating off it. To test it, I spit on the door. It spit back, hotter than a skillet on a stove. I could smell the fire also. Paint, wood, kerosene, with a *frisson of cucarachas*.

I looked around and found some rags. I soaked them in the sink and refilled Mario's hubcap. I splashed the hubcapful of water on the doorknob to cool it down some. It sizzled and steamed. Then, wrapping the doorknob in wet rags, I tried to open it. The knob turned, but the door stuck. The metal had expanded in the heat. I tugged, feeling the heat through the soaked cloth. One knuckle brushed the door by accident, I felt it burn. I went back to the sink, even while figuring that it was a stupid waste of life-and-death time to tend to one knuckle, and ran cold water over it. As long as I was there, I clogged the drain with one of the rags and left the taps open, full. It wasn't much, but it might retard the fire.

This time I wrapped the wet rags directly around my hands. Using both arms and bracing my legs, I was able to start the door moving. The heat came off it in waves. I was close to pain and full of fears.

It opened.

I heard and felt the fire before I saw it. Hungry for oxygen, it sucked air out from my basement room, roaring and screaming all the while. It was ravenous. Red and wild, it filled the hall, it carpeted and surrounded my way out. Someone had been lavish with kerosene. Generous and uninhibited, like a chopper leaving napalm.

I slammed the door shut as fast as I could. Gasping, sweating, and scared. My shoulder, where I'd shoved the door, felt sunburn raw.

The basement was a genuine basement, not half submerged, with windows at street level. I made one more circuit, looking for another door or window or any other conceivable way out. It was getting thick and smoky. Mario dogged my footsteps.

There was no way out. My eyes stung, I was starting to cough, and I had a very vivid vision of becoming a roast.

There was one way out. Through the steel door and down the hall where the fire had been started.

Actually, fire deaths are most often caused by inhalation of smoke and noxious fumes, death usually occurring before the corpse burns. Alive or dead, burning usually takes the same course. It begins with blistering, then charring, at which point the victim is almost certainly in shock. If rescue occurs, and it sometimes does, and the victim does not die from shock, survival is sometimes possible. Rehabilitation and reconstruction are extraordinarily painful processes. If the victim dies, the corpse is almost invariably found in what is known, in the jargon of the trade, as the *pugilistic* attitude: fists clenched, arms raised, and knees bent. This is not because the victim's last moments were spent in trying to punch it out with a fiery and anthropomorphic vision of death, but because the muscles contract from the heat. This contraction takes place even in those bodies already deceased.

145

When a dog dies in a fire, I don't know what position the corpse assumes, though obviously a similar set of contractions occurs.

I could open that door, take a deep breath, because there was probably nothing breathable in the passage, and make a run. If I didn't stumble, if nothing fell on me from above and knocked me out, if I didn't get caught on something or blinded, I might make it out alive. Fricasseed to one degree or another, but with enough left to heal from. I could stay and wait, hoping the fire department battled its way into the basement in time. If they didn't save it for last. Which they probably would. Fires are fought from the top down.

"Here, Mario," I said, calling him over to the sink. Water was pouring steadily over the edge. He saw it and backed away. "You stupid little fuck, I ain't screwing around," I snapped at him. He slunk down low and humble, his Mahatma Gandhi passive-resistance bit. I was not impressed. I grabbed him by the scruff of the neck and dragged him under the slow-falling shower. "Stay!" I said in my most commanding tones. He did. He will do that. Unless he smells a bitch in heat.

I went and got the hubcap/doggie dish and started slopping the water over the both of us. The wetter the better. Then I collected various rags from around the room. I discarded the ones that had paint and what might be oil on them. That didn't leave me enough. I had a T-shirt under my shirt, and I stripped that off. With a knife from my kit, I cut it up. I needed a face mask and Mario needed shoes. I didn't believe that I was making shoes for a dog, but I was. If he survived at all, his coat would protect most of him, but the pads of his paws, tough as they were, would almost certainly suffer. Then he would lie around the house while he convalesced, expecting to be catered to, Joey or me having to carry the son of a bitch out every time he wanted to piss or shit. Not a chance.

Having cut his cute little doggie slippers, I didn't have any rope to tie them on. I sliced up telephone line. The building was going to be out of service anyway.

The smoke kept getting thicker. I was staying low as I could, but it was already stinging my eyes so badly that I was blinking more than looking, and I was holding a rag to my face to breathe through. The dumb mutt was shaking the water off himself.

I tied my face mask on like Jesse James, splashed myself one last time for luck, and tried to think of what else I should do before I made my exit in a puff of smoke. There was something. My hands. I wrapped them in rags. I stuck a couple more into my collar and made sure my jacket was zipped up all the way.

I wasn't entirely sure that Mario would follow me, so I put the leash on him. If he had too much sense to leap into a blaze just because I did, I was going to drag him. Carrying him would be a bit much, but no way was I going to go home and explain to Joey how I'd left the hound behind.

I hadn't closed the swollen door all the way the last time I had opened it. This time it was going to be easier. I tried to breathe deep and ended up coughing and choking.

I yanked the door open. Sure enough, there was a fire out there. Smoke rushed in. Heat hit us in a wave. I made a whimpering sound, then shut it off because I was losing precious air that way, and started to make my dash. After a brief hesitation, probably due to incredulity, Mario followed, then leaped ahead. As long as he was going to do it, he was going to spend as little time doing it as possible. He was brighter than I had given him credit for.

I didn't see much.

My head was tucked down. Smoke and heat hurt my eyes so that I only dared to look in blinks, intermittent strobes of terror.

The footing was terrible. Fallen pieces of whatever littered the floor, and the floor itself was buckling.

I stumbled. My feet went out from under me. I caught myself on my hands and kept going, crouching, slipping, tripping, running, trying to hold what air I had and taking very shallow breaths through the cloth.

It was noisy. Terribly, terribly loud. Around me and in me, as fear-propelled blood pounded in my head. It was not a long time. It was also forever. I was getting dizzy from lack of air, I guess, because I banged into a wall.

But I was doing fine, by the standards of the situation, until I got to the stairs. They were partly burned away and partly still burning. Certain that the center would give way, I went up staying close to the wall. My jacket was starting to go, and I kept brushing my hands over my hair, thinking it was on fire.

Then a step, or steps, did give. I was down, trying to yank my foot out of some kind of mess. Then I think I was crawling, my hands clenched in fists inside the rags to protect them. I didn't want to die.

There was barking. Barking? I had hoped there was sex after death, but dogs? Hands, good, big, strong hands, grabbed at me. They pulled at me. I was up the final bumps and out of the fire. The noise stopped. The big hands still held me. I kept my eyes closed, and someone slapped an oxygen mask over my face. I breathed.

I like oxygen. Some folks like their whiskey, some swear by food, good coke can be a Rolls-Royce cruising, Demerol is peace, the opiates are sweet dreams, acid heads chat with gods, but me, give me that stuff we breathe. Talk about sniffing, my oh my oh my . . .

I sat up and opened my eyes. A very large person with black skin, in one of those costumes—big gloves, big boots, long heavy coat, and a funny hat—was looming over me. Mario was there too. Singed all over, and sooty to boot, but very nonchalant about it. I started coughing and spitting.

"Your buddy here," the fireman said, ruffling the beast's neck, "he saved your ass."

"Yeah?" I said. Mario looked positively smug, considering that he'd lost his whiskers.

"I heard him barking at the basement stairs. Then I seen you stumbling at the bottom and dragged you up," he said with excessive admiration. Mario hadn't made any effort to drag me out himself. But he had made the call. That was something, I guess.

"Yeah," I said. "He's a credit to his race."

"What's your name?" he asked.

"Is this something official?" I asked. The last thing in the world I wanted to do was start filling out forms.

"Nothing like that," he said, so I told him. He pulled off his gloves and took a tiny spiral pad and a little stub of a pencil out of his pocket and wrote it down. He asked me how many s's and how many l's.

"What's that for?"

"Well, you just come out of there, so maybe you know what it takes to go in. For some, it seems it's easier than for others, to keep on going in. For me, it's not so easy. So what I do is, every time I get somebody out, I put their name on my list. See, your name is going on the list now, and that is going to help me keep on going in."

"Yeah," was all I could say.

"Then I give them my card, if I have the opportunity to do so," which he proceeded to do, his big hands fumbling inside his coat to get one. "And I ask them if anything good should happen to them, if they would be so kind as to drop me a postcard and let me know."

"Like what kind of thing?"

"Oh, most anything. They have a baby, or graduate from school, get a better job or"—he smiled—"any job. Or do something good, you know."

Then I started to shake. I couldn't help it. My body was just doing it. And to cry. Tears came down my cheeks and mucus from my nose. I put my hands over my face.

"You'll be all right," he said, patting me on my shoulder. "I got to go back in there now."

16.

The Strange Case of Philip Buono

I was a good boy during my convalescence.

I read the red herring. Which was unfortunate. Before I read it, my distaste was a vague, nonrational thing based on a cluster of half-baked prejudices. Once I had the facts, my instincts were confirmed and I could be righteous. The down payment would exceed what we had on hand. The mortgage payments, plus estimated monthly maintenance, would exceed our rent by 50 percent.

Glenda pointed out that the red herring was just a first offering. That if the tenants opposed it, then Wirtman would have to come back with a lower offer. Get involved! Organize!

That was true. It was also true that the monthly maintenance was only Wirtman's estimate. It was not guaranteed, not stabilized, and would become the responsibility of the new owners. Us. I had one of my apocalyptic visions. A house divided. The Spenders, who want to beautify, improve, maintain. The Savers, who want to save. Then splinter groups. Cold stares in the elevator. Snide remarks in the laundry room. Long harangues from neighbors I've never seen before. Leafleting. Board meetings. Open meetings. Closed meetings. Cabals.

Glenda pointed out that it meant owning something! Rent was money down the drain. We could have something to show for our money! If we couldn't make the mortgage and maintenance, we could turn it around and take the windfall profit, which would be tremendous.

But that only works if you don't live in what you're selling. If you live there, you have to replace it. Where is the profit if the only available replacements cost as much as or more than what you sold?

"We don't always have to live in Manhattan," she said. "We could actually live better, in a lot of ways, somewhere else."

Daddy's gonna be a commuter. Daddy's gonna have a lawn to mangle. And a driveway. I wish she hadn't said it. We all have our perverse tendencies, our dirty little urges. But the courteous thing to do is to keep them to ourselves. I really, really wish she hadn't said it.

I also went to the library.

To read up on Randolph Gunderson. I understood that the downside risk was excessive. But I had just died, almost, on a job where the downside was apparently minimal. Besides, I like reading. I owed it to everyone to make an informed decision.

My sources were the *New York Times,* the *Wall Street Journal,* the pop magazines like *Time* and *Newsweek.* Once Gunderson had his problems, *Fortune* and *Rolling Stone* did the best work.

There must have been an official biography prepared by the White House press people. In the gushy period before the rumors, the special prosecutor, and the Scorcese killing, all the early pieces had come from a single source. Randolph Gunderson was portrayed as the proverbial more or less poor boy, born in the urban equivalent of a log cabin, who made it big.

His grandfather emigrated from Sweden and bought some farmland about twenty miles north of New York City. One imagines that if he had simply hung on to it, the family would have become rich when the area turned into suburban Westchester. But by the time young Randolph was dirtying his diapers, the family was propertyless and living in a small rented house in Yonkers, about a half block from the wrong side of the New York Central tracks.

His father was a clerk. His mother was a housewife. At one point she also worked part time at a dry-cleaning establishment.

The bio went on to say that Randolph had worked his way through school. He attended the City College of New York, which was free in those days.

He applied to law school, but by the time he was admitted it was

1942. Instead he enrolled in OCS, stout lad, received a commission as a lieutenant, and rose to captain by the time he was demobilized. If he had served in combat, or in any overseas capacity, the bios were the sort that would have trumpeted the information. Nothing was said, so I presumed there was nothing worth saying.

Still, he was entitled to the benefits of the GI Bill. With that and a job, he was able to afford Fordham Law. He was not in that elite upper sliver of the class that gets invited to join the powerhouse Park Avenue firms or the great Wall Street squabblers of capital. He became a regular, small-time Bronx attorney, doing what they do—your mortgage, Fred's divorce, Mrs. Mulligan's probate, my accident claim—mostly pulling generic forms from the file and filling in the blanks with a specific name and number.

In the mid-fifties he entered that period of his professional life which became the most highly touted when the advice and consent of the Senate was requested for his confirmation. He became a civil rights lawyer, in the forefront of the battle for housing integration, helping deserving persons of color find homes beyond the black and white lines of the ghetto.

Later, when the policies of the Justice Department seemed to be specifically antiminority, Gunderson and his defenders pointed backward to that period of time, citing it as evidence of his commitment to equal opportunity and proof that the new code words—"anti-quota," "non-compulsion," "reserving remedies only for direct victims of segregation"—were expressions of idealism rather than reaction.

True or false, his altruism did him no lasting harm. It was immediately afterward that his real estate career took form and took off. He started in the Bronx, moved out into the suburbs, down into Manhattan. He got onto what was going up and stepped off before things went down. The PR people had him painted as an astute prognosticator. He was a serious contributor to local political campaigns by then. Real estate money is the leading source of campaign financing in New York City.

Real estate naturally led to construction, development, and management.

By the time he left it all—temporarily and in good hands—to become attorney general, most of his holdings were organized into two companies, Empire Properties and the Sun Group, both closely held. Dun and

Bradstreet, in the year before Gunderson left for government service, reported that Empire, which operated primarily in the Northeast and included Empire State Estates, Empire Administration, Endview Construction, 28th Street Corporation, and several others, had net earnings of $11,000,000 on property valued at $103,000,000. The Sun Group, named for his wife, Susan "Sunny" Gunderson, controlled Sunshine Properties and Sunrise Developments in Florida, Sunview Developments and Sunview Estates in Arizona, Highrise-Sunrise in Texas, and Sunbelt Industrial Parks scattered around a whole bunch of those type states. According to D&B, it had reaped a return of $9,750,000 on $164,800,000.

There was a partner and apparently some limited partners, and there were investors, and then each of those companies that the two main groups had controlling interest in was organized in a different way, some of them even publicly traded. No one but the IRS would know how much Gunderson ended up with officially, and even his own accountants might not know how much he actually netted.

In any case, his self-declared net worth was $18,000,000, making him the second-richest man in the cabinet. That sounded low to me. Maybe it referred to cash on hand and what he had in his NOW account.

Wealth brought a new political awarness. He abandoned his hereditary affiliation with the party of the urban prole and became a true-believing Republican. Excepting local politics, of course, where business is business and ideology is a press release that comes only once a year.

When another semi–log cabin legend who had started on the left then seen the right came along, Gunderson got on the bandwagon. Early. Back when Reagan was losing the nomination to Nixon. And then losing to Ford. Still with him in '79 against a world of nonbelievers. Not many figured that Reagan would ever play the leading man. There were all those chimp jokes. And most of Ron's favorite anecdotes contained errors in fact gross enough to make Gerald Ford sound like a scholar. Back when James Reston of the *New York Times* could say things like: "The astonishing thing is that this amusing but frivolous Reagan fantasy is taken seriously by the media and particularly by the President. It makes a lot of news, but it doesn't make much sense."

Gunderson dug deep into his own pockets, then into his corporate pockets, which were deeper still. When he reached the limit the law allows, he organized some PAC pockets. It added up to $280,000 for the primaries and $960,000 for the campaign against Carter. There were whispers of larger, unrecorded sums, but there always are among campaign gossips, just as movie fans whisper about which star is in the closet.

Ron liked Randy.

He wanted him around. Randy became one of the few Easterners on the transition team, then part of a presidential advisory group. When, a year into the first term, the physicians at Walter Reed diagnosed Attorney General Lamont Reever's cancer, the President selected Gunderson as his replacement.

An FBI background check is standard practice. The Bureau can then alert the President that his man has been arrested in public rest rooms for solicitation, has been a member of the Klan or the Communist party, or has ties to organized crime. The candidate is then sent to the Senate for confirmation. The appropriate committee queries the nominee's competence, qualifications, and views. They want to know if he has been unethical, illegal, weird, or perverse, so the senators call in the FBI, to learn what the FBI has already, presumably, told the President:

SENATE CONFIRMATION HEARINGS

SPECIAL AGENT VERNON W. MUGGLES: The Federal Bureau of Investigation, in a background check involving 4,220 man-hours, has discovered nothing detrimental about Randolph Gunderson and knows of nothing that would serve to bar him from properly undertaking the position and duties of Attorney General of the United States.

Even Gunderson's family came up clean. He was a one-wifer. They were churchgoers. His son had a college degree, a job, no arrests, and since he had a wife and child, was presumed heterosexual. His daughter had never disrobed in front of a camera. The family spaniel mated only under the supervision of an accredited AKC breeder.

Randy was a shoo-in.

That lasted two weeks. Then Phil Buono saw Randolph Gunderson on television. Buono was a banker turned federal witness. Testifying about his money-laundering schemes, drug money, casino money, and political money had become his full-time occupation. He told federal prosecutors that he had met their new boss.

Time

THE STRANGE CASE OF PHILIP BUONO

Philip Buono thinks of himself as an artist.

Federal prosecutors admit that the Ocala, Florida, banker has a "remarkably fertile and agile mind. His schemes have a marked originality." They concede that they would never have been able to indict Philip, let alone convict him, if he had not come forward himself. "But," Bill Parkins, the tough, craggy-faced, senior member of the Strike Force team, points out, "that mind was a mind wasted. Think what he could have done if he had used his powers for good."

Defense attorneys in cases arising from Buono's testimony have a different reaction. Cleveland-based Milt Glaser, representing alleged mobster Steve Susman, uses the phrase "delusional paranoiac." Don Joe Baron, representing millionaire Rafael Ramos Santana de Castro (being tried in absentia while the Justice Department seeks his extradition from Colombia), suggests "premature senility." Aston Johnson Galt (attorney for Don Liccavolo) has retained psychoanalyst Lars Wittgenstein as an expert witness. "I have not had the opportunity to meet with the subject personally. But I have observed him extremely closely, with great acuteness. I have interviewed intensively with associates and family members. What I might suggest is personality weakened by excess, subsequently distorted by religious mania, falling into a semiotic schizophrenic state. Certainly delusional."

It was one of Phil's money-laundering schemes that first linked Randolph Gunderson, however loosely, to organized crime figures.

"A panderer of unsupported, unsupportable, and untrue gossip of the foulest sort," the Attorney General calls him. "It is unfortunate that anyone would take such a flake seriously."

The round-faced, merry-eyed subject of all this secondhand analysis laughs with delight at the descriptions. With one exception. "Loreen. It hurts that she says the things she says."

155

Loreen Lenore Bowdoin, the ex–Mrs. Buono, is prone to tears when she describes Philip. "Boys will be boys," she says, "and my mama, she always says there's certain things a woman has to put up with. But Philip took everything to excess. That first time we were separated he had that heart-shaped pool built. The things that went on there. Teenage girls! Wearing nothing but oil-base mosquito repellent and little-bitty bits of gold lamé!" Ms. Bowdoin is currently in her third lawsuit against her former husband, this time seeking ownership of the Buono family bank when it is released from federal receivership.

"I'm actually happier now," Philip says. "I've found my personal savior in Jesus Christ. Not that I am ashamed of what I did in the past. What I did, I did better than anyone else. A man must have pride in his work. 'By the fruit you shall know the tree.' One of the reasons that I came forward was that I couldn't share what I was doing."

Philip came to Jesus at 3:48 on a Sunday afternoon. He credits Tom Landry, coach of the Dallas Cowboys, who appeared in a TV commercial explaining that his personal relationship with God was more important than football.

Buono was handling skim from a Las Vegas casino, La Puta d'Oro, thirty-two stories high, four and one-quarter acres of slots alone, whose books were always in the red, but it never went out of business. The major hidden owners were (allegedly) the Cleveland mob and the Gonzoni crime family in New York. They were represented, respectively, by Steve Susman and Don Liccavolo.

Randolph Gunderson's Sun Group had a controlling interest in Sunview Estates, which in turn was in a limited partnership in a development called Sunrise Park. It was this last that Buono used for the casino money. Gunderson could make a good case that he had nothing to do with the Sunrise Park arrangements and no way of knowing that any of the money was tainted.

Except that one day he came to dinner. With Buono, Susman, and Liccavolo. At the Golden Phoenix Golf & Country Club. Over after-dinner drinks, Steve or Don put an attaché case on the table. He opened it. It was full of cash. About $700,000, Phil remembered.

Steve then said to Gunderson, "The boys from New York told us you had the Midas touch. 'If it's Gunderson, it's gold,' that's what they say. I'm glad it's in your hands."

Gunderson, Susman, and Liccavolo all denied that the dinner ever took place.

Phil was not the only federal witness who recognized Gunderson. Sal Minelli tied him to the New Jersey Teamsters, aka the Prozzini crime group. Benito Caputo said he'd seen Gunderson with Santino Scorcese. And of course the FBI had tapes of Santino Scorcese talking about, if not to, Gunderson.

The known Scorcese-Gunderson connection was with Empire Properties, the other side of Randolph's holdings.

Santino owned several junkyards. One of his junkyards, near Piscataway, New Jersey, occupied a portion of what was to become the site of a new industrial park developed by the New Jersey Revival Corporation, in which 28th Street Corporation held a controlling interest.

Shortly before New Jersey Revival Corporation entered the arena, Scorcese began acquiring his neighbors' properties. Two things made his purchases easier. One was a series of accidents and fires. The other was an interest-free loan of $300,000 from Empire Properties. Financial records showed the initials "R.G." beside the approval of the disbursement—that is, it had been approved by Gunderson himself.

By the time Gunderson was appointed attorney general, Santino "The Wrecker" Scorcese was in prison on unrelated matters. Fenderman, the special prosecutor, called him to testify. Frank Felacco, Fat Freddy Ventana, and an unnamed driver met with Santino's son, Arthur. During a conversation in which they allegedly asked the younger Scorcese to influence his father not to testify, they shot Arthur.

Felacco and Ventana were members of the Lupino family. I had a passing acquaintance with one member of the Lupino family, Michael Pollazzio, aka Mikey Fix. Pollazzio was on favor-trading terms with Vincent Cassella, my father's older brother.

The Cleveland group represented by Susman was alleged to have ties to the Teamsters Central States Pension Fund, controlled by Jackie Presser, Successor to Mike Fitzgerald, successor to James Hoffa. Presser, like Gunderson, had been a member of the presidential transition team.

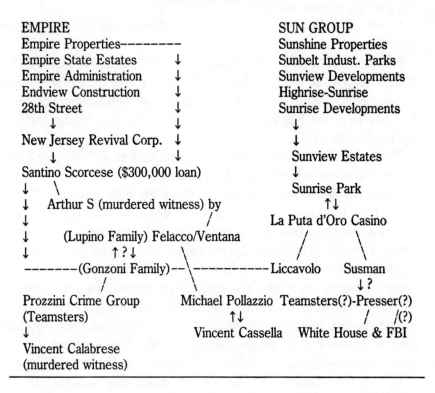

The aftermath of the Scorcese killing was also in the papers.

The police started looking for Frank Felacco right away. He had gone to the Bronx in his own car. Carlos Ortiz had written down the license plate. And for Freddy, because when someone says Felacco and a fat guy, it's Freddy. They found Freddy and put him in a cell on Rikers Island. His cellmate was a federal informant. Another one. The informant was referred to by police spokespersons as Mr. T.

Freddy knew that Mr. T was a federal informant because Mr. T told him so. Apparently he said that his crime normally carried a seven to fifteen year sentence, but by becoming an informant, he'd gotten it reduced to one year. Freddy thought that was a great deal. Freddy said to Mr. T, "This is what I done," in detail, and "What kinda deal you think I could make?" Mr. T immediately told all of that to the D.A. The D.A. shared it with the press.

It seemed like an open-and-shut murder case. And the ultimate pop of the Gunderson balloon.

Frank Felacco was not arrested. He turned himself in. Accompanied by attorneys, of course.

Frank claimed that his automobile had been stolen the night before the event, and at the time of the event, he and several cronies, including Fat Freddy, were at home playing pinochle.

It was not a terribly credible alibi. Except that the tape logs of incoming phone calls to the Long Beach Police Department confirmed that Felacco had reported the theft of his car before the murder.

Mr. Ventana, after meeting with Mr. Felacco's attorneys, recanted his conversation, explaining that only someone very stupid would tell such a story to someone that he knew was a federal informant—true enough—unless, of course, he did it as a joke. "You know, kinda like a put-on, it was. I tol' him all that stuff about Gunderson to make the [expletive deleted] Feds go nuts, you know, this way and that way, about, you know, Gunderson."

The government's key witness, Carlos Ortiz, was an ace on the getaway car and license plate, but not much on a people ID. The testimonies of Inez Rodriguez and Estelle Kalmanowitz were worth even less.

There was only one real mystery about the whole thing. That Randolph Gunderson—and the administration with which he was associated—had emerged unscathed.

17.

Reaganomics

Straightman called me again. As I expected.

I agreed to meet with him to discuss the matter. Once again, he wanted to background everything with partisan politics.

A lot of what he said was familiar from the preceding days in the library. Gunderson had sent a general memo that the Justice Department would back up any department that refused to open records under a Freedom of Information Act request. Gunderson's Justice Department had consistently appeared in court against desegregation, most notoriously in appearing for Bob Jones University, a segregated Baptist college that wanted a tax exemption, but also in school cases in Seattle, Nashville, and East Baton Rouge.

> We are not going to compel children who do not want
> . . . an integrated education to have one.
>
> RANDOLPH GUNDERSON

> The mere finding of some statistical pattern that indi-
> cates that once upon a time, in bygone days, there
> had been injustice is not what we are here to rem-
> edy. But make no mistake, this government is com-
> mitted to Civil Rights in any and every case in which
> there is intent to discriminate and we can find reme-

dies for the direct victims of discrimination.

RANDOLPH GUNDERSON,
explaining Justice Department opposition to court-
ordered affirmative action in the New Orleans Police
Department (*Williams* v. *City of New Orleans* [#82-
3435 5th Cir.])

"Your issues are not what the issues are for me," I said.

But the congressman wanted to recite his list of social justice issues. Reagan had cut or was trying to cut Social Security, the Legal Services Corporation, milk for schoolchildren, food stamps, Meals on Wheels, low-income housing, education for the handicapped, the minimum wage, environment controls, parks.

The one thing he said that struck a chord, in spite of myself, was that union busting was high on their list. According to Straightman, the PATCO strike was a setup. The air traffic controllers had been led on by the administration so that Reagan would have a union to bust. My father, very much an idealist, had been a union organizer. He had been driven out of his own union by the mob in collusion with the government.

"My decision," I said, "is going to be based on money."

"You're willing to do it," he said eagerly.

"My price," I said, "is one hundred thousand dollars."

"Anthony." He sighed. "I want you to get what you deserve. But I know what you can be had for. It's more like two-fifty a day."

"It's gone up," I snapped. "Blame it on Reaganomics."

"A hundred thousand for four months or less is quite a lot."

"What's four months got to do with it?"

"It all comes down to one day," he said. "One day. November 6. They walk into the booth, close the curtain, and pull the lever. We need the indictment early enough for it to grow into an issue. The minimum would be thirty days. But my target day is Labor Day. September third, 1984."

"The special prosecutor, he had all the time he wanted and a million bucks. Now you're quibbling about a hundred grand. Forget it," I said, and stood up. "So here's what I'm gonna do. I'm gonna walk on out of here and mail you a bill for two days of jerking me around."

"Wait a minute."

"What?"

"Maybe we can come to some kind of terms."

"Are you really up for this, John? Forgetting about my fee, start thinking about the expenses. The expenses are going to be huge."

"We're committed," he said. "What it takes is what it takes."

"Who's we?"

"I can't tell you that. For their sake and mine."

"And I don't work for people I don't know who they are."

"How can I explain this? . . . If you think of the money as coming out of the same place as the Democratic National Committee's television budget, that would give you a good idea of where the money's coming from. From contributors."

"Then my hundred thousand is cheap."

"You're right," he said. "When you're right, you're right. If you expose Gunderson, and if that swings the election, I'll meet your price."

"Swing the election? Forget it," I said. "You're gonna run Mondale—"

"That's not settled yet."

"—which is like the Midwest reruns of Jimmy Carter."

"It could well be someone else," he said.

"Who? Jesse Jackson? Gary Hart? You're going to beat Reagan with a Negro? Or a yuppie? You hire me to nail Randolph Gunderson. Period. What that does to the election, I don't know. It's way beyond my control."

"Let's be reasonable," he said. "Let me try to formulate this so it's good for both of us. We're talking about four months. Sixteen weeks. That's twelve thousand five a month. That's fifty thousand dollars."

We fenced back and forth about it. "A minimum of fifty guaranteed," I said. "Let's say I nail him in one day. Or even in one month. Then I'm motivated not to tell you, to sit on it so I make more money."

He finally agreed to that. Then I said, "The bonus is one hundred thousand."

"Wait a minute . . ."

"You want me to gamble for it. Then it's double."

He sighed.

"It's take-it-or-leave-it time," I said.

He frowned. Then he nodded. "I think we have an agreement in principle." He even manufactured a smile—a rueful one—and held out his hand to shake.

I didn't take it. "In principle is one thing. Let's nail the details. I want the bonus in escrow. With instruction that it be turned over to me when I present information that makes Gunderson indictable. And," I said, "I want it in a Swiss bank."

"Why in a Swiss bank?"

"Because," I said, telling the truth, "it has style."

"To be turned over when he is indicted," Straightman said. "So long as it's before Labor Day."

"Come on. October tenth. After I do my job, some D.A. is going to have to prepare a case. Then take it before a grand jury. Then they have to return the indictment. Besides, nobody gets serious about the election until the first debates."

"Yes they do," he said.

"The politicians, maybe, but not the voters."

"Try to make the Labor Day date."

"I will," I said. A wonderful thought came to me. Possibly the greatest I've ever had. "The only thing left is that you should know that we're marking up expenses thirty-five percent these days."

"Don't kid a kidder," he said, "and don't press your luck. I've had bills from you. You don't mark up expenses."

"Didn't, John, didn't. Our accountants really got on our ass about that. It costs us twelve to fifteen percent to process expenses, bookkeeping, overhead, audits, interest paid and interest lost. So you take that, and also nobody should be handling money for free."

"You're pushing it, Tony."

"For you, John, thirty percent."

"Twenty. Period. Nonnegotiable. And you'll make out like a bandit on that."

So I would. "All right," I said grudgingly. "But no bullshit, no nit-picking. I'm straight with expenses, and a lot of this stuff, there won't be no receipts."

We shook hands.

Gerry Yaskowitz drew up the agreement within the week. He suggested two addenda. One was that I be employed by an attorney for

Straightman so that I would be protected, however slightly, by extension of the attorney-client privilege. Straightman passed a dollar across the table and named Yaskowitz his legal representative in this matter. That was fine all around. The second was that in the event of my death, the bonus be paid to the beneficiary of my choice. The congressman countered with a suggestion that he would pay the additional premiums required to increase my life insurance by that amount. That was sensible. Wayne would remain the beneficiary, with Glenda as trustee.

The Swiss account was opened with a $100,000 deposit. That's a lot of money. In New York you can buy one room of your average condo with it.

18.

Game Plan

```
Owen,                         Owen Levy
Thanks for one life.          Engine Co. 323
I'm doing what I can.         210 Madison St.
Just took on a new job.       Bklyn, NY 10378
Best money ever, lots of
challenge.
              Tony Cassella
```

I was so thrilled with my newfound prosperity that I even attended a tenants' meeting with Glenda.

She was pleased. "I can't believe you're actually coming. I thought you'd avoid it forever." We kissed and rubbed our hips against each other.

165

"Got a good, good piece of business in," I told her. "Lot of money, and four months' work, guaranteed."

"What is it?"

"Complicated. It's really convoluted. I'll tell you later." We walked into the meeting with our arms around each other's waists.

We discovered that Wirtman had refinanced the building just before he filed the conversion plan. In effect, he was selling the building twice. Once to the bank, then to us. Leaving us to pay off the bank, at 18 percent rather than the 9 percent the old mortgage had been. In addition, we were buying a building that was 90 percent mortgaged instead of 30 percent. It was going to take an extra ten years to pay it off. It was going to cost us, Glenda and I personally, an additional $136 a month just to service the debt. All of which confirmed my worst suspicions.

"I don't understand your attitude about this," she said. Her lust to own was undiminished. "Why do you have an attitude about this?"

"If we have a choice between renting and owning, we should be aware that there is a price for owning. Is it worth—"

"You love to talk about costs and numbers, as if you're ever so rational," she said. "That's one of your macho things, pretending everything you do is rational. But you should see the look on your face whenever the subject comes up."

"Whatever the look on my face, it doesn't change the numbers."

"Is it the money? That you think we can't afford it?"

"Well, actually . . ."

"If that's what it is, maybe it's time to look at some other things objectively."

"Actually, at the moment, we can afford it. I wish it were six months from now. I would have a better idea if it was going to stay that way."

"Anthony, you're exceptionally bright. We all know that." In good-girl school, they teach them to always say something positive before they offer criticism. The result is that whenever she says something nice, I cringe at what's to follow. "Why do you choose to live this way? Not knowing from month to month, from day to day, how much money you're going to have?"

"I just got the highest-paying job I've ever had," I said.

"I just think you should . . . you should take a look at yourself. You did well in law school. You've said it yourself, you're a better lawyer than most of the lawyers you work for. You know you could go back. Or finish at night. You've made yourself less than you're capable of."

"Thank you, Miss Social Woiker."

"There's no need for sarcasm."

"In point of fact, I'm making good fucking money now."

"Oh, Tony . . ."

"O-o-h-h, To-o-n-n-y . . . What?"

"This case is a lot of money. But what about after it?"

"If buying this fucking apartment is what our life is about, go ahead and buy it. Put it in your name. Don't worry, I'll pay my share. But I don't want every day of my fucking life to be going in circles around are we gonna buy this apartment."

"Don't talk to me that way. It's not necessary."

It was necessary. Because I kept the truth locked in my trunk of silence. I was animal inarticulate, shaking my rattle and raising my hackles.

Apologies were made, angers packed away, so we wouldn't be wearing them when we got back upstairs to say good night to Wayne.

Joey had taken time off for an extensive physical. I went to see him at home. He looked worn out. From the exam, he said, but it was all good news. All thumbs up, everything working, from brain pan to prostate. In turn, I gave him my good news: We were about to be rich and famous!

"Watch this," he told me. "Watch good." He held his fist high in the air. "Mario," he said. The mutt came bounding into the room. He spied the fist, came to a screeching halt, and went into his intelligent-hound-as-beggar act: hindquarters down, one forepaw up, ears up, tail twitching, what was left of his whiskers quivering, and his eyes locked on Joey's fist.

Joey opened his hand, turned it over, and showed Mario there was nothing there.

Mario slumped to the floor, his head sinking between his forepaws, doggie eyes gazing up into eternal sadness.

"That's you," Joey said to me.

"Not only is the money good," I told him, "but Straightman is right.

We're small-time because we make ourselves small-time. We're nowhere, going nowhere."

"Some things there isn't enough money in the world for."

"Which is OK for you," I snapped, angry and out of patience, "fine for
you. You got your pension, you got your rent-controlled apartment,
your kids are grown. You got nothing to go forward for. But it's not fine
for me. My life isn't fuckin' over yet."

"These kinda bastards," he said, shaking his head, old and sad. "What
these kinda bastards, they'll do to you . . ."

"So if you don't want to go along, then fuck you. I'll take this one on
my own hump."

"You stupid, stubborn little bastard," he said. "You're like your
goddamn old man." He stuck his finger out at me. "Your old man, you're
lucky you had him. Sonuvabitch stood by me when . . . when I had
problems. So what? So that puts me in this with you."

"What are you talking about? What kinda problems?"

"You stupid sonuvabitch," he said without anger. "Get me a beer and
we'll sit down and look at what we got here and how we're gonna do this."

I got two bottles, pouring out a sip for Mario.

"You know," Joey said, "I was gonna take a vacation. Go down to
Florida."

"Yeah, well, maybe you can go down to Ocala, see this Buono guy,"
I said. "Then we can bill the trip to Straightman and make it a deduc-
tion."

"Yeah. Maybe."

"Hey, lighten up, Joey. We're gettin' lucky here. Paris for me.
Disney World for you. It's time for us to get on the gravy train."

"Let's see how this lays out," he said.

I had my notes and my chart. I also had two ideas pretty set in my
mind. One was that if there was a blueprint for the investigation, it was
the special prosecutor's report. The complete, unexpurgated version.

"You didn't make a copy?"

"What for?" I said. "That was the end of things, not the beginning.
And by the time it arrived, it was all I could do to make delivery before
my flight. I need the thing. OK, maybe Fenderman did a bad job, maybe
there's a cover-up, but if there's a blueprint for what we're looking for,
the report's it."

"So get it again."

"I figure it was Bronstein sent it to me. I figure. I don't know for sure. But I do know for sure that if it was Bronstein, she sure as shit did not want to be seen giving it go me," I said, thinking out loud, and realizing: "I got to get to Des. Get it back from him."

"Des don't exactly like you these days."

"True, but I think I know how to hook Desmond Kennel."

"Kennel ain't a stand-up guy." He said it without emphasis, but it was a final judgment, like a feminist slapping on the "sexist" label.

"Yeah, well"—I shrugged—"he's got something I need."

The other thing I was convinced of was that Santino Scorcese was the key.

Joey suggested that we use Miles Vandercour for the paper chase. Miles was the tag end of an old Dutch New York family and a lawyer. Miles wasn't all-around bright. He ended up the fall guy for someone else's scam and was disbarred. In his disgrace he found his glory. Friends, throwing him a bone, or looking for cut-rate legal services, started hiring him to do research. He discovered that his brilliance was patience. He became a paper chaser. He had come to know his way through the bowels of every record room in the city better than he knew the face in his mirror.

Joey agreed to go down to Ocala to see if we could get more on Phil Buono than was in the papers. I felt we were together on the thing. It was taking shape. We were getting a handle on it. It felt good. It felt right.

"We got a good enough business as it is," Joey said suddenly. "Silverman, he don't want to use nobody but us now. He thinks you're the greatest."

"He thinks I'm the greatest?"

"The cops grabbed Elijah, running out of the fire. You know that."

"Yeah . . ."

"Well, it was our case, I figured we should get the money. So I went out t' Brooklyn. Well, the Snake, he's real impressed with you now. He figures a guy who would torch a joint just to bring in a skip, such a guy is real committed."

"Wait a minute . . ."

"Yeah." Joey grinned. "Real committed. That the republic can only survive 'cause of committed people like you." He stopped grinning. "So we could go ahead and drop this Gunderson thing and still get ahead. Still make a living."

"No," I said. "You're still not gettin' it. We do take Silverman's stuff, and we farm it out some. Even if we only take—what?—twenty, thirty percent of the fee, we still make out, as long as the Straightman thing is also coming in. Then anything from the Snake, it's gravy. We are going to be a business."

"No, *you* don't get it." He was adamant. "These kinda people, they'll strip you down to nothing. Nothing." We were back to that. "If I could stop you, I'd stop you," he said.

"Good night," I told him, tired of it, ready to leave.

"If you knew the things I know . . ." he said portentously.

"What? What is it you know?"

"All right," he said, sounding very resigned. "Yeah. All right. I don't know what it is. People got things they got to do. Got to do 'em. That's the way it is, isn't it? You more than most. Even me. I got things I got to do too."

I called Alicia Bronstein. She didn't return my calls.

I called Des. He didn't return my calls. I went to the studio. WFUX security had orders not to let me in. So I waylaid him outside his apartment building the next morning.

"Get away!" he cried when he saw me.

"Hey, cool it, Des," I said.

His head swiveled, as he looked for an escape route. I kept trying to talk to him: He scuttled blindly backward. Someone had failed to scoop his pooch's poop, as required by the New York City civil code, and Des's foot went flying out from under him. I jumped forward and grabbed him as he fell. "It's about your TV show," I said, my arms around him.

"I'm going to call a police officer," he said, with his feet flailing for purchase and his torso twisting to break my grasp, "and have you arrested for assault."

I clamped down. "I got someone who wants to back your TV show," I said in his ear.

"Is this serious?" He stopped struggling.

No. It wasn't. But I had someone who would pretend it was: mystery

Israeli millionaire Yakov Felstein, who owned a small videotape facility in midtown Manhattan and peddled arms from the back room. Not Saturday Night Specials. The real thing—assault rifles, armored vehicles, tanks, land-based missiles. He had catalogs with glossy full-color action photos. "Mail order," he said, "like Sears Roebuck." He had once hired me to investigate a buyer. Yakov's instincts were sound. The buyer was an FBI agent trying to set up a sting. But I didn't think Yakov's motive for helping was gratitude. He doesn't like the press, and the idea of putting one over on a member of the Fourth Estate pleased him.

He had a most impressive conference room. He convinced Des that he would back the show as an indie and put it in syndication. All that was needed was a socko pilot. Something to make the world sit up and take notice. Yakov quoted figures and projections, and Des dazzled himself with avaricious dreams. So much so that when the idea of making Gunderson the subject of show number one came up, Des didn't flinch. If Yakov liked it, Des loved it.

His only problem was time. For a piece of the action—and a featured role—I was willing, I said, to do the actual investigating.

Everyone left the meeting delighted with the arrangements.

Des even promised me real press credentials. They would be indistinguishable from what I could have had made up for twenty-five dollars. Except that an entire television station was now prepared to vouch for them. Which was a nice bonus. Being an actual reporter gave me some latitude and protection. Not a lot, but some.

"Right, let's start with the special prosecutor's report," I said to Des, getting to what I really wanted. "Get me a copy, will you?"

"I don't have it," Des said.

"What do you mean?"

"The Feds took it."

"Come on Des, you must've made a copy."

"I gave it to them."

"Notes?"

"They had a warrant, Tony. It asked for the notes."

"And you gave them your notes? Where the hell did you grow up? Didn't your parents teach you anything? Didn't your father tell you you're supposed to lie to the cops?"

19.

Santino Scorcese

I tried out my new press credentials. I learned that Felacco and Ventana were still on the streets. The D.A. didn't want to put them on trial for the murder of Arthur Scorcese until he was certain he could convict. But why hadn't Santino "The Wrecker" Scorcese done something about them?

There is a great deal of talk about people in organized crime taking care of each other. Certain criminal groups have acquired the designation "family." This is mostly from Mario Puzo and very misleading. They are strictly financial organizations. They have as much heart and family feeling as your average brokerage house. Felacco and Ventana were on the outside, making money for people. Santino was inside. Not making money. That's why Felacco and Ventana were still walking around.

I tried to approach Scorcese through his attorney. No, Santino Scorcese did not want to talk to a reporter. Even when I said there was a book in it and a movie deal.

I drove up to Dannemora. A long and tedious trip. I was prepared to offer Santino cash for information. But not through his lawyer, who was the attorney for several other mobsters in the same "family." One of the correction officers would carry a message in for me. For cash. COs have the same attitude toward corruption as any other public official. Most of them will participate in it if it's profitable, and they can convince themselves it's harmless, and they think no one's looking.

172

Unfortunately, someone remembered my face. From the old days when I had been a CO myself, and had investigated and convicted several fellow officers. Even though I had been city and these fellows worked for the state and it had been a long time ago, they still felt antagonism. So that plan fell through.

Joey had returned from Ocala. He'd taken Mario Cuomo with him and was bitching about how bad the fleas were in Florida. I told him how lovely the Adirondacks had been.

"This guy Buono," Joey said, "he's like the papers said, a genius and a flake. Except that he's bent, he's a fine example of our Italian heritage. Smarts. Even with the guy testifying against himself, the Feds don't know if they can convict him."

"You talk to him?"

"Federal Witness Program," he said. Which meant no.

When the phone rang, I answered it. It was my uncle Vincent. He'd left several messages, which I hadn't returned.

"You got to come see me," my uncle Vincent demanded.

"What's this about?" I asked him.

"Come see me," Vincent commanded.

"Is this something we can't talk about on the phone?"

"Are you gonna come see me or not? It's for your benefit."

"What is?" I asked.

"Either you come or you don't," Vincent said.

"Yeah, well, I could try to come out next week," I said.

"That might be too late," Vincent said.

"For what?" I asked my uncle.

"You coming or not?"

"I told you," I said to Vincent, "I'll try to get out there next week."

"When?" he demanded.

"I don't know," I told him.

He hung up. It had been a typical conversation.

"Who was that?" Joey asked.

"Vincent."

"What'd he want?"

"What he always wants: to see me."

"You're so concerned with money, making money, maybe you should start thinking about seeing him."

"Fuck you," I said.

"What are you, too proud to do his business?" Joey said, laying the sarcasm down with a trowel. "He told you he got business for you. Legit, he says. Nothing illegal, he says. He's just a construction guy, he says. What are you, too proud?"

"You want to do his business?"

"No. But I ain't the one in a hurry to make money. I got a pension and my rent-controlled apartment and no kids to worry about no more. I got all I need. You're the one's got needs and urges—"

"What the fuck is it with you? What is this strange shit with you?"

"With me?" he yelled.

"Argh! Argh!" Mario barked.

"Call off your dog," I said.

He put a restraining hand on the mutt's neck. "I'm trying to figure out what it is made you take this job. I keep going around and around about it. You got to know that you're just asking for trouble. So all I come up with is it's the money. And if it's the money, there's other things we can do."

"Are we gonna have this fucking conversation every time I see you?" I said. "Scare you so much, whyn't you go your way, I'll go mine." Which is the kind of thing people say when they're fighting. Lovers, husbands and wives, and partners. Sometimes it's what you got to do. Most of the time it's the last thing in the world you want, and you know if you did there'd be an emptiness you'd never fill.

"Like for example," my partner said, "I met an old friend down there. Lee Fazio. He's a P.I. now. Jesus, he's living good. Got an El D' custom convertible, pool out backa the house. More work 'an he can handle. Maybe it's time to give up this New York thing, which costs like it breaks your back and hurts my bones in winter. Down there, we can make more and spend less to live better."

"Retire if you wanna retire," I said. "But do me a favor. Before you do, tell me what you found out about Buono."

"Not much to tell." He sighed. "Thing is, federal prosecutor, sent down to Ocala, you gotta know he's not exactly major-league material. Ocala, it's not even triple A. These are not guys that management is planning to bring up to the majors. Everything, everything they got, they leaked to the papers. Swear to God, it turns out that they brought in the reporters and showed them the entire grand jury minutes. I got the clippings, you can go over them. And some reporters' notes, though most everything got printed."

"Is it worth finding Buono?" I asked him, though digging out someone buried in the Witness Protection Program is tough.

"Well, it is and it isn't. On the one hand, I don't think he's much use. He seems like the kinda guy who never looked beyond his own thing. The only time he ever knew anything about Gunderson was that one dinner."

"Yeah. So why's he worth going after?"

"Loreen," he said. "The ex. She wants him served a subpoena. Federal Witness Protection Program or not. Can't sue him if she can't serve him."

"To hell with it," I said. "We gotta find a way to get to Scorcese."

"You don't fucking listen to nothing," Joey said. "Do you?"

20.

Panty Hose

Last thing in the world I want to do is drive up to Dannemora.

Thought the Fla. thing would hook him. What it is is restlessness? Or is it ambition? Or self—destruction. The Fla. thing a good thing. Much $ down there. Much divorce. Small—town type. Doing it to the neighbors. The closer to home the more the hate the bigger the legal fees. Also lots of real estate deals, double—X's. Lots of paranoia. Drugs does that. Tony around drugs? Think he's really clean now. Not AA clean but just past it. Is that possible?

Lee Fazio getting old. Not as fast as me. But getting old. More business than he needs. Without even looking for it. We—he—Tony—could hook up fast down there. Cost of living's lower. Lifestyle. But I sold it wrong. Didn't sell it at all is what I did. Maybe I can guide him back to it.

Less beer, more percs.

T says to do the Loreen Buono job if *I* want. He's getting off on multiple jobs. $ on top of $. He's probably right. But not that one. Too far away,

176

complicated. Better if I stay close. Though the
last thing in the world I want to do is drive all
the fucking way to Dannemora.

From the Notebooks of Joseph D'Angelo

I rode out to Brooklyn, standing like I used to, as a kid, looking out
the subway window, as we went over the Manhattan Bridge. Dusk sky
and building lights, it was again as wondrous a thing as urban man can
make. Vital dreams levitated as real as granite. Money, money, money,
on the tip of Mammon's ideal island. God got his shot on the Brooklyn
side. The Jehovah's Witnesses announced the *Watchtower* with a sign in
lights, ten feet high, sixty feet long.

Down to the courthouse on Schermerhorn Street, where, I thought,
I would find Alicia Bronstein.

They had her doing arraignments. Grunt work. Her, a judge, a Legal
Aid lawyer, and a never-ending supply of criminals. In Brooklyn they
get them arraigned at a rate of one every 3.2 minutes. When the judge
finally called it a day, I rose in anticipation of Bronstein coming to me or
me going to her.

She strode up the aisle and out the doors like I didn't exist. I followed
her. She turned right when she left the courthouse, along the back side
of downtown Brooklyn's shopping district. She went into A&S, the
department store where my parents bought me my first suit, for
grade-school graduation.

I came up beside her on the escalator.

"What do you want?" she asked me.

"Hey, how you doing?"

"Fine," she said.

"Still in arraignments," I said sympathetically. We got off at ladies'
lingerie. "You didn't get back to me," I said.

"That's true," she said, her head framed between mannequin legs.

"Let me take you out for a drink. Sit down and talk things over."

"What do you want?" she said as we passed the bras for full-figured
gals.

"Always direct, to the point," I said. "The report. I need it again."

177

She turned away from me and marched to the counter. "Panty hose," she said to the Puerto Rican clerk.

"What kind?" the girl said.

"What's on sale?" Alicia asked.

The salesgirl said there was a special on Lady Femmes at $2.39 a pair.

"Fine," Alicia said. "I'll take a half dozen."

The girl went to gather and bag the merchandise. "Can I get it from you?" I asked her.

"Maybe," she said. "Maybe."

"It's important," I said.

She shrugged.

"Look, I got a new thing going. A TV show. For real. With Des Kennel. On crime. Magazine format, feature-style news. It would be real easy to do a feature on a . . ." I almost said "lady," then "woman," then settled on "female prosecutor. Without hitting the female part. Just a D.A. story that happened to be a woman."

"I'll give it some thought," she said dryly.

The girl rang up the sale. Alicia signed for it. "We can do each other a lot of good," I said. "Lemme buy you a drink."

"No," she said.

Alicia took her panty hose. I went home to Mother.

The smells coming from my mother's kitchen were wonderful. A Sicilian poem, sharp as Romano, soft as Ricotta, erotic as real ripe tomatoes mated with sweet basil. Emphatic as garlic.

Which was unusual, because my mother can't cook.

"My friend is cooking," she said.

"I'm glad you got a friend who can cook, Ma," I said.

We walked into the kitchen. "This is Guido," she said. "Guido, meet my son, Tony." The man standing at the stove, wearing black slacks and a white T-shirt, turned around and smiled at me. He was older than my mother, about seventy. Fine-boned and slender but for a small round potbelly—from his own cooking, to judge by the smell—thin white hair over a Piedmontese face, deeply lined only around the weary eyes. His nose was thin but beakish, his teeth were either excellent or false, and there were liver spots on his hands.

He put down the wooden spoon long enough to shake hands. His were soft.

"It is a pleasure to meet you," he said. It was an educated, even elegant voice, soft. The faint traces of accent matched his face. "Your mother has told me a great deal about you. She is very proud of you."

"She didn't tell me anything about you," I said. Whenever I had asked her about men, or suggested that she find one, she had always dismissed it. As if it were something that just wouldn't happen. An attitude sadly grounded in reality. There aren't a lot of men around for widows of sixty. I was delighted to see that she might have one of the very few.

We started with a tortellini salad, news of the neighborhood, a little endive, and some politics. Mother had written off Gary Hart. He'd changed his name. Guido had used distinctly fresh basil in the dressing. Unfortunately, Walter Mondale had all the sex appeal of *polenta*. Ronald Reagan, she said, was very good on television. "Mr. Nice Guy," she said. "If you want to not believe him, you have to work very hard. How are regular people supposed to know what is true and what is not? TV is not good for politics."

> The "big lie" tactic can work because TV and the
> media do not concentrate on the content but simply
> supply the medium for delivery.
>
> KEITH BLUME, *The Presidential Election Show*

"I don't know," Guido said. "This time it works for someone you do not like. Other times it worked for things you did like. For Kennedy."

"It makes things shallow," my mother said.

"People are shallow," Guido said. "They were shallow when we had radio. They were shallow when we had only newspapers. Only a very few people want to think things through, to distinguish between their prejudices and the facts. That is difficult and . . . and painful."

"Yes, Guido," she said gently, "it is."

He laughed. "Not everyone is as strong-minded and independent-minded as your mother," he said to me.

"That's true," I said.

"An important position, a person they've got a responsibility," my mother said, clearing the salad plates. "Like a lawyer is supposed to work for his client, a newsperson you would think they should work for the truth." While Guido brought in his veal and eggplant Milanese, zucchini marsala on the side: "This is a very complicated world, this modern world. To know what is true or not true, you need a staff to look things up. A computer. I don't think the television people are doing their job."

Guido looked at me. I grinned at him. "They certainly could do better," he said. "Doing a good job is a rare but excellent thing. Even a humble job, it's unusual to see it done well. . . . You, I understand, are very good at what you do."

I made my modesty noise. I bit into the veal.

"Of course he's good at what he does. But he could have been an attorney. Yale Law School."

"This," I said about the veal, "is superb."

"Anna," Guido said, "a man's profession is not to be sneered at. It is never to be belittled if it is honest labor and well done."

"Thank you," I said.

"Personally, I envy your choice of professions. What you do must be quite exciting," Guido said.

"Usually it's boring. I talk to a lot of people who don't know anything. I sit and watch buildings, waiting for someone to come out and go somewhere. Then they decide to stay home and watch *Dallas*. It's not like TV."

"Nothing is like TV," my mother said.

"But you are a doer," Guido said to me. "The actor in your drama, not the audience."

"Sometimes," I said.

"Also," he said, "the things you did in your previous career, with the prison department. This shows you are a person of integrity. And courage."

"Hey, Ma," I said, "what'd you tell this guy? You must of laid it on pretty thick."

"Your mother," Guido said, "probably does not tell you how proud she is —"

"Guido," my mother admonished. "Too much praise is not good for a child."

"How did you do this zucchini?" I asked. "It's wonderful."

He launched into his recipe. Between the brief steaming and quick sautéing in olive oil with garlic, my mother started in again on the pernicious effects of television. "That's why people love this President so much. He tells them the world is like a TV show. We have complications now, but he's going to get the writers to put in a happy ending at the end of the episode."

Dessert was hot zabaglione. Rich. Luscious. I sat back with a full round stomach and savored it spoonful by spoonful. Something nice was going on between Guido and my mom, even if I didn't know exactly what it was.

After dessert, Guido brought out espresso and Strega. Mom wanted to show everybody old pictures. Again. Why not? She asked me to get them for her. They were on the top shelf in the hall closet.

When I opened the door, I saw Guido's jacket hanging inside. I pulled up a chair and stood on it to get the photo box. Looking down, I saw something underneath the jacket. White. I climbed down and pushed the jacket aside. There was a rabat underneath it. The stiff white collar and black dickie of a priest.

My mother was seeing a priest.

My father would have died. Except that he was dead already. What would he have said? He would have said what Garibaldi said. Just for starters.

> A priest is an impostor, and I am devoted to the sacred worship of truth.
>
> GIUSEPPE GARIBALDI

> I have been certified an anti-Communist by the CIA. Therefore, I am permitted to point out that in its historical context, the Marxist hatred of religion has a certain justification. When the church reaches a concordat with the state, it becomes the willing co-conspirator with, if not the instigator of, every oppression, every murder, every violation of human rights that the state could commit. I saw them do it

in Poland. You can see them do it in South America, Vietnam and the Philippines today.

The church that opposes abortion today is the church that opposed anesthesia during labor because it said that the Bible said that women should give birth in pain.

The history of progress, of science, of medicine, of civil, human, and political rights, is the history of overcoming the opposition of organized religion.

STANISLAW ULBRECHT, 1972

Toleration made the world anti-Christian.

John Cotton (1584–1652),
Puritan clergyman,
"The Patriarch of New England"

There are plenty of people who really believe, no matter what. A lot who just hedge their bets. A lot go through the motions for public appearances.

Me, I can't do it. All the contradictions, hypocrisy, obvious untruths, all the pain, stupidity, and oppression that occur in the name of Christ—or whatever else they got—stand up in my mind like rocks in the middle of the ocean. They're there. My mind keeps hitting against them. If that shocks my friends and neighbors, if people want to use that against me, and they do, if they think I'll recant on my deathbed, or claim that I must have prayed in the foxholes, so be it.

Truth is truth. Bullshit is bullshit. That's the ultimate human right, and maybe mankind's highest destiny—to discern truth from bullshit.

MICHAEL CASSELLA

"Mom. Ma, can I talk to you a second," I said. "Privately."

"Certainly," she said.

We went into the bedroom. I closed the door behind us. "What the hell is going on?" I said.

"What do you mean?"

182

"He's a priest," I said.

"I know that," she said.

"What the hell are you doing with a priest? Huh? Is your brain going soft?"

"What are you so upset about?"

"Look, you gotta understand. If you're with a guy, I'm happy for you. I've been hoping you would find someone. . . ."

"I have a right to live my life."

"Yeah. Yeah. You have every right. But, Ma, a priest. Next thing, are you gonna start having plaster saint statues in the window? It's one thing to sleep with the guy, but, Ma, is something theological going on here?"

21.

Confession

T made a funny story about his trip up to Dannemora. Figured he could get to Scorcese through a
corrections officer. Not a bad idea. Spoke to a CO
named Earl. Good country name.

Met Earl at a roadhouse.

They're country here. Think they're hard. The
fucks still remember. T made a funny story out of
it. He was sober, they were drunk. He made it to
the car. The only thing that got punched out was
his headlights. Ha—ha. He ran over someone's foot.
Ha—ha.

T doesn't learn. He can't see the connection
between this and that. COs selling dope to in-
mates, cops on the pad, *federales* doing break—ins,
don't see themselves as criminals, don't accept
the people who bust them as just the other half of
the game.

Couldn't face drive. T said fly Plattsburg, rent
car.

Spend money. No question expenses this one. He's
right. Unfortunately. We spend, we profit.

Is T taking good care Mario while I'm away?

Confession

```
    CASH
    Misc. $5.68
    Gas $10.45
    Bkfst $2.10
    CO P.K. $100 carry message
    Lunch $5.30
```
Evening beverages $5.00 (while I wait for CO P.K. to return Hennessey's Utopia Bar & Grill with an answer, maybe, to offer to Scorcese: $20K for Gunderson info).
If this is utopia, let me die in Newark.

Call son. Who is son? See grandson. Should mean more. That's the truth. Take a vacation.

———————————————

From the notebooks of Joseph D'Angelo

Guido came to see me at the office. He was in uniform. Black and white. He was very polite. "Excuse me for interrupting, I'm sure you're very busy."

"Yup," I said. I was waiting for Joey to get back from Dannemora.

"I think there is perhaps some confusion. About the relationship between your mother and me."

"Look, *Father,*" I said, "the only confusion is your whole life."

"You feel strongly about this, don't you," he said mildly, more amused than anything else.

"Let me make this as clear as possible. You got a religion that beats people up for fucking. I happen to be the kind of person thinks fucking is good. A positive good. On the other hand, a mass murderer can come in, get his feet oiled, make a brief apology, and you'll tell the sonofabitch he's gonna go to heaven when he dies.

"People got to be responsible for what they do."

> I never met a mobster didn't have plaster saints on his windowsill.
>
> MICHAEL CASSELLA

185

"It is refreshing to talk to you," he said. "As it is to your mother."

"What is between the two of you, and when will it stop?"

"You see, not only do the two of you have very strong opinions; they are thought out and informed. You feel passionately about them. That is unusual. Difficult to find. So the relationship with your mother is very important to me. And I would like to clear up what stands between you and me."

"The history of Western civilization," I said. Rather pretentiously.

He laughed. I found it disarming.

"Look, Father—"

"Guido."

"Yeah, well. Maybe I'm flying off the handle a little bit. Maybe I'm not giving you a chance," I said. "So I'll tell you how it is. People like you busted my father's chops his whole life. Now, for a lot of his life, I think he enjoyed it. You know, being the iconoclast. But towards the end, he was getting tired from telling the truth. And when things were bad for him, it made the pious Catholics in our neighborhood very happy. When he died, one of the nuns at Saint Mary's told my cousin Carmine he couldn't get out of school for the funeral. Told Carmine that my father's death was God's punishment on an unbeliever. Then she mentioned that my father, who was as good a man as I've ever known, was going to burn in hell forever."

"I'm sorry," he said.

"Don't be. Carmine came anyway. Carmine even managed to reconcile it with being a good Catholic. Until he went to Nam. He claims he fragged the chaplain. It didn't bother him, he said, when the chaplain used to say, every time a guy died, that it was God's will and he would go on to a better reward. But then some guy, Carmine's buddy, lost his eyes and his dick, all at once. The chaplain said it was a blessing in disguise. He would be without the temptation to sin. The blind, dickless guy, that is. That's when Carmine fragged the chaplain. He says."

"Catholics are a lot like regular people," Guido said. "A lot of them are assholes."

Mario, who had been napping in the corner, barked. He's got different barks. There's the food bark, the warning, the walk-me. This was the happy bark. Joey was back.

Mario ran to the door and stood there like an anxious idiot.

"I got business," I said to Guido.

"I envy you," he said. "I was raised in a family that believed strongly. It is easy for a young man, who is sensitive to ideals, to romantic notions, to get swept up by religion. Now, as I approach the end, I envy someone like you. I would like to know more about what it is to lead a real life."

The door opened. Mario jumped for joy. As if he had been deprived, or beaten, as if I hadn't fed him and walked him twice a day and even patted him on the head from time to time, once or twice.

"Oh yes-s-s, oh yes-s-s, that's a good boy," Joey cooed obscenely as the mutt lopped saliva all over his face. "What's a matter? Didn't Tony take care of you? Didn't he feed you or walk you or pet you?"

The mutt barked "Yes." Lying little bastard. Joey glared at me.

"How'd it go?" I asked.

He stood up and shook his head. "Scorcese said no."

"Didn't even ask for more money? Or anything?"

"You're barking up the wrong tree," he said. "Whatever secrets Santino got, he's keeping them close."

"Santino Scorcese?" Guido asked.

"Yes," I said.

"The alleged organized crime member, as the television refers to it?"

"Yes, Father," Joey said, respectfully.

"He's a very bad man," Guido said.

"Yes, he is, Father," Joey said.

"So we hear, Guido," I said.

"Oh, it's very true," Guido said.

"Thank you for that information," I said. Joey gave me a look. For being disrespectful to the father.

"I know that he is," Guido said. "I was his family confessor. At Saint Anthony on Fordham Road. Many years ago. I might be able to help you reach him."

Then, the second day in a row, I had to go out to Brooklyn. Gene Petrucchio wanted to have a talk. Gene doesn't like to talk on the phone. Except about the weather and the Brooklyn Dodgers. We met at Dom & Angie's Luncheonette. I asked after his family.

187

"Anita, she's got a boyfriend. He's a nice boy. An accountant. Me, I'm happy for her. The wife, she's all upset. What if they wanna get married? They can't get married in the Church. It's all the same to me, long as they're happy, but not to the wife. They'll be living in sin, that's what the Church says, so that's what the wife says. If they have kids, the kids'll be bastards. I tell the wife, what kinda bullshit is that? Of course I don't say bullshit, but that's what it is. So she's in an uproar, and she wants Anita should go back to her husband. So Anita's in an uproar. Otherwise, maybe I woulda had you over the house."

"That's OK," I said. "This is a nice luncheonette."

"Well, they make good coffee. Also they sweep the place every week. Check the phones, everything. For the convenience of the patrons. My nephew Eddie does it for them."

"What can I do for you, Gene?"

"It's what I can do for you," he said. "You have a problem."

"I have a problem?"

"I hear," Gene said, "you get in trouble over women."

"Jesus, not anymore," I said. "The truth is, I'm ashamed to admit, that I lead a very monogamous life. These days."

"Well, you did something to that broad, she hates your guts."

"Which broad?" I asked him.

"The D.A. broad. Bronstein. I don't know what you did to her, but she's out to hang you. You're lucky you still got some friends. Also that she doesn't."

"Who're my friends?" I asked him.

"I am. When the broad went to Landsman—"

"Bronstein went to Landsman?" I said in surprise. Landsman, the designated successor to the D.A.'s office, should have been the last person she would go to.

". . . Landsman went to Alfonse, because Landsman doesn't wipe his ass unless Alfonse says its OK to put it on paper. Alfonse called me."

"What I don't understand," I said, "is Bronstein going to Landsman. She hates him."

"If you can't fuck your friends, you fuck your enemies," Gene said. "Some people are like that. It looks like Bloom isn't going run for D.A. So your friend decided to play ball. She'd have offered Landsman gratuitous sex, but Landsman can't spell it. She had to bring in something. She gave Landsman you, so Landsman could give you to the Feds. There's a lot of Feds in Brooklyn—grand juries, strike forces, special task forces. It could save somebody's ass someday to have a line on who the Feds are investigating. She says there's a lot of charges they could bring you up on. Suborning an officer of the court, violating the grand jury process, attempted bribery.

"I want to protect you if I can, because you're one of my people in this thing. So tell me what's going on, and maybe I can fix things for you."

"What I was asking Bronstein for," I said, "was the special prosecutor's report that she worked on, on Randolph Gunderson. There's some people that think that the special prosecutor didn't do a real good job and that Gunderson could and should be indicted. In time for the next election."

"Is that it?" Gene asked.

"That's it."

"You offer her a bribe?"

"I told her that I would get her favorable press. That I had a hook at WFUX. That if Bloom did run, I could get Des Kennel to make a big deal out of it. Which was bullshit. But there was no offer of money. I told her she should give me the report for the public good. Technically I could even say I was working for WFUX."

"It's understood that I look out for my people," Gene said. "So what I'm gonna do is have Landsman told that there's nothing to this and I think we can keep it under control. But you better figure she still might go to the Feds."

I had been wrong. Very wrong. Alicia Bronstein had not sent me the report. She'd sent me the FBI. It was that coincidence that had them following me when I went to the offices of Finkelstein-Magliocci and why they had picked me up on the way out.

"This thing you're working on . . . if it any way affects my people, it's got anything to do with Brooklyn," Gene said, "I figure I'll be the first to know."

"Absolutely," I said. "Has it got to do with Brooklyn? With Alioto?"

"As far as I know," Gene said, "it doesn't. But that's not the point, is it?"

"No, it's not," I said.

"My nephew Eddie Alfoumado—the Alfoumados, that's my wife's family—he learned all this countersurveillance in the Signal Corps." Gene gave me his nephew's card. "He's real good. You ever use that kind of thing, you might call him."

22.

The Badlands

It had to be Sydney Coberland.

When I called his office, they informed me that he was no longer with the firm. I asked if they knew where I could reach him. They said they didn't.

I staked out his house. He came out at 8 A.M. He wore a tweed jacket, pink shirt, blue tie, denim pants, and a funny little helmet on his head. He mounted his bicycle, in a precise and neat way, and pedaled off against traffic. When he got to the end of the block he turned left and disappeared.

I stood there. I had never tried to follow someone on a bicycle before. But it was obvious that it couldn't be done on foot or with a car.

Of course, I, too, know how to ride a bicycle. I rented one and was ready the very next morning. It had ten speeds, those handlebars that curve down, two wheels, and everything. Even a lock and chain. I was fully liable if the bike was stolen. When Sydney mounted up the following day, I was ready. I followed him the wrong way up the block and turned left on Lex. He cut sideways through the traffic to the right-hand side of the street, then a right, then a left to go south an Park Avenue.

On Park Avenue I got doored. Doored is what happens when you're riding as fast as you can and someone opens a car door immediately in front of you. The front wheel hits the door. The bicycle stops. The person continues.

My head went over the car-door window. My shoulder hit the window, which broke. I continued, airborne. Somehow I tucked my head and hit Park Avenue with my hands and then my shoulder.

I heard the screech of brakes. Someone was being polite enough to stop rather than run me over.

I looked up. It was a taxi. The driver stuck his head out the window. "Are you all right?" he asked.

"Yeah, I think so," I said, feeling for broken things.

"Then will you get outa the road," he yelled.

My injuries did not require medical attention. But the bike shop held me liable for the wheel. Clearly, this job, so simple at first appearance, required special expertise. I hired Speedo.

Speedo trailed Syd to the Gay Alliance Health Crises Center on Christopher Street. He called me. When I got down there, Syd was still inside. I paid Speedo and went in.

Oversize posters recommended safe sex. Cartoon drawings were graphically explicit about what was safe and what was not. A slender young receptionist with a blond Frito Bandito mustache sat at the front desk. The sign above his head said: "It's time to learn about living with death."

"Hey, guy," I said, "is Syd around?"

"Do you have an appointment?" he asked me. Like a receptionist anywhere else.

"It's personal," I said, a little shyly, "and I'd like to surprise him." I smiled my nicest smile. A nice surprise.

He smiled back, displaying Hollywood caps and flirtatious hazel eyes. "I guess it's all right," he said. "Over there."

There was a new sign on the office door, which said: "Legal Services." Syd didn't look up when I entered. But he did when I said, "Hello." He didn't appear pleased to see me.

"It's about the special prosecutor's report," I said, seating myself in the client's chair beside the desk.

"It would be better for both of us if you leave now," he said. He even stopped looking at me and continued making notes on his legal pad.

"It took me a long time to figure it out," I said. "It never occurred to me that it was you. But now I know it was."

"Frankly, I have no idea what you're talking about."

"The Gunderson report," I said, in a manner that I thought conveyed conviction and relentless determination.

"Whatever your name is," he said, "I think you should know that the Federal Bureau of Investigation is interested in any attempt at obstruction of justice in the federal judicial system. I am about to call them. I suggest you depart before I finish dialing." He lifted up the phone with one hand. He tore a page from his notepad with the other.

The page, which he held up for me to read, said: "Tonight. 8. Christopher & West St."

The corner of Christopher and the West Side Highway used to be tucked in damp darkness, heavy-leather bars on the east side, piers of desperate assignation on the west. Then the highway fell down. The city removed it from Forty-second Street to the Battery, rediscovering a fine wide street, with sun and the river breeze. The derelict warehouses have been torn down and the piers paved over, creating a nonchalant park with a river view.

That side of the street is for light cruising.

The howling wolf—banner of The Badlands—hangs over the northeast corner. The heavy-cruising corner. Everybody's in a costume from a butch Baptist's nightmare: leathers, macho mustaches, hot hankies, chains, and lace—an explicit code declaiming categories of lusts.

Vanity Fair

THE LURID LOOK

Fashion goes downtown again.

Nothing beats the gay underground for sheer macho depravity. Three hot young designers are turning to the leather and stud set that can be seen lounging around the alleys of the West Village to bring a new look uptown.

"The straight world has abdicated masculine image making. I will bring it back!" is Hugo Von Diedle's bold claim. "Even men who like women will dare to look like men again."

Esther della Vacheria says, "It is inspiration. All inspiration. My inspiration is the real men who once populated the cinema. What woman doesn't want a John Wayne, swaggering in his costumes militaire. Or the silent cowboy

strut of Randolph Scott. Every woman laments, Where are
such men today? Should only men have them?"
    Lancelot Westbrook III is even franker.
    "Let's talk hot. Brando in leather was hot. Hoffman in
drag is not. In the last ten years, the only men who dared
to look hot were in the Mineshaft or at the Saint. Come on,
you straight guys. Come out of the closet. Add a little explicit hot to your haberdashery."
    . . . What we ask is: can that heat be translated with
the new cross-back fashions? And do we want it to be?

Ayn Atlass

An outsider like me assumes that the code has a refreshing clarity, a
certain unabashed honesty. But maybe not. Maybe presentation di-
verges from performance, style is a promise that no one means to keep,
and man-man routines are as full of lies as man-woman games.

I looked for Syd. They looked at me. X-ray visions imagining my
body. I felt their fantasies creeping between my legs and across my
chest. Dorian Gray's portrait came down from the attic, with its pale,
ravaged face, dyed hair, eye with a tic, and put a hand on my arm.

"Come on inside," he said.

Anything could be going on inside—pulling a train on a virgin from
Waycross to the fist-fuckers' regional playoffs. "Do I have to?" I asked,
terrified as a Baptist coming face-to-face with a vagina.

He gave me a big broad wink. It was not reassuring. "You're looking
for someone, aren't you?"

"If you mean that in the specific sense, yeah. If you mean am I looking
for *someone,* no!"

"Your specific someone is waiting for you," he said.

I followed him, keeping my mind closed. It was dingy inside. Syd was
leaning against the wall in back, with a bottle of beer in his hand. He still
wore his tweed jacket and tie. He looked distinctly understyled, given
the surroundings. To the left of him, two guys dry-humped and French-
kissed passionately. Another guy sucked frantically on his own mustache while receiving a hand job under one of the small tables. It was
like the good old days. In prison.

Syd's friend, who had never relinquished his hold on my arm, guided
me through.

194

"Here's your hunk, sweetie," he said to Syd, both of them relishing my discomfort.

"Thanks, Fred," Syd said. "Tony and I want some privacy, you understand."

"Sure, Syd. I was just hoping I could watch," Fred said, and gave us a wink as he backed away.

"Jesus," I said, "did we have to meet here?"

"Why not? I'm out of the closet now. Are you ready to come out?"

"Fuck you, Syd. You know what I want to talk to you about. You sent me the special prosecutor's report—"

"Me?"

"Yeah."

"What makes you think that?"

"Not think; know. I showed your picture down at City-Speed. Someone ID'd you."

"You're lying," he said coolly.

I was. Nobody at City-Speed had been able to tell me, or the FBI, who had brought them the mystery package. But I didn't feel like he was challenging me. More like he was telling me that lying was a mistake. That he might deal with me if I was up front. I admitted that I was figuring by process of elimination.

"Why do you think I did it? If I did it?"

I thought he did it out of fear. But I didn't say that. I said, "I don't know."

"Fear," he said. "But not of what you think. Not of your cheap blackmail. You know, you're a sonofabitch pig; you're slime for what you did to me."

"I did what I had to do. I hit on some other people some other ways. You do what you have to do."

"But one thing I'll admit: You used it straight. You did what needed doing with it, which is bring it out. The report was a bad piece of work. I know that now. I could have done a better job. Or quit."

"What do you mean?"

"You want a beer?" he asked, a mockery of flirtation in his voice, from our first go-around.

"You did send it?"

"I got so upset, so enraged, and so humiliated after you took the gun from me—not that I can believe I was that crazy that I pulled it out to begin with—I got sick. I have a history of asthma. I got what seemed to be bronchitis. Or maybe pneumonia. Look around." He gestured at the room. "Every one of us has fucked someone infected with death. Then look around at your own life. Maybe you have too. Assuming you haven't slept with men, and I figure you haven't—God, you suckered me—think of your women. Any of them ever shoot up? Or get a blood transfusion? Or sleep with someone three years ago who shot up two years before that?

"Think about it. Makes your skin crawl, doesn't it? Your stomach knot. Are you going through the list? Did you perhaps have a sore or a cut on your cock or your finger where her juices could slip into your blood?"

There was a harsh moaning breath to my right. I looked. One of the dry-humpers was coming in his pants, his hands digging into his partner's leather vest and neck, his body rigid except for its moving center.

"I thought about it," Syd said. "Thought about it and thought about it. With every breath that I had trouble breathing, I thought terror.

"Finally, I got hold of myself. More or less. And I decided I had to face things. Truth and consequences. Look it in the eye. I had a blood test."

The Village Voice

Dear Problem Lady,

I always had a terrible problem when I asked a simple question like "How are your parents?" or "your spouse," or whatever, and then discovered the person I was asking about had—how shall I put it?—passed on.

Frankly, Problem Lady, I never knew what to say. "I'm so sorry" is très stupide.

Gradually, I stopped asking after anyone that I had not heard from within the previous month. Still those embarrassing moments would crop up! I simply ceased asking about anyone at all, unless they were standing in front of me, as large as life and actually exhibiting speech or motion.

In recent months I have become afraid to ask even "How are you?" So many people reply, "Terminal." "I'm so sorry" seems even stupider when you are talking to the soon-to-be-dead than about the absent dead.

Since almost every conversation seems to require a "How are you?" I don't speak to anyone anymore. This has had a noticeable effect on my social life. Which, no matter what anyone says, used to be *excellent*.

What should I do? Should I move to a foreign country
where I don't understand the language? Or is there a secret, special response superior to "I'm so sorry."

(signed) Desperate & Silent in Manhattan

"I tested positive," he said.

I didn't say anything.

"It's a curious thing," he said, "being sentenced to death. Particularly
as a result of your own sins. I blamed myself, of course. For my
unnatural acts. Do you want me to be more explicit about which ones
they were?"

"No. That's OK," I said.

He smiled. "I come from good old-fashioned New England Method-
ists. I bought into everything I was raised to be. Protestant, Republican, and better than *them*. All of them. Specifically these"—he gestured
at the room—"*them*. It's not a particularly unique reaction," he said.
"Have you ever heard of the RPQs? Or the Thirteen Club?"

"No," I said.

"An informal little group down in D.C., the Rich and Powerful
Queens. I've been an honored guest. You'd be amazed who drops in to
fuck with us. We're talking cabinet-level cock. The Thirteen Richest
Fairies. They're against everything they are. Many of our leading
fag-baiters are fags. From a former chairman of the National Conser-
vative Political Action Committee to one of the louder television evan-
gelists. I think of them as Turks. Turks despise homosexuals. But they
define it differently. A Turk will fuck a man in the ass and then boast to
his friends, 'I fucked a fairy today.'

"I loathed myself. I was certain that I had brought about my own
death through my own despicable sin."

"How could you know . . .?" I said.

"Oh, I knew. I knew that it was sin. Degeneracy. That's what
attracted me to you. You look so straight. Which of course you are."

"Sorry about that," I said, insincerely.

"A curious thing happened. I have a very good doctor. While I was
wallowing in my misery, he ordered a second set of tests. There's a
twenty percent or better margin of error in the blood tests. The second
test, and the third, came up negative. This body is clean. This body is

going to wait to be run over by a car, or have a heart attack. But I am not going to die of AIDS." Syd laughed. Then he said, "I was livid. I let myself get angry at the straight world for the first time in my life. Instead of at myself. For making me despise myself. For turning a virus, a microbe, into Sin. Let me tell you something: In Africa, this is a heterosexual disease. It's the plague. None of this picking and choosing the underclasses, the dope users, and cocksuckers.

"Which," he said, "is why I sent you the special prosecutor's report. To tear up the past. So that I couldn't go back. I'm some kind of radical now, I think," he added shyly. "I quit my job. I do largely volunteer work. The estates of the soon to be departed. If they're substantial enough, I take a fee. Fighting landlords to let the stricken keep their homes. I told that bitch I married that she could have half of whatever I make. However little that is. There's work that needs doing, and I am not going to waste my life protecting the fortunes of Fortune 500 corporations so that she can have two houses and a Mercedes.

"Her lawyer sent a threatening letter. I sent back a copy of the first blood test." He laughed. "That shut her up. Of course, a few years from now, when she discovers I'm still alive, she'll be furious and sue again. But I'll worry about that when I come to it."

"I need your help again, Syd," I said.

"Sure, Why not?" he said. "Since I don't owe you anything but a kick in the ass. You know, I could announce that you're a fag-basher. And let the whole gang jump on you. . . ."

"Cute," I said.

"But"—he sighed—"I'm not that flipped out yet. Let me watch a couple more people die of opportunistic infections, sores oozing all over their bodies, and maybe I will be."

"I need the report again," I said. Someone passing by patted my butt. It took all the control I had not to turn around swinging. Or shriek.

"Why?" he asked.

"I'm going after Gunderson. To get him indicted."

"Interesting. But I can't give it to you."

"Why not?"

"I don't have it. Nobody has it, as far as I know. After your friend did his broadcasts, the FBI showed up. They not only questioned me, they confiscated my copy of the report. They confiscated everyone's, I think. Except, maybe, Fenderman's."

"Is that legal?"

"I don't know. It didn't occur to anyone to argue about it at the time. Certainly not to me. That would have been pointing the finger at myself. Which I was not about to do. It was not exactly a pleasant interview. They knew I was . . . homosexual. They felt obligated to act super-butch."

"We go along in America and mostly it feels like politics is bullshit," I said. "Ford or Carter. Hart or Mondale or Reagan or Bush. I mean, what the hell difference? And most of the time, what you think you're voting for, it's the inverse of what you get. Vote for Reagan you get bigger deficits; Nixon made friends with the Red Chinese; Johnson and the war. But sometimes you see a line, and that line, you really gotta say, Which side are you on, boys, which side are you on?" I was speaking to motivate Syd, but as I talked I couldn't help hearing myself. "There are people running the country who are not part of the solution. They are the problem. These guys owe their election to the Falwells, the Pat Robinsons, the haters, the fag-baiters. They're your enemy. This federal government is not going into court to support the civil rights of people who sleep with people of the same sex. They're not going to fund a crash program in AIDS reasearch."

> [We are] facing the future with the Bible. [Within it]
> are all the answers to all the problems we face
> today—if we only read and believe.
>
> RONALD REAGAN

". . . You watch," I said. "What they're going to say we should do about AIDS is stop fucking. And pray. Which side are you on, boy?"

"I think the FBI is watching me," he said.

"Me too," I said. "But please, Syd, let's find another way to evade them than meet in The Badlands. Please."

23.

A Proposition

When I left The Badlands, I was kidnapped.

It was simple, classic, and Cadillac. I didn't notice the Caddy creep up behind me. One guy got out. He slammed the door. I glanced over my shoulder and saw him. By then the Caddy was shooting forward. When it was beside me, the driver cut right, up, over the curb, onto the sidewalk. The hood behind me had his gun out.

As instructed, I got in the backseat. The wise guys rode up front. We went north.

"Hey, what's happening?" I said.

"They didn't tell us you was a faggot," the driver said.

That hurt. Maybe they were going to kill me, but I wanted to go with my masculine image intact. I started trying to explain that I wasn't one of *them*. I had only gone to The Badlands on a case.

"Get a case, you mean," the gunman said, and laughed at his own wit. "Haw haw, uh uh."

"Hey, whaddaya do? Suck 'em or fuck 'em?" the driver said.

"I don't do either," I said, sounding like an inane twelve-year-old. Feeling like one.

"You one of them leather types, or do you do it in thoth little lathy numbers?" the driver said in a heavy-handed imitation lisp. "Haw haw, uh uh, haw."

200

A Proposition

"Just shut up, you guys," I said. I hadn't been that embarrassed since that first time with Maria D'Aquisto, when I melted in her hand instead of her mouth. And she laughed at me.

They laughed some more. Then they started talking about the horses, Atlantic City, and lying about their winnings. I asked where we were going. They ignored me.

We went over the George Washington Bridge, to Englewood, New Jersey. Lush elms and maple shaded the winding suburban streets, larger and larger homes set back from the street. When we turned in, I recognized where we were. The fellas had brought me to see my uncle.

There is an area of ambiguity here. Or willful blindness.

What I do know is that Vincent is worth a lot of money and that the money comes from construction. This may only be what Ray Donovan, Reagan's secretary of labor, called the "New Jersey Syndrome," when he was being investigated by a special prosecutor. That is, "If you are in the contracting business, it seems in this country you are suspect. If you are in the contracting business in New Jersey, you are indictable. If you are in the contracting business in New Jersey and you are Italian, you are convicted." Ray meant to imply that this was a public myth that obscures the reality. Rhythmic and pithy, it may instead be a poetic statement that captures the truth.

Presume that the contractor is as honest in his heart as Abe Lincoln. But he is surrounded by corruption. The government sits on his left, the unions on his right.

> There are only two reasons to be labor leader.
> One is because you believe that workingmen have
> a right, a priority, to the profits of their labor. All the
> intellectual structures that support such a belief come
> from the left. Communism, Anarchism, Socialism,
> Whathaveyouism. Certainly not from investment
> bankers.
> The other is to make more money than you can
> make actually working. If you're in it for the money,
> then you'll do other things for money. Like sell out
> the people you represent.
> Even a working stiff can tell the difference.

In order to stay in power, the guys who are in it
for the money have to rely on force. The people who
deal in force, they like the unions. A union is a cow
with two udders. You milk the members. You milk
the employers.

When the gangsters are attacked by the idealists,
what do they do? They call the government and say,
"We got commies to get rid of." When the businessman comes up against a union he can't buy, he calls
the government and says, "We're dealing with a
bunch of communists." So the government comes and
kicks the commies out—or anybody they can call a
commie, or have to call one because he has the integrity to stand up to the bosses and the guts to
stand up to the gangsters.

Who's left? . . . The government, the businessman, and the gangster.

MICHAEL CASSELLA

One of the people who got cleaned out was my father. Afterward he
turned away from the union and went into business for himself. A small
construction business. His older brother, who had taken a very different
path and was already a big shot, came along and they went into partnership.

They quarreled, bitterly, and never spoke again.

About what? "Vincent and I had very different ways of doing business," my father said. In what way? "He would have called it business
as usual. Living in the real world. I think you have to make a choice:
doing things right or not doing them at all." I accepted that answer. Only
later, looking back, did I see how explicit it wasn't.

It is easy to see how a businessman who will not do business under
the table—payoffs for "labor peace," bid rigging, bribing inspectors as
well as mayors—can't survive against one who will. That doesn't
make it right. Another question remains. Whether a particular businessman, such as my uncle, simply does business with them or is one
of them.

And now the trail from Gunderson seemed to lead back home. How?

202

Through Scorcese? The Teamsters? Frank Felacco? Michael Pollazzio, aka Mikey Fix? I didn't know. I figured I was about to find out.

We went to Uncle's favorite room. Mine too. It faced the long, sloping backyard. High arched windows from floor to ceiling made the outdoors part of the in. The garden was illuminated. Spotlights glowed on the early blooms—tulips, daffodils, lilacs: red and white, yellow, purple. A red Japanese maple was lit from beneath. There was one major change in the room since the last time I'd been there. A bed had been installed. A hospital bed, with cranks and adjustments, and a call button beside it. A soft, warm breeze came from one opened window. But the floral aromas that drifted in were overwhelmed by another smell: hospital.

Vince sat in a chair beside the bed, a blanket across his lap; he was pale, shrunken, and small. A uniformed nurse sat in an easy chair by the window, knitting.

"Zelda, outa here," my uncle said. The nurse rose, wool and needles clutched in her hands, and left us alone.

"Why you no ahave akids," he said, his beady eyes glaring at me, cheeks twitching or wobbling. "*Infamia.* You one a those people. Alla time I wonder. Now I know."

I laughed.

"Whata for you laugh? You got no shame? I shoulda spit on you, my blood or no, I shoulda spit on you."

"Is that what those assholes told you?"

"Theya tell me where they find you," he said with a sneer.

Why I cared what he thought, I didn't know. Maybe it's the one defamation I compulsively felt I had to refute. And I did. "I'm on a case. And the guy I need to get information from, that's where I had to go to find him. If I had to go to Jerusalem, it wouldn't make me a Jew. You able to follow that, Vincent, or is it too complicated for you?"

"Thena how come you gotta no children?"

"I don't know that that's any of your business."

"It'sa my business. I hadda no son. Your father had only one son. That leaves you. You're a bum. But you're all there is to carry on the family. I wanta you to carry on the family."

"What?"

"You heard me. Why you got no children? Why I got no grandnephews from you? Tell me something—how mucha money you make last year?"

"None of your business."

"The year before that?"

"Look it up in Dun and Bradstreet."

"If you had a kid, you couldn't afford a kid."

"I got a kid," I said, "and I support him." What he said hit me in places that I kept hidden. Money was a lot of why all of it had happened. The relationship with Glenda, not having a child with her. Or leaving to have one with someone else. If that was what I wanted instead. Not that that was an option anymore. Wayne was too much my son.

"If I made it so you could afford a kid, would you have a kid?"

"I got this case," I said, "and I got some questions to ask you."

"Raising a kid, it costs a lotta money these days."

"How deep in the mob are you, Uncle Vincent?"

He waved that away with his hand. "Thirty, forty grand a year? Is that enough?"

"Is Mikey Fix your boss? Or are you his? You in the Gonzoni family? Do you know Santino Scorcese?"

"You tell me what it costs," he said. "We're runnin' outa time here."

"What costs?"

"You having a kid. You're still capable, aren't you? You still gotta the stuff, huh?"

"It's time you told me something. What happened between you and my father?"

"I tell you that long ago. Long time ago."

"You told me bullshit, Vince. You told me nothing. You told me he didn't know if he was a commie or a saint. But you didn't tell me what the quarrel was about."

"You go to church anymore?"

"I never went," I said.

"I'm thinking I'm a gonna leave alla my money, the house, everything, to the Church. The priests, they're leeches. But giving to the Church, that's a good thing. Charity."

"It's your money. You do what you want."

"Where you think I'm going?" His head twisted as he looked around the room. "You think I'm gonna go to hell? Lookit me. Whaddaya see?

I tell you what you see. You see a dead man. I gotta get things settled."

"What was it about? What did you do to my father?"

"Do? I didn't do nothing. I tried to make him some money. Your father, he had problems. He thought money was immoral. Money got no morality."

"This is getting nowhere."

"You tell me, now. Your gun still shoot? You can still do the deed?"

"Yeah, old man. My gun still shoot."

"I got a proposition for you."

"What?"

"You getta the girl. The girl you got, different girl. Don't matter." He stopped to breathe and to wipe the dry spittle from his mouth. "I pay for the kid!" he announced, proudly.

"I'll give it some thought."

"You lissen a me, Antonio. You lissen. We do this right. You getta your lawyer. He meets with my lawyer. Draw up the agreement. You getta the girl pregnant, you get plenty of money."

"Right, Vince."

"I got conditions. You gotta marry her. I don' wanna no bastards. You find the girl. Both of you got to get tests of fertility. I don't want no misfires. I come to the wedding. To see that it's legit. As soon as she gets pregnant, you get the money. Forty grand, fifty grand a year. For eacha one. That's a lotta money."

"I promise you I'll think about it. I'm gonna go now," I said.

"You lissen to me. This offer, it's only good for ninety days."

24.

June

People been watching. I can feel it.

get a box? stash the money?

where am i going to go? heaven or hell. Is it like
they told us? This world certainly ain't. Does T
believe in anything at all? How can he live if he
doesn't? Do I? The Priests/Nuns, they lied about
everything. How can I believe them? Was Father
Cappiello doing it with ''young Father O'Connor''?
We didn't think those things back then, but looking back . . . does being a cop twist everything?
me, coming down to the wire, seeing everything and
everybody as perps and perverts.

what do I care about? who do I care about? My
brother is shit. He beats up on his own kids. his
wife. or he did. I don't think he got the strength
anymore. I think he's gonna beat me out of here,
cirrhosis or DWI. Two sons and both bums. My
sister. She started good. Too good. I think. Looking back. Married a bum. If I'd known. If I'd
known, I would have fixed him. I would have
straightened him out. Hurt him. the way he was
hurting her. But she kept her mouth shut. Good
Italian girl. Good Catholic girl. Let her husband

use her as a toilet bowl and never say a word. Or would I? She come to me, maybe I would have said, ''That's your husband, he's the king of your house.'' That's what I thought.

King of the house. Not in my house. All I learned from that is doing good don't pay back good. Being right don't buy nothing. Scratch one more, two more, three more people to care about. Ex-wife. Ex-son. Ex-daughter. One did me wrong. Two left me before they knew me so well that it mattered.

Who do I care about? Mario & T. Now that's what I call a wasted life!

From the Notebooks of Joseph D'Angelo

"Some men came to the house yesterday," my mother said. "They wanted to talk to me about you."

"Who were they?"

"They said they were FBI."

"Were they FBI?"

"They said it several times. When I didn't let them in. They held their wallets up to the peephole."

"What did they say?"

"They said to let them in, they just wanted to ask me some questions. I said that my husband told me never to let anyone in when I was alone. 'But we're the FBI, ma'am,' they said. Like anyone would let them in. That's when they put their plastic cards up to the peephole. To tell the truth, I couldn't read them. My eyes, Tony, they're not what they used to be. They said it would be beneficial to everyone if I talked to them. I told them they would have to come back when my husband was home. I wouldn't let them in till then. Did I do right, Antony?"

"Ma, you did wonderful."

"What should I do if they come back?"

"Tell them the same thing. You can't let them in until your husband's home."

"And if they find out I'm a widow?"

"Just keep saying the same thing. If they have a warrant, which they won't, keep saying it. Then give them the name and phone number of your lawyer."

"Come to dinner," she said.

"Mom, I'm real busy right now. . . ."

"It's because you don't like Guido."

"I'm real busy is what it is," I said.

"You'll come next Thursday," she said. "He really likes you. And he's very intelligent. Give him a chance."

I'd given him a chance. That's how I knew he was slightly wacko. He had taken to dropping in on the office unannounced. He'd even gone to Dannemora to make contact with Scorcese. The warden must've spent his spare time watching old Pat O'Brien movies in which the "fadder" gentles mad-dog psycho killers with trust and a prayer. Guido did get to see Scorcese. When he returned from his second visit, he was visibly excited. "We had a great meeting," he said.

"Oh, that's good. Did you give him absolution or something?"

"He has agreed to tell all!"

"Really?" I said. I was skeptical.

"There are conditions," Guido said.

"Conditions?"

"This is exciting," he said. "The last time I had such an adrenaline flow was when I was cerain that I had detected underlying fallacies in the *Summa Theologica*. That was a half century ago. And of course"—he sighed—"I hadn't."

"What's with Scorcese?" I asked him.

"The first time, I told him that I would help him appeal to the parole board. That was to establish rapport. This trip I turned the discussion to his son. As soon as we touched on that, I knew I had found a way to reach him. He said that Felacco and Ventana were going to pay. I said it was wrong to take vengeance. The Lord would take vengeance. We're supposed to say that sort of thing. Santino said, 'But, Fadder, he won't enjoy it like I'll enjoy it.'

"Then he said, and this is the important part," Guido said, " 'I'll tell you what, Father. If you would do the job on Felacco and Ventana for me, I would tell you anything you want to know.' So. What do you think?"

"What do you mean?"

"He'll talk!" Guido said fervently. "He's willing to talk under the right conditions. But we have to work together on this. I don't know how to find these Felacco and Ventana people."

"I'm sorry. Did I miss something, or are you talking about murdering two people?" It was definitely time to get him away from my mother.

"Oh, no. I couldn't ask you to do something like that."

"Oh, that's good," I said.

"I must have gotten ahead of myself. You see, once he said that, I knew we had him. It's rather like the conversation Mr. Bernard Shaw had with one of his actress acquaintances. He asked her if she would sleep with him for a million pounds. She said, 'Of course.' Then he asked her if she would do it for five pounds. 'What do you think I am?' she said with outrage. 'Madame,' Shaw said, 'we have already established *what* you are. Now we are merely haggling over the price.' "

"I don't get it," I said.

"We established that there was a condition under which he would talk. Then it became merely a question of negotiating that condition."

"I see," I said. I didn't.

"Which I did. All we have to do is find Felacco and Ventana. Then Scorcese will talk."

"We find them? I didn't know they were missing."

"Yes. They are. I'm not sure why, but they've gone into hiding."

"And then what?"

"Oh," Guido said airily, "we give that information to some person that Santino designates. Or to Santino."

"I get it," I said. "We don't have to do the hit. Just finger the victims."

"Is that what we would be doing?" Guido said innocently. "Do we know that? As a moral certainty? Particularly when we consider that such information could be used to serve the ends of justice in a lawful and legal manner, such as turning over the information to the authorities. Really, it's only a matter of establishing our *bona fides,* creating an atmosphere of trust, of give and take, in which communication can flourish."

"Argued like a priest," I said.

"Yes indeed, my son, there are few places like the Church for circuitous and specious logic. It is a grand school for hypocrisy."

I put him off. I wasn't happy about doing a mobster's dirty work or about working with a seventy-year-old priest aching to enter a Warner Brothers film noir detective fantasy. And I still didn't understand what the relationship was between my mother and the father.

Actually, everything else was so unproductive that I might have done something with Guido's deal. Except that I couldn't find either Felacco or Ventana. I couldn't even determine exactly why they were missing. Joey, with his police contacts, had picked up two different stories. One was that the Bronx D.A. finally had something on them that would have them trapped between perjury and a murder rap, so they disappeared before he could bring them in. Entirely possible. If the Bronx D.A.'s office leaked enough for us to hear about it, it leaked enough that all of the five families could discuss it over espresso and anisette.

"Scorcese, he's getting it together to get revenge," was the other story Joey had heard. From a friend at the NYPD Organized Crime Bureau. "Scorcese's making nice with the Soul Association, which is the most current gang for blacks don't want to be Muslims. Trying to do, maybe, what Joey Gallo tried to do. Which I, personally, don't think it's gonna work."

Although we weren't making progress, we were making money.

As I told Straightman again, it was a slow and expensive proposition. We talked to reporters, lawyers, wise guys. We spoke to Gunderson's college professors and people he'd gone to school with. We needed more manpower than just us two. Mostly we used ex-cops, friends of Joey's. Or friends of his friends. Plus I had Miles Vandercour digging away day by day, tracing the Gunderson empire, billing me week by week. I even had a guy working in Vegas to see if there was a way to tie Gunderson directly to the skim from Le Puta d'Oro. It felt like he was just yanking my chain, but a lot of detective work seems that way until the answers appear.

I sent out one of our guys, Billy DeVito, to see if any of the grand jurors felt like chatting about his or her experience investigating Randolph Gunderson. The day after he made his first contact, the FBI visited Billy at home. Before breakfast. To notify him that it was considered a federal faux pas.

Joey was splitting his time between the Gunderson job and what Silverman sent to us. Silverman paid cash. Plus we had a couple of maritals. I put two of Joey's buddies, named Farrell and Dentato, on that. They called themselves the SAD squad. Special Anti-adultery Division. We paid them fifteen dollars an hour and billed the clients thirty dollars.

The paperwork was killing me. I called my accountant, Sam Bleer. I said, "Help!"

"Maybe," he said, "it's time for you to get someone in there, to do the books and watch the billing." I agreed. "I might even have somebody for you," he said. "Came in to see me last week. Just got a bookkeeping degree from a junior college. Types ninety words per minute. Smart. And very, very cute."

I had a short but delicious fantasy. The one about the secretary under the desk. "You know what?" I said. "My significant other couldn't handle a just out of junior college and very, very cute. Send someone aged, overweight, with a hint of a mustache."

"That's why Hal didn't take her." Sam sighed. "I'll come by end of the week. Get you squared away for now and figure out if you're ready for someone full time or part time."

I also dug out Eddie Alfoumado's card. Gene Petrucchio's nephew. If he was good enough to sweep Dom & Angie's Luncheonette for listening devices, he was good enough to sweep Cassella-D'Angelo. The FBI has microphones like dogs have fleas. We came up clean. Eddie suggested that we have the office swept weekly. It's what all the best people do. I thought it was a good idea and billed it to Straightman.

The following Thursday, I went out to Brooklyn for dinner. As I had promised. Mother was fine.

Guido had been back to see Scorcese. He was excited again. "We have to get on this," Father Guido said.

"What's the rush?" I asked him. "Scorcese's gonna be where he is for another five or six years. The soup is delicious."

"Where he is," Guido said, "is in the hospital!"

"It *is* good," my mother said, also tasting the soup.

"He was stabbed," Guido said. "They're out to get him."

"How," I asked, "do you know? And who are *they?*"

"Santino reserved *The Prince,* by Machiavelli. On my recommendation. When it finally came in, he was so pleased that he went to the library without his bodyguard. He had his back to Science Fiction, and someone assaulted him with a homemade 'shiv.' The assassin struck from behind, in a most cowardly fashion, but he also struck too high and hit the shoulder blade. Not very competent. You see, if you must attack someone from behind, you should strike low, for the kidneys. That's the easiest target. Or, of course, attack commando style, slitting the throat."

"I didn't know they covered that in seminary, Father," I said.

"Sometimes," my mother said to me, "you mistake rudeness for wit."

"Santino's actually quite lively. He required only twelve stitches. Normally they prescribe Tylenol for knife wounds, but he has plenty of cash and was able to obtain morphine."

"That's a relief," I said. "I'd hate to think of Santino Scorcese in pain."

"It's a very long trip. Very tiring," my mother said. "I told Guido that he ought to bill you for his expenses and perhaps you could get the money from your client. He kept all his receipts."

"So you can see the urgency of the situation," Guido said.

"No. Actually, I can't."

"Is everyone finished with the soup?" my mother asked.

"They're certain to try again," Guido said while my mother collected soup bowls. "Felacco and his people that are behind this. They want to eliminate Santino before he can strike back. Would you like some salad?"

"Yes," I said. "I'll help myself."

"We can't let them get away with that," Guido said. "A dead witness is no good to us. I told him about us. And how we would find Felacco for him."

"Oh, you did," I said, a little dryly. "Was he thrilled?"

"He was pleased, I thought. But not overwhelmed. He already has some people looking for them. So you see, it's sort of a race. Obviously, if the others find them first, Scorcese won't tell us anything."

"This salad is excellent," I said.

"When do we start?" Guido said. "I am ready to go at a moment's notice."

"Guido, you're a friend of my mother's. You've been a great, great help. Really. But you're what? Sixty-five? A little more? Without insulting you, I don't think you're quite fit for this kind of thing."

"Frank Felacco, do you know his age?" Guido asked.

"Age often means wisdom, knowledge," my mother said.

"I am exactly the same age as our quarry," Guido said.

"Our quarry?"

"At what age do you propose that people should be put on the shelf?" my mother said.

"I thought you might be on my side," I said to my mother. "The people we're dealing with here are very bad people. For real. Not like when they come to church with their families and it's 'How are you, Father?' 'How are your adenoids? Your hemorrhoids, I hope they're better.' 'My daughter, she's so thrilled to be making her first communion.' And all that crap. Fat Freddy Ventana, he looks like a joke. Felacco told him to hit Arthur Scorcese, and without blinking he put a bullet through the back of Arthur's head. It wasn't his first time, either. Frank, he's into loan sharking. When he leaves church, he goes and has some guy's legs broken. If he still doesn't pay, he drops 'im in the bay.

"Let me put it this way, Father," I said, turning to him. "You're too old to die. These are bad people."

"I am fascinated with this entire business," Guido said.

"Look, I don't want to be rude. Out of respect for my mother. But the answer is an unequivocal *no*."

"Do you know where to look for them?"

"Not exactly," I said. Though the real answer was that I hadn't a clue.

"Do you want some dessert, Antony? I have ice cream," my mother said. "Carvel."

"I know," Guido said. "Not to pinpoint it. But I have a general idea where they can be found. I had some conversations with Mrs. Ventana's parish priest. She doesn't know exactly where Fat Freddy is. But she knows approximately where he is."

"Where are they?" I asked him.

"Anthony, Santino Scorcese won't even speak with you. Your only contact to him is through me. Your only hope of finding Felacco and Ventana is through me. I hate to impose myself on you," Guido said with that calm, infuriating smile, "but what option do you have?"

25.

Men of the Cloth

It was his football.

I hoped my mother would talk sense. But she supported him. So I took Guido on, reserving the option to get rid of him at the first opportunity. He was the type, with his pleasant, innocent manner and his clerical ways, that invited disasters to happen to other people. I put my foot down about one thing. No black suits and white collars. Guido got that helpless look on his face. I gave him a C-note and told him to buy himself some clothes.

Even then, the sly bastard didn't tell me where we were going. Only that we would go somewhere from Miami.

I was supposed to pick him up to take him to the airport, but at the last minute Jerry Wirtman called. I tried to get Joey to cover it. But he'd been on surveillance late the night before, and he was tired. "What I need is a vacation," Joey said. "I got to take some time. Like maybe a month."

"A month?"

"What's been wrong with me, it's some kind of low-grade virus, is what the doctor said. Rest and sunshine. That's what I need. And no work. So I got to get away, like for a month."

"When?"

"What I was gonna ask you, you take care of Mario for me. Also the car. I'll leave the car for you. Well, I should do it soon. You know. Couple of weeks. Soon's you come back, maybe."

So I told Guido to meet me at La Guardia, and that he could borrow cab fare from my mother if he didn't have it, and I went to see my landlord.

"I've been very pleased with the work you've done for me," Jerry Wirtman said. "That Bergman thing, I have to admit, I doubted you when it took so long. And when you went to Paris, I was certain—I'm sorry, I'm a suspicious person, the world we live in": he sighed in Yiddish—"that a vacation you were taking on my money. Such terrible thoughts. I know now that you are an honest person. Even if there is no such thing as a detectives' union, is there?"

"In a more perfect world," I said.

"The FBI came to speak to me," he said, "about the Bergman case. They said that the French police were interested."

"Yeah," I said. "They said they were going to try for extradition."

"For a goy, you have a *Yiddisher kop*," he said. It's a great compliment for one of them to say a Gentile has a Jewish mind, since they're convinced we're all as intellectually dull as Midwesterners. "So from one *Yiddisher kop* to another, I'll tell you something. This gonif shyster . . . Madigliani?"

"Magliocci."

". . . who was stealing my money under the pretense of being a Bergman. Him. He was not the only person they were interested in, these FBIs. I think they were interested in you. A lot of questions they asked that had nothing to do with Magliocci. With you."

I thanked him again, this time genuinely.

"Such bad thoughts that I had about you before." He shook his head. "I would like to make that up to you. A free-lance person—pardon if I am being presumptuous, but banks often do not understand. The days when a banker would look at a person as a person, and say this is an honest and hardworking man, a man of his word, if such days existed, they are long gone. All they have are profiles and formulas. So perhaps if you and the young woman, the two of you are planning to make a purchase of the apartment, you may find—again pardon my presumption—difficulty in dealing with the mortgage. If that is the case, I would be willing to carry the mortgage. This is not in any way charity," he added. "It is a very shrewd maneuver on my part. If you were to default, I would be obtaining the property at the insider price and make an excellent profit."

"Thank you," I said. What he didn't say was that it was important to him that we buy the apartment. He needed two or three more votes to get approval of the conversion plan. Glenda was one of the more vocal holdouts. "On what terms?" I asked him.

"Oh, whatever the going rate is."

"OK," I said in my most disinterested tone. If he wanted us to make a private deal behind the backs of our neighbors, he was going to have to add the sellout bonus.

He understood. "Certainly better than Citibank will give you," he said. "No bank closing costs and handling fees and all the other things they stick on. Maybe even a half a point, a point, lower."

I promised to give it serious consideration. I didn't have a chance to mention it to Glenda before I left.

When I arrived at La Guardia Airport, I didn't recognize Guido. He was wearing a straw hat. A purple bougainvillea print wound down from the collar of his mostly orange shirt. To have said he looked like a caricature of a Puerto Rican grandfather on his way home to Mayagüez would have been an ethnic slur, however accurate.

It was because I didn't recognize him and was looking around so hard to find him that I saw Vernon Muggles. Muggles was very busy pretending not to look at me. There were the two agents with him, a salt and pepper team. They were also pretending not to look at me. Another black man, I was certain, was staring at me from the other side of the terminal.

I thought life would be a lot simpler if they didn't follow us. Wherever we were going. I thought of a scenario to lose them. It depended on not letting them connect me with Guido.

"Hey, Tony!" Guido yelled, waving a skinny arm, the orange shirt flapping like a flag. We all turned to look, me and the FBI.

"That's strike one," I said.

"What?" he asked.

"Never mind," I said. "I'll make a new plan. We'll let them follow us to Miami and then we'll lose them. Where are we going from Miami?"

"Them? Who?" His straw-hatted head swiveled all around in circles.

"Never mind," I said. As we walked through security, I looked back. Salt and Pepper were behind us. When we checked in at the boarding gate, Salt stayed, while Pepper ran back to get their tickets.

Boarding was announced. Guido was eager to get on. I told him to wait. I watched while the gate attendant got a phone call. "Don't worry," I said to Guido. "They're getting instructions to hold the flight for a special passenger."

"Really? How do you know? Who?"

"The people traveling with us are VIPs. And probably, if you weren't with me, I'd be able to dump them."

"We're being followed!" the priest said. Thrilled beyond belief.

I got up, Guido behind me. I looked back, and sure enough, Pepper was dashing up the corridor like O. J. Simpson.

When we stepped into the DC-10, I asked the stewardess if we could upgrade to first class. Salt and Pepper would panic for a while, marching up and down the plane looking for us. But they'd figure it out. So it was mostly spite, knowing that they were in steerage while we of the private sector wallowed in first class. The stewardess brought complimentary preflight champagne. "I don't know how I'm going to cover this one when I put in my expenses," I said.

"Don't think small," Guido said.

"Easy for you to say. You don't have to answer for it, which is always the way in your profession, I would guess."

"The problem with you," Guido said, done with his first glass and signaling for a second, "is that you're still fighting your father's battles."

"I hope you have some different clothes," I said. "Though it'd be better to change your age or get rid of you entirely. I wish you'd believe me when I tell you this may turn out dangerous for you."

"Anticlericalism may have been a worthy position," he said, "a century ago. But today it seems oddly dated. The Church is withering on the vine."

"Fasten your seat belts," the stewardess said, coming by to look at our laps.

"An organized religion is dangerous and stifling," I said. "With secular power, it's oppressive and murderous."

"I don't think it's because we went to the vernacular mass," he said. "I spend a certain amount of time lecturing at seminary. On Aquinas.

I'm not terribly good at it anymore, since I lack the faith. However, I find the level of the contemporary seminarian appalling."

"Just because your crowd is slipping," I said, "doesn't mean the principle doesn't apply. So this year the inquisition is Islamic. It's just a question of opportunity. You'd bring back the auto-da-fé if you could."

"In my day, at least the seminarians were masculine. And occasionally there was one with a brain. But that was in another country, and another time as well."

"Do you have some other clothes?" I asked him, still thinking of escape.

"Anthony, I am disappointed that you don't like my shirt. Your mother thought it very youthful."

"That's my mother's way of insulting you when she wants to be polite. What's between the two of you anyway?"

"I'm really not your enemy," he said. "I doubt that I believe any more than you do."

The engines throttled back, the jumbo jet shivering in its boots, feeling its own gravity-hugging heaviness and champing at the bit at once. The pilot released the brake and we lumbered up the runway, pouring a flood of fuel into the fires, desperate to have enough speed to rise before the end. Just as thousands of planes do every day.

Guido reached a fingertip to his breast. He saw me watching. Whether he had intended to make the sign of the cross or not, he didn't. He took out a pack of Camels.

"I didn't know you smoked," I said.

"From time to time," he said. "Losing my faith was a long and painful process. I thought it was a failure in myself. A fault of character. Like someone who likes sex too much or not enough. 'Father, what's wrong with me?' " he mimicked a thousand unnamed parishioners. " 'I have these de-zires.' 'Father, am I supposed to *like* it?' 'Well, my child,' I would say, 'it's a great deal more pleasant than pestilence, war, and famine.' At least it was in my very limited experience."

"Just how limited is your experience?"

"Are you speaking here as your mother's son?"

"I'm making conversation, which is probably a mistake. You know they show movies on this flight. We get free headsets because we're spending an extra one hundred eighteen dollars each, give or take."

The No Smoking light went off. Matches were struck all around the cabin, including Guido's. He lit one of his short, stubby cigarettes and inhaled. "Watching movies," he said, with a reflective puff of smoke. "That's what it's been like. Or the television. Which is worse. The same thing over and over. The same troubles, tragedies, whimpers, and whines. All other people's, a curtain between themselves and myself," he said.

"Can I have a set of earphones?" I said to the stewardess.

"A voyeur's life," Guido said. "But no more. I'm quite fit, you know: all that abstinence. Except for my knees; prayer takes its toll. I feel ready for whatever may befall."

I plugged in the headset and started flipping through the music channels. I waved at the stewardess.

"This headset doesn't work," I told her.

"Oh, I'm sorry, sir. The sound system is broken in this seat."

"In first class!" I said, aghast. "An extra hundred dollars and I can't watch a truncated four-dollar movie."

"That's deregulation," she said. "You can blame Jimmy Carter. Things will get better now. You'll see. Let me get you a drink."

"Your mother is a remarkable woman. A woman of strength and character," Guido said.

"That was my father's influence," I said. "She'll tell you as much."

"She has. I would like to have known him. He sounds a most interesting man."

"My father treated my mother as a person. Which I'm beginning to understand was a rare and unusual thing."

"Indeed it is," Guido said agreeably.

"Maybe," I said, "that's what the hell's wrong with my relationships. Every other guy I know, they have a wife stuck out in Queens, with the kids. Which they don't go home to, not too much anyway. And they got the regular girlfriend in Manhattan and the occasional lay out in Brooklyn. They can do that because they're all Catholics and don't eat fish on Friday. So why can't I live like that? It sounds a lot simpler, doesn't it?"

"To have had a wife," he sighed, looking at his drifting smoke, "and children. I may have a son. But I think that's mere romantic yearning."

"So I'm involved with a woman in a goddamn modern relationship. Or

219

one that's supposed to be like my parents', but it isn't, because it's half-assed. So as good as what my parents' thing was, and right, being right is fucking me up."

"Sounds like fun," the priest said.

We could see the clouds hugging the Florida shore as we began our descent. They had an ugly look, and the PA system commanded us to strap down for turbulence. When we started bouncing through the clouds—that sickening rise and drop—I looked at Guido. "Tell me," I said, "in case we crash, you die and I live, where to look for Felacco and Ventana."

"Anthony, I know you would like nothing better than to be rid of me. . . ."

"Then why do you persist in tagging along?"

"Naturally, I am reluctant to lose my only hold over the situation."

"At some point, Guido, you have to trust somebody. At some point, we wanna lose Salt and Pepper, our federal escort. Now until I know where we're going and what we have to do to get there, I don't know how to do that. Are we traveling by car? By plane? Domestic? International? North? South? come on, Father, gimme a break."

"Will you give me your word," Guido said, "that you'll let me see this through with you?"

"Insofar as that's possible, absolutely," I swore. A nice flexible, jesuitical turn of phrase, I thought, that could mean anything I wanted it to.

"My boy, I was trained by Jesuits. Possible absolutes and absolute possibles are the phrases we used to betray entire populations. Do you think I'm weak-minded enough to fall for that?"

"Yeah, yeah, yeah," I said. "You can see it through."

"Your word?"

"Don't you want me to swear to God or something?"

"Your word will do," Guido said.

"You have my word."

"Freeport, in the Bahamas," he said, as the jumbo jet dropped six feet like a stone.

Someone shrieked.

"Shit," I said. "We gotta do something about passports. And we should lose those assholes as soon as we can. And do you have anything else to wear?"

"Well . . ."

"Well, what?" I asked.

"I am cognizant of your feelings, and I respect them. But I actually don't have a very wide wardrobe. And you'd be amazed at how useful those things are."

"You brought your collars?"

"Yes, I brought my collars."

"How many collars?"

"Two. I always take two. For when the other one is being cleaned, you understand."

The wheels dropped through the cloud shroud and collided with an invisible runway. We bounced, the way lead does. Then we were rolling comfortably into the terminal. It was one of those flights where the passengers break out in spontaneous applause at touchdown.

Rank hath its privileges. For one hundred eighteen dollars, you too can have a free drink and a five-dollar lunch and get off the plane first. We deplaned at Gate 12. I grabbed Guido and dragged him down behind the unused boarding attendant's podium at Gate 8. I took off my sweatshirt and shoved it over his head, hiding the orange abomination. "Go, get a cab," I told him while I started pawing through his bag. "Go to Monty's in Coconut Grove. I'll meet you there."

He hesitated. "I gave you my word. Now move it," I said, shoving him out. "But slowly," I hissed after him. "Speed is conspicuous."

Then I did what I had to do. I put on one of his shirts. The kind with a stiff white collar.

I forced myself to wait, peeking out from behind the pedestal until I saw Salt and Pepper dashing down the corridor looking for an old man in an orange shirt with a young one in a sweatshirt. I stood up and strolled out behind them. I stopped at the newsstand and bought a pair of sunglasses.

The last time I'd been out of the country had taught me to bring either my own Vaseline or a false passport. Pete Palmeri was a high-school buddy. A paisan from the neighborhood. We'd hung together because

221

we were white people whose first language was English. In Fort Greene, those are distinguishing characteristics. Pete went to Brooklyn College, studied numbers, and became an accountant.

He discovered cocaine a couple of years ahead of me. He also discovered, trying desperately to hide, disguise, bury, and shelter income for several dealer clients, how lucrative it was, as a business. While I felt guilty and out of control, he felt it was time to move on up, from grams, to zees, to keys, and finally he moved to Miami, where he could tap the main vein.

I still had his address and phone number. I dialed from a pay phone. When I heard his voice answer, I hung up. I wanted to know that he was home. I didn't want to tell the DEA that I was dropping by.

I ambled away from the phone booth. I spotted Salt upstairs and then Pepper downstairs, looking for me. Pepper looked right at me, and through me. I stepped outside in the thick, hot air, rain thudding down beyond the concrete canopy, and found a cab.

By the time we reached Monty's, out by Sailboat Bay, the storm was over, the clouds had fled, and a tropical sun was making the puddles steam. The fare was twenty-four dollars. I asked for the clerical discount.

I found Guido, then phoned for another cab.

Pete had done well for himself. A big house on a substantial piece of property. The security system alone—cameras, infrared, sound detectors—was in the 75K range. I rang the bell and smiled into the camera above the door. A voice came through an external speaker: "Sorry. We gave at the office."

"Hey, Palmeri, you asshole. It's me, Cassella."

"Holy fucking Jesus," Pete said through the speaker. "What happened to you?"

"You gonna let me in?" I said to the door.

I heard beeps and clicks. "Door's open. Come in, we're out back. . . . Holy fucking Jesus, Cassella a priest."

We passed through a central room two stories high, Mexican tile on the floor, white pine walls, *Casablanca* fans turning lazily overhead. Pete was by the pool, looking cool in his tan, shades, and shorts. The pool was surrounded by lush tropical growth, trees, vines, flowers. It was just like a TV show. Including the three girls. There was a progression there, of sorts. The first one was fully dressed. She wore a bikini. The second was topless, the third topless and bottomless and painting her toenails.

"I can't get over this," Pete said. "Come on, sit down, let me get you a drink. You a priest! What're you drinking?" He had a couple of chairs around him and a table beside him. The table had a phone and a TV.

"Piña colada," Guido said.

"Rita, get a piña colada," Pete yelled. The topless one put her feet into high-heeled sandals and swayed toward the house. Guido watched her, goggle-eyed. "What you havin', Tony? Hey, one thing I know about priests—they drink."

"Club soda," I said.

"Wow," Pete said. "Something must've really happened to you. Strange-o . . . Rita," he yelled, "and a club soda."

"Nothing happened to me," I said.

"Uh huh," he said. "Long time no see. How you like the spread? . . . Hey, girls, say hello to my paisan from the old neighborhood," he yelled. They more or less looked up. "That's Annette, my Mouseketeer, and Caroline, her friend. . . . Girls, this is Tony, but you can call him Father. . . . Oh, man. The last person in the world. Who's your buddy?"

"This is Guido," I said. "And, Pete . . ."

"Hi there," Rita said, coming up with two tits and two drinks on a tray.

"I'm enjoying the trip, Tony," Guido said. He reached forward. Rita put his piña colada where his hand was going. He blinked.

Rita came over to me. Close enough that I knew her breasts had neither stretch marks nor implants, her areolas were a little browner than her tan, her nipples small, with tiny nubbles. I took my drink. She came even closer.

"I've never done it with a priest before," she said.

"Uhh . . . really," Guido said.

"I have to be honest, my child," I said, patting her lightly on top of a tit. "This is just a disguise."

"Oh," she said. What little animation there was in her face left.

"A disguise, a disguise," Pete said, laughing. "That's my man, Tony. That's my paisan. Oh, shit, I thought you'd really gone weird on me."

"Uhh . . . *I'm* actually a priest," Guido said to Rita.

"Oh," she said, and wandered off. Several emotions rippled over Guido's face.

Pete looked at Guido, then at me, asking.

"Yeah," I sighed. "Don't ask me to explain."

"You don't want to explain," he said, a coke dealer's flash of paranoia about any unanswered question.

"If you want me to, I will," I said. "Just to give you an idea of how weird it is: to start with, he's going out with my mother. I think."

"Oh," Pete said.

"Yeah, oh," I agreed. "You still . . ."

Pete looked at Guido again.

"Guido, could you give us a little space here," I said.

"Take a walk around the grounds, Father," Pete said. "We got some dynamite landscaping here. All kinds of tropical shit you won't see nowheres else." He pointed off to the right, "Star fruit, key lime, all kinda horticulture stuff. Probably in'erest a man of the cloth."

Guido looked down at his drink, which he had finished.

"You wan' another?" Pete said. "Just go in the kitchen, help yourself, or get one of the girls to help you."

"So what's been happening?" I said, as Guido went inside.

"Hey, I made my pile," he said, "and got out. I got pizza parlors now. New York Pizza and Ray's Real Brooklyn Pizza, five o' the first and franchising the second."

"So you're not doing business no more," I said, looking around.

"And you, what're you doing?"

"Still a P.I.," I said.

"Man, I love the disguise. You here on a case? My ex looking for me, or something? Or something?"

"What I'm hoping, I'm hoping you know somebody who can help me get a passport. Not the State Department, but one of the private issuers."

"Piece of cake, paisan, piece of cake," Pete said. He picked up the cordless and punched in some numbers.

"Two," I said. "I gotta take the father with me."

"Pablo," Pete said, "I got a little thing maybe you could do for me. . . ." He looked up at me. "Rush?"

I nodded yes. It was hot. I reached behind me, unsnapped the collar, and shrugged out of the shirt.

"Whyn't you come over? . . . Whaddaya need? A Polaroid, I got a Polaroid. . . . Whyn't you come over?"

"Yeah, you're outa the business," I said.

He winked at me. "You wanna toot?" he asked.

"No," I said.

"Me neither. I just keep it around for the girls. But just snortin'. I don't want no crack, basin', bazouko, any o'that crap around. Tootin's nice, you wanna party, but that other shit, you got zombies, might as well get one of them three-hole blow-up dolls. Take a bimbo, plug her any way you want, it don't matter; all she wants to do is suck pipe. Disgusting . . . Sure you don't wan' a real drink?"

"No, that's OK."

"Damn, it's good to see you, paisan. The streets, the streets, the streets of Brooklyn. Shit. We've come a long way, baby."

"This guy you got comin'. He good?"

"The best. I don' know what he's got on hand, but he can give you, usually, U.S., Venezuelan, Canadian. That's real popular, Canadian. It's just like U.S. for getting into the U.S. but like cleaner with everyone else."

"Yeah, you're in the pizza business," I said.

"For real. I am," he said. "Every now and again, for a select few, just for cash flow, you know."

"You amaze me," I said.

"Howzat?"

"You been doing that thing for ten years. You're alive, well, and not in the slam."

He tapped his forehead. "It's 'cause I got it up here. Numbers. I'm an accountant at heart, you know, not a fuckin' cowboy. I don' make a move unless I analyze profit against downside risk. Most fuckin' people do this, fuckin' cowboys. Or junkies. You know, wired-out weird on the white lady. I get over two grams a week, personal use, I put myself out to the farm, take the cure. Get clean. No point doin' business when you're movin' faster than you're movin'."

"So that's the secret?"

"That's ninety percent of it. You ever make the scene down here?"

"No," I said.

Guido came out of the house, glass in hand. He looked over at us. Then at the girls. Wistfully, he turned toward the gardens and went that way. Pete watched him go and took his bottle out from a drawer in the table that held the phone.

"You sure?" he asked. "This is Peruvian flake. Alpaca pura."

"No, thanks," I said.

He tooted rapidly. The Mouseketeers, with their radar ears, looked up. He waved a hand at them, saying, Forget it.

"Awww," Rita said.

"Later," Pete told her. He sniffed it back. "Oh, yeah. We're talking Rolls-Royce. Cruising speed. . . ."

"Hey, Pete," the girl with the blond bush and freshly painted toenails whined.

"All right, all right," he said. He took a couple of good-size hits, screwed the cap back on tight, and tossed the bottle across the pool. Six tits bobbled frantically as the girls jumped up to catch it.

Pete laughed again. "I got another bottle here," he said with a wink. Guido had returned, a little peaked from the sun and the booze. He looked over at us, then at the girls. He opted for them.

"So you got no problems," I said, just making conversation.

"You really wanna know, paisan, what the secret of success is?"

There was laughter from the other end of the pool. Guido wiped sweat from his brow. Apparently, the heat was too much for the father. He got up and went toward the house, Rita and Annette, the one almost dressed, going with him.

"Yeah," I said.

"Federal informant," he said.

"Yeah?"

"I'm a federal informant. They think they're playing me, I know I'm playing them. I give them this guy, that guy, a little something from time to time, and I do whatever the fuck I want. It's a license to steal, a license to deal."

"This passport thing you're doing for me," I said. "Is that a little something you would give the Feds?"

"Hey, paisan," Pete said, sounding hurt. "What're you talking about? You're my people. I only give 'em spics."

"Oh, that's all right then," I said.

A set of chimes played "I can't get no sat-is-fac-tion." Pete flipped on the TV. The front door showed up on the screen. "That's Pablo," he said to me. He picked up an electronic control box and unlocked the front door by remote. We could see Pablo enter on the TV.

"Come on," Pete said, getting up. I followed him into the house. Pablo was coming in the front door. Guido was off to the side, on the couch. His third drink was in front of him. Rita was on his right, Annette was on his left. His eyes swept back and forth as he tried to decide whether to fall into the tits to his left or to his right.

Rita was laying out lines on the coffee table, snorting them through a rolled bill. A flashback to my own bad old days. The other girl was patting Guido's thin white hair.

"I'm a little sleepy," Guido said.

"Here, honey, this'll help," Rita said, handing him the tooter.

"Guido," I said, sternly, "give that back."

The girls laughed. Pete cracked up.

"I've never done this," Guido said.

"I'm not having you doing coke," I said. Sternly.

"What are you," Annette said, "his *father?*"

Everyone thought that was hilarious.

"Guido," I said, making my way to the couch, "it's time to cool it. Let's not get carried away."

"A man should try everything once, before he has to say goodbye to this world," Guido said. "I'm going to try it."

"Damn it," I said. "If you so much as touch that shit, I'm gonna have to tell my mother on you."

26.

Reggae

Pablo didn't have any Canadian passports. Pablo suggested birth certificates since that's all an American needs for the Bahamas. Pete thought passports were better, on principle. I agreed since I wasn't worried about getting in as much as coming back. We got Irish passports. Pete thought it would be amusing if we were Irish priests, Father Gregory O'Malley and Father Anthony O'Hara.

"The best way," Pete said, "to get to Freeport is on a gambling junket. Friend of mine sets 'em up. I'll tell him I got a couple of high-rolling priests from the auld sod. I'll get you comped and everything." He even drove us out to the flight.

The charter flew out of Opa-locka Airport. The plane had propellers, and I think it was the same one on which Ingrid Bergman flew away from Humphrey Bogart at the end of *Casablanca*.

"I got to thank you. For everything," I said when I got out of the car.

"It was worth it to see you in a collar. Man, Tony Cassella, cocksman and cokehead, in a collar. You shoulda put it back on and done the girls. That's the kinda thing they think is kinky."

"No, I mean it," I said. "All of this was above and beyond. I owe. Anytime you need a favor, you got it."

"I'm glad you said that," Pete said. He went around to the trunk and opened it up. He took out a small suitcase. "You ain't got a lotta luggage, so I was thinking maybe you could take this with you. Take it as carry-on."

"And then?"

"You got reservations at the Royal Princess. A guy, he'll come by, for Father O'Hara, he'll pick it from you. It's locked and all. Not that I don't trust you, 'cause you're from the neighborhood and all that, and you're a wop. But this way, nobody got to even think about it."

"And what if they want to open it at customs?"

"They won't. I been on these. They just walk you on through. But if they do, you just play the forgetful padre, you know, absentminded, start looking through your pockets for the key. And 'Oh, dear, I must 'ave lost it while I wuz on me knees prayin' at the sacred statue of our holy sainted mother of somethin' or other.' Then you can ask for a locksmith to help you get it open."

"And then?" I asked.

"And then, if you convince them you're sincere, they'll get irritated and tell you to find your own fucking locksmith at the hotel. Or they'll get one for you and open it."

"Do I worry about them opening it?"

"No," Pete said. "It's only money. They want you to bring money into Freeport. That's what it exists for."

"How much money?"

"You don't wanna know, Tony, you don't wanna know."

He was right. I didn't want to know. I decided not to worry about it. I let Guido take it through customs.

The first night in Freeport, we did nothing. Except check into our two-bedroom, complimentary, three-hundred-dollar a night suite, hand over the suitcase, and sleep. The guy who came for the money was named Eddie. I asked him if he knew where I could pick up a piece. Just in case.

In the morning I ordered a lovely room-service breakfast. OJ, eggs, Irish bacon, toast, fresh pineapple, a day-old *New York Times* for me; two aspirins for Guido. I signed for it. It was lovely, sitting on the balcony, feeling the morning breeze, looking out at the sea, seeing Guido in pain.

When the busboy came to clear away, he brought up a package from the hotel desk. A SIG P210 automatic. Swiss made. Very expensive. Very classy. Thanks, Eddie.

I went out dressed as a real person, not a priest, to the casino in the next hotel. They were delighted to give me a couple of thousand on my credit cards. In chips, of course. I played blackjack and roulette for two hours. Lost ten dollars. Then turned in the chips for cash.

Then I went out and took a wind-surfing lesson. I was terrible. I got up on the board, lifted the sail, then fell over. Then I climbed back on the board, stood up, and fell over. Back up on the board, I stood, tugged on the sail, it spun around and knocked me over. This went on for about an hour. The water was gorgeous. It's the blue that people rave about. We never had water that color at Coney Island. I suspect it's because there's less shit in the Caribbean.

Then it happened.

I got the sail in the right position, drew it in close with the correct hand. And sailed. At least fifteen yards before I fell over. Clearly, it was what life was really about. I was born to be a yachtsman.

It was a wonderful, lazy couple of days. Making casual inquiries about Felacco and Ventana around the casinos and restaurants. Sunning, wind-surfing, snorkeling, eating expensive food, spending expense account dollars.

We'd only been comped for two days. After that the Princess wanted money. When I went to prepay and settle up for the incidentals, I got to see our phone bill. There was a call to the 518 area code in the States. Upstate New York.

"Who did you call in 518," I asked Guido.

"Santino," he said, "to let him know we were on the case."

"Did you tell him where we are? Did you?"

"Yes," he said.

"Oh, shit."

"What's wrong?"

"You know, you may not see anything morally wrong with what we're doing here," I said. "But I do. And I had a perfect jesuitical solution to the dilemma. I mean a real fish-on-Friday answer. And that's how we're gonna play it. If we still can. There's a warrant, an active warrant, out on Felacco and Ventana. Now the minute we know where they are, I call NYPD Organized Crime. My partner, Joey, he's working with a guy there. And what I want to happen is for the NYPD to pick up Felacco and Ventana. Bring 'em back to New York, put 'em in the slam or whatever. Now if Sorcese wants to hit 'em in the slam, which is a pretty good place to do that sort of business, then he can.

"But at least . . . at least I can say that we handed 'em over to the duly constituted, you know, and when they're inside, which is where they're supposed to be, it's someone else's job to protect them. And our hands are clean. Sort of. Mostly."

"But my agreement with Scorcese . . ."

"Well, what I was gonna do was let you call Scorcese just before the cops came in. Then we held up our end of the deal, just he was slow to pick up on it. He doesn't have to know that the reason he was slow is we made sure the other guys were quicker. Which I hope they are. But if they're not, I can still blame the murder on bureaucratic bungling. Instead of on myself."

"You're right," Guido said, with his mild smile. "You could have been a Jesuit."

"Do you know if Santino sent anyone down yet? What did you say to him?"

"I am aware that the prison telephone is hardly a secure system," Guido said. "I spoke as his priest. Our conversation, the gist of it, was that he was eager to see me to discuss spiritual matters and I would come to see him as soon as I returned from vacation, in Freeport. I think the authorities will find that very innocuous."

"Oh, man," I sighed. "Well, maybe we're only half fucked."

"How about some lunch?" he said.

"Yeah, come on. We'll eat at the pool."

The sea breeze was a slight saving grace in the June sun. The water was a set of blue color cards, light and luminous at the shore, neon past the chop, then IBM blue, and finally navy at the horizon, below the high stacked clouds. Back home they just had clouds. Here they had illustrations from my grade-school textbook. Cumulus, stratus, stratocumulus, cumulonimbus, nimbus. It was noon. The clouds would come in at two, rain at two-thirty, be gone at three. As the guidebook promised. Unless they decided to hang out and give us a full tropical storm.

I ordered the tropical fruit salad and iced tea. Guido ordered pompano.

"Have you been to South America?" Guido asked me. "Peru? Bolivia? Colombia?"

"No," I said, watching the wind-surfers catching rides on the rising wind, wishing that I could be as graceful. Given sufficient money and leisure, I would.

"We, I mean the Church, had a problem," he said. "This is back before my fall, when I was at the Vatican. The problem was liberation theology. Radical priests. I was sent on a theological fact-finding mission, of sorts. The doctrinal questions are quite complex."

Another junket jet must have just landed. A fresh group of tourists, with that just-landed look, came out to the pool. I noticed one of them simply because he was black. While there were plenty of blacks around, they were almost all staff. He was vaguely familiar. Like the man I'd been paranoid about at La Guardia. I wrote it off to they-all-look-alike racism.

"In reality, my mission," Guido said, "was to discover what dogma had developed in this peculiar hothouse of Latino *barrios*."

The fruit plate arrived, artfully arranged, arcs of pineapple around arcs of citrus around slices of mango around balls of melon, topped with half of a yellow star fruit, point pointing upward. Guido's pompano was grilled light, crusty with butter, served on white china, with green slices of lime on the side.

"The poverty, ignorance, disease, hoplessness, and sheer stupidity I saw down there was appalling. Truly appalling," he said, flaking off a piece of fish with his fork. "This, by the way, is delicious. Would you like a taste? This is really quite perfect."

"Yes, thank you," I said.

He broke off a piece and put it on my bread dish. "I was in Colombia for three weeks. Now there's a place where anticlericalism is a living political reality. As is clericalism. And the obsession we call Marianismo. The theologically inspired female prostration before machismo."

"You're right," I said. "This fish is incredible."

"Isn't it?" he said. "I was depressed, seriously depressed. At last I escaped. High up in the Andes. Bolivia. And it was worse. The Latin American world is one that the Church had a leading hand in building. It is our creation. Our priests are either part of it—arrogant, ignorant, Chaucerian prelates—or arming themselves for revolution. Or falling off

232

the edge with the mad sadness of it. That was my choice, sadness. I went to a monastery, some fifteen kilometers outside of La Paz, and asked for a cell in which I could meditate. I was checking myself into an asylum. I prayed. I cried. My God, what had we wrought?"

"The fruit is really good too," I said. "You want a taste?"

"If you could put a few bites aside. I like it after the fish."

"Sure," I said, picking out one bite of each for him. The clouds were marching forward over the water and the boats were starting to turn in, back to harbor. People were looking up, trying to judge how much tanning time was left.

"Given the reality . . . given the reality," he said, "all I could do was recommend some sort of marriage between the Church and liberation theology. Precisely the opposite of what I had been sent to do. There was no way I could watch that suffering and say it was God's will, see that systematic diminishment of humanity and say we ought to be part of the system," Guido said, while I watched a forty-two-foot sports-fishing cruiser slide between the wind-surfers and the catamarans.

"I went back to Rome and made my report," Guido said, and started on the fruit. The big cruiser pulled into the hotel pier. A couple of harbor boys rushed over to receive and secure the docking lines. "I was ordered to revise it. I refused. The report was ordered repressed. I was certain it was the Truth and must be published. I started sending out copies. Writing letters. Knowing that I was destroying my career."

"That's them," I said. Frank Felacco and Fat Freddy Ventana, spiffy in resort wear, looking frisky and ready for a little roulette, stepped off the cruiser and onto the dock. "I'm gonna follow them. You sign for the meal, then get the name of the boat. Who owns her. Where she's kept. Got that?"

"Yes," he said. "Are you sure it's them? My eyesight isn't that good."

"Yeah, it's them." We weren't the only ones who'd noticed. The black guy I thought I'd seen at La Guardia was in motion too. "Now do what I said and no more."

Gambling in America is like being in a machine. Ignore the advertising. You are not king of the castle. Beneath the thinnest layer of glitz money can buy, it's Chaplin's *Modern Times*, a spinning wheel factory, the patrons lined up like cows, the machines at their teats, milking the money out as efficiently as possible.

The Caribbean casino is less obsessive. The air and the psychic noise are less tobacco-stained. Maybe because you can't get there by car or bus.

Frank and Freddy looked real relaxed. Frank's silvery hair was freshly blow-dried and set. He wore a turquoise Ban-Lon shirt, yellow golfing slacks, and white patent-leather shoes with a webbed top. Except for the gold bracelet with half-inch links, the gold chain thick as a finger, and the diamond-studded watch, he looked just like a golfing WASP. Freddy wore madras Bermuda shorts in extra wide. And a sport jacket to cover his gun. Frank and Freddy sat down at the alcoved high rollers' black-jack table. There was a third guy with them, that I didn't know. Not only did the black staff wait on their every whim; even white people came out to service them. VIPs indeed.

The casino manager, in his white Bogie dinner jacket, dropped by to chat. I looked to the doors, wondering where Guido was. When I looked back, the manager was beckoning one of the employees over, a croupier I had talked to when I was looking for the two mobsters. The manager, it seemed to me, was instructing the croupier to tell Frankie something.

Right.

Time to fade. I slithered toward the doors, heading out the way I came in. I saw the third man rise from the table. He was going in the same direction. I held back and let him get ahead of me, then I followed him out.

On the patio, a reggae-for-whites band was doing the island version of a White Rapper song.

> *Sunday suburb gone to seed,*
> *Tuesday's child growing weed,*
> *On Wednesday Reagan did decreed*
> *that old morality must succeed.*

The third man walked past the bandstand. Heading toward the dock. Guido was chatting amiably with one of the dock boys. A deckhand stood at the bow of their boat. He held a rifle.

Reggae

Thursday's child is overseas.
Back on Friday with the keys,
Oh. Crack-crack.
Moral disease,
Oh. Crack-crack.
Mommas cryin'
babies please
don' wear
dose dungarees
first step to degeneracies.

The third man walked up to Guido and began speaking to him. About two sentences were exchanged. He put the arm on Guido. I started moving forward, but by the time I reacted, Guido had been hustled aboard.

I knew it. From the moment I saw his collar, he was bad news. Now I had to go after him. Whether I wanted to or not.

When something happens to a man's partner, he's supposed to do something about it. It doesn't make any difference what you thought of him; he was your partner, and you're supposed to do something about it. Then it happens we were in the detective business, when something happens to one of your organization; it's bad business to let someone get away with it. It's bad all around—bad for that one organization, bad for every detective everywhere.

My gun was in our suite. Which would be the next place they'd be looking for me. To beat them there—and avoid the elevators—I took the stairs. All four flights. No one had gotten there yet. I went to the gun first. A clip was in. I chambered a round, put the safety on, put it in my belt. Then I grabbed a small travel bag. I shoved all my cash in the bottom. The phone started to ring.

I didn't answer. It continued to shrill while I stuffed some clothes on top of the money. The phone stopped. Passports. I put the passports in the bag. Someone started knocking at the door. "Housekeeping," a voice called through the door. But the voice was male, white, and New York.

It was time to leave.

I went out on the balcony. Two-thirty, right on schedule, the cloud cover was darkening the beach. The first drops of rain fell.

I was, quite frankly, a little hesitant about the stuntwork involved in an exterior departure from the fifth floor. I heard the door opening inside the suite. To convince myself that I had to do what I had to do, I tossed my bag onto the balcony below. There was four grand in it. Even John Straightman wouldn't accept an expense item: *$4,000—cash misplaced.* I had to follow it down.

I dropped down and hung by my hands. A Bahamian gardener looked up, regarded me with amusement, and carefully stepped away. Just in case I missed. I swung in, released, and landed beside my money. Without mishap.

In the movie-of-the-week version there is a beautiful actress—hair by Jonathan, wardrobe by DeMille, breasts by Silicone—waiting in that room. Ready, after one look at my honest brown eyes and hunky shoulders, to aid and abet me. Whilst satisfying my every lust.

I got an empty room. I'm not complaining.

The glass balcony door was locked. I tapped a hand-size hole with the butt of the SIG, unlocked the doors, stepped in, walked on out the front, and went down the stairs. I found my way, by smell, toward the service entrance and exited beside the garbage. Outside, it was coming down. Thick and steady, like a locker room shower.

I made for the dock.

The storm was growing. We were in for more than the fifteen-minute-as-advertised tropical special. More rain, more wind, more waves. That was going to help. Everyone had headed for shelter. Including the guard in the bow. I could get to the boat without being seen.

If there were no more than two of the opposition on board, I might be able to get Guido out. I had a gun. And no desire to actually fire it. It's not that I don't enjoy killing people. Anyone who has ever watched TV knows that once it's been clearly established that the victims are bad guys—dope pushers, toxic-waste dumpers, crooked lawyers, IRS agents—slaughter is a lot of fun. But if the Bahamian police had not been watching the same shows, I would be stuck with attorney's fees, a time-consuming and probably embarrassing trial (those false passports), and incarceration for fifteen years to life.

The difficulty was getting on board without alerting anyone.

There was a gangplank. If I crawled up, spreading my weight, it would cause a less abrupt shift. For Guido? Did I owe it to Mom? I thought back to those nights, a child sick and feverish, my mother staying up, soothing my fevered brow, spoon-feeding me that awful soup she used to make from a can. Yes, Mom, I got down on my knees and crawled up the gangplank in the drenching rain for you. We're even now. At least for the soup.

It brought me up near the rear of the cabin, the bow to my left, the stern and the entrance to my right. I dumped the luggage bag there, then slithered across the deck, keeping my silhouette low. I reached the cabin in just four slithers. Rising slowly, I tried to get a look inside. Then I heard a noise to my right. I slumped down to a prone position, gun out in front of me, and began crawling toward the stern.

At the end of the cabin wall, I gathered my feet under me but stayed as low as I could.

The rifle appeared first, before the man.

That was my moment. I could reach him before he saw me. I rose, leaving my gun on the deck, and made a grab for the rifle barrel; got both hands on it and rolled back, ripping it away from him. I'd meant to do a neat judo-class rollover, but my feet slid out from under me. I reached out with my right hand to grab something, but there was nothing, and I went down hard. He yelled. I grunted. My elbow hit the deck just after my back. My left hand went numb, and the rifle flew away over my head, sliding on the wet deck. I tried to get up, but it took a beat before my lungs could get enough air to let me do it. Up on my hands and knees, I went scrambling for the SIG. Not knowing where he was.

I got the pistol, then went skidding around the corner. He was disappearing into the cabin. I went after him. Without thinking. Which is the only way to do something like that.

Inside the cabin I saw Guido on one side. It looked like he'd been hanged. But I didn't pay a whole lot of attention, because the other guy was going for another weapon. It was one of those squat, ugly things—an Uzi, or a MAC-10, or one of their cousins—that burp out six hundred rounds a minute. So much firepower that even a dead man can kill with it.

I charged. Hoping, I guess, that the clip was out, that the safety was on, that something was wrong enough that I would get to him before he could fire.

He was slow. A few beats later, after I'd hit him, my brain realized what my eyes had seen. He was operating with one hand. My weight slammed him into the cabin wall. The breath blew out of him. Then his lunch, which had been largely liquid. Regurgitated rum and Coke cascaded down over my head and back.

I jumped away. He continued to vomit. He couldn't breathe. And he was trying to nurse the wrist that had snapped when I took his rifle. I thought it was safe to leave him be. I picked up the Uzi, put the SIG in my pants, and took a look at Guido.

"Hello, Anthony," he said, with that same calm, placid smile that I hated. He had one rope around his scrawny neck; a second tied his hands behind him; and both were fixed to a cleat near the ceiling. "I don't want to die."

It was a good knot. A bitch of a knot. Eventually I just gave up on it. I found a knife in the galley, then cut Guido down.

The guy on the floor was getting it together. I caught his movement out of the corner of my eye.

"Move, you asshole, and I'll kill you," I said, informationally.

"Drop it, you asshole," Fat Freddy Ventana said from behind me.

I dropped the Uzi. It fell loud. Then I turned slowly. There were three: Freddy with his .38, Frankie, and the one I didn't know. He held a Clint Eastwood magnum.

He went down first. With a very stunned look on his face.

The next bullet hit Frank Felacco from behind. Frankie screamed. Which was the first sound of violence, the first anyone of us knew that someone was shooting from outside the cabin door. Freddy turned, slowly, the way a semi does. The next bullet hit him, but he kept going. The guy I had beat up grabbed the Uzi off the floor.

I pulled out the SIG and fired at him. I think, by then, Freddy was shooting. My shot was right on. I got the guard in the head. The far side of his face exploded. But his hands clenched, convulsed in reflex, and the Uzi started emptying its clip. The recoil moved his dead arm in an arc. Glass and metal and wood shattered and split and flew around the room along with the bullets.

I shoved Guido to the floor and threw my body over his.

It was from there that I watched the automatic fire from the dead man cut Fat Freddy in half.

Finally it was over. Silence, silence. Then the sound of rain came through the silence. Reality seeping back in. I stood up and rushed for the door. It was still coming down thick. I thought I saw, through the storm, a man slow from a run to a walk. He was black, and maybe he was the man I'd seen at the airport in New York, who may have been the tourist I spotted earlier in the day. Sent by Santino Scorcese because of Guido's call. Then again, maybe that was three different people.

I grabbed my suitcase from where it still lay, beside the gangplank, then I went back in and started checking bodies. Frank Felacco was still alive. Not very alive, but doing that last-breath number.

When somebody arrived, if somebody arrived before we disappeared, I wanted to be found as a priest. An innocent priest. I fumbled in the bag. Yes, the passports were there. Real and phony. And two black short-sleeved shirts with collars. I tossed one to Guido, while I squeezed into the other. He didn't react.

"Put it on, put it on," I told him, and he began to do so.

I knelt down in the blood and took a closer look at Frankie. He saw the collar.

"You really a priest?" he said.

"Why did you hit Arthur Scorcese?" I said.

"Father . . ."

"Come on, come on, Frankie tell me about Arthur."

"I wanna make confession," he said. "I'm dying. I know I'm dying. Fuckin' Freddy, so fuckin' slow."

"I'll handle this," Guido said, back in costume.

"Yeah, yeah, go ahead. Find out about Scorcese."

I stood up and watched Guido kneel beside Frank. He took a cross from somewhere and held it up to Felacco.

"Confession . . . and the last rites, Father . . . You gotta."

"First you must make confession," Guido said, leaning close to him.

It was an eerie scene. The old doubting priest kneeling among the dead. Felacco with the life visibly draining from him. The cross held up. A pond of blood flowing around them. The madness had shattered all but two of the small, low-voltage lamps. The light was dim and soft.

The senses return one by one. I became aware of odors, and of hot and cold. The man I didn't know had died pretty clean. But the guard's brains and much of his face were spread across the floor. Blood drained from his head, urine from his crotch. The blood was hotter than the tropics. All that blood raised the temperature of the cabin. Freddy was worst of all. Most of the fire had hit him in the back, after he turned, and the exit wounds, the big ones, were in front. Body fat, intestines, organs, were all falling out of him. The room reeked like an abattoir.

It was the tropics. The smell grew fast and it grew thick. And the flies had already begun to find us. Even through the rain.

I stepped outside. I wiped the SIG clean of fingerprints and threw it overboard. They would probably find it. But by then, hopefully, we would be clear. Still the rain came down. Still no one came.

Back inside, Felacco had lost the strength to talk much more. It was time for us to be gone anyway.

I bent low and said as much to Guido.

"Father, the rites, the last rites," Felacco said, with all of the little life he had, a desperate whisper.

"No," Guido said, "not yet."

"I made my confession. Forgive me, Father, forgive me in the name of Jesus."

"I have to tell you," Guido said calmly, "that I won't forgive you. You have been a terrible man. A killer, thief, drug peddler. You have fed on the flesh of others. Frankly, Frankie, if there is a God, and he has any sense—"

"You ain't no priest," Frankie gasped.

"Yes, Frank Felacco, I am. And I am here to tell you that if God has any sense, he won't forgive you, either. If there is a hell, you will burn in it forever, in immortal agony. But there may not be. So the least I can do is let you go to your death in a state of fear and terror."

27.

Santino Speaks

I called Pete and asked him if he knew someone who might make the run in a small boat. Of course he did. It cost us two thousand dollars. Cash. And we weren't the only cargo. But it was a fast boat, leaving late and scheduled to arrive in Miami before dawn.

Things finally caught up with Guido while we were at sea. Exhaustion, shock, his age. He passed out. He got very pale. It scared me. But I covered him with blankets and he came around before we reached the mainland. Pete met us and took us to the airport. I destroyed our false passports, then caught the next flight to New York.

I took him to my mother's. He was going to need some rest before we went up to see Santino Scorcese to claim our reward.

There had been a long talk about computer camp or baseball camp. Wayne had decided on computer camp because it had all the camp stuff—including baseball—plus computers. He was into a real rationalist phase.

"What if I stayed home this summer?" he asked when I put him to bed. He sounded troubled.

"Why would you want to do that?"

"I want to stay home," he said in a statement.

"If you want to stay home," I told him, "you can. It would save me some money."

"Can we afford camp?" he asked.

"Yeah, champ. This year we can afford it. De money's in. Big bucks, ya know what I'm sayin'. If you go to computer camp, I'll get you a computer of your own when you get home."

"You think if I go to computer camp I'll be a nerd?"

"You don't have to be just because you use your brain. I'm sure there are plenty of brainless nerds."

"OK," he said. "I'll let you know."

"Good," I said, tucking him in. I turned out the light.

"Tony," he said, in the dark, "if I go away . . ."

"Yeah, kid?"

"If I go away for the summer . . . when I come back . . . when I come back, will you be here?"

"Yeah," I said. "I'll be here."

I closed the door behind me, went to the kitchen, and got a beer. What a wonderfully normal thing to do. I shivered. With a kind of relief. So very far from the madness in Freeport. I considered telling Glenda what'd happened down there. But I didn't want to hear about it myself. A refrigerator. A kitchen. Quiet. Homelike. Good stuff.

Glenda said, "Why didn't you tell me about Jerry Wirtman's offer?"

I'd left in a rush. But I'd spoken to her several times from Freeport. I could have told her. I said, "How did you hear about it?"

"Why didn't you tell me? Is that something that doesn't matter to *us*?"

"I didn't get around to it. Besides, it doesn't matter. Until we get down to cases. I don't know . . . maybe I was saving it as a nice surprise."

"Maybe," she said, "you're still avoiding whatever it is you're avoiding."

Maybe I was. "There I was, in the Bahamas. All these bikinis parading around, micro-mini things, and I was true and it's been a long time. How about it?" I said.

"What kind of sluts wear micro-mini bikinis for men to slobber over?"

"The point was that I didn't do anything."

"Well, why not? I thought out of town and under five minutes doesn't count. But that's right, you never do it under five minutes."

"Here I am, telling you I was good."

"A funny way to tell me. Do you think I want to hear about your escapades?"

"The ones I didn't have. That was the point."

"The ones that you thought of having. How could you resist micro-mini bikinis?"

"I wasn't even tempted. Come on. It's been a long time. I've just come back from a dangerous mission. I got sunburned. Is this the greeting I get?"

"I did miss you," she said. "When I wasn't mad at you. Did you miss me?"

We looked at each other and it wasn't there. But we tried. Because it was supposed to be. Our emotion tracks were on tapes so tired that entire chunks had flaked off, big glitches in the melody and irregular gaps in the rhythm. She would lapse, I would lapse, an alternating pattern. My biggest blank was while I waited for her to put in her diaphragm and the strange slush that goes with it. We managed.

I was under five minutes. She was out of town. Did it count?

"I made an appointment to see a lawyer," she said while I surreptitiously dried my postcoital penis on the sheets.

"About what?"

"Buying our apartment. I have the contracts for her to go over."

We had our first full-time bookkeeper, Naomi Pellegrino. Sam Bleer had found her. "A nice Jewish lady," is how Sam described her, "who married a bum, an amateur wise guy. Who, thank God, left her a widow. She can keep books, type and keep her mouth shut. Plus she worked at a private nuthouse on Long Island, so she can cope with you and your partner." Naomi had white hair. Glenda would be happy.

Joey was irritable. Which he'd been a lot lately. It was worrisome and annoying. He had been waiting for me to get back so he could go to St. Louis for Snake Silverman. Something he had promised he would do, personally, before he went on his continually postponed vacation. He showed me where the dog food was. And the doggie treats. The flea collars and the doggie shampoo. Mario and I drove him to the airport. I commented on how tired and even ill he looked. He agreed. A vacation. He needed a vacation.

I got back from the airport in time to meet with Miles Vandercour, who finally, after more than two months of digging, had an interim report. He was a pale, lumpy sort of man in his late fifties or early sixties. He dressed in a manner that I could only call natty and spread classical references and allusions over his speech like oelomargarine on rye.

Miles had a rosebud in his lapel. He had a map of the Bronx. And of Manhattan. And of Brooklyn. All carefully marked up.

The maps cross-referenced to three books of records, each four inches thick, of deeds, title searches, and property records.

"What the hell does all of it mean?" I asked him.

"We are in Plato's cave," Miles said, stroking his map of the Bronx. "See here, these are but the shadows of men. Or are men but the shadow of this, their maps, their charts? Charcoal scratchings on the wall of the cave."

"Oh," I said. "Um. Uh. Is there anything in particular that I should pay attention to? In these shadows and scratchings?"

"The Bronx map is the most interesting," he said, pointing out several of the notes he'd penned directly on it. "Notice how many holdings were in places where there are no longer places. How many people do you think live, these days, in the center lane of the Cross Bronx Expressway? These"—he pointed at another spot—"are now a low-income housing project. Some people do very well with property that lies in the way of government plans. Perhaps Gunderson was born under a lucky star. Said star guided him to those real properties. You might look at that.

"Also note, if note you will, this sort of trill, in Morrisania. This I really don't understand," he said. There were five properties marked with numbers. "The numbers are the number of times Gunderson owned those properties. This one three times, that four, and so on. I suspect there is a much larger pattern there. It took two weeks merely to find the first series, however. Even then I only found it by accident."

"What does it mean?"

"I don't know. But it's unusual. Property values are not that volatile. They almost never go up and down like the stock market. So it's rare for someone to buy, then sell, then buy back, then resell, then do it again, with one piece of property.

"As time goes by," he said, "I think I will find more of these."

244

"What does it mean?" I asked again.

"You tell me," Miles said. "In any case, I have my current bill to submit."

I introduced him to Naomi. I told him to give the bill to her. She smiled at him, brightly.

With a cough and some confusion, Miles unpinned his rosebud from his burnt-sienna jacket and presented it, gallantly, to Naomi. "I am charmed," he said.

"I'm the new bookkeeper," Naomi simpered. She blushed to the white roots of her hair.

I met Glenda at the end of the day so we could meet the real estate lawyer, Pauline Felder. By the time we got together, Guido had had a long talk with my mother, who had a long talk with Glenda. It was like a game of Telephone, except that it was the attitude about the story that changed. Guido thought I was a hero. Mother thought I was crazy. Glenda was livid. And grievously insulted that I hadn't told her every detail.

"There was nothing to tell—"

"You were almost killed. You killed someone."

". . . that wouldn't have upset you."

"Don't you have any reaction? Don't you feel something? How can you not tell me?"

"I don't tell you because I don't need this shit."

"What am I to you?" she said. "Somebody to keep you company when you can't find anything else to do?"

"I haven't thought about it," I said.

"You haven't thought about our relationship?"

"I wasn't talking about that. I was talking about what happened in Freeport. And I don't want to think about it. It was out of town. It was under five minutes. It really was. It doesn't count."

"You have to face these things. Oh, Tony, what are you doing with yourself?"

"Oh-h, Ton-n-ny," I mimicked her. "This is why I don't talk to you. Because I don't like going around and around. . . . It's garbage. Just garbage."

"Why are you doing this to me?"

"*To* you? *To* you? I'm doing it *for* you. Like any good semihusband should. I'm bustin' my hump, risking life and limb to bring home the bacon or beans or whatever it is it takes to own a condo these days. You wanted success? You wanted bread? I got bread. That's why we can go talk to your lady lawyer. And buy the condo without scrimping and saving and eating ricey leftovers to do it. And keep Wayne in camp and private school—"

"Which my ex—"

"Which your ex sometimes pays for, but not entirely, either. So I ain't doing squat to you. I'm doin' for you."

"Then how come it doesn't feel good?" she asked.

"Good fuckin' question."

We went to the lawyer's office. We looked over the deal. The deal was sound. Our attorney would contact Wirtman's attorney and set a date for the closing. Our attorney charged only $150 an hour.

I couldn't find anyone to walk and water the mutt, so I had to take Mario upstate with us. He and Guido got along well. They both liked automobile rides. They didn't have to drive.

The motel was a motel. Dinner was greasy. Breakfast was worse. Mario was happy with the leftovers. After we ate, I drove Guido, in his uniform blacks, to the prison gates. Then I waited.

I put on the radio low and made myself relax. Just drift. Just think about $100,000 in a Swiss bank. The Olympics were coming. *Time* magazine said America was going for the Gold. Right on. Me too. And a Cadillac. With all the options: AM-FM/tape deck/quad, sun roof, whitewalls, cruise control, respect and admiration. America. We have the dollar, and our dollar has muscle.

I would feel better about me. Glenda would feel better about me. Admitted, she was a good person, who didn't want to judge people by income. In particular the man she lived with. But she was human. And a woman. So, of course, she did.

I had two thousand cash in my pants pocket. Packed thick and warm. With my eyes closed, I felt the money grow around me, releasing me from old illusions. Allowing me to embrace new ones. Back to the Bahamas. In February. With a large-breasted companion who I could dislike because she was only with me because I had money. Like

Kimberly. Or. Rita plus Caroline plus Annette the Mouseketeer. I would buy a borsalino and make guest appearances on *Johnny Carson* and *Miami Vice*. When my ship came in.

Guido came shuffling down from the prison gates. Mario barked a greeting. I got out and stretched.

"He lied," Guido said. "He lied to me."

"What do you mean?"

"He's not going to talk. We kept our part of the bargain. He's not keeping his."

28.

Conversion

When I got home, I did major mea culpas. I begged forgiveness. I took out my needle and thread and sewed big patches on my relationship with Glenda. After we sent Wayne off to camp, we even took a couple of days just for ourselves. We stayed at a bed-and-breakfast near New Paltz, where we got semisweet. It was called the Nieuw Olde Haus, a restored seventeenth-century Dutch stone building. We even managed, by taking a vow of silence, to perform two reasonably exciting and satisfying acts of intercourse.

Which was nice. Since we would soon be owning property together.

When I got back to the office, I had to face the fact that every real lead was dead. Except, perhaps, for the abstract that Miles Vandercour had seen. Turning it into something useful was going to be a tedious, frustrating, slow, boring business. Cop work. Which was who we had working for us, ex-cops. The best of the lot were "Fast Frankie" Farrell, Eddie Mazzolli, and Billy DeVito. I'd made the mistake of paying DeVito everything we owed him, so he'd taken off for Atlantic City and wouldn't be back until he'd lost it.

So that's what we did. Farrell, Mazzolli, and myself. Going back to those neighborhoods. Talking to people. Who didn't know anything. But who might know someone who did. Then finding that we couldn't find the next person in the line.

New York is not America, and from Manhattan, the Bronx is a foreign country. So was the Brooklyn I grew up in. It's realer. The problem with reality is that it's ugly, smelly, and ominous. Reality is garbage, and the hotter it gets, the more aromatic it is. The kids squall louder. The diapers have more reek. In the center of the city there are more people on the street, but they're going somewhere. In the slums and ghettos, they're standing still. Waiting. Maybe Ron in his TV-land White House thinks that white cops don't still go to the neighborhoods and hand out beatings to blacks who act bad. If he does, he's wrong.

Malevolent eyes stalked me. And Farrell and Mazzolli. Who came back talking "nigger" this and "spic" that. To keep my own mind from being infected with racial fears and contempts, I had to keep telling myself that a black walking through the white zones of Howard Beach and Ozone Park would get the same. Still, I felt more comfortable carrying a gun. Or having Mario with me.

Joey came back from St. Louis. He reached me by leaving a message with Naomi. I was in the Bronx. The number was the pay phone at Snake Silverman's.

"How was Saint Lou?"

"Piece a shit. Guy ain't there. Where's Mario?"

"Win a few, lose a few. The mutt's with me. Actually, except for that he sheds, he's a pretty good partner."

"Better 'an me, prob'bly," he said.

"Farrell's got Mazzolli. I got a dropout Alsatian."

"I ain't even been to the office. Everything OK? We making money?"

"Yeah, we making money. Naomi's got a check for you. July fourth bonus or something."

"Yeah, well, you hold it for me. Unnerstand? Me, you know what? I ain't even go near there, or a phone. I'm going home, snatch a bathing suit, and no one's gonna hear from me—two weeks, a month, even. That's if I can trust you to take care of something as simple as a dog."

"Dog'll be all right. You just lay off the booze. Lay around. Maybe even get yourself another checkup."

"Nah, I'm sounder 'an a dollar. . . ."

"You go to the supermarket, fuckin' dollar's more like a peso these days."

"Ain't it the truth."

"That's when I first realized I was getting old," I said. "First time I said to myself, 'I can remember when the dollar was worth a dollar.' "

"What I'm gonna do is get my stuff, go straight to the airport."

"Hey, partner, where you going?"

"You know what? I'm not gonna tell you. I tell you, you're gonna be all the time pestering me, to tell you how to do your job. Which you don't need no help to do, 'cause you can do it. As good or better than anyone. You remember that. And don't get into trouble. And don't let that go to your head. Me, I'm gonna go and fish a little. Also drop by and visit my wife for a couple of minutes, to remind myself that I don't like her."

"How about I drive you to the airport? Which one you leaving from?"

"I'll take care of it," he said.

"Please deposit another five cents for five more minutes," a machine said.

"Take good care that dog. Or I'll have your ass," he said, and hung up.

Two days later, Jerry Wirtman and I and Glenda and his attorney and our attorney met. We'd accepted Jerry's offer to finance the deal. There was still a $25,000 down payment, plus a $1,000 check for Pauline the lawyer. I didn't believe that she had that many billable hours on the job, and I thought we were being victimized by sisterhood. I wisely kept my mouth shut about it. Signatures were signed. Papers were witnessed, notarized, and sealed. Glenda seemed to hold her breath through the entire business. Everyone shook hands and congratulated.

Finally, when we were downstairs and out of the building, she breathed. She took my arm. "Oh, Tony, isn't it wonderful. I feel so much better. Our own place."

"Yeah," I said, "it's great. Lemme take you out, someplace nice, to celebrate. A nice dinner."

"But we just spent all that money," she said. "I couldn't. I couldn't add another dollar to that. I feel like, I don't know, happy, but I have to live up to it. Why don't we go home and I'll cook something special."

"I'll buy the champagne," I said. "Good stuff. Real French label."

"Wonderful," she said, hugging me closer.

I spent sixty-two dollars on a bottle. Over Glenda's protests. But what the hell, I was a guy who could afford conversion. A big shot.

"I feel so differently about it," she said when we walked into the apartment. She moved through it, looking at the walls, fixtures, furniture. A paint job and rebuilt kitchen were coming for certain. And more. It grew smaller and tighter around me. I knew what I was going to do. When night came, in the darkness, I would write a note and explain it all.

But I couldn't even wait that long. "I'll keep up the payments," I said. "I will. But I can't stay. I promise I'll keep up the payments."

She wanted to talk. Her first thought was that it was another woman. Would that it were. Her second, that it was a joke.

> No marital separation since I broke the story that Mary Pickford, America's sweetheart, was leaving Douglas Fairbanks had the effect of the parting of the Reagans. . . . Jane and Ronnie have always stood for so much that is right in Hollywood . . . that's why this hurts so much. That's why we are fighting so hard to make them realize that what seems to have come between them is not important enough to make their break final.
> LOUELLA PARSONS, *Photoplay*, April 1948

"Call it temporary, if you want. Yeah," I said, "call it temporary. To get used to the idea that my feet are nailed to the floor. That I'm set in concrete."

"If you're that crazy, we'll sell it," she said, tears streaming down her face. Mascara tracks. Why don't women wash before they weep?

"Just a couple of days or weeks or something. You know. I gotta take care of the dog."

"We'll sell it."

"No we won't," I said, pushing her arms off me. "We keep it. You keep it. I have to leave."

"Why? Why? Why?"

29.

Letter to the Times

Peace flooded through me.

Even when the inner dialogues began—was I right? was she wrong? am I bad? what else could I have done?—they halted of their own accord. A weight I hadn't known I carried, gone.

Maybe it would never have happened if Joey had not been away at the same time that the signing took place. Maybe it wouldn't have happened if we hadn't bought the apartment.

I did talk to Glenda the next day. I did one of those "just need my space for a little while, there's nothing wrong but I have to sort out my feelings" raps that women do so well. Since they do it, they believe in it. It's like selling to a salesman. When you're really sure you're insulting their intelligence, they're sold. What was I going to do? Tell the truth? The truth: We had met when I was down. Then, to stand up, I built a scaffold around you and Wayne. Then I put my hands on a crossbar and held myself up. I closed my nose to keep from snorting. That took a couple years. Then I thought I didn't need the support. I stepped out. Watch out for that first step; it's a killer. And I stepped right off the edge. So back I crawled. You still had the scaffold. You almost forgave. You never forgot, and that kept your center a little dryer than it used to be. Your tongue a little sharper. Your nerves more raw.

Reread the story. There's one line missing: "I fell in love." Cared. Liked. Respected. Owed. Needed. Used. Gave. Took. Lots of things.

252

But not that one thing—delirium? delusion? decision?—that transforms the rest, the daily days, the quarreling idiocies, the turned-down possibilities, into one long double helix of endearment.

Joey's apartment was available.

There I was. Happy to meet me. In an apartment that belonged to someone else. Alone but for someone else's dog.

Space. I just needed some space. That's what I told her.

In mid-July, *Time* said Geraldine Ferraro was "A Historic Choice." The next week the Los Angeles Olympics was "America's Moment." We had a couple of small cases, matrimonials. I put the other guys on them. Joey called a few times. I missed him. But when he returned I would have to move back with Glenda. I did see her. We drove up to see Wayne on parents' day. And pretended that nothing was wrong. I was good at it. I'd been doing it all along.

It was also possible that someone was following me. I twice saw a salt and pepper team behind me in a government-issued sedan. And I spotted Fergie the FBI gorilla on the street outside the office. If they were watching, they were being disappointed. The big case was going nowhere. I was reduced to following up a letter to the editor in the *New York Times* as a lead.

For Blacks: Friend or Fraud

I read with dismay, and amazement, the once again uncontradicted claim that Randolph Gunderson was ever a friend to the black race. Or friend to minority persons of any type. I am personally familiar with the period, "the early days before the Civil Rights Movement had begun to move," to which our Attorney General refers. I am personally familiar with his conduct during that period.

It was reprehensible. It was exploitive. It was consistent with his record today.

The standards of objective journalism should be no excuse for lazy journalism. Where are people who check the facts? Are this man's words to be accepted like biblical prophecy and not to be challenged? Or has your august journal, the newspaper of record, joined in the day's inversion of rhetoric in which war is called a peace initiative and racism is called civil rights?

Rev. C. D. Thompson, Sr.

Charles Dickens Thompson was getting on. He walked with a cane. A stout and sturdy, polished piece of wood. But his teeth were his own. And his voice was strong. He lived on Edgecombe Avenue, in Harlem.

It was a warm summer evening, the late light was gold. The brownstones on the block, which were built well, large and ornate, looked genteel and comforting. If the yuppie march north finally pushes white people over the invisible border, or money somehow comes into black hands, it will become prime real estate. I'd bet on the yuppies.

I showed him my news credentials. It was all it took.

"Umm-hmm. Oh, yes, I know Mr. Gunderson. Mr. Randolph Gunderson. Attorney at law. Attorney General of the United States." The soul needs music, the tongue loves glory; the reverend was a Baptist. Words came like the Lord's own flood. I didn't hear the amens, but the amens were there, like a cadence in the air. "Oh, yes, indeed. I bought a home from Mr. Gunderson. I lost a home to Mr. Gunderson. And that home no longer stands. The land on which it was built barely stands. It is as a land sown with salt. A wealth and a richness made desert. Oh, yes, I do know Mr. Gunderson.

"Those were the days when we walked with our heads bowed low. We had Robeson, we had Robinson, we had Louis, Joe Louis, in the ring. But it was 'yassuh,' 'nosuh,' and you had Jim Crow. There was Truman, who integrated the Army. Yes, sir—said a black man was fit to die with a gun in his hand in that Korean conflict, on an Asian land. Something that even Mister Roosevelt didn't dare to do. Black was black, white was white.

"Then there was Mister Earl Warren; you know they still, still curse his name. The white men who hate the black men. Because it was Mr. Warren who said 'separate but equal is not equal.' When a man sees the truth he is blessed. When he speaks the truth, he is a pariah. Mr. Earl Warren dared to say that a black child is a child just like a white child. That we must teach him. That we must allow him books. Teach him numbers. Mathematics. History. Even science. Imagine, a black child, beside a white child, delving in a text of physics. Quantum mechanics. Nuclear theory.

"Dr. King dared to dream. We dared to dream. I dared to dream.

"My dream was to lift my family out of poverty. Which I did. You see their pictures there, on the wall. Yes, see them there on the wall. My son Charles Dickens Thompson, Jr., lieutenant colonel in the United States Air Force. In uniform . . ."

I looked as he pointed. They were studio portraits. Posed. Paid for. Pridefully maintained.

"Joshua Paul Thompson, in uniform, first lieutenant, United States Marines, died in action in Vietnam. My daughter, Mary, who teaches high school in San Francisco, California. Her husband is a college professor at the University of California.

"My dream was to take my children out of the ghetto. Away from the evils of the streets. Into a clean place, a clean and well-kept place, high in aspirations. Not rich in material things, but wealthy with dreams, with the coin of ambition.

"That's how I met Mister Gunderson. Randolph Gunderson, Attorney at law. And through the blindness of my desire, through the desperation of my hopes, through the greatness of my need to do right by my issue, I became a pawn for his evil.

"Evil. I do call it evil. A harsh word. A strong word. But a biblical word and the right word. Randolph Gunderson is a man of evil.

"I tried to buy a home in a good neighborhood. When I came to look, they jeered at me. They threw stones and bottles at me. They scandalized me. And they would not sell to me, for no matter how green my dollar was, my skin was blacker.

"Then Mr. Gunderson came to me. How he found my name, how he knew my aspirations, I do not know. But he came to me. He made me an offer. He would buy a house for me. Of course, I could not see it, except perhaps to drive by, but he would buy a house for me. With his white face. And my green money.

"Of course he made a profit. I expected him to make a profit: ten percent, fifteen percent. I don't know how much profit he made, but I know that it was more than twenty-five. I know that it was more than thirty. It may have been fifty. Fifty percent profit. On a transaction for which he risked not a nickel."

It was more than Thompson could afford. Gunderson helped arrange financing. At a point or two over the market. Thompson went for it.

And Mr. Thompson was not the only black family that Gunderson assisted. He liked to bring in two per block. They called it block busting. It was in the interest of the real estate dealers to fan the flames of fear.

Get the residents to panic and sell at panic prices. The middlemen made out very well.

But the prices were high enough that a lot of the purchasers were certain to default. Then the brokers, or the lawyers, or the banks, would repossess and resell. Very quickly, the buyers, in order to make the mortgages, broke up one-family homes into two or three apartments. Or rooming houses. The prophecy that blacks would bring down property values was self-fulfilling. Half of the Bronx, hunks of Queens, huge chunks of Brooklyn, went down the tubes.

"He was there when we bought, he was there when we sold, and in the end, when there was nothing else left to take, when the udder had been milked dry, when the land had been overplanted, he burned it down for the insurance.

"He burned so many down."

"Mr. Thompson," I asked, "can you prove that?" Because if he could, we had Gunderson.

"If I had proof, oh, if the good Lord had placed proof in my two hands, legal proof, evidence of the sort that brings weight in the courts of law, then Mr. Gunderson would long ago have gone to a better place for such as he."

"It's a serious charge," I said.

"We in the black community, we are not surprised by it. Oh, no. It's part of the language. Up here, out there on the streets, they call it 'Jew lightning.' You ask what happened, when the family is standing naked on the streets, their pitiful collection of material goods char and ashes, smoke and ruin, before their eyes. They say, 'Hymie the landlord was smokin' his cigar.' But that's a form of racism too. Gunderson was not a Jew.

"Randolph Gunderson. Let him be as full of fear, as full of despair, as full of care, as I was when the bank came and foreclosed on my hard-won home, when the bank came and confiscated all my worldly goods, when his bank came and made me bankrupt, with three babes in my wife's arms, Lord rest her weary soul.

"I have something greater than proof. I have the truth."

I didn't tell him the truth was nothing. He already knew that.

Or that racism is not a lawbook crime. That exploitation is not a crime. Buying low and selling high is a virtue. Real estate speculation is the national sport. George Washington preferred it to fox hunting.

I needed an indictable offense.

Which arson is. It is also one of the most difficult crimes to prove. It was worse when it happened twenty years ago.

It was dark when I finally left. And warmer rather than cooler. The breeze was dead. The air sat. There were a bunch of kids on one stoop, laughing and sassing. Across from them, two men drank from a wine bottle, while a momma fed the infant on her lap with a bottle. A large, shirtless teenager danced with a fifteen-pound tape deck on his shoulder. He shone with sweat, and rap screamed down the block. I saw the tight blue pattern of flame from a butane torch reflected in an automobile window. Someone was squatting between the cars, sucking up a crack pipe. There was a silver Mercedes with smoked windows down where I had parked. Four or five brothers were hanging around the driver's side, looking for action.

I walked up the block.

The minute they turned toward me, I knew. It was in their walk, in their eyes. Dark, shiny eyes that thought four on one was fun. They were gonna get some manhood by cutting pieces out of mine.

They spread, two to cut me off, two to get around behind me. The headlamps on the Mercedes flicked on. An invisible man behind the smoked-glass windows put it in gear and it purred slowly down the street, leaving me to his friends.

SCENARIO #1

Q: So four guys walked across the street, more or less in your direction?

A: Correct.

Q: Then you pulled a gun?

A: Correct.

Q: I see. Did they have weapons? I mean, visible to you?

A: One had a baseball bat.

Q: He was also in a sweatshirt. With a team name on it. So he might have been hanging out after a game in the park?

A: I didn't think so.

Q: Now, did any of these four hit you?

A: No.

Q: Throw something?

A: No.

Q: Utter threats?

A: No.

Q: Did you know any of these people previously?

A: No.

Q: Four guys, actually two groups of two, cross the street, at a walk, carrying no weapons, except possibly a baseball bat, which might well have been used for playing baseball. They do not commit battery, assault, or even say anything to you. Then you draw a .38 caliber revolver and begin firing. You kill one and injure two.

A: Wait a minute. You don't understand. I knew by the look in their eyes.

Q: Tell me, Mr. Cassella, are you in the habit of committing murder because people walk across the street? Did you think that that side of the street was yours?

A: I mean, what it is, if I waited for them to get close enough to assault me, four to one, it would have been all over, the other way. I was the intended victim.

Q: Or is it because they were black and you have some paranoid racist fantasy that all black people are criminal assailants? This is not South Africa. This is not Nazi Germany. We don't permit that, Mr. Cassella. Which is why you're under indictment for murder.

SCENARIO #2

Witness: Well, Officer, dey was dis whiteman, don' know what all he's doin' here. He jus' bobbing along, you know. They they's these brothers, you know, they's on the other side of the avenue. Up and a sudden the whiteman, he starts flyin'. He's screamin', "Feets, don't fail me now," or some such. I don' unnerstan', you dig. Then they's these other dudes, brothers, you dig, you hear me, man, they start goin' after the whiteman. Don' ast me whys, I don' know whys, alls I knows is they's flyin' behind. Until they catch him, 'cause you know no whiteman go'n beat four brothers in no foot race. Get one of them Ferrari cars maybe outruns the brothers. Anyways, then he was dead meat. Right there. Dead meat. I sees it. . . . Who they was? I don' know nobody. Not me, Officer, I don' know none those people. Prob'bly from Jersey, Georgia, someplace like that, you dig.

SCENARIO #3

With one hand I drew my gun, flicked the safety off, and pulled the hammer back. With the other, I pulled out my wallet. I flopped it open like I was showing my shield. Little bits of paper fell out. Receipts. I didn't bend down to collect them.

"Don't even fucking think about it," I said.

They stopped. All four of them. Their eyes locked on me. The way a Doberman stares when his master says, "Watch him!" I put my wallet back but kept my piece out. "You two," I said to the brothers on my left, "beat it. You," I said to the ones on my right, the ones between me and my vehicle, "up against the car. Assume the fuckin' position. You know the fuckin' position. You been there."

They had. They knew. They did.

I edged around them, keeping my eye on the other two, who strutted extra slow, just to show they weren't intimidated. Fine. When the strutters were far enough away that they couldn't cause me trouble, I moved in on the two leaning against the car. I kicked their legs wider apart and made sure they were too off balance to move. Then I started patting down the first of the two. I tossed his wallet on the ground. There was a big hunk of metal in his front pocket. A Saturday Night Special. I relieved him of it. As I moved to the next one, someone yelled, "White motherfucker," and something hit me hard as hell in the lower back. I stumbled into the second guy. His hands slipped off the car roof and he started crashing down. His legs tangled in mine, and I went down on one knee.

Half a brick sailed over my head and through the car window. I got my gun around and just about fired at two kids. They were no older than Wayne. "Motherfucking whitey," they yelled, running away.

259

I didn't have time to sigh with relief for what I hadn't done, when the first guy hit me in the head. Which was really stupid. He broke his hand. Which is what usually happens if you hit someone's skull hard enough.

It knocked me to the side. That was good too. Because the guy below me was waving a blade. Whatever part of me he was aiming at, he missed. His forearm and fist hit my shoulder. I saw the blade. It made me really angry. I shoved backward hard, using the full power of my legs and all my weight. He slammed into the car with a grunt, a thud, and a moan. I turned my gun on the other one, who was moaning over his busted knuckles. His eyes went wide and his mouth went slack.

God, I wanted to shoot him. He saw it and started to scramble backward, waving his good hand in front of him, like it would ward off a bullet. The son of a bitch beneath me was still trying to stab me. I stumbled around out of his range, then kicked his arm. He dropped the knife.

My arm was wet. I realized he had cut me. With my mind screaming "Nigger"—yes, the garbage of the world catches up with me—I stomped his hand. Stomped it hard. To hurt the bastard. Then I shoved the gun in his face.

"Oh, man, oh, you motherfucker—I wanna make you eat this. I wanna make you swallow a fucking bullet and fucking die! You hear me? Now tell me who the fuck told you to come at me."

"Don' know."

I tapped his head with the gun. Just like a real cop would. Seething, boiling, sick with rage. He moaned and put his good hand to his skull. I hit him across the knuckles. That hurt even more.

"Don' know the man. White man."

"What'd he want?"

"Said to hurt you, hurt you bad."

"Pay you?"

"Yo, he pay. He pay."

"Show me," I said.

He tried to pull out less than what he had. I snatched at his pocket and came up with two hundred-dollar bills. I kept them. Two hundred each, eight hundred total. The man in the Mercedes had wanted me more than hurt. "You were supposed to off me," I said.

"Hurts bad's what he say. Hurts bad."

Somebody had been following me. And wanted to stop me. Why now? Because of Reverend Thompson? The attack gave his information a whole lot of weight. A whole lot. "Stupid motherfucker," I said about the Mercedes white man. "He paid retail."

There were sirens. Someone had maybe called the police. So I left the guy who'd cut me there and walked away. Though the sirens could have been going somewhere else entirely.

Some guys like to kill. Some like to hurt. A lot of people take comfort in despising other people for the where or way they're born. My daddy raised me different. I thought. So where did the garbage that had filled me come from? It was a white man set them on me. Why was I seeing niggers? Why do we do that?

The adrenaline goes sour afterward. It turns into adrenochrome. That makes you feel sick. Nauseous. I swallowed it down, but I tasted myself. Tasted my garbage.

I stopped in front of a deli as soon as I got far enough south for the streets to be white. I took a look at my arm before I went in. It was all right, but a mess. I went in and bought a roll of antacids and some aspirin. The guy behind the counter kept looking at my arm and wondering about its connection to antacids. I was close to home. My real home. The one with Glenda.

Then I decided to go to my other home. The one with the dog.

30.

Je Ne Regrette Rien

" 'Ello," she said, dropping the *h* that doesn't exist in French. "Do you remember me?" Which I absolutely did. "I am in New York now. I have just made the arrival."

"Where are you?" I asked.

"At an 'otel, with my friend."

"Oh, which friend?" I asked. Not because I knew Marie's friends, but to find out if it was Jean-Paul, Jean-Luc, Jean-Claude, or one of the other hyphenated Jeans.

"Valerie," she said, to my great relief, but added, "and Jean-Claude."

Jean-Claude turned out to be Valerie's. He wanted, mostly, to go to Tower Records to buy unpleasant rock 'n' roll albums. I met them that afternoon and did the walking tour of Central Park. The next day I took them on the Staten Island ferry, the world's cheapest sea voyage. On the ride out, they stared at Lady Liberty. On the way back, as the sun came down over Jersey, magic-hour light painted the towers of the World Trade Center low gold, and the stubby skyscrapered tip of the stockbrokers' city looked like the closing credits for the world's best urban love story.

I watched her black curls dancing in the breeze and stared at her Anna Magnani face.

We went to Little Italy for dinner. The East Village for music. Which, being young, they adored.

She had gone to college but hadn't finished.

She told me about the man she had gone out with, whom she left for the man she fell in love with, who went back to the woman on whom he had fathered two children. A man, a girl, a boy, a heart or two broken. It was sad, it was amusing, and every time her eyes met mine, Edith Piaf sang *"Non, Je Ne Regrette Rien."*

So now she had no boyfriend.

"A girl like you," I said, "must have many boys. If I were in Paris, I would chase you."

"Paris is not good for a girl," she said. "All the boys like the boys. It is terrible. . . ." She stuck out her tongue, a pretty tongue. "Terrible." New York women say the same about New York. But with the wrong accent, it just sounds like whining.

"In New York, the boys look more at the girls, I think so," she said. Her eyes said more. But no more than *"peut-être,"* not "yes," not yet.

She did not particularly like her job, selling cosmetics. But for her a job was a means to money. She didn't need a Career in order to stamp the ticket that would validate her stop in the parking lot of life. Maybe it was because her English was not so good and my French was nonexistent, so we could not discuss subtleties, but I sensed a simpler version of life. A more secure sense of identity. Boys were boys, girls were girls, life was for living, it didn't have to be measured against Cybill Shepherd's wardrobe.

The case went on. Slow, plodding, frustrating. But at least the search had a focus. Arson.

Thompson was very willing to talk to me a second time. He liked to talk. I brought Miles Vandercour with me, and his maps. Which buildings did Thompson think Gunderson had owned? Which had been disposed of by fire? Miles also asked the reverend if he knew about any similar situations in the East New York section of Brooklyn. Miles had been tracking another set of probable Gunderson properties over there.

No matter what, I would have checked Reverend Thompson's story. But when we hit dead end after dead end, which we did, I would have dropped it and turned my attention to something else, if it had not been for the attack. Someone was trying to keep me from something. It gave the search a sense of surety.

The fifth night, listening to blues on Second Avenue, I put my arm around her. When I pulled her to me, her mouth turned to mine.

Then Marie-Laure came home with me.

It was straightforward and awkward, both.

She was twenty-two. Heavy breasts, full bottom, too much flesh for mannequin magazines. All of it firm and all of her strong. Her kisses were soft and her breath fragrant. Her pubic hair was thick and black. The taste of her was fresh and clean.

The next night the awkward part was gone. We fell asleep entangled. There was no light from the windows, no sound from the streets, when she woke me with soft wet kisses on my back and shoulders. I turned to her, my mouth still acrid with sleep. But it didn't matter to her. She was fresh enough for both of us. Her flesh was warm and solid. She opened to me. It was so damn simple. August city heat wrapped us, and sweated us, slick and sliding. And it was good.

We ate breakfast at the Greek diner around the corner, and I dropped a hundred dollars buying her dinner. One was as right as the other.

There was one small ax that was waiting to fall.

Joey would be coming back to his apartment. It would transform this casual drift through a humid season into a real, and cold, decision.

He called a couple of times—from Arizona, where he went to see his kids and grandkids. He liked the look of the land, he said, but he didn't sound happy. And from Florida, where he was fishing and had said hello to his ex-wife—without any indication of when he was returning.

The city was my city again. Showing it to Marie gave it back to me. Summer heat. Languor waiting to ripen to the color of lurid. And I was seeing the women. There's this natural urban cycle, as clear and dramatic as anything that happens to the trees in the hills of New England. But in reverse. In spring the trees put on leaves and hide their shape. The women peel their coverings and shapes emerge— breasts, buttocks, and cinched waists. As it gets warmer, while the leaves grow thicker, the shirts and skirts get thinner and shorter. Flesh appears, toes and ankles to as high as the thigh, bare midriffs, shoulders, and halves of breasts.

I hadn't been noticing. For years. Glenda's commands had closed me down more than I was aware.

Even when Marie and Valerie were off to Wyoming for a week to see cowboys and mountains, I didn't lose that sense that this is a garden of earthly delights, lavishly flowered.

Even when I had lunch with Glenda, the sense of pleasure remained. I could see, for the first time in a long time, how pretty she was. Her hair was as black as Marie's, but very different. It tumbled in rich, careful curls to frame her face, accentuating the whiteness of her skin and the fine-boned Welsh witchery of her features: small, straight nose, delicate lips over small, even teeth, and startled gray eyes. I told her how lovely she looked. Which she did. She'd meant to.

She was tentative, and angry underneath. I was at my most charming and gracious. I told her, again, that it was the shock of being a property owner that got to me. That I just needed time. Besides, I had to take care of Mario. And I swore fervently that there was no other woman. Then I swore it again. We got cozy. Over one slice of cheesecake with two forks, I suggested that we take the afternoon off.

"Cute, very cute," she said. "And a tiny bit tempting."

"Only a tiny bit?"

"Yes. When you're good, you're very good. And it has been a long, long time. But I do have to be at work this afternoon."

"How about tonight?"

"Tonight," she said with great delight, "I have plans."

"Cut-in-stone, unbreakable plans? Something I couldn't coax you out of?"

"Well, if I'd known that tonight was the night that you wanted me to be at your beck and call," she said a little bit sharply, though not nearly as acidly as I probably deserved, "I'm sure I would have kept myself free. But that's what happens when people need their space."

"OK, OK," I said.

"You certainly didn't expect me to sit home alone every night and wait, did you?"

"Well . . ." I said. Though the idea of her going out was not unappealing. It would clear what little conscience I had. "Seeing somebody, are you?"

"That's none of your business," she said archly.

"How about tomorrow night?" I asked, actually feeling desire.

"Call me, in the afternoon, and we'll see," she said. "I have to check."

"I will," I said, reaching below the table to take her hand. Labor Day was coming. When Wayne would return. I would have to find my way back home by then or find a way to tell her the break was final. If I could think of some way to explain it to Wayne, which was altogether more difficult. Her hand was trembling.

We kept working in pairs. Me and Farrell or Mario in the Bronx. Mazzolli with DeVito in Brooklyn. They scored first.

Mazzolli took me to see Mrs. Mary Murphy, a widow of seventy-eight. She spoke with the brogue mixed with the Brooklyn. "I seen it," she said, "no matter how they try to lie about it. I seen it. They did their dirty deed in the night. It was in the summer, like it is now. It was August," she said.

"When? What year?" Mazzolli prompted.

"The dog days," Mary Murphy said. "We didn't have the air conditioner, the like of which I have now. My Brian, he was asleep, from working all day on the ships. Backbreaking work it was, not like being a policeman, like my uncle and my father's cousins, and it took a real man to do it. But at least he had the sleep at night from a clear conscience. August of '74.

"It was terrible hot, so I went out on the fire escape, for the air. Of which there was precious little. A man come running out the back door of the building across the way."

"Across the street?" Mazzolli asked her.

"No, out the back. Just across the way. In the middle of the night it was, and he was running. It was clear to anyone with half an intelligence that he was up to no good. No good at all.

"Now it's forgetting my manners I am. Would you like some tea?"

Her little apartment was neat as a pin and very busy. Saints and doilies. Tea in a proper pot, with a creamer, and plain cookies on sale from the A&P.

"Tell us about the man," Mazzolli said, while he stirred in a spoon of sugar. "The man who ran out the back."

"He was a terrible man. I knew who he was. One of those eyetalian devils. One of those who interfered with my Brian at the docks. A terrible beating he took from them once. I'm no informer, but I went to

266

the Brian that was my uncle and his cousins and I had a few words with them, I did, about such and like, and it never did happen again."

"Who was he, Mary?" Mazzolli said gently. Mazzolli was convinced that he had a special way of relating to old ladies. That was because his mother still loved him.

"I knew him," she said. "It was a terrible thing. All those babies. Wee little tots. The screaming and the crying, the weeping and sadness. I could feel the heat on my own face, I could. There was the O'Quinns. Her husband was a bit of a brute, when he had the drink in him, but she was all right to my way of thinking, with the baking and such for St. Mary's. There was the Fazios; the husband, he was eyetalian, but she was Irish. Everybody said that wouldn't work, mixing the two, but it wasn't so bad. No worse than mixing with a Jew, certainly. They had three children. All three got out, but one had the burns all over the face. The girl, more's the pity; on a boy, ugliness doesn't matter so much. Lots of ugly men there are, in the Department and on the docks, making a fine living. But who wants to marry a girl that you can only look at with the lights out?"

"There was a fire," Mazzolli said, "after the man ran out?"

"Oh, there most certainly was. Right after. The man came running out of the basement, I saw him, and not more than five minutes later there was flames a-roaring up from the bottom to the top. A terrible fire.

"It was me what called the Fire Department. I had a cousin of me own over in the Fire Department. But it wasn't him that come. He was in a station way over in Canarsie. Michael his name was. A fine big man, but lazy. A Flaherty. The Flahertys are like that.

"I talked to him later, Michael Flaherty, about the whole affair, when I seen him at the wedding of his brother Frank and that Cavanaugh girl from over Jersey City. And Michael, he says that it must've been kerosene, providing it was true that I smelled what I smelled, which I thought was gasoline. It was almost an explosion like, it was that fast."

"Mary," Mazzolli said, "how many died?"

"It was three that died," she said, and sniffed. "Little Patrick Cavanaugh, eighteen months, a lovely little lad. Reddish hair like his mother, and curly. It was because they were on the first floor. In the apartment that was directly above the fire, do you see. And two next door. I didn't know them. They was Puerto Rican people. Garcia, maybe. All of them, they call themselves Garcia.

"It wasn't in the fire precisely that they had their death. It was later, in the hospital, from the terrible burns that covered all the parts of their bodies. It was from them sleeping naked. Otherwise just their faces would have burned away."

"Do you know who owned the building?" I asked.

"It was the landlord owned the building. They own all the buildings," she said.

"It was a Gunderson building. It's on Vandercour's list," Mazzolli said to me. Then very gently he spoke to Mary. "The last time I saw you, Mary, you told me you had a name for the man you saw running out of the building."

"Oh, I knew him, all right. I don't know his proper Christian name, but for certain I know what it was that they called him. He was one of those wicked kind that won't use their own name, for if they were to see themselves with their own name that their mother and their father gave to them, they would die from the shame of it."

"Yes, they would," Mazzoli said. "So what was the nickname?"

"It was 'The Wrecker' he called himself."

> Suddenly the bass came in again like John Henry driving steel and the treble notes ran through the night like the patter of rain.
>
> CHESTER HIMES, *The Heat's On*

Santino "The Wrecker" Scorcese.

The drinks were on me. We gathered up Miles and DeVito and Farrell and sat down to drink a few and congratulate each other. Not that we had a case. Just that at last we had something.

DeVito kept up on mob gossip. Not as well as Joey, but OK. He pointed out that there wasn't much to connect Scorcese and Gunderson before '74.

"I think maybe that cemented things between them," I said. "This is the way I figured it set up. Gunderson's got landlord-tenant problems. So he contacts someone—I don't know who—to take care of it. At that point, Santino 'The Wrecker' Scorcese is just a soldier. Maybe even a free lance. I mean, I don't think this was the first. I think maybe it goes back further.

"But in this one, three people died. And Scorcese, who is pretty smart and ambitious, he uses that to move himself closer to Gunderson. It's after that that he starts participating in real estate deals. Like that New Jersey Revival Corporation thing out in Jersey.

"Even though we don't have the death penalty in New York—"

"You can blame that on our Italian governor, Mario Cuomo," Farrell said. "Can't even fry a cop-killer."

"It was a matter of conscience. Which I don't agree with, but I respect," DeVito said, "which is more than your Irish politician ever heard of."

"Important point, DeVito," I said. "Anyway, Scorcese is not going to talk about a murder he committed. Unless he happened to have immunity. Which he might have had with the special prosecutor's grand jury. Which is when the intermediary, the capo or whatever, gets nervous and wants to make sure Santino doesn't talk. He sends Felacco and Ventana to communicate through Arthur.

"Unless of course," I said, "Gunderson and Scorcese were dealing direct all along, and I'm just making things too complicated."

"The only thing wrong with the theory," Miles Vandercour said, "is that the record does not support it. Yes. Thompson's house did eventually burn down. But he no longer owned it by then. And neither did Randolph Gunderson. Yes, the apartment building behind Mrs. Murphy's building burned down. There was an investigation into each." He had his brief-case, which would have done for someone else's traveling bag. Thorough man that he was, he dredged out copies of the arson reports.

"The cause of the fire in the Thompson home," Miles said, "which had been converted to an SRO or boardinghouse, was determined to be a cigarette. One of the tenants fell asleep, smoking in bed. The autopsy indicated opiates in the body."

"Another fucking junkie," Mazzolli said. "That's such a junkie thing to do, nod out and sleep through your own death."

"The arson investigation of the apartment building behind Mrs. Murphy's shows the cause of the fire to be electrical. Loose wiring, caused by a tenant tapping into a building line to steal electricity."

31.

The Tortoise

Another theory blown out by reality. I had to tell Straightman about it. He was already tense from rerunning Ronald Reagan commercials on his VCR. He made me watch with him.

> Just about every place you look, things are looking
> up. Life is better—America's back—and people have
> a sense of pride they never thought they'd feel again.
> And so it's not surprising that just about everyone in
> town is thinking the same thing: Now that our coun-
> try is turning around, why would we ever go back?
>
> Reagan campaign commercial

Am I really that good?

RONALD REAGAN, seeing campaign commercial

It was driving John to drink. Not that afternoon, particularly, but at least since Mondale's nomination, and it showed. Broken blood vessels and puffiness in his face.

"It's the stress," he said. "Of telling the truth and watching nobody listen. Television and truth are so confused that dealing with facts, it's like kicking a river of molasses. You get sticky stuff all over you, and the gunk rolls on."

The commercial that bothered the congressman most was "The Postman." It was filmed in one darn cute town, and the postman, who's a warm and friendly ol' cuss, he's delivering the Social Security checks, with the new increase. The one that Ronald Reagan fought tooth and nail. Then the friendly ol' cuss of a postman, he tells all us folks that Ronnie should get the credit for the increase.

"We're close," I said. "We almost had him, but it slipped away."

"Christ," he said. "You been watching what they're doing to Ferraro? This tax thing. Not her own taxes. Her husband's taxes. And the press is crawling all over her. They won't let up. It's front-page. Every day. No matter what Reagan does, it doesn't matter. Just once, just once, I'd like to read a headline, instead of 'President Says,' it would say 'President Lies Today.' That's objective journalism."

"I thought I had him," I said, "Gunderson. But it slipped away."

"There's something strange going on in America. Television is reality. You ever been on TV?"

"Not much. You know, once or twice, during the Correction Department thing."

"Are you going to get Gunderson, or am I just wasting time and money?" he said.

"The Ferraro thing," I said. I desperately did not want him to give up. "What it shows is that you've been right all along. Look at the way the media's onto it. It shows that if we throw the press the right bone, they'll gnaw on it and keep on gnawing until they get to the marrow, and if there isn't any marrow, they'll keep dragging at it and kicking it around anyway. As long as it's the right bone."

"I want to think it's true," he said.

"This is America. Dreams do come true," I said. "Tape at eleven."

That was sheer bravado. We kept on keeping on. But it was makework. We were dead in the water.

I returned to the arson reports, again and again, because that's where the investigation had died. I couldn't see anything wrong with them. But they didn't feel right. Miles said it was his job to find them, not critique them. DeVito shrugged and said, "I did twenty years on the force. Homicide for ten. You know, I never hardly seen an arson report before."

"Me neither," Mazzolli said. "Arson, we turn that over to the dalmatian-and-slicker set."

"I got a couple o' cousins, Farrells," Farrell said, "in the FD. I could maybe ask them."

"It's been said," DeVito said, "that the Irish is the dumbest race in the world."

"Do I gotta hear this again?" Farrell said.

"And the indisputable proof of this," DeVito said, "is that if you read the names of the firemen, all you got is Murphy, O'Brien, Callahan, Farrell. And it is an exceedingly dumb thing to want to spend your life walking into burning buildings."

I needed someone to whom an arson report would mean something. Tonto. The story, as I remembered it, was that the Indian had saved the Lone Ranger. The Indian felt obligated by that. That was why he followed the masked man from movie set to movie set. It made sense when I was six, and no one has questioned it since. So I called Owen Levy, the fireman who dragged me from my inferno.

We met for breakfast at Junior's, in downtown Brooklyn.

Without his slicker and boots, the big black man looked just as big and just as black. "The best breakfast special in town," Owen said. He ordered juice, coffee, a three-egg onion omelet with home fries. He smacked his lips over the juice. "I likes my OJ fresh. I bought a squeezer for the station."

"I used to come here. Me and my two best friends, Kenny and Petey. When we were kids. Three of us and one banana split," I said, wondering if they were still as big as they seemed back then.

The waitress knew Owen. She was generous with the potatoes. The basket of rolls and miniature Danish was heaped with the fireman's favorites. "Sometimes, when I got weekdays off—they don't have the special on weekends—I wakes the kids early. Oh, they bitch and moan, 'Here come Daddy and one of his breakfasts.' And I bring 'em all here. Before school. Once they're here, they enjoys it. Especially the Danish. Kids like sweet stuff. Me too."

"How many kids you got?"

"Three," he said. "One thing good about being a fireman. When you're on, you know you got to live in the station. Round the clock. But when you is off, you is off. Which means I got lots of time with my children. To make sure they're doing right. To make sure they're doing their homework."

"They in public school?" I asked.

"No. I got 'em in parochial school."

"You're Catholic?" I asked him. "I figured you Baptist being black or Jewish being Levy."

"For the discipline. I can't afford no private school 'cept parochial school. St. Agnes—the kids calls it Saint Anguish—costs me three-fifty a semester. A real private school, that's three, four long a year. Not for a fireman, not with three kids. I'm sort of a lapsing Baptist. It's a money thing, St. Agnes."

"There's a case I'm working on, involves arson." I handed him the reports. They spanned twelve years; the last was Mary Murphy's fire in 1974.

"I don't know what I can tell you about this. I'm a grunt. A hose, an ax, and suck the smoke. Arson, that's a very technical matter. The arson investigators are scientists. They can look at ash, put it under a microscope, tell you what it used to be, what temperature it ignited at, and how long it took to get from a thing to ash."

Nonetheless, he looked. He read ponderously, every word, from the date at the top to the signature at the end, dark eyes moving in stops and starts, heavy lips forming soundless words. It was like watching a prisoner tunnel out of the Château d'If with a spoon.

He paid no attention when the waitress cleared away.

We sat there for close to two hours. I had a certain admiration for a willingness to work that hard, though I couldn't understand how anyone could read that slow. It was a condescending admiration.

"What do you think?" I said when he was finally done. "Is there anything wrong with them?"

"Sometimes, when you go in, you know. You smell the paraffin or kerosene or gasoline. But when all you're looking at is cold, dead ash, that's a different thing. That's why arson investigators, they are experts. I can't tell how good this guy is. You're investigating this guy, right? On behalf of an insurance company?"

"Something like that," I said. "In spite of the different names, all the buildings were owned by the same guy."

"Oh," he said. "I thought you were maybe after the guy did the reports."

"No," I said. "The owner."

"That's the only thing I noted," he said, shaking his head, disappointed. "That all the reports, they were done by the same man."

"What's that?" I said, finally hearing him.

"All of these reports, they were done by the same man."

The turtle had just beat the hare.

The dead end had turned into a new lead. Ralph S. McGarrity. Investigator in the Bronx, according to the title below his signature, promoted to inspector after his transfer to Brooklyn. The reports were a second pattern. The fires—at least the ones we knew of—had moved with him.

When I got back to the office, Eddie Alfoumado was there. On his knees among plaster and paint dust. Digging out microphones. He'd found three. There was also a tap on the phone.

32.

Mortgage Payments

Alfoumado was back the next day, trying to sell me an entire counterespionage system: sonic alarms, minicams with minicorders, a safe with a computer-generated random-access code, and a secure phone system. All of this could be done for a mere $26,947.95, including an extended warranty and service contract, plus sales tax. Only 10 percent down, two years to pay. Or I could enjoy the tax advantages of leasing.

I asked him if he could determine, from the equipment, who had put it in. He couldn't. There was no way to know if it had been the FBI, the Friends of Santino Scorcese, or Glenda.

He talked me into the secure telephone system. But I balked at the rest. It was time, I decided, for Mario to earn his Alpo. Whatever his failings, he was large, loud when he wanted to be, and he had lots of teeth. No one was going to spend an hour or two installing microphones in carefully concealed positions with a full-sized German shepherd prowling about.

Then I went to lunch with Glenda.

She looked great, especially when anger lit up her eyes. She thought I should shit or get off the pot. It was about time. August 28. Six days before Labor Day. The day Wayne would be home. Home to us together. Or to some very difficult explanations.

"Maybe what I needed was to get away for a while," I said. Stalling, still stalling. "So I could learn to appreciate you more." If I did go home, I wanted us to be able to live together. Part of me liked living alone. I could breathe. But life needs a center. But there was Wayne.

"Lots of men think they would like to appreciate me," she said. "You're not the only one enjoying a little space."

"Have you spoken to Wayne?" I said. "I called him at camp a couple of days ago. He sounded like he's having a good time."

"You're not jealous? You're not wondering what I do when you're not home? I've been going to the beach a lot. With some friends, in the Hamptons."

"I have the money for next month's apartment stuff. Mortgage and maintenance," I said.

"It's great out there. A little tennis. I tried wind-surfing, but mostly lying on the beach and going to parties. It's nice to know this body is still competitive."

"That it is. More than competitive. It's enticing. It's desirable."

"What are we going to do?" she asked. "Never mind. I wasn't going to ask that. I was going to be cool. I've been doing a lot of self-exam-ination. I realize that . . . that my background . . . that I'm a much more uptight person than you are. That's the mistake I've made, isn't it? Being too tense. Too clinging. Well, I've been changing."

"That's OK. You don't have to change. There's nothing wrong with you."

"Yes there is. I've . . . I've gone out with a couple of other men. I want you to know that. And I think it's making me a better person. Not that I want to keep doing that, if, when, if you come back. But I thought you should know. I want things open and honest between us."

"I think . . . Wayne's back at the end of Labor Day weekend, and we'll . . . figure this out by then. I promise. You know, one way or another. Damn, you look good today."

"There's something else you should know," she said. "I fucked one of them."

"Oh," I said.

"Not a relationship. Nothing serious. A very good-looking young man, though. He's from Argentina. A student. On his school soccer team. He's only twenty-two. I was pleased that a twenty-two-year-old boy would be excited by me. So I did what I think you would have done," she said. Part nervous, part brave, part defiant. "I had myself a piece of ass."

"Oh," I said.

"Well, I thought it would help me understand who you are and your type of behavior."

"And did you like it?" I asked.

"I did and I didn't. The truth is, you've spoiled me for other men. But I'm glad to have done it. Just doing it, impulsively, because I wanted to, to score. That was exciting. I see where that might matter to men. So you see, I am changing."

"I see that," I said, "if it's important to you. Look, let's plan on being together Saturday and sort this out." I handed her the checks. Funny, paying the money seemed to be my ticket, in or out. It would lock me in or be the sop to my conscience when I didn't go back.

Either way, I was going to need the $100,000.

33.

So Simple

" 'Ello" Marie-Laure said. " 'Ow are you?"

"Where are you?" I said, thinking: Be 'ere.

" 'Ere. At the airport, Kennedy Airport. Our plane has just made the arrival."

Does the well-lived life need a center? Does adulthood mean responsibility and manhood mean property? "Get in a cab," I said. "Come to the office." Was she my last dalliance before I admitted that my destiny was to be the co-owner of a condo? Or was she the first dalliance in a life of renewed dissipation.

"I will take the train to the plane—from the plane. A taxi is too expensif."

I had to go meet Straightman. "I will leave the keys to the apartment at the office. Come get them. Go to the apartment. Take a shower. Take a nap. Wait for me."

"OK," she said.

"Je t'adore," I said.

"Ah, oui?" A question mark curled on the end. It had me seeing the loose black curls that fell across her forehead, and the liquid eyes that always seemed to add whole stories to simple sentences.

Straightman had his attorney, Dick Gerstein, at the meeting. Gerstein and I had met before, when John had his problems with coke and then with the underage girls. As far as I was concerned, I was the one who had saved the congressional ass and Gerstein was the one who had made the money.

I went over what we had: Mrs. Murphy's testimony, the death certificates of the people who died in the fire, an apparent pattern of arson in Gunderson-owned buildings. And what we were now going after. They key was McGarrity, the arson investigator. He still had to be found. Once found, he had to be induced to testify.

"It's thin," Gerstein said. "Even if McGarrity talks."

"For a conviction, yes," I said. "But not for an indictment. An indictment is what I've been hired to get."

"Prosecutors don't like to go for indictments on weak cases," Gerstein said. The proper caution of a counselor at law.

"Don't be so negative," Straightman said. He wanted it.

"Publicity hounds'll go to court with any kind of garbage," I said. "Besides, once there's an indictment—once they bring it to the grand jury, even—then it's a police matter. They can call people into the grand jury, subpoena records."

"It's terribly important," Gerstein said, "that that phase be handled correctly."

"You better believe it," Straightman said.

"I'd like to handle that, possibly," Gerstein said. "Feeding the material to the D.A., bringing it before the authorities."

"Fine," I said, "as long as you don't make me miss my deadline."

"That won't be an issue," Gerstein assured me.

"Absolutely not," Straightman said. "Absolutely not. Go get 'em, tiger."

One of the rules of my business, maybe of any business, is never trust the client. Not so much their honesty as their competence. Straightman and Gerstein said they would take care of the D.A. and not to worry about the $100,000.

The first thing I did when I hit the streets was go to a pay phone and call Gene Petrucchio. It was time to see if I could feed this thing through the Brooklyn D.A.'s office. Gene said he'd meet me the next day.

The case was falling into place. I wanted my partner in on it. Maybe because I like knowing that he's there to back me up. Maybe because

I wanted him to watch me succeed when he'd made so much noise about the dangers of the case.

He'd been gone so long I was either getting worried about him or getting pissed at him for taking an eternal vacation. I called the number I had for his son in Arizona. The daughter-in-law said Joey'd been and gone. A child cried in the background. I called his ex-wife. She said he'd been and gone.

Of course, I was delighted to have the windfall of his apartment. Particularly when there are French women in the world.

Marie-Laure was coming out of the shower when I got home. She was wearing a towel. The towel fell when I touched it. My clothes got wet when her body pressed against me. I took them off and left them where they fell.

Afterward I asked her, "How was Wyoming?"

"It was very nice," she said. "The moun-tains are very big. And beautiful."

"Are you glad to be back?"

"New York is very nice," she said. Deliberately neutral words, her eyes saying she knew full well all the things she might have said. They were coy, and teasing, and warm, and carefully realistic, all at once.

"Your eyes," I said. "Are they very special eyes, or do all French girls know how to talk with their eyes?"

"Of course I am glad to see you again," she said. "Did you think of me?"

"I thought of you a lot," I said. It felt so good with her. It was not love. I was certain of that. I was certain that I did not know what love was. Was it what my father and mother had? What I felt about Wayne? Was it owning a condo?

"Yes," she said. "Me too."

I kissed her. Her mouth opened, warm. Her breasts were heavy against me. I rolled her over on her back. She opened, warm.

It was so simple.

34.

Joseph P. D'Angelo

I met with Gene in the park behind Brooklyn's Borough Hall. We shook hands, but he seemed very reserved. I asked about his family.

"I was wondering when you were going to finally come to me," he said.

"What do you mean?"

"I mean, you and your guys, you been all over Brooklyn. And I haven't heard word one from you."

"I told you I would come to you if I found anything."

"I took you at your word," he said.

"I got a murder with arson. It's ten years old. Maybe that's what I got. Gunderson owned the building. If it is arson, then he had a bent fire marshal, arson investigator. The arsonist was maybe Santino Scorcese. Maybe it was just what the arson report said, an electrical fire."

"How far up does it go?"

Before the meeting I'd tried to think it through from Gene's point of view. And I'd known that was the question he would ask. "All I need is the arson investigator," I said.

"Nobody else part of the scam? Not the cops? Nobody?"

"Gene, all I need is the one guy."

"You should stay out of it," he said. "You're gonna get creamed."

"Is that a threat?"

"No," he said.

"No?"

"Absolutely not. It's just the truth. Information."

I watched the two girls coming our way. They were licking great creamy ice cream bars. One girl was a dusky Italian kind of white, with breasts the shape of champagne glasses showing through a thin-ribbed cotton halter. The other girl was black, *au lait,* not *noir.* Her breasts were nipple-topped pears, dramatized by the wide leather belt around a trim waist. "Oh, the flesh of summer," I said to Gene. "It's God's way of telling you life is worth living. That's the gospel truth."

Gene laughed. "You're going to go ahead?" We looked at each other. He sighed, then he nodded. "You do what you got to do. I'll do what I got to do," he said.

"What I'm thinking," I said, "is that you might think of the whole thing the other way 'round. As an opportunity."

"Like how?"

"When it comes time to make the case, it would be best to have your people make it. Brooklyn D.A. investigates corrupt fire marshal, or even crooked cops, is a whole lot better than federal strike force brings indictments in Brooklyn, which is saying that the Feds gotta come in because the powers that be are letting things slide.

"But even more important, you're in control. If it's your investigation, you can keep too many extraneous things from happening. I go to someone else with this, which I don't want to do, they could make a circus. Subpoena everybody and his brother-in-law."

"It's worth having some people discuss it," he said. "You keep me current."

"Sure," I said.

Gene got up. He held out his hand. "Always good to see ya, kid." I took his hand and we shook. As I started to turn away, he said, "Hey, Tony." I turned back. "Be careful with Silverman."

"How's that?"

"I don't know what you did with him, Snake Silverman. If anything. That's your business, not my business. My business is to know that first he was gonna be indicted—by federal people—and now he's *not* going to be indicted. You understand."

I understood.

*   *   *

Ralph McGarrity, arson investigator, was retired. That meant he had a pension. Which meant an address to send his checks to. Owen Levy dug it out for me. That was the good news.

The bad news was that it was a post office box. In Faith, North Carolina. I was going to have to go looking for him. Owen was apologetic. He said he would try to get more information, possibly even a real address, which would make it all so much easier. But certainly photos. If life were all business, I would have left for Faith as soon as he found the pictures. But even with my deadline on the case, I had another priority. I'd promised Wayne I would be there when he came back from camp. And I was going to be. Even if it was just so that I could explain in person why I was leaving.

Thursday night I took five Levys—Owen and Elvira, Carl, Paul, and Sarah—and Marie-Laure out to dinner. We went to Jezebel's, at Forty-fifth and Ninth. It looked like New Orleans on the inside. Tastes good too. The Levy family looked sharp. And respectable. Practically Cosbys.

I could see Owen figuring what dinner for seven was going to cost.

"That's exactly why I picked the place," I said, "and we're not going down the street to Blimpie's. I want to spend a little bit on you and your family." I turned to his wife. "Mrs. Levy, would you be so kind as to order whatever it is your husband truly likes, because if you don't he'll try to figure out what's cheapest on the menu. And don't skip the appetizers. And don't skip dessert. And tell me what kind of wine you'd like."

"Well, this is sort of soul food," Owen said, "and the truth is I don't think it's going to beat Elvira's cooking."

"Sure, Dad," Sarah, the youngest, said.

"Do you really live in Paris?" Elvira said to Marie-Laure.

"Oh, yes," Marie said. "Do you know it?"

"Oh, no," Elvira sighed, "but I've always dreamed of going to Paris." Every woman does.

"I want to go to Rio!" Carl said.

"Right on, Rio!" Paul said. "Carnival!"

"I like New York," Marie said. "All the people, also from the TV, make me think New York is not friendly. But it is very friendly. More friendly than Paris."

"Would you mind telling me about Paris?" Elvira said.

"Yes, please," Sarah said.

I watched Owen watching his family with pride. And joy. The kids knew that Dad's eye was on them, and they didn't seem to mind.

And I wished it was me. That I had my own family. Or that I was solidly centered in myself so I could feel that way about my adopted family. Did I want a kid, several kids, of my own? I had an uncle ready to put up the money for it. Assuming that the offer hadn't really run out in ninety days.

After two tentative glasses of wine, Elvira was bold enough to ask Marie about her relationship with me. Her future with me.

"*Qué será, será*. I like Tony. But I live in Paris, he lives here." She shrugged. So Gallic. Her eyes, as always, told stories, asked questions, and knew the answers. I thought I could talk her into staying. For a while. If I wanted to.

"I'm sorry," Owen said to me. "I still can't find a street address for McGarrity. I got pictures. From the retirement ceremony. So they're only a couple of years old. I wished I could do more. Arsonists. That's personal. They're trying to kill me. They don't know that it's me. Well, you . . . you understand that. You and that dog of yours."

"Yeah," I said. "Don't worry about the address. I'll find him."

After dessert, coffee, brandy for the adults, and one sweet liqueur for each child, I didn't let Owen even peek at the bill.

It was one of the loveliest evenings I've ever spent.

On the way upstairs, I picked up Joey's mail. We were alone when we entered the apartment. Not even Mario was there. He was on duty at the office.

I was feeling round and full. I took off my shoes. Marie turned on the TV. I checked the mail to see if there were any bills that I had to take care of for my eternally on vacation and out of touch partner.

There was a fat envelope addressed to me, c/o Joseph P. D'Angelo.

```
Tony,
     They have a typewriter here. One of these
modern IBMs with the correcting ribbon. I would
```

have killed for one when I was on the force. I learned on the old manuals. Where you had to slug the keys. That was the old Department. Where you could slug the suspects too.

I guess they still do. But back then you didn't expect a perp to actually complain about it. And if they did, you didn't expect anybody to care.

I was ambitious. That's one reason I learned to type. A very valuable skill for a cop, typing. And spelling. You look at the old reports, you see everything crossed out, typed over, misspelled. Of course, in those days, they weren't so meticulous, and they didn't throw things out of court for a typo.

There are so many things I have to tell you. About me. About your father. I guess I'll do the hardest thing first.

In the early days I was not a clean cop.

There, that's out. Now that it is said I will defend myself. Briefly. The lines are drawn now. Once they were just understood. ''Honest graft'' —we had honest graft. A store owner wants you to keep an eye on his store, which you would do anyway, which is your job to do anyway, and he wants to slip you a fin—once upon a time five dollars was money, that's how long ago we are talking about—anyone in his reasonable mind will take it. Nobody figured out that like smoking that Mary Jane, it would lead to hard drugs. Which of course it did. Not with me. With the force.

I can't say to you, you don't know how it is, out there alone in the scumbag section of life with the only people who is on your side doing exactly what you shouldn't be doing, and not trusting you if you don't do it. I can't say that to you, because you were there. In scum city. And you didn't fold. You didn't go along to get along. So you know how it is.

That was the hard part. The rest is easy.

I wanted to make detective. Because I was ambitious. And I was a rising star.

It was hard in them days. The Department belonged to the micks. Still does, if you read the names of the upper ranks. They still got The Department. I was a guinea, greaseball, eyetie, black hand. Us, the Hebes too, was like blacks is today. See, I know you always looked at me funny when I said nigger this, coon that. I can relate what we say about them to what they said about us. But the other part of me really believes they is different. How come they haven't come up? How come? With all the helping hands, government programs—which we did not have. Nobody in America lives like they do, they got more junkies, drunks, homos, whores, and no families.

Like I said, that's how the micks thought about us. And they did not want no goddamn guinea moving up in the ranks. They had—have— the Emerald Society, we had the Columbian Society.

A few of us sort of got picked to get the guinea push up the greasy pole. I was one of them. Partly because I was smart. I had a good record, fifth in my class at the academy, some good arrests, a couple of citations for bravery, all that good stuff. Plus I could type and spell. It's amazing how many cops spend so long at making reports and never realize that making reports is a big part of the job. Plus it is the part your superiors get to see. That's what they know you by. Once you know that—which is an obvious thing—it clearly pays to set aside some time to not only get good at it but make it easy on yourself. Like learning how to shine your uniform shoes. (That's not so important these days, but in those days we were much more paramilitary. Shined shoes, clean uniform, polished buttons, standing up straight at inspec-

Joseph P. D'Angelo

tion, all counted for a whole lot.) That's why
I took a typing course.

There was enough Italian votes and enough
Italian politicians—mayors like La Guardia
and Impelliteri, plus councilmen, district
leaders, boro presidents, all of that—that the
Irish had to give us some slots.

I got my gold shield.

I can not tell you how proud I was. I understood all the politics involved, all the bullshit. It didn't matter. It doesn't matter now.
I got the shield with me. The original one.
Polished. It glows when you polish it good. All
the years of polishing have dulled the detail-
ing a little, which gives it a hazy look, like
looking at a streetlamp on a night with fog. It
glows. Bury me with the sucker.

That was in the days when I got real close with
Michael, your old man. He was, as they say, a
breath of fresh air, and an unusual man. No
bullshit. Even his bullshit was no bullshit.

Also, at the same time, I got away from the
honest graft, which as we now know, as I knew
then, was not so honest. That made me feel good.
Clean and good. That is a very impressive feeling. You feel proud as a prelate.

The thing that was so interesting about your old
man was that he had broken with the old ways. Most
of us Italians—and I should really say Sicilians,
because we are not Italians except to America—
most of us took the old ways to the new place and
blended the two. To Michael, the old ways were
crap. Omertà, crap. La Cosa Nostra, crap. The
Church, crap. Keeping women barefoot and pregnant, crap. I always wished I had a relationship—
what a word—like Michael and Anna. I like your
mother. I should have stayed in touch with her.
I never did. I lost touch with a lot of things
after it all came down.

My relationship—there's that stupid modern
word again—with my wife was different. It was
traditional. I was the husband, breadwinner,
king of the house. I won't say what she was,
good or bad, no need to slander others, but you
will see for yourself what she was.

Michael had a fresh vision. It was niave.
(Here I am bragging about my spelling and that
is one word that I can't get right, but it's the
right one.) He did not seem to understand the
venality of man. He thought doing right would
somehow produce a whole race of people doing
right. A very American way to think. He was born
in the old world but made for the new one. In
Sicily they would have stoned him to death,
laughing all the way, hysterical, for such
foolish thoughts. A world of honest cops, honest politicians, honest and powerful unions
which would stand up for workingmen and let
them earn a decent and honorable living. A
fantasy world full of the dreams of men like Tom
Paine, Voltaire, Garibaldi. Something would
come up and Michael would say, ''What would
Garibaldi have done?'' ''What would Tom Paine
have said?'' ''What would Thomas Jefferson have
said?'' He also read and talked about Karl Marx
and Thorstein Veblen. Books you had to hide
under your bed, like something from 42nd Street
with anal sex and dogs. Whatever happens, don't
let Mario fall so low as to do it for pictures.
He should only be with his own kind, and no
pictures. That was a joke. Nothing is funny
anymore.

Gravesend. I better tell you about Gravesend.
Out in Brooklyn.

We got a couple of floaters. I don't know if
you know about floaters, ever seen them, for
real. The body is a sack. After death a lot of
gases begin to form. They swell the body, like

a balloon. If it's in the water it creates
buoyancy. This buoyancy lifts the body to the
surface. That's a floater. In warm water it
takes five to ten days, in cold water it could
be two, three weeks. Before they come up. Identification is difficult. The swelling, which I
mentioned, also causes the outer layer of skin
to split and peel from the body, plus the
effects of water, and whatever else has happened to the corpse during the submerged period, buffeting, feeding upon the body by
various forms of aquatic life.

Finally we do identify one of them. It takes
about a week. What identifies him is that one
leg was shorter than the other, and his clothes,
which matches with a missing persons we got of
four kids from Red Hook. All about 14, 15.

So what the hell is a Red Hook kid doing as a
Gravesend corpse? I ask around and I find out
that it is very possible that the place in which
they come up could be almost entirely unrelated
to the place they went down. Particularly in a
harbor with two rivers, and more if you count
the small ones out of Jersey, and ocean tides.
A floater that started out in Poughkeepsie
could come up the same place as one that started
dead in Coney Island.

Turns out, also, that I know one of the
families, slightly, they being from Red Hook
like me.

So here I am, the young lion, proud as one of
them lions outside the 42nd St. Library, with
my almost brand-new shield, and I am going to be
a hero and find out what happened. Though mostly
what happened, from forensics, is that they
drowned. No wounds, strangulation, nothing.
I'm not thinking major crime, just to find out
what happened.

I do the usual. When and where last seen.
Turns out they were playing hooky, as kids will

do, and they were playing down by the Gowanus Canal. Which is a place kids would play because it's dirty and interesting. Somebody seen them there. I don't remember who. This is a long time ago.

The other thing I find is that there was a water main break, a big one, right about the time they disappeared. Same day anyway. I don't know what made me connect the two, but I did. That's something you are good at. Taking two things that just are and seeing the invisible rope that ties them. You are at your best when such connections truly exist. You miss things when things just are as they are and there is no connection. Your father's mind worked that way also.

You understand that a water main is not just a pipe. It's more like a whole tunnel. One of them breaks, it's like a flash flood. Even when I found the place, which was three weeks later, you could see where the water had rushed to the canal.

It was muddy, it was dirty. What it was, was sewage. I go stepping through it. Wearing galoshes. Because in those days good shoes cost ten bucks, and five bucks was actual money. I found a shoe. I found a lot of things. But among the things was this shoe which was identified by the family as belonging to one of the missing boys. Not one of the two we found. Another one who went missing at the same time.

So what I can see, clear as day, is that here are the four kids, playing in the sludge or whatever, the water main breaks, there's a flash flood, the water carries them out into the canal. You've seen the Gowanus. It is not exactly your babbling brook. The water just sits there, mostly. But the force of the flood must've carried our floaters out into the bay proper, where the tides pushed them along the bottom, then they got snagged or stuck in the

mud near Gravesend, where they waited until
they were gaseous enough to rise.

It was not a major crisis, as I said. Not a
crime at all. Nobody cared except the families.
Now we got one family with two brothers missing, two other families with one kid each missing. One of the brothers is one of the floaters.
So we have two families with children that they
don't know is dead or alive. Of course we're
sure they are dead. But you know what mothers
are. Fathers too.

So I push and I prod and push. Finally we got
teams out there. Dredging with hooks and such.
We found a third boy. His body was wedged into
some pilings. Wedged real good. It took two
days to get the body out. First we punctured it,
in several places, to deflate it. The parents,
they wanted the satisfaction, such as it is, of
burying the kid and having the priest say a few
words and saying how they was all going to meet
again in heaven, where there aren't no Gowanus
Canals. That used to seem real important. Maybe
it still does.

What they had to do was break the body to get
it out. Tore off an arm and half a leg. What the
hell, it was only a corpse.

We never found the fourth kid.

I did find something else. I was looking at
this water main. Just hanging around, watching
them dredge. It was a new one, or a new replacement. The thing was, it was a piece of
shit. Concrete that crumbled in your hand. What
you would call substandard, materials and work-
manship both.

I don't know, if I hadn't known one of the
families, maybe it would have been different.
To this day, I don't know if I would have said
it was an accident. Kids playing where they
aren't supposed to be, and they know it, and
something happens and that's all of it.

But I'm standing there, my shoes all covered with shit and mud, looking at this piece of crap that the city paid for, and this piece of crap, it killed four kids. For a few bucks.

Also, I understand that some inspectors were paid off. Has to be. It's murder. Or, technically speaking, at least negligent homicide.

I am part of the system, the one on paper and the real one, both. So I know what's what. Against my own better advice, I start building a case. I tell myself that I am doing it as an exercise. Because it is a technical thing. But really, it is not that hard. I got the bodies, including the third one, that had come to rest in a direct line where the flood would take it, I got the shoe, and I got a picture of the pattern the water laid down over the mud. I get samples of the materials and get them analyzed. I get an engineer—one who does not in any way work for the city. Here's the negligence. There's the corpses. I go to the records, there's the names of the inspectors, also of course the names of the contractors, and I am able to track down the guys who did the actual labor.

Meantime, I'm in a fight with the families. They want to bury the dead. Naturally. They even sent a priest to see me. But I got a use for them. I want them in the morgue.

I get one of the inspectors down to the morgue, telling him it's about something else entirely, and I show him the body, the one we broke to take out of the water. Naturally he had to barf. I follow him into the john and start berating him. I am all over him. He's on his knees, there's vomit all over the toilet seat and he's got it on his tie and I'm screaming at him that the body in there, that's his responsibility, his fault. He breaks down and he tells me who paid him how much.

292

Thing is, he tells me more than I'm expecting to hear. More than I want to hear, about how he passes on a cut to the guy who is over him, who has to pass a cut on to the water commissioner.

That, right there, was the time for me to stop. I knew that.

What they told me, my lieutenant, then the captain, also my district leader and several other people, was that if I persisted would ruin my career, and I wouldn't make my case anyway. My wife told me that also.

There was four kids dead.

There was only one person who saw it my way. That was Michael Cassella. I told him about it, while it was happening. He agreed with me, and more, that it was murder. He was the only one who told me to go and do what had to be done.

Even after I knew, for certain, and he knew, for certain, that what I was doing was professional suicide.

Which it was. They creamed me. I lost my shield. I got foot patrol. For seven years I had foot patrol. Rockaway in the winter, to freeze with that wind coming off the Atlantic, the Bronx in the summer so I could sweat a little. I wasn't happy about it. I admit that I did some drinking and was tough to live with. But that wasn't why she left me and took the kids, who I never did really get to know again, ever. She left me because she was not going to have the Lieutenant moving up to Captain moving up to Chief that she was promised. She left me because I wouldn't take no more fivers from shopkeepers, or fix parking tickets, or any of the low-end pickings that are there for foot patrol. So we were stuck living in Hell's Kitchen in this cheap apartment which is now an incredible steal.

She left. Found a car dealer in Florida. She was a looker and knew how to turn a man around.

She took the kids with her. My son looks like he's doing real well. The stupid son of a bitch, and that is the best use of the expression I have ever had the opportunity to use, is messed up with Arizona wise guys. Either he thought I was blind or he's a slob. I saw the subpoena on his desk calling him before the federal strike force. My daughter, who made the good marriage and has become a Valium junkie, is more to be pitied than scorned.

I can't scorn the junkies anymore. Not when I'm one. Percodan before I went on my vacation. I've moved up to morphine since.

I'll try some smack when I've finished this letter. Am I telling you too much? Let me go back, because I'm skipping ahead and getting confused myself.

It took me seven years, by then she was gone three, to get the shield back. I never made any more rank than that. Never made the climb up the greasy pole even though I was one of the chosen few picked to do it.

Your father was one of the few who stood by me. The truth is, for a long time I hated him. But then I came to understand that he fought his own battles the same way he wanted me to fight mine. Usually its the guys who sit home in the trenches that scream the loudest.

Like the President. There you and I mostly disagree. I think Reagan is what this country needs to hold its head up again. But I got to admit he talks about war like a guy who has only been to a war in the movies. Not like a guy who has been to a real one. I think about that sometimes. You don't like him because he's a phony. But did you ever think that these are phony times and what the world needs is a phony?

I've done what I could for you. This Gunderson thing. I'm hoping that when the crunch comes you do the right thing. From the day it came in

the door, I saw that it's trouble. Only thing
is, I don't know what the right thing is. You
done the right thing once. It broke you. Nearly.
Now you're on your feet. I done the right thing.
Once. These people, these kind of people, they
can smother you. Take it all away. So I want to
say don't do what I did. Don't stand up to what
can't be stood up to and have the next ten years
of your life, or whatever, go down the tubes and
end up a nothing old man like me.

I tried to stop you. I couldn't. Because
you're ambitious. Which is good. You can climb.
You can be someone. With the money and all the
good things. Remember that.

If you go looking in the dog food—remember how
I told you to only give Mario the Alpo—you'll
find some cans of Kal Kan there. I got them from
the head shop down the corner. You give them a
twist, the top comes off. They're stashes.

It's the cash money, a lot from Silverman,
that I've been siphoning off. Some, just money
I didn't spend. Silverman's not going to open
his books to nobody. So it's good clean unreported cash. It's for you. Fixit money. Getaway
money. Whatever you need. Because if you go
with this Gunderson thing, you're going to need
something.

I don't know if I want to be honest about this.
But there is something about what I did that
still feels good. No matter what it cost. Your
father would probably feel the same way. If he
was alive. Though who we're looking up in the
sky to for approval or whatever that made us do
it, I don't understand.

See, in the end, your father's fight, my
fight, all it did was bring hurt to ourselves
and our families. That's the bottom line.

Now, I've done something else. You will see
the enclosed papers. Adoption papers. I have
adopted you. I don't know if that is legal or

not. You are not an orphan and so forth and so
on. But that apartment of mine, like I said, is
a gold mine, now that Hell's Kitchen is getting
to be Clinton and it's one of the last rent-controlled apartments in the world. Which you can
take only if you are a member of my immediate
family. There are two sets. One current and
semi-legal, maybe. The other backdated to the
year your father died. Use whichever is going
to work better.

Two years ago, when I went in for my operation, I found out I had cancer. They got some of
it. A year later it was back. It's everywhere,
Tony, everywhere. Lymph glands, lungs, liver,
stomach. It even got me by the balls. I knew
that. The vacation, that was for an operation.
They took one look and closed me up. Doctor
practically barfed in me. I tease him about it
now.

My balls hurt. They want to take them off. So
my three weeks or three months or whatever will
be less painful. I want to go out with them
still hanging, even if oversized, slightly mis-
shapen, and killing me. Irony there. We always
thought you were the one whose own balls would
kill him.

Almost forgot. About anything I might have
forgot to tell you, look in my notebooks. I was
always a good detective, because I could type
and took good notes. Meticulous, thorough
notes. In boxes in the bedroom closet of the
bedroom I don't use, marked Salvation Army.

The doc is an OK guy. I asked him what if I
died in my sleep, would there be an autopsy. He
said there wouldn't. I'm a long way from what
the fathers and the nuns taught me. A long way.
Heroin is easy to get up on the block there,
where the apartment is. I've stockpiled. And
brought it with me. This way the doc won't be

embarrassed by stuff missing from the supply closet. Not that I haven't figured out how to do that. I have.

What little life I got left—I got nothing left—is ugly. I'll pass on it. So when I finish this, I'll slip the needle in a spot where there's already tracks.

I don't have to tell you that you are the son that I wanted my son to be. Take good care of the dog.

Joseph P. D'Angelo

35.

A Tacit Bargain

I called Glenda in the morning. While Marie was in the shower.

I didn't tell her about Joey. I just said that I would be home that night. For good.

"You have a lot of 'urt," Marie said. Her lips looked so full and her eyes so knowing. I brushed the hair from her forehead.

"You want to go get some breakfast with me, at the Greek joint?"

"I will make coffee. 'Ow would you like, *au lait* or *noir*?"

"*Au lait*," I said.

"Do you want to say anything to me? There is a lot on the inside."

"Introspection is a disease," I said. "Or a drug. I dabbled in it once. In college. A lot of college girls were into introspection as foreplay." All of which was too fast and too colloquial for Marie. I knew that. But the drivel just kept gushing out of my mouth. Like a comedian in front of an audience that doesn't laugh. "Later on it got easier. In the seventies all you needed to get laid was cocaine. But when you do introspection, you don't do anything else. You enter the cosmic swamp. Meaning becomes obsessively elusive. Naturally, my grades slipped. My father, who used to do things like call my professors to find out how I was doing, found out how I was doing."

She poured the coffee into the hot milk. Standing in the kitchen naked. The sun coming in through the narrow window. All curves, lit

298

and shadowed. I took the cup she offered me. I'd told her about Glenda. And Wayne. "Are you going back to 'er?" she asked.

"My father thought it was serious," I said, "and he whipped my ass back into shape. 'There's a real world out there. With things that need doing. You're a man. You got to be a man. Or you're no son of mine.' That's not what he said. That's an exaggeration. But it's what he meant. He died while I was in law school. He had a stroke. He lay there in a coma. First you hope. When someone has a stroke. Then you begin to worry. The longer they're out, the less there is when they come back. So you think, this is day three, he'll have a little trouble forming words, maybe a hitch in his walk, but with therapy . . . Then week two. You got to figure paralysis down one side or the other. Braces, cane, walker.

"And don't forget the mind. Less and less of it is going to come back. The will. It affects the will. 'It's like practicing veterinary medicine,' the doctor said, 'when the patient can't speak to you to say where it hurts.' Then it was two weeks. Maybe it got to three. When you know that if something wakes up, it's going to be half vegetable. I don't know. Then he died.

"This is good," I said, about the coffee. She looked so sad. Like I should've looked. I put the cup down and put my hands on her hips and drew her body close.

"I don't think she is right for you," Marie said.

"I vote with my feet," I said. "I was out of law school and into the Correction Department before I realized that it was a decision. Too much introspection and you turn into a vegetable. I vote with my feet."

Marie brushed her fingers through my hair. "It is the hour that I 'ave to go to the plane," Marie said.

"You have to go back to Paris."

"Ah, yes, I 'ave to."

"We are out of time," I said.

"We 'ave a little time," she said.

A little time. We made love face to face, kissing. Then I turned her on her side, with me above her, so I could touch the round weight of her breasts and her buttocks. The womanness of her.

She didn't shower again afterward. I walked her downstairs, carrying her bags. She had our sweat on her body, and my semen still inside her. I hailed a taxi.

"Oh, no," she said. "A taxi to the airport is too much money. I will take the train to the plane."

I reached in my pocket and pulled out some bills. About fifty dollars. I pushed it into her hand.

"No. I cannot take it."

"Take it. Take the cab," I said, opening the door. "I'll feel better. I don't know. I'd put you in a limo if I'd thought of it. It's OK to spend a little money." I put her suitcase inside. Then I took her in my arms and kissed her lightly. "A good vacation, yes?"

"Yes. A very good vacation." She lived in Paris. I lived in New York. And all the rest that we didn't say and kept not saying and were certain didn't exist anyway.

"You have a good flight. And don't be sad or anything."

"No. I won't be sad. And you, you will be OK?"

"Yeah," I said. "I will be OK. That's what I tried to explain. I don't think about things too much. I just try to keep on doing."

"Yes," she said. *You boy,* her eyes said, *you are such a boy. Why don't you ask me to stay? Why don't you cry? You are not really OK. You are such a boy.*

I let her go. She got in the cab. I told the driver to take her through the Midtown Tunnel to the LIE to the Van Wyck. No foreigner rip-offs. I didn't watch the cab drive off. I turned and went upstairs. She was a woman. I didn't love her. It was just that she reminded me that I loved women. Which I had forgotten.

Then I went back upstairs to Joey's apartment. His things still filled it, like he was coming back. Marie hadn't understood a word I said. There wasn't much future in it. A great interlude. A fantasy come true. I felt so damn lonely. So damn lonely. I wanted to cry for Joey like I hadn't cried for my father. I wanted to cry because Marie was gone.

Instead I went to the office to take Mario for a walk.

Naomi was there. There had been only one call. It was from Sam Bleer, my accountant. I called him back, but he had already taken off for the holiday weekend. His secretary said he would get back to me on Tuesday. I thought about telling Naomi to get the sign on the door changed from "D'Angelo Cassella" to just "Cassella." And ordering new stationery too. But there didn't seem to be any reason to do that. It was just an additional expense. I told her to close up and take the rest of the day off. That's all I told her.

Then I called the hospital to arrange my partner's funeral. I was a day late. In accordance with his own instructions the body of Joseph D'Angelo had already been shipped out and buried in a veterans' cemetery.

Glenda's office closed early too. I met her at three. I had Mario with me, and we went down to Riverside Park. To see the river or something. I told her about Joey. I told her I was home for good.

"You keep a lot inside," she said.

"I guess," I said. "I'm glad that you're willing to have me back."

"Sometimes we all need space," she said. "I understand that."

"I'm glad that I got this sorted out before Wayne got home."

"When, when you were alone. This last month. Were there other women?"

"Are we going to go back to that crap immediately? The first fucking day?"

"I'm sorry," she said. "No . . . Do you love me?"

I took her face in my hands and kissed her lightly on the lips. She burrowed her head in my shoulder and clung tightly to me. "You never said it very much," she said, "but I always knew you loved me."

> If one settles . . . for a substitute past, an illusion of
> it, then that fragile construct must be protected from
> the challenge of complex or contradictory evidence,
> from any test of evidence at all. That explains Ameri-
> cans' extraordinary tacit bargan with each other not
> to challenge Reagan's version of the past. The power
> of his appeal is the great joint confession that we can-
> not live with our real past, that we not only prefer
> but need a substitute.
>
> GARRY WILLS, *Reagan's America: Innocents at
> Home*

Part Three

AUTUMN
•1984•

"A man's got to do what a man's got to do." I always thought Alan Ladd said that, in Shane. *But it was on WFUX the other night, and he never says it. I wonder who did.*

Anthony Cassella

And Samson slew the Philippines . . .

Ronald Reagan

36.

Faith

"Purple mountain majesties," Reverend Billy Purvis Parker shouted. The white-robed chorus echoed the line. Their voices soared. "Above the fruited plain," he declared. They echoed.

"America, America," he cried fervently, fervently.

Then there was silence. One beat. Two beats. Three beats. Four. "God shed his grace on thee!" A shout. A plea.

"Please, Lord, shed your grace on thee. Show us the way to be worthy. Have we lost our way, Lord?" Billy asked. He looked up. No one else answered, so he did. "God put a special grace on this land. America is a Christian country. America is the Lord's last, best hope for the salvation of the world!"

I looked around, as best I could, through the sea of pale, fervent, white faces, searching for the face that matched my photo of Ralph McGarrity, P.O. Box 733, Faith, North Carolina. Not listed in the phone book or with the Board of Elections.

Faith was a recent real estate event centered on Reverend Billy Purvis Parker's Cathedral of Love's Grace. In the constellation of big-time evangelicals, Parker was rated more fundamentalist than Falwell, though not quite as friendly as Jim and Tammy Bakker or as hard-rocking as Jimmy Swaggert. His finances were a closed book, but he was said to be richer than Pat Robertson.

There were two places to stay in Faith. Both on Heaven's Way, the commercial strip. The Promised Land Motel and Motor Court had facilities for recreational vehicles. So I chose the other one, the Land of Milk and Honey Motel.

My room had two single beds and two Bibles, a Gideon and the Reverend Billy edition.

Among the amenities was a map of Faith. The cathedral was at the center, meeting rooms and Bible study centers in satellites around it. Thousands came by bus, just like they do to Atlantic City. Bus parking was strategically placed so the thousands would have to walk through the commercial strip on the way to and from the cathedral. To the east and west there were tracts for Bless Our Home Houses. The business cards of two recommended realtors were enclosed. Also a schedule of Christian events and two form letters you could send to your congressman. One requesting his vote for the school prayer amendment, the other demanding a balanced budget amendment. I faithfully filled out both and sent them off to John Straightman.

I went to bed early.

In the morning I had breakfast at the motel. It wasn't New York, where the orange juice is fresh squeezed and the coffee contains a wake-up call. The OJ was frozen and reconstituted. I could see through the coffee to the bottom of the cup like it was tea. That's why they hate us. They know our food is better.

Then I went to church. Looking for Ralph McGarrity.

". . . Divorce. Di-vorce. The nuclear family shatters. The center cannot hold. Shattered dreams and broken hearts, we can lay them right at the door of secular humanism. Look in any window, what do you see? Promiscuity! Wife swapping! Orgies! Per-versions to abominable to name. . . ."

I looked down the row to my right. There was a corn-fed cutie hanging on every word, kind of rocking from her center, lips all damp. "Ohh, ohh," the cutie sighed. Her white sweater came right up to her neck, chastely. With a little pearl button.

"Where are our leaders? Where are the leaders who will say, 'Stop! In the name of God.' Our President, he is with us. He is telling us to 'Stop! In the name of God.' Our First Lady, God bless her, is teaching us, 'Just say no!'"

"No . . ." the cutie sighed. Her tongue was pink. Nice, with the pearl.

Faith

"Just say no," the chorus sang.

> *Say no, no, no,*
> *In the name of Christ,*
>   *Just like Nancy.*
> *Just say no,*
>   *Just like Ron,*
> *To bad advice.*
> *Say no to drugs,*
> *Know your duty;*
> *Say no, no, no*
> *to promiscuity . . .*

Reverend Billy had paused to catch his breath. To let the drama build. During that moment of anticipation, she glanced over at me. Our eyes met. Two seekers of salvation. Then she looked away.

"Ah am not going to talk politics," Reverend Billy reminded us. "But we do not believe that the Christians of America will remain silent while the country continues in its slide toward national suicide." He went on to attack homos, inflation, the atheistic separation of church and state, the spend-and-tax Congress, and income tax. He recommended tithing.

That was a cue. The television monitors flashed "800" numbers. "Call now, and for your donation, of whatever size, we will send you . . ." Billy was also asking us. Ushers came up the aisles with baskets on long-handled poles. It was the first break in the service. The ushers glared, in a kindly Christian way, at those of us who rose to leave.

A sign beside the exit said: "Give today. Save our schools from a homosexual tomorrow."

It was good to get out of the cool AC air into the hot, stuffy outdoors. A booth on Cathedral Path sold Mary Jo Parker angel-wing hand fans. Only five dollars. Mary Joe was the Reverend Billy's missus, a heavenly angel of mercy and a Christian mother. I bought one. The woman behind the counter suggested that I also get True Christian Bug-Off, an insect repellent, because the mosquitoes had been real fierce of late. It was ten dollars. I got that too.

The service ended a half hour later. The crowd poured out. The more I looked for McGarrity, the harder it got to distinguish anybody. In New York, everybody, from pimps to bankers, is trying to make a fashion

307

statement. These people were striving, from their double-knit insides out, for commonality.

The cutie spotted me. Our eyes met again. She altered course enough to take herself past me.

"Howdy, good afternoon. Wasn't that an inspiring sermon," I said.

"Well, I have heard better," she said. "I didn't think Rev'end Billy was really up to fever pitch. But it's Wednesday."

"Oh, Wednesday's not a hot preachin' day?"

"Sunday, o' course, that's the biggest, that's the one broadcast live. But for hot preachin', Friday night."

"You from around here?" I asked.

"Uh huh," she said. "You?"

"No. Just visiting. But it sure is inspirational."

"I thought so," she said. "You look a little . . ."

"Swarthy," I said. "Would you like a fan?" I offered her mine.

She accepted and giggled. "I was going to say . . . satanic."

"Oh," I said. "I know what you mean. I get that from daddy's side of the family. Terrible people, my daddy's side of the family. Mostly I inherited just his looks, praise the Lord, and mostly my mother's character. She is an angel, a real come-to-earth angel. So I fight that part of me that's from my daddy. That's part of why I'm here."

She looked interested. Some women like men with inner conflicts.

"Cynthia Lynn," her momma called. Cynthia Lynn made a face, which she showed to me but erased before she turned.

"Coming, Momma," she said. Both parents were glaring, in a sanctified way, at us. Also a brother. A Xerox of Dad. Except that he wore a T-shirt that said "Prayer Warrior" on the back. He had his sleeve rolled up so we could all see "Go With God" tattooed on his bicep. "I'll see *you* later," Cynthia said to me.

She looked so Southern sullen beside her family. Back in the fifties, when the Southern slut was a silver-screen standard, Tuesday Weld became a movie star just because she could pout that way.

I went back to the motel and called the office. Naomi reported that Miles was there with her. Loyal and true, quoting from Plato and looking for an arson expert.

"I have mail and messages for Mr. D'Angelo," she said. "What should I do with them?"

"What you can deal with, deal with; the rest, hold 'em till I get back," I said.

"Mr. Bleer called," she said. "And Glenda."

I called Sam. "You're being audited," Sam said.

I said, "Shit."

"Three years, they want the whole three years."

"Why?" I asked.

"The IRS does not give reasons. The IRS moves in mysterious ways. It makes them feel divine."

"Take care of it, Sam," I said. "I got to do what I got here," I said.

"I need you," he said.

"I need to be where I am. Have Naomi start pulling the records. Get it organized. Then ask me whatever you want."

"It could be problems," he said. "You have a lot of cash expenses."

"You said as long as they're recorded, in my notes."

"I know what I said, but I know they can give you a hard time. If they want to."

"Do they want to?"

"I don't know yet. But if they're auditing three years, it sounds like they want to. You have reported everything, haven't you?"

"Yeah," I said, "I've reported everything. I'm clean. A little inflated, maybe, but clean, honest, and documented."

"You should be all right then. As long as they don't know about any unreported income."

"Don't worry about it, Sam. I reported everything," I told him again. When I hung up the phone, I realized that I had, but Joey hadn't.

I staked out the post office until they closed. McGarrity didn't show up.

I asked the desk clerk where I could find a notary public. He said he was one. He also said that the best place for dinner was the My God Will Provide Restaurant and Milk Bar. It had an interesting menu. Faith Burgers with Fundamental Fries, Self-Control Chili, Gentleness Beans, Love Waffles (our Rise and Shine specials available at any hour), Faith and Fruit Pie (Garden of Eden Apple every day. Ask your waitress for daily special). I had a Friendship Steak. It was tough.

Then I went to a Bible study group. For me it was a trip on the starship *Enterprise*. The alien planets in *Star Trek* adventures were always based on some aspect of earth, but exaggerated, oversimplified, and made universal to that week's fictional world. In Faith, all reality was seen through the Reverend Billy version of the Bible. All events took place as part of a football game between The Good Guys—coached by God, Reverend Billy at quarterback and nearsighted Ronald Reagan at left tackle—and Evil, who fielded Satan, Atheistic Russia, and New York City. I managed to keep my mouth shut. However, McGarrity wasn't there.

The next day I visited Faith's two recommended realtors. If McGarrity had a home, it was probable that one of them had sold it to him. The first one, Ezra Ervin, took me on a tour. There were two subdivisions. Hearth and Home Hills was on the rise to the east. Promised Land Vale, on the flat to the west and south, had a man-made stream—the Little River Jordan—and a pond. The section in between was being held in reserve for a theme park and golf course.

Ezra had high hopes for the theme park. The town's marketing director was a real sincere born-again who had come over from the Disney Corporation. I could see that. Faith was a lot like a Disney World where the people believed in the ducks.

"I'm from New York," I said, hoping he would mention other New Yorkers in Faith.

"I suspected that," he said, with a sell-to-the-devil-himself smile. "It don't make you a bad person, and you sure have come to the right place to live close to the Lord."

"Many New Yorkers here?" I asked.

"No. . . . This is a planned community. All our homes have to be approved by the architectural committee, and you will note, as I drive you through, that they are each and every one as American as apple pie in architectural style."

That did not mean stately Southern mansion, or wrought-iron New Orleans decadence, or New England gingerbread, or Southwestern adobe, or Adirondack hunting lodge. It meant suburban. Even Billy Purvis Parker's house, on the highest point of the slope, had the undistinguished subdivision look of the Ewing home in *Dallas*.

"I'm retired," I said, "from the Fire Department."

"Now how big's your family," he said, "and how much were you considering spending?"

"What's good for my family," I said, "is everything. It would be sort of nice if I knew some folks from back home down here."

"Well, I tell you what," he said. "You got more of you folks coming down to escape from Sodom on the Hudson, you tell 'em to come see Ezra Ervin. Now here's the high school. That there alone is reason enough for moving to Faith for any family man."

The schools had two big selling points. They did *not* spare the rod and spoil the child. And they taught Creation Science.

> It is too early, it seems to me, to send the firemen
> home. The fire is still burning on many a far-flung
> hill, and it may begin to roar again at any
> moment. . . . Heave an egg out of a Pullman window
> and you will hit a Fundamentalist almost anywhere in
> the United States today. They swarm in the country
> towns, inflamed by their pastors. . . . They are ev-
> erywhere that learning is too heavy a burden for
> mortal minds.

> H. L. MENCKEN, 1925

"This teaching of Natural Science minus God has just got to stop," Ezra said. "A man thinks he is a descendant of an ape, he is going to behave just like an ape. Look at the nigras. Maybe they are descendants of the ape, but the Ervins are not. Nosireebob."

On the other hand, he didn't seem to know any retired firemen from New York.

I got a second tour from the second realtor, Sam Hoecher. Sam's pitch was tuned more to what a great investment Faith real estate was. "What we're talking about here is the future, son, your financial future," he said.

"I'm a fireman," I told him. "A couple of the older guys, who were retiring, talked about coming down here. I thought if they were here, I might look 'em up."

"You know and I know," he said, "nobody knows more about money than a Jew. What I always like to say is 'Jesus saves, Moses invests.' Uh huh. This here is an investment."

Both tours, I thought that I saw a blue Ford behind us. Maybe. Maybe not. If it was the FBI, Faith would be the hardest place in the world to pick them out of the crowd.

*   *   *

When I got back to the motel, there was a note slipped under my door. It said: "Cross the River Jordan. The woods. 4:00. Be there or be square."

I hadn't taken a gun because I'd flown into Raleigh and rented a car there. The desk clerk sent me down the block to Earl's Sporting Goods and Gun Shop. "The right of the people to keep and bear arms shall not be infringed" was inscribed in Gothic letters over the door. Earl's also sold uniforms of every type and was the local headquarters for the NRA.

I asked the guy behind the counter if he was Earl.

"Ain't no Earl," he said. "I'm the owner, name's Casper. Thought Earl's was a better name for a gun shop."

"I see your point," I said. "Howdy, my name's Tony. I'm a new neighbor."

He took my hand and shook it firmly. "Always glad to meet a new neighbor." He gave me his full name, Rauberger. When I gave him mine, he deduced that it was Italian. He thought most Italians were Catholic. I explained that I'd seen the light and no longer followed the harlot of Rome with its painted idols, though I looked forward to Christian ecumenicism when the Pope was Born Again.

That settled that, and we got down to the important stuff. A discussion of stopping power, the 9 mm vs. the .45 caliber. He was a .45 caliber man. "U.S. Marines learned their lesson, fighting the hopped-up Moros in the Philippines. Nothing less than a forty-five could stop 'em. Plug 'em with a thirty-eight, they'd keep on coming, waving their spears and such, 'cause they was all fanatical on religion and from chewing them drugs. A nine mil'meter is nothin' but a thirty-eight. Now, I ask you, if nothin' less than a forty-five is gonna stop a hopped-up Moro, how do you expect to stop a cocaine-crazed nigra with a nine mil'meter?"

"But you got a lot more recoil," I said.

"If you're talking about target shooting," Casper said, in tones that made me understand that was for sissies, "it might make a difference. But if you're talking about a real lifesaving situation, protecting yourself or your family, hammer and tongs, face-to-face, it's that first shot, before any of your recoil, that's gonna make the difference. I got some friends, state troopers, they wouldn't carry a thirty-eight or a nine mil'meter if their life depended on it, and their lives do. You get one of them cocaine-crazed nigras, they get hit with a thirty-eight, they just breaks wind, pardon my French, and keeps on coming for more.

"If you're talking survival, you're talking forty-five, three-fifty-seven magnum or forty-four magnum. A man's gun."

"Bless me," I said, "you have indeed got a point. Which one would you recommend?"

"For in the house? In the car? Or on your person?"

"On my person," I said.

"Take a look at this here S and W three-fifty-seven snub. Two-and-a-half inch barrel. This is what your undercover, plainclothes police officer likes to carry. Concealability, stopping power, and manufactured in the U.S. of A."

"I'll take it," I cried.

"Ankle, belt, or shoulder holster?"

"Belt."

"Cartridges?"

"Yup."

"Hollow points, right!"

"Is that what Bernhard Goetz used?"

"Sure did. Now that's a good ol' boy. Best thing that ever happened up in New York. Don't matter if he's a Jew scientist; he's a good ol' boy in Casper Rauberger's book."

"I'll take 'em," I said.

"Cash or charge?"

"Charge," I said.

"All righty. Now you just fill out these here forms, give me a driver's license and credit card, and I'll go tote this up."

I handed over my plastic and began to fondle my new piece.

"This here says your residence is New York."

"I'm in the midst of moving right now," I said. "I'm staying here at the Land of Milk and Honey, and just this morning I talked to Ezra Ervin 'bout buying a house. I got some business in 'lanta, then I'm driving back to New York to bring the family on down. I'd hate to go to 'lanta unarmed."

"Y'all know who to blame for that. Jimmy Peanut. Do you know that when he was guvner down there, he made Martin Luther King Day a state holiday? Made the nigras think they could get away with anything they wanted. Ruined Georgia. No, sir, Casper Rauberger is not going to force a white man to go to 'lanta unarmed and unable to defend hisself. No, sir, not to New York, neither. You just put down there the address of that home you is planning to buy from ol' Ezra, that's what you do."

"You're a good Christian, Casper."

"I try to live by the book," he replied, with deep sincerity.

"Amen."

Suitably armed and dangerous, I made my way, on foot, toward the River Jordan. I saw a blue Ford parked across the street. Then, within a block, I saw two more like it. There's a story about two girls who went to Hollywood. They both blew all the producers they could find. Five years later, one was a star, the other was a cock sucker. Paranoia's like that. You don't know what you were until it's over.

I ambled into a couple of stores and out, then made my way with elaborate casualness to the woods. The mix of large old trees and untended post-swamp scrub was pleasantly chaotic, a relief from all the order that surrounded it.

There were flies, mosquitoes, no-see-ums, yellow jacks, and numerous things that a city boy simply doesn't know the name of. Take my word for it: True Christian Bug-Off does not work.

No one seemed to be following. On the other hand, no one seemed to be waiting.

"Over here," I heard a girl's voice say. I turned toward the sound and saw nothing.

"Where's here?"

"To your left," she said with exasperation.

To my left there was nothing but brush. It sounded like Cynthia Lynn, my cathedral cutie. I wondered what I was being set up for. I made my way through the brush.

The girl knew how to pick her spots. There was a clearing, tree stumps, and granite outcrops. She had her back to the west so the sun illuminated her blond hair and outlined the shape of her body, just like they light movie heroines.

"Are you really from New York?" she said.

"What do you want?"

"Are you really from New York?"

314

"Why do you ask?"

"I checked your license plates. They're not from New York."

"It's rental car. I flew down."

"Are you a reporter or something?"

"No," I said.

"What would you come down here from New York for?"

"Well, it's different. A cleaner, more Christian way of life."

"You really believe that?" she said with a teenage sneer.

"Well, that's what they told me at the motel."

"Are you that much of a sucker? You know what this town is? Boring. Bee, oh, are, eye, en, gee."

"Yeah, well, I could see that."

She moved her shoulders, which moved her breasts, which were too good to work Ninth Avenue. "Ah'd do anything, if you'd take me to New York," she drawled. She'd been practicing in front of a mirror. "Anything aht al-l-l, mister."

I laughed.

That upset her. But she tried harder. "What's the mattuh? Don't you like what you see? Maybe if you saw a little more."

I sat down on a tree stump. I also put my hand on my gun. I had a crawling sensation up and down my neck that if someone found us here and she got one more button of her blouse open, something strange and Southern Gothic would happen to me.

"Be cool," I said, "and tell me what's going on."

"You don't want me," she pouted.

"I don't mean to insult you," I said. The guidebook to the South said be polite. Manners are strongly valued there.

"You don't think I'm good-looking."

"You're very good-looking."

"I'm too unsophisticated for you. I knew it." Underneath the act there was some sort of genuine and struggling adolescent, which was appealing, even touching. The act, and the lines, were something she'd learned from the TV. It wasn't that she'd learned them badly, creating a sad parody of prime-time soap opera. She had it quite right. It was being stuck in reality that made it hollow and meretricious. "Look, mister, I can learn, I'm smart. You take me to New York, I'll show you a go-o-od time."

"I take it you sent me that note because you want me to take you to New York. Correct?"

"Uh huh. I surely do."

"What do you think you're going to do in New York?"

"Ah know what men want," she drawled. And licked her lower lip.

"You want to go to New York and be a prostitute?"

"Wel-l-l, you don't need to be so crude. But ah heard girls make hundreds and hundreds of dollars in a single night. They can go dancing and to the movies, any movie they want, and wear clothes and makeup and everything. And I want it!"

This was the kind of place they came from. And that's how they got to New York, with simpleminded stories and a bus ticket. Maybe some of them made money. Some of them ended up on Eleventh Avenue, competing with the transvestites for the opportunity to give blow jobs to truckdrivers. "Tell me something, Cynthia—"

"Call me Sin," she said, as she'd dreamed of saying.

I didn't laugh. "OK, Sin. You the town slut?"

"No way," she said indignantly.

"You got a reputation?"

"Course not," she said.

"You do much fucking?"

"Wha-a-a!?"

"Much suckin'?"

"Nevuh."

"But you think you want to go to New York and be a whore."

"I know what I want. I know what men want. I just put the two together and it come up four. I'm not dumb," she said.

"I'm not a pimp," I said. "How old are you?"

"Eighteen. I'm a high school senior."

"Unless you were left back, I figure seventeen. Why don't you finish, then either get a job or go to college and then go to New York or wherever, like a real person. Girl, you go up there like this and they'll eat you alive."

"No they won't. I'm real pretty, even if you don't think so, and that means a lot to a man."

"Take my word for it, they'll devour you. And is there some reason we had to have this conversation in a mosquito-infested swamp? Why do people always want to meet me in uncomfortable places?"

"Look, mister . . ."

"Call me Tony."

"OK, Tony. Y'all know what a Faith High School diploma is good for? We only been here three years, so ah been outside, ah been to a real school. Not a real good one, but at least a real school. Alls they teach you here is Bible verses and to be an oh-beed-i-ent wife. Like my mother. Oh-beed-i-ent. Beaten into the ground—that's more like it. Now my mother is smarter than my daddy, but neither one of 'em is evuh gonna admit that. My daddy is stupid. He runs the car without oil, the engine burns up, and he thinks he's got bad luck. He cahn't balance a checkbook. You see those men start giving me hundred-dollar bills, you better believe Cynthia Lynn can balance a checkbook."

"What's the matter, you don't like studying?"

"What's there to study? I been through the Bible twice. I done memorized the nasty parts. 'She lusted for the lechers of Egypt, whose members are like those of an ass and whose issue is like that of stallions.' Ezekiel Twenty-three: Twenty. I done memorized the regular parts too. Now I got to get out of here. You gonna help me or not?"

"Look, Sin . . ."

"You want to see the goods?" Her fingers worked quickly and the blouse fell open. There were two of them. They were big. She was seventeen; they were as firm as big ones get.

"I don't know who's watching," I said to the woods at large, "but whoever you are, all I want is for this girl to button up. I don't want to see anything I shouldn't see, and I don't commit statutory rape. You got that?"

"You think I'm settin' you up for something?"

"Will you button your blouse? Before you get mosquito bites on your tits and have to walk around scratching them." She did as I told her, defeated. There is something very powerful about refusing to respond to a pretty girl's sexual overtures. "And if that's what you really want, why the hell are we meeting in the middle of the woods?"

"If I talked to you in town, Mammy and Pappy will know I was talking to you in about two seconds. Unsupervised. You can't even have a

317

conversation in this town without it becomes a matter of community concern. Then before you know it, you become the subject of a church sermon. How long you been here?"

"A couple of days."

"Then you don't know what narrow-minded is. I got to get out of here."

I stood up. "I'm sorry, Cynthia Lynn. I can't do anything for you." And started heading out of the clearing.

She dashed around in front of me. "What if I holler rape? Huh? And tear my blouse?"

"Gimme a break," I said.

She started to sniffle, then to cry. It was a pleasure to see a girl cry without makeup. Instead of leaving black tracks of unknown substances carving through rouge, looking like the passage of brackish water over red clay soil, the tears flowed clean and bright. She bit at her lower lip. It grew swollen and red. I put a hand out to draw her close. So I could be paternal and comforting. She jerked away.

I sighed. "Look. Let me think on it. If I can think of something." What she needed was a social worker or a pimp.

"Will you? Will you really?"

"Yes, dammit. Stop wailing."

"OK," she said, and began wiping her eyes.

"I got something I'm curious about. A guy I knew from New York, older guy, a retired fireman, is supposed to be down here. You know anybody like that?"

She shook her head.

"Come on, let's get away from here," I said, slapping another mosquito. He'd fed well, and I got a bright red drop of blood on my palm along with the corpse.

"We have to leave separately," she said.

"Fine. I'm going first."

"Wait. Can I ask you one thing?"

"Sure."

"Up in New York, in restaurants, do they really call waitresses waitpersons?"

"Sometimes."

"And the women who believe in the ERA, are they really lesbians who drink beer from cans and wear Jockey shorts?"

37.

Laying On of Hands

I went to church again Friday night.

Friday night was Variety Night. Like the good old days at the Brooklyn Paramount when Alan Freed's rock 'n' roll show came to town. Not just one star and an opening act, but a whole show. Bo Diddley *and* Chuck Berry *and* the Shirelles *and* the Del Vikings *and* Dion and the Belmonts *and* Lloyd Price *and more*. Friday night in Faith cooked. Five preachers. Five backup groups. Miracle cures, speaking in tongues. Friday night drew a different crowd. Younger and older, seedier and livelier. Gimpier too.

A Gran'pa Walton look-alike walked slowly up to the cathedral, leaning on a cane. One of the many white-wardrobed disciples rushed forward to help him. It was a sweet thing to see. She engaged him in conversation. Another ministering angel rushed up with a wheelchair. They sat him down and helped him roll in.

Cyn saw me and Cyn approached me. She was alone. "Usually my brother Bubba comes with me Friday night," she said, "my parents are too old to do anything but stay home Friday night, just to make sure I don't talk to strange men. But Bubba's got a football game, over Westfield. He's gonna come home stomped. Faith always gets stomped by Westfield; they got nigras. You want to come to services with me?"

"I'm kinda looking for somebody," I said.

"You look like you're alone, that's what you look like," she said.

"And satanic," I said.

"Well, hush my mouth. Should I apologize for saying that? It's your eyes."

Services started at six. I hadn't seen McGarrity come in, but it was entirely possible that I'd missed him. So I went into the cathedral with Cynthia Lynn.

"What do you see? What do you see up here before you on the podium?" Troy Woodcock asked the throng. "I'll tell you what you see. A criminal. A desperate, despicable criminal." Troy styled himself "the Mad Man of the Gospel—that's mad as in angry."

"Why doesn't he call himself the angry man of the Gospel," I asked Cynthia, "so he doesn't have to explain what mad means?"

"James Robison already got Angry, so's he's got to call himself something different," she said.

> When I was a kid I planned rapes and plotted crimes.
> I considered everything but murder. I was mean. I'm
> talking about sadistic! cruel! I killed animals . . . de-
> liberately. I killed a dog—just threw it on the floor
> until it died. I killed a cat. Put it in a fire. . . . God, I
> was bad. I was filthy.
>
> JAMES ROBINSON, evangelist

What had made Troy mad, as in angry, was, apparently, having sex.

"I was insatiable. I was a beast. I did not have just one woman. I didn't have just two women. I didn't have just three women. I didn't have just four women. I always had six, seven, eight, or nine.

"White women, Mex'can women, colored women.

"I was a fornicatin' fool!"

> "What makes you think you're called to be a
> preacher?" The country boy just grinned kind of fool-
> ish. "Well, I got the biggest prick in the neighbor-
> hood," says he, "and a terrible craving for fried
> chicken."
>
> VANCE RANDOLPH, *Pissing in the Snow & Other*
> *Ozark Folktales*

"There was no controllin' me! No stoppin' me! If I seed a woman, and I wanted her, there was nothin', nothin', nothin' I wouldn't do till I had her. I would buy her things. I would tell her lies. I would make promises I had no intention of keeping.

"It didn't matter if'n she was married. I'd wait till her husband was away. I would exploit her weakness. I would ply her with whiskey and wine. I would employ the seductive power of drugs."

Cyn was squeezing her thighs together, keeping rhythm with Woodcock.

"You know what I'm talking about. That marijuana weed!"

The drummer hit a rim shot. The congregation gasped.

"I'm talkin' about happy dust! Magic powder! Cocaine! Just one whiff, just one whiff, and I would have a woman sliding down, down, going down the greasy slide to perversions. What kinds of perversions? . . . Anything you can think of."

Cynthia reached what Masters and Johnson defined as the first plateau in the sequence toward orgasm, a flush in the neck and torso, a change in breathing, nipples erect.

So great was Troy's satanic power over women that he, in due course, became a pimp. And did a whole bunch of horrendous pimp things—drove a Cadillac, wore silk suits, drank scotch and milk.

While he steeped in sin, there were two things he held sacred: white-haired Mom, golden-haired Sis. Sis was seduced by one of his associates, a nigra pimp. This event was described in grim and alarming euphemism. Troy made it clear that the vile seducer had, as the legend requires, a larger-than-white penis.

As we all knew it would, the event brought on attempted suicide (Mom), successful suicide (Sis), attempted murder (Troy)—and a miraculous Bible that appeared at the right time. Troy was born again.

Troy had his own backup group, the Woodcock Gospel Four, from Muscle Shoals, Alabama. They were Pentecostal. They were hot. And they ripped off Jerry Lee Lewis something awesome. They took "Whole Lot of Shaking Going On," substituted "saving" for "shaking," and made it Jesus who had the bull by the horn. But it was still down in the barn and it was still low down, just plain dirty, rock 'n' roll. Just like Jerry Lee meant it to be.

Cynthia Lynn pressed a moist hand into mine. "Take me outside for some air, honey, please."

I wasn't the only man walking out with a stiff prick and a wet woman.

The sun was going down, the sky glowed red, and Faith was heavy with shadows.

"Where do you want to go?"

"Just for a stroll, for some air, honey," she said, leading me down the hill. I had an idea where she was going, the darkness between a stand of weeping beeches and a Bible study center.

We edged into a doorway, hidden in shadow. I wondered what the age of consent was in North Carolina. Her body pressed into mine, and each body discovered what the other body wanted to know. Her fingertips made a determination of my size and shape. She humped her pubis against my leg. "Touch me, touch me," she moaned.

She lifted her skirt and guided my hand to her thigh. From there, I knew the way. My hand slid up. Her panties were cotton. And very wet. The mechanics in Faith were the same as anywhere else, clitoris top and center, manipulate rapidly, gently but firmly.

"I'm so bad, I'm so bad," she moaned. "I want it, I want it, I'm a bad girl." Her fingers clamped down around my erection for emphasis.

Climax was marked by strangulation of the word "bad," followed by biting. We did that three or four times. I was feeling very adolescent about the whole thing. My brain was distinctly on vacation. I felt like the two of us were in a throbbing cocoon. It made us invisible. It also prevented reason from entering.

We paused. She tried the door of the Bible study center. "Oh, darn," she said. "Darn, darn. This door is nevuh locked. Doors in Faith are supposed to be open all the time so Billy Purvis Parker can go 'round talking about how doors in Faith is never locked 'cause with all good Christians there is no crime."

"Oh, darn," I said.

"We could go to your room," she said.

"Yeah," I said.

"I just knew you had that satanic look the first time I saw you. But sweet, you know," she said, giving my aching erection a reassuring squeeze. "And you kiss good. Like nobody else I ever kissed. Am I bad? I'm bad, aren't I?"

"No," I said, starting for the Land of Milk and Honey. "You're not bad."

"It never felt that good," she said.

"That's good."

"Afterward, can we talk all about New York City?"

"Sure we can." Anything you want.

"Do they really have libraries there with every book ever written and just anybody can come and take them out without special permission?"

"Yeah."

"I'm so happy," she said. "Look, we better not be seen going down there together. I mean, if we're seen."

"What do you want to do?" I asked.

"If y'all give me the key, I can sneak on down, then you just wait about five, ten minutes and you come along and I'll let y'all in."

"Fine," I said, giving her the key.

"I wish I could just kiss you and kiss you. I love the way you kiss. Hurry along, don't you lollygag."

"No, ma'am," I said. "I never keep a lady waiting."

I gave it five minutes by my watch—that's a long time when you're locked in a burning building or horny—then started down after her.

That's when Ralph McGarrity decided to come to church. He had his Bible clutched to his breast like a haunted man warding off vampires. He'd put on weight, looking heavy and haggard both at once. But there was no doubt who it was.

Of course I hesitated. Of course I cursed him. But I followed him back to the cathedral.

McGarrity craved the loving arms of Jesus. The fervor of the preachers swept him along. He bobbed his head with their rhythms. He gasped and amened in the right spots. He even wept.

I wondered how long Cyn would wait for me.

Then the star of the show came on. Reverend Billy Purvis Parker. The power of Jesus was on him. He was going to do some healings. "Amen," McGarrity cried. "Amen."

Reverend Billy asked if anybody out there needed healing. No one else answered, so Reverend Billy did.

"Grandpa Stoner," he cried, "you got arthritis, arthritis so bad that down the VA hospital they took out your hip. Then they put in that plastic hip. That plastic hip, it don't work right. It never worked right. It hurts you. It hurts you so bad, so bad, you can't walk on it. It hurts so bad that even the codeine doesn't help. Nothing helps.

"But there is something that can help—um hmm—and I feel the power now. Yes I do. Yes I do. Yes I do.

"Somebody help Grandpa Stoner, somebody get behind his wheelchair. Somebody wheel him right down here. Where I can lay my hands upon him. Where I can touch him with the power of our Lord Jesus Christ. Wheel him down, wheel him down, wheel him down."

One of the white apostles wheeled him down. It was the Gran'pa Walton look-alike I had seen walk up the hill to the cathedral.

"Now wai-i-it a minute," Billy cried, like the Isley Brothers do in "Shout." "Have we ever met?"

"No, sir," the old man said. "I can't rightly say I've had the pleasure."

"And what's your name?"

"It's Stoner, sir. Eliot Stoner."

"Is that the name I called you by? Is that the name I called you by?"

"Well, yes sir, it is."

"Now how did I know that? How did I know that?" Reverend Billy said, like he didn't know how he knew. "I swear to you, that name just came to me. It just came to me. Out of the air. No, no. Not out of the air. It came from Je-e-esus."

"Yes, Lord," McGarrity cried. "Yes, Lord."

Then the reverend asked Mr. Stoner if he believed in the power to heal. Which Stoner did. Billy closed his eyes with coital intensity and laid his hands on the plastic Stoner hip. After which he commanded Stoner to rise and walk. Which of course Stoner did. With no more effort than he had displayed on his way in.

There was great jubilation. McGarrity was almost overcome, close to tears at bearing witness to the miracle.

Several more healings followed.

Then there were savings. McGarrity got saved. He rushed to the front. He told the Lord he was a sinner. He gave himself to Jesus. He was reborn. Tears of joy streamed down his face.

He looked sincere. He looked like he'd been saved lots of times before.

I got saved too. To stay close. I fell to my knees, waved my hands in the air, and in general behaved like Groucho Marx in blackface. Nobody questioned my sincerity.

At last it was over.

I followed McGarrity through the throng as we exited. He made straight for the parking lot. I knew I was going to lose him as soon as he got in his car. It didn't matter. Once I knew what he drove, which was a blue Seville, and the license plate, I could find him again.

When I got back to the motel, Cynthia wasn't there.

There was a note in a sealed motel envelope. I tore it open. It said:

Dear Friend,

. . . right now, your tax dollars are providing America's schoolchildren with some of the dirtiest, filthiest and perverted books and films on sex education you can imagine! . . . Let me share with you some shocking, downright disgusting facts. For example, did you know your tax dollars are teaching school-age children to:

French kiss and masturbate

enjoy the roles of being a homosexual or lesbian?

draw the sex organs of men and women and the act of intercourse . . .

Dr. William A. Block's *Do It Yourself Illustrated Human Sexuality Book for Kids* . . . depicts a nude "Sex family" . . . including gutter terms for sexual organs and the sex act.

I wish I had more time to share with you all the horrible things American children are being taught about sex in the classroom. . . .

P.S. Originally I had planned to enclose a sampling of the crude street language and drawings used in Dr. Block's sex book. . . . However, they are so disgustingly graphic that I decided not to send them unless requested to do so. If you want to see what your schoolchildren are being exposed to, just enclose a self-addressed envelope along with your donation.

Taxpayers Against Sex Education
A Project of Christian Family Renewal, Inc.

38.

An Archangel

I called home early on Saturday. Wayne wanted to know when I would be back. Glenda wanted to know if I was being good. I said I'd heard that song before, and it was too old.

"I'm not allowed to ask questions when I haven't seen you for a week?"

"Hey, I've called you three times since I left."

"You said you liked Southern sluts. I've heard you say that."

"That's because I never met one. I grew up in Brooklyn. I saw them in the movies."

"I want to refurnish the living room."

"There's a battle of good and evil," I said, "and in Faith, good has triumphed. Even the pornography is religious."

"I thought they didn't have pornography there."

"It's a matter of degree. Before they invented miniskirts, men used to get hot over ankles."

"I don't want to fight with you. We've done so much of that. I'm happy we're back together."

"So what do you want to do with the living room?" I said.

"Some good oak pieces, I think. Maybe we can go antiquing when you get back."

"Wow," I said.

"I want you involved. It's your home too."

"You know what my dream home is? A Holiday Inn room. Good showers. Small closets so you can't accumulate too much. And somebody else cleans. Maybe with a twenty-four-hour library and saloon next door."

"Somebody else does clean," she pointed out.

"Yeah, but in a motel I don't feel like I'm supposed to help."

"Under that veneer of being hip, you're really a bit of a sexist," she said.

"You don't know what sexism is until you live in Faith. The first commandment is: Thou shalt obey your husband. The second is: Thou's husband is always right. The third is: Shut up and obey your husband. I wish to hell you'd enjoy me."

"I love you," she said.

"Yeah," I said, "but is that any fun?"

"Do you love me?"

"Do I love you? What else would I come back to a condo for? Is Wayne doing well in school? The first weeks are critical. If the teachers think he's brilliant in the first two weeks, they think it's their fault if he hits a slump in midseason. You gotta get ahead of the game."

"Will you be home soon?"

"Sure. Maybe. Will you get a new tape?"

I staked out the supermarket. The Seville arrived in midafternoon. The driver was a washed-out woman in her mid-thirties. When she came back out, I followed her.

McGarrity's house was up in Hearth and Home Hills. It had a lawn and rosebushes out front. Two four-year-old pines were planted alongside the driveway. A white picket fence surrounded the backyard. His new name was on the mailbox. It was Rolf McDonald.

I went back to the motel. Rolf McDonald's phone was listed.

The woman answered.

"Mrs. McDonald?" I said.

"No," she said. "You want to speak to Mr. McDonald?"

"Isn't this Mrs. Anne McDonald?" I asked.

"Isn't no Mrs. McDonald," she said. "Mr. McDonald, he's a widower."

I apologized for calling the wrong number. I figured her for a housekeeper. They weren't living together. Not in Faith. I was going to take him either late at night or early in the morning. Somewhere between sleeping and waking, not in dreams but close to them, where you can see into your own mind, where the demons play.

I went back to Casper Rauberger's store. He sold uniforms for sports, for gas stations, for choirs. I bought a choir robe. White with lots of gold trim.

The phone rang. It was Cynthia. She spoke low and anxious.

"I got to talk to you," she said, sniffling.

"Sure."

"I can only talk for a second. They're coming back. When are you leaving?"

"I don't know; maybe tomorrow," I said.

"Will you take me with you?"

"Look, Cyn . . ."

"Darn, darn, they're coming back. Listen, we always go to dinner Saturday night . . ."

"My God Will Provide?"

"Yes. At seven o'clock. Same time every Saturday. Now there's an alley out back. Would you be there, honey? Please? Pretty please, with sugar and honey and sweet things on top," she said. Then she hung up.

I swam in the motel pool. Then went over the McGarrity file. There was still time to kill. I went to The Word newsstand and bookstore. They didn't have the *New York Times*. Or the *Washington Post*. Or anything else I cared to read. I took a walk.

Down the bug-ridden bridle path. It was still hot and thick. I longed for even a rumor of autumn. I thought about Cynthia Lynn. Got thick in my cock. I touched myself and felt the weight. What a fun toy. What a pleasure. What a delight. What a great way to get close and communicative. What was it about it that so terrified the residents of Faith?

I got to an open area, where the sun shone down. I unzipped and stroked it erect so the sun could see. I closed my eyes and the brightness left sunspots on my lids. I made up pictures from them, like people are supposed to do with clouds. Great penis blimps sailing over Rev-

erend Billy's Christian Community. The residents screaming in terror.
They scramble for their fallout shelters.

T. K. Jones, Deputy Under Secretary for Strategic Nuclear Forces,
is there to organize things. "Dig a hole. Cover it with a couple of doors
and then throw three feet of dirt on top. It's the dirt that does it. . . .
Everyone's going to make it if there's enough shovels to go around," he
says.

They dive in. And discover women are waiting there. With functioning vaginas.

All die of hysteria. I alone march out and tear down the attorney
general, who is the third corner of a pedestal on which the President is
standing. The blimps ejaculate, in new condom colors. From everywhere there is applause. From women, union leaders, blacks, from the
literate, from fiction writers who can be clear once again about what is
nonfiction.

I tucked myself back in, with the humble realization that if the future
of the country were in my hands, we'd be as bad off as we were with
Reagan. I needed for things to be over with. I was getting strange.

I got to the alley promptly at seven. My gun in my holster, my piece
back in my pants. There was no one there. The Dumpster was aromatic. Seven-ten. No one there. Dumpster still aromatic.

Seven-twenty. I heard her voice calling my name in a stage whisper.
But I didn't see her. "Over here," she called. I looked around and saw
her face sticking out of a window.

"I'm in the ladies' room," she said. I looked in. She was. "Please, I
got to go with you."

"Look, you're seventeen, you haven't finished high school, what the
hell am I going to do with you? I have a family. I can't bring you home."
Even as I said it, I realized I could put her in Joey's apartment.

"Somebody saw me going away from church. Last night. Natcherly,
they just had to tell my pappy. I want so much to be somewhere where
nobody pays no never mind to nobody else's business. I want you to see
what he done to me."

She stood up on the toilet seat so her hips were about where her face
had been. She turned her back to me, lifted her long skirt, then dropped
her white cotton panties. Lovely buns. Round, firm, tender. With great

red lash marks across them. Mostly weals, but some broken skin, crusty with dried blood and scabs. Older scars were beneath them. I could also see wisps of pubic hair. Very blond.

"OK, put your clothes back," I said. "I'm probably leaving tomorrow. In the morning."

"My folks go to church at seven. I can pretend to be sick. I make myself feverish and then I vomit. I've done it before."

"Can't I just give you money for a Greyhound ticket?"

"You still don't get it, do you? They watch the bus station."

"Cyn . . ."

"If I don't get out of here real soon, bad things are going to start happening, as sure as Reverend Billy is a millionaire."

"All right. But I want to be out of here early."

"I'll be there by seven-fifteen. Seven-thirty at the latest. Bye, honey. I got to go, before they gets upset. Thanks, honey."

"I don't believe I just agreed to that," I said to an empty ladies' room.

Around eleven, I drove by the house of Ralph/Rolf McGarrity/McDonald. It was an early-to-bed town. Only three houses had their lights on. His was one of them. I drove on. An hour later I drove by again. Only two houses had lights on. The other one was far in the distance.

I parked in front of the house. I checked my .357 snub. Then I put on my white choral robe with gold trim. It was just too silly. I was sure any reasonable person would be smitten with hysterics when they saw me. Then I remembered I was in Faith.

I got casually out of the car and strolled up to the front door. I was shocked. It was locked.

But the kitchen door was open.

The living room was ordinary. Overpoweringly ordinary. Wall-to-wall carpeting, a couch, two armchairs, a coffee table, Reverend Billy and Ronald Reagan on one wall, Jesus Christ on the other. McGarrity sat in one of the armchairs, a standing lamp with a cream and russet shade throwing light from over his shoulder onto the Bible. Reverend Billy's blessed and personally autographed, commemorative, limited-edition, calfskin-bound, genuine-parchment-style-paper, twenty-color-plate, one-hundred-dollar-tax-deductible-contribution Bible.

I set my voice deep and hollow and intoned, "Ralph McGarrity."

He looked up. Startled. Frightened. But he didn't say "Who are you?" or "What do you want?" or "What are you doing in my house?" He said, "It's Rolf, with an *o*." Then he stuttered over "McDonald."

"It's Ralph," I said. Authoritatively. "And it's McGarrity, not McDonald."

"No, no. It's Rolf McDonald. My friends somethimes call me Mack."

I raised my white-draped arms on high. Nobody laughed. "Do you believe in the Lord?" I shouted.

"Yes," he said.

"Is Jesus Christ your personal savior?" I cried.

"He is, he is. I gave my soul to the Lord. I took Jesus into my heart. Jesus Christ is my savior."

I stalked toward him. I stood over him. I glared down in his face. "Do you lie to your Lord and tell him that your name is not your name?" That flustered him. He probably did. Religion is strange. But he got his pension checks in his real name. He could lie to his neighbors. He could lie to his friends. But he could not lie to the City of New York Civil Service Pension Fund! "You think God doesn't see!" I grabbed him by his shirt and yanked him out of the chair. "Get down on your knees," I yelled in his face, then shoved him down to the floor. "Pray!"

He did. He began to mutter, " 'The Lord is my shepherd, I shall not want . . .' "

I put my hand on his head and took hold of his hair. "I want the truth now. I can see into your heart. I can see into your mind. Nothing is hidden from me."

"Who are you?" he asked at last.

"I am the Sword of the Archangel Michael. I am the avenging angel. I am the messenger. I am the blood of the lamb!"

"I am a sinner," he said. "I am a sinner."

"You are a murderer. There is blood on your hands."

"I've come to Jesus," he said. "I've been cleansed of my sins. I have. I have. I have," he chanted like a child.

"Flames! Do you see the flames?" I moaned, waving my floppy sleeves. "Hellfire. Hellfire and damnation. Do you want to burn in hell?"

"No. No. I want to go to a better place. I'm going to go to the better place. I gave myself to Jesus."

"Not enough," I said. "Take it from the Archangel Michael—it doesn't cut it, Ralph. What we need here is some earthly atonement."

"What? What? I tithe. I pray. I don't drink anymore. Not much anymore."

"The flames," I roared, fluttering the sleeves for effect. The robe was great. "Three dead in Brooklyn. What about them, Ralph?"

"That was in my previous life. My sinful life. Before I was born again. It doesn't count."

I thrust out my finger and pointed at him, a living portrait of accusation. "Bullshit," I cried. "That's bullshit in the eyes of the Lord. And the Lord don't love bullshit. The Lord wants full confession. And he wants it in writing."

It didn't take much more. McGarrity had not become McDonald and buried himself in Faith because he was hiding from the law. He was hiding from himself. He was trying to shut the inner eye that persisted in seeing visions of fire. The story poured out. With a lot of excuses. And self-pity. He had more expenses than he could handle. But it wasn't the gambling or the drinking that did him in; it was because his wife chose to get sick at the wrong time. Otherwise he could have paid his gambling debts.

"Tell it, brother!" I cried. And other things of that sort.

Then along came this guinea, called himself Mr. Fix. Mr. Fix knew someone who could help McGarrity with his troubles.

It was a real job. A consulting position with a New York company that was doing a lot of building in the South and Southwest. "Fire codes in New York, and fire prevention—we were much in advance of down South. This company wanted to build better, safer, more fireproof buildings. That's the job I took. Saving lives, that's what it was about."

"The Sun Group?"

"You know everything," he gasped.

"Yes, but you must confess it, you must cleanse your soul."

He dealt with Mr. Gunderson himself. A very sincere and dedicated man. Committed to building a better America. In the days of real dollars, when gold was thirty-five dollars an ounce, the salary was enormous for a part-time assignment—ten thousand dollars.

Before he even got his first check, he was visited by Mr. DeStefano, a vice-president of Empire Administration. McGarrity was the arson investigator assigned to a fire that destroyed an Empire Administration building. Mr. DeStefano was very gracious and very pleased to meet him. After all, McGarrity was about to become an employee of one of Empire's sister companies, the Sun Group. Mr. DeStefano was certain that McGarrity's report would show that the fire in his building was an accident.

When DeStefano walked out the door, the collectors walked in. To remind McGarrity of his gambling debts.

McGarrity had become a capitive arson investigator. An employee of the people who were burning New York. "No one was ever hurt. That first building. It was practically empty. Falling down. Useless. If it weren't for government overregulation, they could have torn it down like it should have been torn down. When the government regulates things, everything gets screwed up. Now who knows better how to run a business, the businessman whose business it is or some paper-pushing bureaucrat in Washington, D.C., who's never worked in the real world a day in his life?"

"And the fire in Brooklyn?" I said. "Three dead."

"That wasn't supposed to happen. You know that wasn't supposed to happen. That was an accident. I've come to Christ. People get killed in accidents all the time. You're making steel, guy trips and falls into the—the thing they make steel in, you don't crucify U.S. Steel. I've been Born Again. Things have to get done, and when government regulation gets all in the way, sometimes you have to do it different ways, and who is to blame? I came to Jesus. Those people, they're not my fault. I didn't kill them. I came to Jesus. I am Born Again."

Then I had to get him to put his words in writing. By five, it was done. Six pages of handwritten confession. Including being hired by Randolph Gunderson, personally. Gold. Pure gold. I could open a Swiss bank account with it.

At five-thirty, with a befuddled and weary McGarrity in tow, I pounded on the door of the Promised Land's desk clerk and notary public.

"Come back later," he moaned.

"Open up," I said.

"Wha' . . . what is it?" he said, coming to the door in his pajamas.

"I need something notarized. Now."

"You . . . Later. Later."

"You don't understand," I said, looking him square in the eye, as deadpan as Dan Aykroyd. "We're on a mission from God."

I used the Xerox machine in the motel office to copy what he'd written. Then I drove McGarrity back to his McDonald home. I kept the original and one copy of the confession, mailed one copy to myself, the other to John Straightman. I was excited enough that I called him as well, even though it was before six o'clock in the morning. Of course I got his answering machine. I left a message saying that I had the goods on Gunderson.

A few minutes after seven, Cynthia Lynn woke me up. She was all bubbly and ready to go. I was on top of the bed, still dressed, except for the choir robe, with my gun butt digging a hole in my hip. No sleep makes me irritable, and one hour's sleep makes me meaner than no sleep at all. "Just shut up," I growled, stumbling into the bathroom to brush my teeth and splash some water in my face.

The phone rang. I was certain it was Glenda. "Don't take that," I spluttered, with a mouth full of foam. I raced out to the bedroom to get it first. She was smiling at me, the top two buttons of her blouse open. I answered the phone, swallowing toothpaste. It was Straightman. I told him to hold on. I rinsed my mouth and came back. He asked me what was going on. I looked at Cynthia. I told John to hold on again. "Wait outside," I told her.

"Outside?" she said, beginning to protest.

I took her by the arm. "Now wait outside," I barked.

"Where?" she whined.

"I don't give a shit," I said, shoving her out the door. "Go to the coffee shop. Get me a coffee to go." My brain was starting to function again, enough to say, "Milk, no sugar," and "Better make that two." I closed the door, with her outside.

I went back to the phone. "Hey, John, I got a sworn and witnessed and notarized statement. The arson investigator was on Gunderson's payroll. He admits that he covered up the Brooklyn fire and six of the other nine we knew about and eight more."

By the time I hung up, he was ecstatic. I was going to be also, as soon as I had my coffee.

The door burst open.

A bunch of people were coming into the room. All I saw was that they had weapons.

I rolled over to the far side of the bed, drawing my gun as I did. I peeked over the mattress. "Freeze, you fuckers!" I screamed. The obscenity, which is part of the rhythm of New York street speech, rang harsh and loud in Faith. It was the first time I'd heard it in a week. I think it was that, more than the gun, that brought the four of them up short.

I now had time to see who my guests were. Bubba, the brother in the Prayer Warrior T-shirt, had a deer rifle. Pappy had a baseball bat. There were two other guys I didn't know. One Bubba's age. The other in his mid-thirties. He looked FBI. But everybody in Faith looked FBI or overweight.

"Now this is a three-fucking-fifty-seven magnum," I said.

"That's a three-fifty-seven magnum," Bubba said. Thrilled and impressed.

"I thought they were bigger," the other teenager said.

"It's a snub-nose, you asshole," I explained.

"I seen Dirty Harry's," he said, shaking his head.

"Make me prove it," I yelled. "Come on, sucker, make my day!" I said.

"Wh . . . where is she?" Pappy said.

"Who?" I asked.

"Mah daughter. You got my daughter."

"Who?" I asked. "You have a daughter? Do I know you?"

"His daughter," the FBI-like person said. He had an especially undistinguished tie. "You are planning to abduct his daughter and sell her into white slavery in New York City."

"You people are on drugs," I said, hoping that the little ditz didn't choose that moment to walk in with my two coffees to go, milk, no sugar.

"You got her," Bubba said. "We know you got her."

"Who the fuck are you talking about?"

"Watch your language," Pappy said.

"Watch my language?" I yelled, standing up and cocking the hammer on the gun. "Watch my fucking language? You four fucks break into my room, which is like my home, and that entitles me to shoot you for breaking and entering and trespassing and being all-around bad people, and if you don't back the fuck up and get the fuck out of here, I'm gonna start blowing people away."

"Wh . . . wh . . . where is she?" Pappy cried.

What the hell. I let one go into the ceiling.

The sucker was loud. I mean thunder. That big, clapping echo noise that a low cloud lets go of when it's right over your head and the dogs go and cower under the bed and little children cry. Thunder.

Plaster tumbled down on their heads as they tripped all over each other, stumbling for the door. I fired again. What a great noise!

My suitcase already had most of my stuff in it. I didn't bother to go and collect my toothbrush and such. As soon as they were out, I just grabbed what was packed. I stepped out, waving my Smith & Wesson in front of me. They were huddled together about twenty feet away, conferring.

"Back, you weirdos, back," I yelled. They moved back. Keeping my eye on them, I moved toward my car. I opened the driver's door and tossed my things in. Cynthia Lynn came out of the coffee shop with two coffees to go. She stared at her father and brother. They stared at her. I hopped in the car. Turned it on. It caught right away. Thank you, car rental folks. And I floored it out of the parking lot.

39.

The Empire Strikes Back

I was in the friendly skies.

> You may have been good. You may have been bad.
> You may be going to heaven. You may be going to
> hell. It doesn't matter. If you die in the South, y'all
> have to change planes in Atlanta.
>
> *Folkways of the New South,*
> Oral Anthropology Project
> William and Mary College, 1979

I was on the wings of man.

It depends on the winds. And who else is up there. Sometimes the
flight pattern is over Long Island, which is a lot like anywhere else. But
sometimes the flight comes in over the harbor. That's the sight that's in
photographs and movies and on TV. Bridges and boats, rivers and
lights, towers and traffic. Manhattan stands there like it thinks it's the
center of the world. It is.

> *don't come back unless you win,*
> *'cause losing is a sin,*
> *that cannot be forgiven,*
> *so if you wanna keep on livin',*
> *get that gold*

> *and come on home,*
> *get the gold*
> *and bring it home.*
> *America.*
>
> *America loves you when you win,*
> *don't do the Vi'tnam thing again,*
> *show 'em that we're greater,*
> *take 'em like we took Grenada.*
>
> *go out and run your race,*
> *there ain't no second place,*
> *come back standing tall,*
> *come back first or not at all,*
> *get that gold*
> *and come on home,*
> *get the gold*
> *and bring it home.*

The White Rapper (H. Stucker),
"Olympic Fever"
(© Honkey Tunes, Inc., 1984)

I was bringing it all home.

I walked into the apartment with that nice afterglow you get from a good workout—real tired but sort of floating, free of pain. Glenda wanted to tell me everything that had happened when I was gone and hear everything that I'd done. I wanted to make love and go to sleep.

I remained good-humored. Friendly. Tolerant. Loving. A new me.

I gradually brought her around. Without a foreplay fight. It was pretty good too. Not as hot as a Troy Woodcock sermon on perversion. Not as jolly and free as loving with Marie. But good.

I got up in time to walk Wayne to school. I wore a loose shirt to cover my gun. It felt familiar now. It never really had before. I didn't like that. I promised to quit work early so we could play some ball.

"Have you ever considered a computer," he said, "for your office?"

"You'd rather have a computer than play ball?"

"I was thinking of the many benefits a computer brings to a small business," he said innocently. "Of course, I would help teach you to use it. And I could use it too."

*   *   *

Everyone at the office was glad to see me: Miles because I had to sign his check; Naomi because she had three years of expenses and invoices that the IRS wanted to see and that she didn't understand; Mario because he's like that.

I petted the mutt and even let him lick me. I told Naomi she was doing a great job, to continue, and I would start tomorrow.

"You're gonna get a bonus," I said.

"I'd settle for overtime," she said.

I gave Miles the confession so he could integrate it into what we already had and start digging out the support data on those parts of it that were new to us. Then I called the congressman.

"Hold everything," he said again, "except preparing the material, until."

"When is until?"

"I'll fly to D.C. tomorrow. I think I'm only asking you to wait until Thursday. Three days. I'll call you and confirm that tomorrow, from D.C."

"Three days?" I said.

"You have done an incredible job, a great job, an unbelievable job," Straightman said. "Now it's time for me to do my job. You understand that. Let's just hope I'm as good at it as you are."

"You're the client," I said.

I sent Miles off to slave in the bowels of the record rooms of Kings County and Bronx County. "Your Naomi," he said, "is a treasure." I went out for a stroll down Madison Avenue, enjoying the hustle of people with money to make and money to spend. I saw a couple of shirts I liked in a shop window. I saw a woman watching me watching the shirts. "You think I'd look good in that?" I said. "Yes, I think you'd look good in that," she said. A brief moment without security guards marching all over our faces. Eyes, smiles. She thought about saying that I'd look good in anything. I would've said it would be sweet to feel your fingers unbuttoning my collar. Then she slipped shades down over her interest.

The shirts were $74 each. I bought both. Then I dropped another $190 on a silk blouse for Glenda. Then I saw a computer store. An IBM clone, two floppies, color monitor, printer, cables, DOS and word processing included, a space game, a detective game, $2,795, plus tax and $25 for delivery. I wrote the man a check.

I figured Mario deserved a treat too. I bought him some leather bones, then took him with me when I went to the park with Wayne. Mario and Wayne were a boy and his dog waiting to happen.

"Can we keep him?" he asked. "Please."

"Yeah," I said, realizing that he was mine now. Both of them were mine. "But you have to remember, he's a working dog. Not just a play dog."

"Uh huh."

"See, one of his jobs is guarding my office at night."

"So he can't come home with us?"

"In a couple of weeks," I said, "he probably can. Right now I want to make sure nobody gets in. But in the meantime, you can visit him after school and walk him and make friends and all that. OK?"

"Sure. Wow," he said, and put a headlock on Mario. "You want to be my dog, Mario?" He made the dog's head move up and down. Then he stuck his hand in Mario's mouth, grabbing his jaw and yanking it back and forth. The mutt seemed to like it.

Wayne stood up, his hand full of slobber. "Mario Cuomo is a funny name for a dog," he said, with the mutt leaning against him.

"You can change it if you really want to. He could probably learn a second name. He's a school dropout, but he's not stupid."

"That's what Uncle Joey named him," he said thoughtfully, "so we should probably keep it."

"Yeah. I think that's a good idea," I said. Grown men don't cry.

"What did happen to Uncle Joey?"

"He was sick. He had cancer," I told him, as I had before. "It was very bad and it killed him."

"Did he tell you about it? He never told me about it."

"No. He didn't."

"Why not?" Wayne asked.

"Good question. It was, I guess, a question of dignity."

"Dignity?"

"Yes. Joey was a certain kind of guy. You know, a cop. He was a pretty big guy, and pretty tough. I think it was important to him to stay that way. At least in front of us. He didn't want us to think of him as weak, and sick."

"Why not?"

"Because that's the way he was."

"I miss him," Wayne said, switching, instantly, as a child will, from frank, open curiosity to sadness. And maybe fear.

"Me too," I said, and put my arm around him.

"Look," Sam Bleer said, "you have to start taking this seriously." *This* was the stacks of papers that covered Naomi's desk.

"Sam, gimme a break. I've been working my ass off. I need a couple of days, to breathe and to get this Gunderson thing in the bag. Then we can worry about it."

"Sam's right," Gerry Yaskowitz said.

"He had to bring you into this?" I said.

"Tony, Tony, you have to understand—how shall I put this? You can't fuck around with the IRS."

"Look," I said, out of patience, "I'm not a dummy. I know I can't fuck around with the IRS. Just stall them a couple of weeks. That's all I'm talking about."

"The IRS," Sam said, "wants what it wants when it wants it."

"A week? Can I have one lousy fucking week, before I dive into that pile of shit over there?"

"Silverman," Yaskowitz said, "Snake Silverman. Does he have anything to say about you?"

I paused. I had a vision of money stashed in cans. Of Joey rolling off hundred-dollar bills. *Both* of us putting them in our pockets. Neither of us reporting. On a certain level, it's best to tell your attorney everything. So he knows how to defend you. But Yaskowitz and Bleer could only advise me to declare the money as fast as possible and pay the taxes and the penalties. I had the letter. A dead man would take the weight. "I practically never dealt with the man. Joey dealt with Silverman. And since my partner's demise, I haven't even spoken to him. You," I said to Sam, "set up a separate accounting thing for that, right?"

"Yes, I did," Sam said. "But as the sole surviving owner, you're responsible. With your structure, you'd be liable anyway."

"I haven't looked at the books," I said, "for that part of things."
Thinking I might very well have a need for the money. The empire had
not yet struck back. But they would. "As soon as I get a chance, I will,
then I'll tell you. Sam, you start, then you give me a list of questions,
or whatever."

"Tony," my accountant said, "I've done that."

"I've got to go to Washington. Thursday. It was just confirmed. We'll
talk when I come back."

"What do we do with him?" Sam said.

"He's the client." Gerry shrugged.

I'd made a promise to keep Gene Petrucchio up to date. More
important, I wanted to make sure the Brooklyn D.A. was interested in
prosecuting the case, in case whoever my client was lining up failed to
come through. I drove out to Brooklyn and gave Gene Petrucchio an
edited version of what was going on. He looked disturbed.

"What if I tell you to put a lid on it?"

"What it is, Gene, is that someone is gonna rock the boat," I said.
"Now if that happens, you want your man to be the one doing it. That
way at least you can control who goes overboard. You see what I'm
saying."

"You know me; I got nothing to hide. But there's people running
around this town, they're into this and that, and"—he made his finger
and fist into a gun—"they're like that. You know what I'm saying." He
shrugged.

"You know something I don't know?" I asked him.

"Nah," he said. "You take care of yourself."

"Yeah, you too. My love to the missus. And talk to whoever, about
letting your D.A. be the hero on this one."

"I heard you the first time," he said, genially. "Take care of yourself."

To hell with them all. I had my priorities in order. I drove home and
took Wayne to the park again. A breeze came off the river, the sky was
a solid cobalt blue, the air smelled like real air and the sunshine was
clear. How many days like that are there in the world?

A day like that, you could marry a woman you don't exactly love.

Knock her up and have a kid of your own blood to go with the one you already had. You could forget that status is measured in cash, and about going for glory, and winning. Forget about the gun under your shirt. Leather gloves and a white ball. Imagine that you're a rookie phenom with a 96-mph fastball and a good breaking curve and a forever world of grass-green summers in front of you. Never imagine that if you were a rookie phenom you might have troubles too. The bone spur growing in the elbow. The woman you don't love and the pretty new one you love too much. Too many buddies laying those white lines down, hoisting the brew, blue flame in the pipe.

There's sunshine. There are women to love. Kids and slobbering dogs. And what the hell is life for anyway except getting in and out of trouble?

The empire struck back on Riverside Drive.

We were laughing and I had my arm around Wayne as we crossed the six lanes at the wide sweeping curve at Ninety-sixth Street. We had the light, and no one was trying to make the turn from the exit off the West Side Highway. The silver Mercedes with smoked windows came rocketing at us, pedal to the metal. Wayne was between me and the car. I screamed. I lifted the kid bodily and tossed him out of the car's path.

Then I tried to jump out of the way myself. He swerved after me. I hit the ground with my hands. Half rolling, half scrambling, I squeezed under the middle of a parked car. The Mercedes smashed into the car over me. It bounced up. I waited for it to come down on me. Something slammed into my back. It bounced up again.

Was Wayne all right? Was Wayne all right? Was Wayne all right?

I dragged myself out. Was Wayne all right? Was Wayne all right? Was Wayne all right?

"Tony, Tony," he was calling. I lifted my head, looking, my legs still underneath. There he was, running to me. Scared for me. Like me for him. I jerked myself out, stood up, and enveloped him in my arms.

"AreyouOK?AreyouOK?AreyouOK?" My voice repeated over and over, while a horn howled. The Mercedes had crashed. After it hit the car I was hiding under, it had spun around and smashed into the next car. "I'm OK," Wayne said. "Wow."

The horn was blaring. Rage filled me. As great and terrible as the fear that had filled me a moment earlier. People had come after me before.

That was one thing. This motherfucker, this sonofabitch cocksucker, this slime who would eat his own mother's womb, had been willing to kill a kid, Wayne, my kid, to get at me.

The gun came out of my belt into my hand. My hand took the safety off. I pushed Wayne behind me. I didn't give a flying fucking shit if this motherfucker was FBI, a cop, or what. What he was now was a dead man. A fucking corpse.

I stalked toward the car, gun in front of me. I yanked the door open. He was lying twisted, his head smashed forward over the steering wheel. The horn blared. I took aim at his head.

"Tony, Tony," Wayne cried, tugging at my belt.

I paused. "Tony, Tony," he said again, and I heard the tears in his eyes. Some kind of reality was coming back. The thundering in my head was going quieter. I still wanted to kill. But I knew I wouldn't.

I reached into the car and pulled his body back from the steering wheel. The horn stopped. What sweet silence. He moaned. Alive, but limp. Hurting bad, I hoped. It took a couple of moments before I recognized him.

Dominic Magliocci. The shyster lawyer with the Bergman scam.

I woke him up and questioned him before the police arrived. The French had moved to extradite him. To charge him with the murder of Samuel N. Bergman. Extradition is a long process. It had been going on for months, as well as disbarment, several civil suits, and a prosecution for fraud. Magliocci, spitting at me, said that he had tried once, tried twice, and he'd get me the third time.

It had been him. Up in Harlem. The attack that convinced me that Reverend C. D. Thompson's arson charges were real. Which they had been. But the attack had nothing to do with it. I'd been attacked out of revenge for exposing an illegal sublet in apartment 12C.

Clearly, there was a murky lesson in that.

40.

Flawless

Glenda didn't see me as saving Wayne. She saw me as the cause of the event.

There was a short debate over whether or not to put a bandage on his scrape. Wayne insisted the wound would "breathe" better without a bandage. Actually, he wanted to show it off. Then she fed him hot chocolate, a method of getting him to drink hot milk, with its soporific effects. By then, the reaction was setting in, and his protests were no longer convincing.

I understood, perfectly well, when she started in on me, that it was out of fright and concern for her son. I tried to allay her fears. I pointed out that this had all come about over an illegal sublet. The problem was not my job. The problem was that Magliocci was crazy.

"No, no, no. This is all because of the business you're in."

"Which is finally making us a ton of money so we can buy condominiums and computers. Hey"—I smiled—"didn't you like your silk blouse?"

"What computer?"

"It's coming on Saturday. For Wayne."

"How much did you spend on that?"

"What difference does it make? He's smart. He can use it. He will use it."

"Without consulting me?"

345

"Fuck you," I said, and walked into the bathroom.

"That is not a meaningful thing to say. If that's the way you want to talk, then 'fuck you' back."

"Where the fuck is the aspirin?" I said, staring into the medicine cabinet.

"Are you all right?" she asked.

"I'm all right enough I don't have to go to the hospital. I'm not so all right I can live without aspirin. Where the fuck is it?"

"It's right in front of you."

"Oh, yeah?"

"Yes," she said, and reached into the cabinet and pulled it down from right in front of me.

I swallowed two and marched back to the living room.

"How can you keep living this way?"

"I have less injuries than any player on the Jets," I said.

"That's . . . that's facetious."

"Can't you give it a rest?"

"Not when it involves my son."

"I'm making money," I said. "I like making it. We're finally going somewhere. Jesus Christ, Glenda, this was over an illegal sublet. Not about me being a detective."

She didn't buy it.

So I tried something different. "Just for once," I said, "I'm doing something that's worth doing for its own sake. Reagan, and Gunderson, and the fundamentalists down in Faith, they're marching backward to the glorious past. When it was a rich *man's* world. I have seen their future, and it's the past. Bible teachers running the schools. Women in the kitchen and hush your mouth. No knee-gros need apply. No unions. I like the idea that I'm doing something about it. And I'm not going to stop. Not for them. Not for you."

She didn't buy that, either, though it might've been true. "Even if it means my son gets killed because of it?" she said.

"All he got is a scrape. Dammit, the kid's proud of it."

"Will they miss next time? Who will they get? You? Me? Wayne? Who do you think you are? Somebody in a movie who's got a stuntman? And everybody goes home to their hot tubs when the director yells cut?"

I took two more aspirins. I was hurting so much that I lay down on the

couch. And I was so tired that I fell asleep. Otherwise I would have lost
my temper and stalked out to Joey's apartment.

In the morning she apologized. She told me she loved me. We hugged
and kissed. Then she suggested that if I was making as much money as
I seemed to be, maybe it was time to go back to law school. I laughed.
I didn't intend to let anything bother me.

I took a long hot bath, getting the ache and stiffness out. I wasn't
moving too well, but I looked good. There was close to a thousand
dollars on my body. One of the new shirts, a silk tie, a raw-silk-and-linen-
blend suit, and a pair of Bally shoes, Swiss.

I went to the office and went over everything with Miles. He had done
a hell of a job. I gave him an extra grand. Naomi flushed with pleasure.
I sat down and typed up a two-page summary. I'm not as good a typist
as Joey was. I had Naomi retype it. I ran off four copies of everything.
My appointment was for five. I took the three-thirty shuttle.

John Straightman had a town house in Georgetown. His attorney,
Dick Gerstein, was there with him, waiting for me. Straightman was
drinking brandy and soda. Gerstein was drinking Scotch and water.
Gerstein went over the papers. Straightman looked at the clock.

"Excellent," Gerstein murmured.

"That's a great suit," Straightman said. "You're looking good."

"Thanks," I said. "Are we waiting for someone?"

"You should dress like that all the time. You look like success."

"Very, very good work," Gerstein murmured again, more to himself
than to us.

"Yes. We're expecting someone," Straightman said. "Let me give
you a drink."

"A little Scotch for me," Gerstein said.

"Fine," I said. "Brandy and soda. And a couple of aspirin."

"Headache?"

"Hurt my back," I said. "Among other things."

"What, playing squash?" the Congressman asked, pouring drinks. He
went off and got me my aspirin. "What do you think?" he asked his
lawyer when he came back.

"Yes," Gerstein said. He raised his glass. "I think," he said to me,
"you have earned your bonus."

Straightman grinned. He raised his glass. "To you, Anthony Cassella. Dragon-slayer."

I raised mine. We touched glasses. We drank. Straightman looked at the clock again.

"Who are we waiting for?" I asked.

Gerstein looked to Straightman. Straightman looked at me. "There's been a couple of things happened," he said. The doorbell chimed.

"Yeah? What?" I said. Not feeling exactly thrilled.

Gerstein got up to open the door.

"Don't worry about it," Straightman said with some urgency. "It's all going to work out, and I can about guarantee your bonus tonight."

"All right."

"Just follow my lead. OK?"

"You're the client, John."

"I am. And paying very well. So I can rely on you to go along with me."

"You probably can, John," I said.

With that, I guess I wasn't surprised when the attorney general of the United States, Randolph Gunderson, came through the door. He was taller than I expected. He looked well-rested.

Straightman introduced us.

"Mr. Cassella," the attorney general said.

"Mr. Gunderson," I said. We didn't shake hands.

It didn't even surprise me to see Gorilla Ferguson.

"You." He sneered.

"Fergie, baby." I smiled.

But what the hell was Stanislaw Ulbrecht, old Flawless Slawless, doing there?

"Tony," he said.

"Dr. Ulbrecht," I said. "How've you been?"

"Very well. You were an interesting student. I remember," he said in a pleasant professorial way, his *Mitteleuropa* accent unchanged.

"I thought you were in the Philippines," I said to Ulbrecht. "I saw a picture."

"I am a roving troubleshooter," Ulbrecht said, enjoying himself.

"It's my understanding that this conversation is off the record," Gunderson said.

"Entirely," Straightman said.

"Entirely," Gerstein said.

"You don't mind if my man does a brief security sweep," the attorney general said. It wasn't a question.

We all stood while Fergie stalked around the room with his detector kit, looking for microphones or recorders. When he failed to find anything, he scratched his head in bewilderment. Then he chewed his lip.

"Nothin'. They're clean," Fergie said.

"Wait in the car," Gunderson said.

"Drinks, anyone?" Straightman said.

"Bourbon and water," Ulbrecht said. "I love it. It is so American."

"The same," Gunderson said.

"Please sit down," Straightman said from the bar.

Stanislaw found a big armchair and flopped down in it, looking very at home and at leisure. Gunderson remained standing. Straightman brought the drinks around.

"Dick, why don't you explain?" Straightman said.

"Actually," Gerstein said, "the report and the documentation speak for themselves." He stood up, papers in hand—"Mr. Gunderson"—and proffered my report to the attorney general. Gunderson took it.

"Here," Stanislaw said, requesting a copy. Gerstein gave him one. The attorney general read every page, like an attorney. Ulbrecht read faster and only glanced at the documentation.

"Very good, clear prose, Tony," Stanislaw said. "Simple. Direct. Not like me, eh? I gave you kids a devil of a time with my lectures, did I not?"

"Yes, you did," I said.

"Oh, I was a son of a bitch for a professor," he said with delight. "I followed your subsequent career, or that portion of it that was reported in the press. Under cover. Exposing corruption. It all sounded very heroic. Very American. Was it a learning experience? Did it relieve you of some of your naïveté?"

"I'm so tired of that," I said, irritated. "That's something I did. And I'm tired of it following me around my whole life. It's not my whole life. You get much off the wiretap in my office?"

"Only a dog howling," he said. "Alfoumado is an excellent technician."

"Yes, I've read it," Gunderson said flatly, and tossed the report back to Gerstein.

"Very impressive, very thorough; it would be a bitch in court," Straightman said, swallowing his drink, then pouring another one.

"You are not an attorney are you?" Gunderson said coldly. "Any competent defense would tear this tissue of lies and garbage to shreds."

"The jury would decide that," Gerstein said. "But as a practicing criminal attorney, I can certainly say I've seen less credible lies and garbage convince a grand jury to indict. For a person in your position, going through a trial is damaging enough to avoid the entire matter if at all possible."

"Yes," Gunderson said. "If I can avoid being slandered, I prefer to avoid being slandered. If I am slandered, in spite of all, I am perfectly capable of bringing suit."

"It's academic," Gerstein said, "but it is extremely difficult for a public figure to win a slander suit. Or a libel suit. Almost impossible."

"That wouldn't prevent me," Gunderson said.

"I've always felt that the best thing an attorney can do is keep his client out of court," Gerstein said. Gunderson was silent. Hanging tough, forcing Gerstein to continue. "That's what we are here to discuss," Gerstein said. "Settling out of court. You have this matter, my client has a nuisance suit pending. An IRS matter. He is as innocent of those charges as you are of these."

"I have no jurisdiction over the Internal Revenue Service," Gunderson said.

"Bullshit," Straightman blurted.

Everyone looked at him as if he had said an indelicate word. Instead of the truth. And the truth, I understood, was that Straightman was faced with going to jail. Again. This time for income tax evasion. The truth had to be that it was not a new wrinkle; it was why he'd hired me in the first place. It had never been political.

"Criminal proceedings are traumatic and terribly expensive," Gerstein said in a matter-of-fact attorney voice. "For persons of prominence it is worse. The media attention is constant and embarrassing. A prosecutor will indict just because there is a media situation. A prosecutor who would normally drop a weak case if the accused were a normal person will, instead, go to greater lengths to secure a conviction, because there is media attention. He knows the world is watching.

I speak of professional prosecutors, not a special prosecutor like Mr. Fenderman."

Gunderson kept his mouth shut and his eyes hard. The expression that Negroes use on *Spenser: For Hire* to show the audience they're really tough.

"Oh, I think there must be some person over at IRS we could have a chat with," Ulbrecht said. "Don't you think so, Randolph?"

"I would not want to interfere in the proper working of any department," Gunderson said. Coldly. It seemed to matter very much to Gunderson that he stay above it. Even pretend there was no deal. It was a typical real estate negotiator's routine. The principal pretends to be a total hard-ass, ready to stomp out if he doesn't get his deal. The sidekick, in this case Ulbrecht, plays a mediating role, trying to find a way to make the deal possible.

"Congressman Straightman," Gerstein said, "has no objection to paying his taxes. But what he's perturbed at is that he is accused of criminal evasion. Which is not the case."

"Bureaucracies," Ulbrecht said. "Some overenthusiastic underling cranking the wheels of overregulation, taking this rule and that rule, and some other pettifoggery rules, not realistic at all and crushing the citizen. If this business were looked at by someone sensible, Mr. Gerstein's view would certainly prevail on the merits. It could happen, don't you think, Randy?" Ulbrecht was providing a rationale. "It could be done without impropriety." He was enjoying it. The academic gets to work in the real world.

"Without impropriety," Gunderson said.

"Of course," Gerstein said.

"Yeah, you call off the goons at the IRS and then all this arson and murder by arson and Mafia stuff stops right here. Everybody goes home at night. Nobody goes to prison," Straightman said. "Deal?"

Everyone looked at him as if he had just announced that prostitutes peddle pussy instead of providing a utilitarian social service. The silence ticked until Ulbrecht laughed.

"Let's make a deal," he said. "America, I love you. Blunt. To the point. Let's do business. OK, OK, let's make a deal. Something satisfactory to everybody. Everybody protected."

Gerstein smiled.

Straightman poured himself another drink and said, "All right!"

Gunderson nodded soberly, silent agreement in principle. "I have some pressing engagements." He looked at his watch.

"The business of the nation," Ulbrecht said impishly. "My time is less valuable. Perhaps if I could have another bourbon, I can stay and chat about the details, ramifications, the necessaries of our coming to terms."

"You gentlemen," Gunderson said, "will excuse me." He had no intention of being present for that.

"I won't," I said. My voice came from somewhere through the numbness around my mouth. I knew I was doing what I shouldn't be doing, but the silence wouldn't hold.

"Remember what I said, Tony," Straightman said.

"Fuck off, John," I snapped.

Gunderson turned his back and began to move toward the door. I stepped around in front of him, blocking his way.

> There is sin and evil in the world and we are
> enjoined by Scripture and the Lord Jesus to op-
> pose it with all our might.
>
> RONALD REAGAN

Gerstein got up as if he thought it was necessary to restrain me. Straightman swallowed some Scotch. My old professor looked irritated.

"I don't think there's a deal." I said. "I think there's a triple murder by arson in Brooklyn. I think there's uncounted people pushed around, lost their homes, got ripped off, by you. I think you tore up neighborhoods and made back-door deals and fucked up people's lives, so you could make a nickel. I think it's time for you to stand up and face that. It's time for the world to see what you are."

He was good. And more in control than I was. Maybe because he was getting what he wanted and I was the one having the ground cut out from under me. He stood still and unflinching and looked at me with his face frozen.

"Tony . . . come on, Tony. You're gonna get the money," Straightman said, tugging on my arm.

I pulled my arm from his grasp, then shoved him away. He bumped into the wall and spilled his drink.

Gunderson thought before he spoke. "I don't think there is a need to explain myself to you, and I don't think my conduct needs any defense. But in the interest of clarity, I will address myself to a few points.

"In the first place, there is hardly anything immoral in making a profit. This is America. Not Communist Russia. The business of America is business. Building and maintaining housing is an extremely useful and socially valuable task. We in America do that better than anyone in the world. What our people consider inferior housing would be palatial for someone from a Third World country. There would be riots in the streets if middle-income housing in New York even resembled a Moscow apartment. People of your mentality may consider calling someone a landlord a form of insult. I don't. It is something I am rightly proud of.

"As to these charges. You have assembled a group of coincidences. I, too, wish that accidents didn't happen. But they do.

"You have tied them together with conjecture and the statements of two of the most unreliable witnesses that it has ever been my misfortune to hear of. Mr. McGarrity, as his confession makes clear, suffers from religious mania. Mrs. Murphy is an elderly widow whose testimony meanders and wanders. She clearly relishes the fact that anybody is willing to listen to her. I suspect that she would say anything, simply to be listened to.

"I think it is time for you to step back and look at your material objectively. The congressman and Mr. Gerstein understand that already. You may pursue it at great cost and embarrassment to all parties, including yourself. I will sue for libel. That is not an idle threat or, I point out, an illegal or a criminal one.

"You may think that the suit is unfair. But that will not prevent it from costing you every nickel you have in legal fees to defend it. An onerous burden on top of the legal fees you must already be committed to in order to face your own tax audit."

"You son of a bitch," I said. "Shit like that is not going to stop me."

"Slow down, Tony," Gerstein said. "Say what you have to say, if you like, but restrain yourself. Control yourself."

"Shove it," I said to him. "I'm going to take you down," I said to Gunderson.

"You won't succeed," the attorney general said. "And it would be regrettable for everyone if you made the attempt. I really do"—he looked at his watch—"have to go."

He stepped around me. At the door, he turned and looked at Straightman. With a faint trace of a sneer, he said, "I assume you can cope with your own operative." Then he left.

"Let's sit down and talk this through," Gerstein said.

"No," I said. "There's nothing to talk about. You paid me to do something, and it wasn't this. Now I'm gonna go and do what you paid me to do. I'm going to go to the D.A. and put that bastard away."

"Tony," Straightman said, "if it's the hundred grand you're worried about, you got it. You got it."

"You're damn right I do. I'm gonna have an indictment by October."

"Tony, you are so impatient, so rash, so full of enthusiasm," Ulbrecht said. "You must be more exacting. More research before you conclude."

"Hey, Flawless," I said, "I've done my research." I waved my report at him.

"Listen to your old professor," he said. "McGarrity will not testify."

"McGarrity will testify. Under subpoena if necessary and with the prompting of God and his conscience."

"Call him up, Tony, dial his phone. There will be no answer."

"What did you do, have him hit too? Like Scorcese and Calabrese?"

"No. He is alive. Comatose but alive. Tubes—they do things with tubes and monitors. I think I have here . . ." He fumbled through several pockets, pulling out scraps of paper and bits of this and that. "Ah, yes. The telephone number of the hospital."

I took the number and dialed.

"Ask about McDonald, not McGarrity," Ulbrecht said.

I asked for Rolf McDonald. They told me that unfortunately Mr. McDonald couldn't answer the phone. Was he comatose? Yes, he was. What was his prognosis? He was stable. I hung up the phone.

"What did you do to him?" I asked. "Come on, Flawless, what did Gunderson have done to him?"

"Tony, I swear to you, nothing. It happened two days ago. After you left Faith, McGarrity's blood pressure—he had high blood pressure, you know—started rising and he complained of headaches. As a true believer, he did not seek medical advice. He went to one of Reverend

Parker's healing services. McGarrity proceeded to the altar. The reverend proceeded with this laying on of hands—a very interesting phenomenon; perhaps you would like to do a paper on it?—The reverend raised his eyes to the ceiling and commanded, 'Heal! Heal!' McGarrity convulsed, his eyes rolled into the back of his head, and he had a massive cerebral accident.

"Gunderson had nothing to do with it. Ten million people saw it happen, broadcast live on the Christian Broadcasting Network."

"Hey, Tony," Straightman said. "We won. Relax and enjoy it. You get rich, I stay out of the slam."

"Not a chance, John. I don't buy into this."

"Jesus Christ, Tony," Straightman said, on the verge of a complete breakdown. "Dammit, I don't want to go to prison. That's all. I just don't want to go to prison."

"You made a major error," Stanislaw said to Straightman. "It is so difficult, and very expensive, to make one man betray himself."

"I don't want to go to prison," Straightman said. "Would you?"

"It is always possible to get one out of a group to betray the others," Flawless Slawless lectured the congressman. "But to rely on one man to turn on himself, and to ask him to do it when he is looking in the mirror . . . Bah! What you should have done . . . it's academic, but what you should have done was hire Mr. Cassella for exactly what you wanted him to do. To get information with which you could . . . should I say blackmail or should I say barter? Cassella would have found his own rationalization. For the money. For the game. Professionalism. But instead you have a problem. And it is a big problem. Because Mr. Cassella is going to do his very, very best to destroy the attorney general. And if Mr. Gunderson goes, of course you go also.

"But I get carried away with this urge to teach and enlighten. I was always like that in class, wasn't I, Tony?"

"Yeah, you were flawless, Slawless."

"Come on, Tony," Straightman said, pleading. Then he twitched and ran to the bathroom. He'd needed a deal, had his deal, lost his deal. Down, up, down, the world crashes on.

"You really should reconsider, Tony," Gerstein said. "What can we do to satisfy you here, congruent with arranging things to everyone's satisfaction?"

"Nothing," I said.

"You are such a child," Ulbrecht said. "An absolute child. It is time for you to step back from your obsessions and your ego and your adolescent theatrics and look at the situation objectively.

"On the one side you have your pride. Ego. Pride is nothing but ego. Yes, you can embarrass Gunderson. What will that do? He has been embarrassed before. And survived. Will it embarrass Mr. Reagan? Nothing embarrasses Mr. Reagan. Will it affect the election? Not according to our polls.

"This is what it will be," Ulbrecht continued. "Your client will go to jail. Perhaps you, too, will go to jail. Yes, the IRS will press its suit. Nothing personal. But we both know that to be a small businessman is to be vulnerable about taxes."

"I'll fight it," I said.

"Perhaps you will. Even with success . . ." he said. "At what cost? Will you sell your newly acquired condominium—or is it a co-op? these things confuse me—to pay your legal fees? I suggest that you will have to. How will your business fare as you spend all your time defending yourself? You're a man with family responsibilities.

"Add to that criminal charges, minor ones—destruction of property, reckless discharge of a firearm—in Faith."

If that was all he was talking about, it meant that they hadn't hooked me up with the slaughter in Freeport. Not that I was guilty of anything there, but it was an unholy mess. That could really cost me. "Garbage charges, and you know it," I said.

"Suppose someone connects you to the death of Francis Fellaco and Federico Ventana in Freeport? Garbage also. I know it. You know it. Everyone knows it. But just as it has cost Mr. Straightman many dollars to stay out of jail, and it has cost Mr. Gunderson many dollars to stay out of jail, it will be very expensive for you to refute these garbage charges. The difference is that Gunderson and Straightman can afford lawyers, private detectives, and long court battles. You cannot.

"On the other hand," Ulbrecht said, "you can win."

"That's right," I said.

"The way you win," Ulbrecht said, "is by letting go. First you get your hundred thousand dollars."

"Immediately," Straightman said.

356

"Then the IRS will drop this audit. Then you can concentrate on all the success that is coming your way. Mr. Straightman and Mr. Gerstein can't help but be impressed by your work. I am certain more investigations and new clients will absolutely flow from them. We, too, are impressed. There are people in this government who do have use for outside agents. Very, very lucrative work. I'm certain some of that would flow your way. Not as a bribe. Not as quid pro quo. Not at all. Because people are impressed with your talent. And after all, isn't that why you really, in your heart, went all out on this? To prove yourself. To let people see just how good you are."

"You gotta listen to him," Straightman said. "He's telling it like it is."

"Fuck you, Straightman," I said.

"I guess I deserve that," the congressman said, shaking his head. "But—"

"Stifle yourself, John," Ulbrecht snapped. "You've made an ass of yourself on this from the beginning. Don't continue.

"As I was saying, Tony, we are all impressed. Including myself. I don't know if the idea of working abroad interests you. But if it does, I can arrange that for you. When this is all over and you've taken a vacation or whatever, we could do some fascinating things. Have you traveled much?"

"I've been to Paris," I said.

"America is a wonderful place," he said, "but there is a big world out there. The Middle East, still as dramatic as it was in the Middle Ages. Asia, so different, utterly fascinating. That's another subject, and I could lecture for hours, weeks, on it."

"Are you done?" I asked.

"Yes, I think so."

"Goodbye," I said, "and good luck."

They all started trying to talk to me at once. Flawless Slawless cut through all of them with his "Stifle it, people."

"So," he said, "you are going to go ahead."

"If the D.A. won't play, TV will."

"I'm not going to fight you about this. You will make up your own mind, I understand that. I am going to ask one thing from you. Only that you not be rash and adolescent. That you reserve your decision for twenty-four hours. Sleep on it."

"I'm not going to change my mind," I said.

"Fine," he said.

"What's going to happen to me on my way home? Is that it? You want time to arrange for me to . . . disappear?"

"No one will harm you." He sighed, as if I were being paranoid.

"You tell that to Scorcese and Calabrese?"

"Don't be ridiculous. As far as we can determine, those were exactly what they appeared to be. The Scorcese boy was killed because Fellaco and Ventana were stupid. Calabrese was killed because the Prozzini people thought he was going to talk about them. That is as much as we know. You may know more. But I don't believe that Gunderson had anything to do with it.

"So will you wait until tomorrow to tell us all what you are going to do? You cannot act on the decision until then, in any case."

"Yeah, why not?"

41.

Shaggy Dog Story

The real crisis we face today is a spiritual one; at root, it is a test of moral will and faith.

Ronald Reagan

I refused to say much when I got home. Glenda started talking about how I didn't open up and share. I said that was an old record and we'd better find a new one if we were going to keep on keeping on. It was late anyway, and there wasn't enough zest in the conflict to keep either of us from feeling the gravity against our bones. So we just went to sleep.

I was up with the light. Needing to think. Not what I was going to do, just how. I was going to bring Gunderson down, the question was how to survive the process. I slipped into jeans and a sweatshirt and walked down to the office in the ambiguous light of a New York morning.

The office door was open. It was clear that it had been broken in with a crowbar. Mario was dead.

A cursory examination showed that he'd been shot three times. Once in the throat. Twice in the chest. There was a lot of blood on the rug. It was a cheap rug and it was time for a new one, probably. Paper was everywhere. The files were open. They hadn't gotten into the big old safe, where I keep the cameras, sound gear, and such. It didn't look like they'd even tried. I went to the Gunderson file. Most of it was gone. Including the original of McGarrity's confession.

I didn't examine much else. I called the police. Not that I expected them to do anything. Just for the record and the insurance and to ask them how one gets rid of a dead dog.

It wasn't like we lived in the suburbs or something and could have a doggie funeral in the backyard. There had to be laws about burial ceremonies in Central Park.

They suggested that I call the ASPCA. Or the Sanitation Department. They had no interest in fingerprinting or photographing the room. So I did it. Numbly and halfheartedly. I wanted to remove Mario before Naomi arrived. It seemed to be the right thing to do.

I called the ASPCA. Their facility was out on Linden Boulevard in Brooklyn. They don't pick up. I called the Sanitation Department. They don't answer. I realized that veterinarians must have facilities for this situation. I dragged out the yellow pages. Veterinarians are listed only alphabetically, not by location. I had to read all the listings to find the nearest one. It was on Thirty-sixth Street between Eighth and Ninth avenues.

I tried picking Mario up in my arms. Blood, bits of flesh, and hair came off his body. He was awkward to carry, and it didn't seem right to walk through the streets with a dead dog in my arms. A large dead dog. I went down to the basement and got a plastic garbage bag from the super. Mario fit in it OK, and I put him over my shoulder and proceeded to walk to the vet's.

When I got there, I peeked in. There was a waiting room. Must've been pet flu season or something, because it was full. I thought it would be tasteless to parade death in front of the assembled animal lovers, who were certainly, at that very moment, in a state of anxiety about the fate of their own beloved beasts. I tied the top of the garbage bag and set it down gently outside the door. Then I went in. The receptionist was behind a plastic shield, with a small hole for speaking and a larger one for paying.

"I have a dead dog outside," I said in hushed, mortician's tones. "Do you have facilities to handle that?"

"Yes, we do. Bring the departed in and go right to the back."

I went and hefted Mario back up on my shoulder. The receptionist held the inner door open for me and I walked quickly but quietly through. The vet came out from an animal care cubicle and took my burden from me. She hefted it in two hands and said, "About eighty, eighty-five pounds. But let me weigh it." She took Mario away and came back a moment later. He'd been eighty-five pounds.

I went to the receptionist's desk. She was already making out a bill. "That will be three hundred forty dollars," she said.

"You're out of your mind," I said.

"It's four dollars a pound," she said.

"By the pound? For what?"

"We can't help it. We get charged by the crematorium by the pound."

"Crematorium? You're gonna send a dog to a crematorium?"

"Yes, sir. Would you be interested in an urn? For the ashes."

"Three hundred and forty dollars?" I said.

"Without the urn," she said.

"Forget it," I said. "Give him back to me."

"Certainly, sir," she said.

She got up. I got up. She went in back. The vet came out, carrying Mario.

"I want my garbage bag back too," I said.

They were kind enough to return my garbage bag. I set it on the floor and shoved Mario back in. Then I hefted him on my shoulder again and left. I had seen some construction on the way, and I decided that the thing to do was put the corpse in a Dumpster. Sentiment is one thing, but $340 and a crematorium seemed too unrational. While I was standing on the corner, waiting for the light to change, the bag broke and Mario fell out.

It was New York, and most passersby ignored me while I tied a knot in the top, then turned the bag around to stuff him back in the way he'd come out. With the reversed bag over my shoulder, I walked two blocks to the renovation site. As I approached the Dumpster, a man standing in front of the work area turned his glare on me. He knew I was going to try to steal space in his Dumpster.

I walked on past, searching. Block after block, no more Dumpsters. But I did spy a large lidded trash bin, about three feet deep, four feet high, six feet wide, outside a restaurant. I lifted the lid. It was empty. Restaurant trash is picked up daily. Perfect. Mario would not become a health hazard.

"Don' do dat," someone yelled from the doorway.

I had never realized before how possessive people get about their trash receptacles. I saw myself as an urban version of the Ancient Mariner, doomed to wander Metropolis, eighty-five pounds of dead dog as my personal albatross.

I set my burden down and thought. Then I hefted him back on my back and retraced my steps to the vet.

"OK," I said to the veterinarian's receptionist. "You win. Three hundred and forty dollars." I put the dog down, took out my checkbook, and began to write.

"We don't take checks," the receptionist said.

"I'll tell you what I'm going to do," I said. "I'm going to write a check for three hundred and forty dollars. I'm going to slip it in your little slot here. Then I'm going to leave this dog, this dead dog, on your doorstep. What you do from there is up to you."

Sam Bleer was in the office when I returned. Naomi was hysterical. "All my work. All my work. And you destroyed it!" she said to me.

"What are you talking about?" I said.

"Tony, come on," Sam said. "You can't beat an audit by stealing your own files."

"Stealing my own files? What are you talking about?"

"Everything I've been working on, for over a week, with overtime— which you don't pay, not at time and a half anyway—" Naomi said, "is missing. . . . Are missing? . . . Is missing."

"Wait a minute," I said. "What's missing?"

The bulk of three years of financial records was gone. Sam and Naomi were convinced that I had stolen them. Sam started lecturing me that it would only screw me with the Feds.

"Why would I steal my own records? Why would I kill my own dog?"

"Who else would?" Sam said.

"You killed that wonderful, sweet, kind animal?" Naomi shrieked.

"I didn't kill. I didn't steal. Stop!" They stopped. "I came in early. I found the office a wreck. I saw that the Gunderson file was gone, part of it. I didn't realize the financial records were gone. Mario was shot. I called the police."

"I don't believe it," Sam said.

I glared at him.

"You I believe," Sam said defensively. "I believe you didn't steal your own records. But I don't believe that someone else did. The IRS won't believe it, either. It had to be you, even though I know you and believe you and it was someone else."

"So what?" I said.

"So what?" he said. "I don't want to tell you what. I want you to hear this from your attorney."

So we got Gerry Yaskowitz to come over. And I went through the whole story again.

"So tell him," Sam said.

"You can't fix this one," Gerry said. "You destroy records in the middle of an audit, you go to prison. You're going to do time, Tony. You shouldn't have done it, even though I believe you when you say you didn't do it."

"Now I know why Flawless wanted me to wait a day to decide. What this is," I announced, "is political." The assembled multitude was underwhelmed.

"Of course it is," Gerry said.

"Don't you see? I can cut a deal with Gunderson: I lay off him, the IRS lays off me."

"Hey, if you're on speaking terms with the attorney general," Gerry said, "why bother with a little guy like me?"

"I'm not going to do it. I'm gonna bring the bastard down. Once I do that, we can prove this was political."

"It doesn't work like that. Just because he is guilty doesn't mean that you are not guilty."

"I didn't steal my own files. I'll get the dog back and get ballistics on the bullets, if they're still in him. Then we can prove—"

"Nah," Gerry said, shaking his head.

"I'm not going to let them stop me."

Sam scratched his head. Gerry looked up to the ceiling, where the Jewish God is.

"Gerry's right," Sam said. "If you can cut a deal, you better cut it. I've never, in my whole life as an accountant, had one this bad."

"Sam's right," Gerry said. "They got you by the balls."

"Well, maybe I'll take my chances."

"You're going to go to prison," Gerry said. "As your attorney, I am telling you that as a fact. Not advice. Not opinion."

"So I'll do the time."

"What's Glenda and the kid gonna do?" Gerry said. "While you're on the inside, who pays for the apartment? What the hell are you gonna do when you come out? You sure as hell won't have your license anymore. What are you gonna end up with—other people's scraps, like Miles Vandercour?"

"You leave Miles alone," Naomi said. "Miles is perfectly good."

"Sorry," Gerry said, "but we're discussing Tony here. And, Tony, the Feds already told you they want you in the pen in Atlanta, not in a country club like Allenwood. You might not come out alive."

"Just get me some time," I said. "Some time to clear myself. To get some leverage."

"I can't get you time. I can get you the weekend. I'll wait till four thirty-one to call the IRS so they won't get back to me till Monday. Is that the kinda time you need?"

"There's a guy in Washington." I handed Stanislaw Ulbrecht's card to Gerry. "I don't want to talk to him. You call him. Cut a deal. Money talks, everybody walks.

"I'm not a kid anymore. Once upon a time. I'm not a kid anymore. I got responsibility. . . ."

"Sure, I'll call him for you, Tony."

"I still score the hundred grand, which means I get to pay everybody's bill. That's important. It's not up to me to save the world. Just do my job. Take care of my own."

"You're making the right decision, Tony."

We all read the comic book
from the comic book store,
it said you better exit laughing
because you can't buy forever more.
The times they have changed.
I don't know them anymore.

The leaves got stuck
on a calendar of the year of eighty-one.
Everybody decided to live forever,
but they all stopped having fun.

Nobody wants to touch the sky
on the way out the door.
Nobody's laughing,
they don't accept the score—
not anymore.

"Nashville" Katz, "Decades A Go Go"
(© Pussykatz Muzic, Inc., 1983)

42.

The White Rapper

*It is by the goodness of God that in our country we
have three unspeakably precious things: freedom of
speech, freedom of conscience, and the prudence
never to practice either of them.*

Mark Twain

Glenda told me not to be upset. That I had done very well. That I had
made the right decision. The adult decision. She was proud of me.

I went to Joey's apartment to think, reflect, look at my life and
myself. I stayed there from early morning until ten or eleven each night
for the next four days. I went home at night only to avoid having to
prove to Glenda that I was spending my nights alone.

At one point, I tried to reach Des Kennel. To see if WFUX wanted
to run with the story. There was no indictment, but he certainly could
use the word "alleged" a lot. But he was out of town. For a week. At
a Life Plan Way Full Realization seminar.

There were several anxious calls to the office. Gene Petrucchio and
Syd Coberland each called twice. Uncle Vincent called. Wirtman called.
Gerry Yaskowitz called late Monday, when he got back from D.C. He
told Naomi to tell me everything was A-OK. I didn't call him back until
late Tuesday.

"That Stanislaw Ulbrecht is a very strange fellow," Gerry said. "But
we had a nice conversation on the ontology of English common law.
How many people these days care about the nature of things?"

"So?"

"The deal. Whatta deal. Has he got a deal for you. First, as a sign of
good faith, your audit has already been postponed. For ten days. Business days. In two weeks you can apply for a thirty-day postponement.
Which will be granted. Then they will drop the case."

"Who came up with that schedule?" I asked. "The reelection committee?"

"He also has in his office . . . It's a nice office; lots of books. I tell you, Tony, when I retire I could retire to a room like that. So much to read. Wonderful . . . an internal FBI memo which makes it clear that you were only defending yourself in Faith. Just in case you should ever need such a statement."

"Fine," I said.

"Straightman's case is also postponed. They are discussing a settlement. In November the settlement will be accepted. No criminal prosecution. After he releases the hundred thousand dollars to you. Ulbrecht wanted to hold that up until after the reinauguration. He thinks you tend to be volatile. I insisted that you get yours before Straightman gets his deal.

"January sometime, you go down to Washington if you want. Stanislaw—that man is very well connected—guarantees to arrange another hundred thousand dollars' worth of contracts to go your way in fiscal '85. . . . I think we did pretty good."

"You did fine, Gerry," I said.

"You don't sound so happy about it," he said.

"So?"

"You got money, you got your health, plus you got a great attorney. What more can anyone ask out of life?"

"Thanks, Gerry," I said, and hung up.

I went home. Wayne was zapping aliens on his new computer. He asked me if I was ready to learn how to use it.

"Not yet," I said.

"Oh," he said.

"You want to go to the park? Throw a ball around?"

"Sure," he said. "Male bonding."

"You're awful short for a wise-ass," I told him.

We went to the park. It was a muggy day, and we didn't seem that into baseball anyway.

"What's wrong?" he asked me.

"It's pretty complicated. I haven't figured it out yet."

"Is it Mario?" he asked. "I'm upset about him too."

"It's more than that," I said.

"That's what upsets me the most," he said. "I wish we'd had a backyard to bury him in."

"Would you like a new dog?" I asked him.

"Maybe. But not yet."

"OK," I said, listlessly.

"Will you snap out of it," he said.

"Look," I told him, "this is a lot more complicated than you can understand. I'll try to explain it, if I have to, but basically I have to figure some things out."

"You know what I think?" he said.

"What?"

"I think you're sulking."

"You're awful small for a wise-ass," I said, "but when you're right, you're right."

Wednesday, I went into the office and went back to work. As part of my new adult, post-sulk, self, I decided to make the least pleasant call first.

Uncle Vincent wanted to know why I hadn't come to see him. he explained that I was a "bum."

"I apologize for it. I've been busy."

"The greata man. Always too busy. You gotta the full appointment calendar."

"I can come over now, if you want."

"You sure a that? I'ma not taking you away from affairs of state? I figure a busy man like you, you got an appointment with President Reagan. I wouldn't want to interfere widda that."

"No," I said. "Mr. Reagan and I, we settled our business. My calendar is open now."

"Yeah, sure a you had business with President Reagan. I'ma glad you got it settled. Now you gotta time for your family."

"So I'll come on over now."

"Oh, the busy man, the busy man, he findsa the time. You come if you wanna. You don' come if you don' wanna. I don'a care."

I drove out to New Jersey, not really knowing why I went. Maybe it was to look at his money. Maybe I would like living in a home like his. Great trees shadowing winding streets, green grass on sloping lawns.

He wanted to talk about me having Michael's grandson, a blood nephew. While he talked, I nodded and grunted and let my mind drift, drift transatlantic. I had a fantasy about Marie. She seemed fixed in herself as a person, though adrift in terms of job and career. The opposite of an American woman. And there was—whether I was perceiving or projecting, I didn't know—a different attitude about the husband-wife, man-woman relationship. I saw myself going to her. Telling her about my uncle's offer. Guaranteeing her thirty or forty thousand dollars a year, or whatever, to be a mother. To let me be the father of her child. What kind of husband and wife we would be, how long it would last, we would figure out as we went along. I would have my cake and eat it too. She would be fixed for life.

I told Vincent I would give his offer every consideration.

"Hurry up," he said. "I don't got much time. I'm running out of time."

I went back to the office. I called Gene Petrucchio. He asked me to come out to Brooklyn around seven. I said I would.

Jerry Wirtman had called while I was out, to tell me to expect a call from his nephew on his wife's side of the family, Matthew Silverstein, about business. The nephew had in fact called. He called himself Matt E. Silver and he was an A&R man at 21st Century Sounds.

"You the P.I.?" he said.

"I'm the P.I.," I said.

"My uncle says you're good. He's an old guy, but sometimes he's pretty sharp. Whyn't you come over here and we'll take a look at you. How's right now? Yesterday would've been better."

"Yeah, why not," I said.

21st Century Sounds was in the Brill Building, a short walk from my place. Their offices were small, physically unimpressive, and energetic. They ushered me into the office of their president, Ron Tower. He had a potbelly and a sports jacket. He must have been close to twenty-nine. He was the elder statesman of the place. Matt E. Silver sat on the edge of the desk in baggy pants and a T-shirt with the sleeves rolled up.

"You know the White Rapper?" Tower asked.

"Of course he knows the White Rapper. Everyone knows the White Rapper," Matt said.

"Not necessarily," Ron said.

"I know of him," I said.

"Of course he does. I made rock 'n' roll history with the White Rapper. The first rap act to play CBGB's. The biggest rap record contract in the industry. A five-record deal. Rock 'n' roll history."

"He's gone missing," Ron said.

"No gratitude," Matt E. Silver said. "I made him."

"What's his real name?" I asked.

"Real name? Does he even have a real name?" Matt said bitterly.

"You see," Ron said, "the Rapper really is Matt's creation. He's a concept, and we got writers to write the songs and we made up a real name for him, Harold Stucker, and we copyright all the songs under that name, then we found a funny-looking guy—"

"Isidore Danielovitch," Matt said. "Do you believe Isidore Danielovitch? This schmuck was wandering around the streets looking for a job as an actor and didn't even have the sense to change his name. I found him."

". . . and got him a choreographer. Then we got a couple of our black acts to work with him to teach him to rap."

"I could do it again," Matt said. "Let's just find a new guy. We can do makeup. We can say he had an accident." Suddenly he jumped up. "We could do great PR on the accident. . . . Visualize it. All wrapped up like the mummy man. He's had plastic surgery. His face was ruined in the accident. Then we have a dramatic unwrapping. Live press coverage. The bandages come off. The White Rapper's new face is revealed! Dig it—we video it, the unwrapping, then we do a rap video around it."

Ron smiled, proud of his protégé. "You can see why we at 21st Century call Matt the Boy Hustler. What a guy!" he said.

"So you wanna forget old Izzy?" Matt said.

"As a last resort," Ron said. "If Tony can't find him, we'll make a new one."

We discussed price, and I agreed to take the case. They gave me photos, his address, the name and address of his girlfriend, the first name of a groupie he was known to be hot for, and the name of his connection. On the way out, Matt offered me the White Rapper's latest album. "I'll autograph it for you, personally. Hey, you want a White Rapper T-shirt?" He grabbed one from a stack. "Lemme do you a real favor," he said. "I got T-shirts from the Porcine Porkers' Japanese tour. They're rare. A little piece of rock 'n' roll history. And they're really good, hundred-percent cotton, none of that fifty percent poly crap."

Before I went to Brooklyn, I returned Syd Coberland's call.

"Remember the missing pages you were looking for?" he said, a discreet reference to the unexpurgated special prosecutor's report on Randolph Gunderson. "I got 'em."

"Too late," I said, "too late."

"What'll I do with them?"

"Syd, don't force me to make obscene suggestions."

Dom & Angie's Luncheonette was the same. Eddie Alfoumado was there, checking the pay phone. He said hello. Gene recommended the meat loaf, if I was hungry. I wasn't. Ralphie announced the phone was clean. When he left, Gene said, "You got that Gunderson thing ready to prosecute yet?"

"I thought your people wanted to shut it down."

"Did I say that?" he said, smiling.

"It doesn't matter," I said. "The case is dead."

"I was counting on it," he said. Not smiling.

"Why?"

"Edith Bloom changed her mind. She's going to announce in January that she's running for Brooklyn D.A. We ran a quickie poll. Her against Landsman. Nine to one. Fifteen to one among the Jews. A lot of that is simple name recognition. Who knows Landsman? We figure . . . we put our heads together, and we figure what he needs is that one big case. Put him on the map. What's bigger than the attorney general?"

"I'd love to help you, Gene. But I can't. My client sold me out. And Gunderson's got my balls in his pocket. They fixed me good, and I could go down on an IRS rap. . . . Besides, my key witness is in a coma."

"I didn't think they could get to you," Gene said. He sounded sad. Almost as if he pitied me.

"Fuck you," I said. "They have me in a box. I'll tell you what my choices are, then you tell me what I should do. I go after him, get destroyed in the process, and not get him. Or I let it go and I make out. Understand? It's 'They win, I lose,' or 'They win, I win.' So I did the smart thing for a change."

"Yeah, I guess. Most of the people I know, they do the smart thing. Why should you be different?"

"Hey, who's talking? Every day of your life is a deal."

"Most people I know," Gene said, "they got what you call variable integrity. Somebody comes around who's different, I find it refreshing. Like your old man. We were on different sides a lotta the time. But I always respected him. It was refreshing."

"I told you what my choices are. You tell me what you would do."

"You're right," he said. "We all gotta do what we gotta do."

Nobody I talked to had seen the White Rapper. Wherever he was, he would still want pussy and drugs. That made it mostly a surveillance case. Follow the dealer, watch the girlfriend's place. Two teams.

I called DeVito. Naomi spoke up. "I think you should use Miles," she said.

"He doesn't know anything about it," I said.

"He's smart, he's a hard worker. Besides, I want him to get out of file rooms all the time. He should get some air. He should get some sun. He's a wonderful person, but he's turning into a mole."

"Look, I already got two guys to sit on the girlfriend. I'm going to cover the dealer."

"You should work with a partner. What do you do when you have to go to the bathroom?"

"That's what bottles are for."

"Oh," she said, and blushed.

"Yeah, why not," I said. "I'll put the other two guys on the dealer. Watching the apartment isn't too difficult. He can't screw it up. I don't think."

"That's a wonderful idea. You can train him."

"I'm doing this for you," I said.

"Thank you. I think I deserve some consideration."

"What've you been doing, taking Assertiveness Training?"

"Yes," she said. "With LPW. The Life Plan Way."

So I put Miles on. And when, despite what I'd told Syd Coberland, Speedo showed up with the full, unexpurgated version of the special prosecutor's report on Randolph Gunderson, I took it along. With two of us on the stakeout, I would want something to read.

The report was only moderately interesting. What they had taken such pains to hide was barely worth hiding. But in portions that had been public all along, there was evidence of a clear and conscious pattern of discrimination in housing.

FENDERMAN: Low-income housing was going to be built in your district.

DISTRICT LEADER AUGUST WALBY: That's right. We was forced by the city to accept that.

FENDERMAN: It is my understanding that you were influential in pushing the contract to build and manage to the Empire companies.

WALBY: Yes. They're good at it.

FENDERMAN: There were several lower bids.

WALBY: So what?

FENDERMAN: Did you accept any financial inducements, any favors, in order to swing the contract to one of Mr. Gunderson's companies?

WALBY: No.

FENDERMAN: Yet there were lower bids, from other reputable companies. It doesn't make sense to me. Explain it, please.

WALBY: Look, the city forces us to accept this—this invasion. Nobody wants it. We got a nice neighborhood there. What do they want to shift all the bums and muggers out to us for? So I figured it would help if somebody got the contract who would take good care of things. I look out for the interests of the people in my district. Anybody says different is a liar.

FENDERMAN: What do you mean, "take good care of things"? Take care of you?

WALBY: Don't keep implying I take bribes. I don't take no bribes. I got a good insurance business. I don't need 'em. You want me to spell things out? OK, I'll spell it out. Somebody doesn't make a lot of money, that doesn't make 'em a bad person. My parents, they didn't make a lot of money, but they were clean, decent, hardworking, churchgoing people. Now Mr. Gunderson, his operations, they have a reputation, a good reputation, for keeping things right. So we talked to him and he made it real clear that he would see to it that the place wasn't loaded up with coloreds, and not ruin one of the last good and decent neighborhoods this city still got.

It seemed to me that a case for violation of the city's Fair Housing Act could be made fairly easily. And nailing the attorney general on a civil rights violation had a certain appeal.

I sat on it for two days. It was a stupid idea. Self-destructive. Then I drove to Brooklyn. Gene and I strolled over to the promenade in Brooklyn Heights. Looking out over the harbor, I told him that there might be a case. It would be a technical violation rather than what the public conceives of as "crime." That they could certainly indict, but maybe not convict. Was he interested?

He was interested.

"If I give it to you, will Landsman run with it? I have to know, Gene—I'm putting my ass on the line."

"You have my personal guarantee."

Then I asked my lawyer and my accountant to come to the office for a meeting. I laid it out for them.

"Why don't you take a vacation?" Gerry said. "Let your brain slowly return to normal."

"But," I said, "this case can be made entirely without me. They don't need the information from me. It's right there. In the record. So how can Gunderson blame me?"

"You realize that you're kidding yourself," Sam said.

"Of course he realizes," Gerry said. "He just asked us here to tell him that he's kidding himself. So that's what I'm going to do. . . ."

One of my father's favorite plays, and mine too, when I was growing up was *Cyrano de Bergerac*. My father was a terrible romantic. Cyrano has a great death scene. Mortally wounded, he sees an anthropomorphic vision of Death:

CYRANO: I'll meet him on my feet.
  [*He draws his sword.*]
    Sword in hand.
  He sees me. He dares to mock me! . . .
  What do you say? That it's useless? . . . I know that.
  Do I fight because I think there's something to win?
  No. No. The most beautiful battle is the one I know I have to lose.
  Who comes here, who are all of you . . .?
  Oh, I recognize you now. All my old enemies.

The Lies—
    [*He assaults the air with his sword.*]
    Take that, and that. You, Compromise!
Prejudice! Cowardice!
    [*He strikes.*]
    Will I make a deal?
Never. Never. . . . Ah. There you are, you, my Pride and Vanity.
I always knew it would be you who finally took me down.
    [*He swings wide as a windmill, and stops, panting.*]
Yes, you took it all away from me, the laurel and the rose.
You've got it. Take it.
But there is one little bit which I take.
And tonight, when I enter the House of God,
My salute will touch the sky,
Because in spite of you,
I take something that is clean,
something that is without a stain
    [*He raises his sword high.*]
and that is—
    [*The sword drops from his hands. He totters, he falls.*]
My white plume.
My pride, my pose, my lifelong masquerade.

Dangerous stuff to raise a child on. We're better off with Rambo and Mr. T.

". . . Tony," Gerry said, "you're kidding yourself. If Landsman indicts Gunderson, you go to prison. So does Straightman. Maybe you can be roommates."

"Let me ask you one question," I said. "A technical footnote. If the indictment comes down by October, can I still claim that hundred grand?"

"Yes," he admitted hesitantly. "But—"

"Tony, it's stupid," Sam said. "You can't spend the money in the slam. If you had it, which you won't, because the IRS is going to take it. Take the deal, you make twice as much again within the year. And you can even keep some of it."

"I just don't like it," I said. "This guy is mobbed up. We know it. Everyone knows it. But he's just going to go on and on. I had him. And

I lost him. I'm having a lot of trouble living with that. What I see, is me going on for the rest of my life, and looking back, all the time, and saying, I could have done something about it. I could have done it. But I let it go. Because I was scared—"

"Because you were sane," Gerry said.

"Because they bought me. Because I folded in the clutch. Because they bought me."

"Look, Tony, I know you want to agonize about the purity of your soul, but it's time to get on with things."

"All right guys, let me put it to you another way. Just sit back and think about it, coolly and logically," I said. "What would you say if I told you that it was already done—that it was in the works, in front of a grand jury, and an indictment is going to be announced in a couple of days?"

"You didn't . . ." Sam said.

"You're a *meshuggener*, a schmuck, an asshole," Gerry said.

"Hey, hey, guys, slow down. I didn't say it's done. But I want you to tell me what advice you would give me in that hypothetical situation."

"I wouldn't give you advice," Gerry said. "I'd say get a new lawyer. Who needs *meshuggener* clients."

Sam just shook his head.

"Seriously, guys. I want a real answer here," I said.

They looked at each other. Exchanging grimaces.

"Me, I would say," my accountant said, "flee the country."

"And while you're at it," my lawyer said, "change your name."

Epilogue

When Assistant Brooklyn District Attorney Landsman announced the indictment, Randolph Gunderson resigned from office.

It made headlines. For a few moments. But the only place that really picked it up and ran with it, along with the long list of other Reagan appointees who were investigated, indicted, forced to resign, was *Doonesbury*. Mondale was still unable to make the "sleaze factor" a campaign issue. The Reagan steamroller steamed on and, in November, flattened his opponent.

The President nominated one of his closest advisers to be the new attorney general. That nomination was, in due course, presented to the Senate for confirmation.

Time

Senators Grill Meese About Possible Conflicts of Interest

The question sounded facetious. "Was there anybody who had either given loans or financial aid to you or your family who wasn't subsequently given a federal job?" asked Vermont Senator Patrick Leahy. Laughter rippled through the crowded Senate Judiciary Committee hearing room. Presidential Counsellor Edwin Meese grinned. But Leahy was serious. Meese hesitated, then came up with a name: James Schmidt, a senior vice president of California's Great American First Savings Bank, which had loaned Meese $423,000 in mortgages and loans secured by houses in California and Virginia. Leahy tartly reminded Meese that four other officials of the bank had received federal appointments. . . . An internal memo from two lawyers in the Office of Government Ethics claiming that Meese had violated rules governing the conduct of federal employees was disclosed by the *Wall Street Journal*. . . .

The 385-page report of the special counsel, Washington lawyer Jacob Stein, cleared Meese of any criminal acts but did not pass judgement on the ethics of his conduct. . . .

Meese was finally confirmed by the Senate in February. The Justice Department policies moved, if anything, even further to the right.

Gerry Yaskowitz was correct. The Swiss bank turned over the money without hesitation. In person. There was also a total of $75,000 in Joey's apartment. Cash money. That, of course, I gave to Glenda, which will cover the condo payments until I figure a way back to the States.

I found the White Rapper for 21 Century Sounds. But Matt E. Silver is infatuated with his concept of the near death and subsequent resurrectional unwrapping of the New White Rapper. If Isidore Danielovitch pulls his disappearing act one more time, the Boy Hustler promised me, I will be the first one they call as a replacement. So that's a possibility.

My mother, of course, was very understanding.

Getting out of the country and truly disappearing required some imagination. Guido was of great assistance. He helped me find this temporary retreat. It's pretty strange wearing robes and living in a cell. But it's not all bad. I enjoy the theological debates. They think I'm quite funny. Though they know quite well what I'm doing, they don't seem to mind when I disappear for afternoons with Marie. The climate is sunny, and it was raining in Paris, as usual, so she is happy to be here too.

I feel the money has settled my debt to Glenda.

> How very foolish for a man to kill himself for one woman when the world is full of women. When a woman takes my fancy, I say: "Do you love me? I love you. You don't love me? More fool you!"
>
> GARIBALDI

I do love women. Like I love the sky and seeing the leaves fall and the rain come down and new shoots rising. Except more so. As much as my honor. Which I didn't know I loved.

Epilogue

THE NEW YORK TIMES

It's no longer remarkable to find the U.S. Attorney General under investigation by a special prosecutor. The case of the Wedtech Corporation marks the third time that an independent counsel, appointed by a court under the Ethics in Government Act, has scrutinized Edwin Meese's conduct—twice at his own request. What is remarkable is that Mr. Meese continues to denounce as unconstitutional the law that makes such inquiries possible.

The only thing I miss, and my only regret, is Wayne. That's not an owing that I clear from my conscience with cash. I explained as best I could before I left, and I have written him, at length, subsequently. I hope he understands.